# THE LAST NOCTURNAE

# MICHAEL TERRANCE

ATROCITIES OF BLOOD & MOON

# THE LAST NOCTURNAE

A NOVEL

THE LAST NOCTURNAE.
Copyright © 2024 by Little Yellow House, LLC.
All rights reserved.



Cover design by Kerry Ellis

Edited by Lenore Appelhans, Bethany Lauren James, Sara Kelly, Jenna Lee, and Emily Young.

Library of Congress Registration No.: TXu2426448

ISBN 979-8-9904673-0-9 (ebook)
ISBN 979-8-9904673-1-6 (hardcover)
ISBN 979-8-9904673-2-3 (paperback)

First U.S. Edition: 2024

Published by Little Yellow House, LLC
www.michaelterranceauthor.com

For my mother and father,
who encouraged me to write this story.
I will forever miss you.

# Content Warning

# THE LAST NOCTURNAE

ATROCITIES OF BLOOD & MOON, BOOK ONE

# PART I: NOCTURNAE

# 1



THE ICY WINDS whip through the streets of Washington D.C., but I barely register the cold. I'm too hungry to notice it. A man walks past me carrying his sleeping daughter and I can't help but think of all the things I'd do differently if you were still alive…

Laughter catches my ear as a party of five enters the tavern across from the U.S. Treasury Department building. Famished, I decide to stop in for a bite and a drink while I wait.

As I push through the revolving gold door of the Old Ebbitt Grill, conversation and roaring laughter punch me in the face. Roughly four dozen people scattered throughout the establishment continue in their own little worlds, without an inkling of what horror just came in off the street.

White linens cover each table, which will serve nicely as the canvas for my next masterpiece. I'll use the patrons as my paints and pastels, and I will call it, *Blood.*

Polished silverware gleams atop green cloth napkins.

Fucking silver.

I weave through the pods of bar patrons and find a seat in the farthest corner under the watchful eyes of taxidermied animals, supposedly victims of President Teddy Roosevelt.

The bartender approaches with a smile. "Good evening. Can I get you something while you wait?"

"It'll just be me," I say, sadly eying the empty seat beside me.

The last of my kind, condemned to dine alone for eternity.

"Very well, sir. What can I get for you?" The bartender places a cocktail napkin in front of me.

A pint of B-positive would be wonderful right now.

"Do you have Michter's Single Barrel Rye?" I eye the bar shelves.

Sometimes I miss the good old days.

"Of course, sir."

"Manhattan." I fluff a small purple flower pinned to my lapel. "Three shakes of bitters, not two. Stirred and served up."

I miss those days. Those days with you.

"Sure thing."

Humans claim Nocturnae drink to curb the craving of blood, but in all truth, I drink because I like it. The complexity of cocktails reminds me of human blood—everyone tastes a little different. Drinking also has the added benefit of allowing me to go unnoticed as I wait for the right morsel to present itself.

Back in 1856, when this place first opened, I had an easier time picking off a human from the herd. I didn't have to contend with security cameras and fucking cellphones.

Using the mirror to my right, I glance around the room. Groups of businessmen and women, politicians and their staff, and members of the armed forces blanket the establishment. I also note a handful of students, tourists, and couples. And a woman in a lace dress seducing a gentleman with a stained tie.

The bartender carefully places a stemmed glass garnished with two brandied cherries on my napkin. "Here you are."

"Thank you." I don't look away from the mirror.

"Can I get you anything else?"

A blood sampler: the young faux-blonde in the mint dress, the brunette gentleman with two-day-old scruff, and the little number sulking to herself off in the corner—I wonder, did she lose someone too?

"That'll be all for now. Thank you."

I study the herd.

"I'm doing great mom," a young girl says.

Your quickened heartbeat says otherwise.

"You're sure you don't need money for rent?" her mother asks.

"Nope. Paid it yesterday."

There it is again, liar.

In a way, I envy them. It's been a little more than 600 years since I saw my family. I'd give anything for a cryptic word or a white lie. I look at myself in the mirror and down at the purple flower. It's been even longer since I saw you.

Too many tables with kids in here. I swore never to feed on a child again.

Four frat guys opposite me slam their shot glasses down and high-five one another. I don't need another drunken night clouding my mind.

I scan the bar once more through the mirror. Two suited men in the middle of the bar catch my eye. One sweats too much and struggles to breathe; the other has his arms crossed and is focused on the TV.

You don't wear an American flag pin on your lapel unless you're involved in the government or the defense industry in some way. Not so strange in these parts, but there's something off about him.

I tune out the rest of the room. Everything around me fades to white. The overwhelming noise goes mute and I can only hear the two men.

"Sorry for being so weird on the phone," the sweaty man whispers.

"What's going on? Why did you call me *here* of all places? I was in a meeting on the Hill."

"You were right." The sweaty man wipes his brow. "I'm so sorry I ever doubted you, but you were right."

"Right about what, Stephen?"

Yes, right about what Stephen?

Stephen rips a pen from his jacket pocket, grabs a cocktail napkin, and quickly writes nine letters on the makeshift paper. I can't see what's being written, but I can hear the pen grinding over the wooden bar as it makes the unique sound of each letter.

A nine-letter word—Nocturnae.

He slides it to his friend and runs his finger over the word. "Her."

Impossible. Could it be?

Without thinking, I quickly look at the napkin. My quick movement must have caught Stephen's attention because he looks up at me and my eyes flash crimson.

"Shit!" he yells, shoving himself away from the bar and spilling his beer.

People stop and stare.

"What the fuck?" his friend shouts.

Stephen runs for the door, but collides with a woman behind him. Her martini goes flying through the air and the two of them tumble onto the floor. He looks at me, scrambles to his feet, and makes for the door.

That's my cue.

I down my drink in a single mouthful and leave a fifty on the bar. In the chaos, I head further into the establishment. Leaving the main dining room, I step into Grant's Bar with a breath-taking ceiling mural and a nude painting over the bar. Noticing the waitstaff disappearing behind the door, I follow and find myself in the kitchen.

Dinner to go.

I quickly shuffle through the kitchen and exit through double white doors onto Northwest G Street. I turn right and head east.

Hell of a night for the lights to be out in the alcove of Metropolitan Square.

I step into the shadows and wait. It isn't long before Stephen comes barreling around the corner, looking back over his shoulder every third step.

Huffing air, he blindly runs past me. In one smooth motion, I grab his jacket and pull him into the alcove. "Not so fast, Stephen."

He gasps and his heart rate skyrockets at the sight of me. I cup his mouth, silencing his screams and bite his neck. The world around me quickly slips away, and I step into Stephen's mind. Time stops as I join Stephen in his memories.

A dark hallway with three doors at the end comes into focus. The small viewing window in one door opens, revealing an emaciated figure cowering in the center of the room. A flashlight beam illuminates the figure's long scarlet hair. The figure turns her head and her eyes flash crimson.

Quickly, I pull myself away from Stephen, severing the connection.

"She's alive," I mutter, wiping the blood from my lips. "She's been alive this entire time…" I press Stephen firmly into the concrete pillar behind me. "If you even *think* of screaming, I'll rip out your tongue."

He gulps the air and gives a shaky nod as his feet search for the ground.

"Where is she?" Stephen doesn't answer. I break his third rib under my thumb. "Ah. Don't scream."

"Wright-Patt," he groans through his teeth.

Wright-Patterson Air Force Base. Ohio.

"Which building?"

He's quick to answer. "Hangar-4."

"Thank you, Stephen," I utter with a smile and snap his neck with one hand.

I clutch his lifeless body like I'm holding up a drunk friend. I walk him to the staircase across the street, setting him upright against the railing so a passerby would think he was homeless or passed out drunk.

Shoving my hands in my pockets, I walk down the street, away from Old Ebbitt Grill and the man who gave me a second chance.

Military base, means training and guns. But holding a Nocturnae means silver. Do they know that? It's a huge risk. I'll probably die.

I turn the corner and hear a woman scream from the far end of NW G Street. "Help! This man is dead! Someone call 9 – 1 – 1!"

But she sacrificed herself to save me.

"I'm coming, Claret."

# 2



THE PHONE GREW heavy in his hand, and suddenly breathing became difficult.

"Okay thank you." Dr. Eugene F. Shelley returned the phone to the receiver. "Breathe in, two, three. Hold, two, three. Breathe out, two, three."

He threw open the bottom drawer, pushing papers and books out of the way. From the very back of the drawer he pulled out his estranged friend, Jameson Irish Whiskey.

The shimmering emerald bottle taunted him. "Six months and four days sober … again."

Quickly, he removed the cap and filled his empty coffee mug halfway. He wet his lips in anticipation of the sweet release from his anxiety. Then, he caught a glimpse of an old photograph on his desk and stopped. Those dark eyes could always see right into his soul.

"Sorry honey," he offered weakly, then slammed the whiskey

with a single gulp.

He picked up the phone and hit SPEED DIAL 4: DR. JEAN ALLICINES. Tipping the bottle again, the whiskey splashed sloppily into the mug as he racked his brain, unsure of how to begin.

"Hello?" Jean yawned into the phone. "Eugene?"

"I'm … I'm sorry … I'm so, so sorry to have called you this late." Eugene stared at a folder on his desk labeled SUBJECT 252-7-38.

"It's okay." She sighed. "Is everything all right?"

"No, no everything is not all right."

"Are you okay? Has there been an accident?" Blankets rustled in the background.

"There's been an *incident*…"

"Who got out?" Jean groaned.

"After the first incident, we improved the containment cells, increased security, and beefed up our passive deterrents and countermeasures. Hell, we even transferred Subject 053-8-79 to our maximum-security facility to ensure it never happened again! But this…"

"But *what?*"

"It's not who got out …" Eugene took another sip of his whiskey. "…it's *who got in.*"

"What do you mean: Who got in?" By her tone, he could tell she was concerned they'd get their funding cut by General Grissom again.

"A male Nocturnae broke into the facility this evening." A weight lifted from his shoulders and he felt like he might float away from the sheer shock of it all.

"…you're shitting me."

"I wish I was."

"A Nocturnae broke *into* our facility? For what? How?" Jean asked, quickly.

"The southwest entrance."

"But we don't know *why*?"

"No," Eugene snapped. He gulped his whiskey. "That's what I need you to find out. We captured him alive. He'll need to be interrogated."

Jean paused for a long moment before responding. "Is everyone alright?"

"Multiple casualties and even more injured, most in critical condition."

"What about Subjects Delta and Gamma? Are they contained?"

"Yes, and we believe they're unaware of the break-in." He slumped his shoulders. Eugene hated this part of his job—the constant coded messages about classified topics over unsecure lines.

"But, you're sure there was no contact?"

"I DON'T KNOW! I don't fucking know." Eugene slammed his fist into the desk, spilling his drink. "I called you first because I need help. I … I just can't. I need to assess the massacre, call in Henry—like he needs something else to worry about—debrief the security forces and get their reports, oversee transport of the casualties to Base Hospital and the Valley, inform the Director and the General, prepare a briefing to give them in the morning, I … I …"

"Just breathe. My mind is spinning just as fast as yours. I can do the interrogation," Jean said in an encouraging tone. "Take that off your plate."

Eugene knew Jean had never come face-to-face with a Nocturnae. She didn't know how truly terrifying they could be. How their eyes looked through you as if you were nothing but their next snack. But then, her condition could be an advantage—she'd never have to know.

"Thanks. You'll be fine Jean. I guarantee it," he lied. "As a precaution, it's bound and restrained according to Apex Level guidelines. Oh, and wear sunglasses."

Jean snorted as if he'd told a ridiculous joke. "Sunglasses? Is that really necessary?"

"You can't be too careful around these monsters."

"Glasses it is. Do you think he'll talk?"

"I don't know ... I doubt it," Eugene said nervously and looked to the far corner of the lab. "Remember, though, you're the one who asks the questions. Don't let him manipulate you into telling him anything personal or anything about The Company or our research."

"Understood. Do you want me to handle the victims of the attack for you? I'm already awake, and there's no way I'm going to be able to fall back asleep, not tonight. Besides, maybe the victims can give me something that could help me interrogate the Nocturnae."

"Hm, that's a good idea. If you don't mind doing all of that, yes ... that would be a huge help. Do you have the safety procedures for an Apex Level event with you?"

"No, they're in my office," she said.

"Okay, I'll email them to you. Listen to them on your way in. And Jeanie…"

"Yes?"

"Good luck."

He hung up the phone, took one more swig from the bottle, and returned it to the bottom drawer. "You'll need all the luck you can get," he muttered to himself.

Was he a coward for sending her in his place? Yes. But he just couldn't do it again, not after what happened last time. He slumped into his chair, opened his email, and began typing:

*This email is classified TOP SECRET. Compartmentalized under PARANORMAL INTELLIGENCE caveat within The Company. All contents within the email are not releasable to any foreign country or entity. All United States personnel with the proper NEED-TO-KNOW must be cleared SENSITIVE COMPARTMENTALIZED INFORMATION, maintain an updated Full Scope Lifestyle polygraph, and be read into the appropriate Unacknowledged Special Access Programs before divulging or alluding to any of the information outlined below.*

Dear Members of The Company,

I have just been informed by Security Forces there has been an Apex Level incident. Though there have been casualties, it is unclear how many have died or the extent of structural damage to the facility. However, I am happy to report that we have captured the Nocturnae intruder—male in his late 20's to early 30's, roughly 5'5", black hair, pale skin, well-built.

From this point forward the Nocturnae will be referred to as: Subject 076-7-46.

In response to this event, I am calling for an emergency meeting of all parties tomorrow at 0900. Dr. Jean Allicines will be interrogating Subject 076-7-46, and I will have an official report of her findings and our next steps in your mailboxes by 0800 Tuesday, January 22nd.

The Gamma and Delta Level Subjects remain unscathed and, as far as I can tell, completely unaware of the events that have transpired. Research continues as normal. See you in the morning.


Eugene hit SEND and slumped back in his chair with a heavy sigh. Interlocking his fingers behind his head, he stared down the bridge of his nose at the blurred image on his desk. His glasses slid down his face with a twitch of his nose, bringing the woman in the photo into focus.

His eyes locked onto hers and the warmth of her gaze cured him of his anxiety and unease. He smiled. "You always knew how to calm me down."

# 3



IT'S QUIET.

Too quiet…

My eyes aren't adjusting to the darkness … I've lost too much blood.

The air is eerily still, disturbed only by my breathing.

I should be able to hear something else, *anything* else … footsteps, a mouse, a rattling pipe but all I can hear is an annoying humming sound. It's more of a ringing … what is that…? Oh, right … the shotgun that went off at close range.

Strangely, my senses are off; I can't see in the dark. I have the hearing of a human. And then there's the throbbing pain in my head and hot burning sensation over the majority of my body.

Ow.

If I were human, I'd be terrified right now.

But I'm *not* human.

UGH, I MUST have fallen asleep.

I wince in agony, pulling my head left to ease the pain of what feels like a boiling metal finger digging around in my right shoulder. I can feel the object moving around inside my muscle, carelessly scraping against my bone.

Due to the major blood loss, I can't heal from these wounds and push the objects out. Not any time soon at least. At this rate, I'll be here for weeks. That's not an option.

Why do my wrists hurt? Better question: Why can't I move them?

Shi…

I SQUINT AND can make out a figure. Huh, perhaps my senses are coming back.

The human lurking in the corner thinks I am oblivious to his presence—probably because I've been in and out of consciousness; I must give the presence some credit, its breathing is low. Slow. Resembling someone who has been trained to control their respiratory and circulatory systems. A technique not widely utilized or practiced outside of martial arts or elite soldiers.

I think I'll sit here, motionless, and observe…

MUST HAVE PASSED out again.

How long have I been out? Hours? Days?

The air in the room has shifted. I can only assume my silent friend's legs are falling asleep, they have to urinate, or exhaustion is setting in. It doesn't seem like they're sitting, so they must be standing or less likely, squatting. Special Forces. They must be. Standing nearly motionless for an extended period is a challenge not many humans could undertake.

My eyes still haven't fully recovered, but it's more than enough to see the edges of his shoulders. They're larger than the average six-foot-tall man. It's easy to tell a man's build when his traps converge around his neck.

Now the room … it's still too hard to tell. It's large though, maybe thirty-by-thirty feet.

My wrists, ankles, and every inch of my skin touching this goddamn chair burn as if exposed to white-hot coals.

Silver.

The object in my shoulder must be silver too—safe to assume anything shot at me was silver. But that's not enough to cause this much damage … not anymore, not since France.

Something else then?

Why can't I remember?

While my soles sizzle, the sides of my feet stay cool and wet, like I'm immersed in a puddle.

Is the floor silver? Is it somehow in the water? My Maker, is it in the air?

The hairs on my neck stand on end, sending a cold shiver coursing through my body, and I'm suddenly short of breath. *Don't fall into this trap. Snap out of it.* I grip the arm rests, welcoming the exchange of sudden panic with the pain of my burning hands. I grimace, but I don't cry out.

FUCK, that hurt. At least I'm thinking clearly again.

"Hello, my friend," I say into the darkness.

The man's heart stops for a second, and he quickly opens his eyes. If I didn't already know where he was, I would now—a silent flutter to humans is a symphony of sound to a Nocturnae.

"You can come out, my friend," I say softly into the darkness. "I know you are there."

The mercenary continues to ignore me.

Minutes pass and my frustration grows.

I hate being ignored.

"Come now, don't be shy. You're in the corner to my right."

I may have struck a nerve with that one; an electric current zips down his spine, forcing his heart to race.

He doesn't react but continues staring into the darkness, eyes straining intently in the thick air. Slowly he stands, shaking the fear and stiffness from his body. There is no room for doubt in his mind; after all, I taunted him. More than once.

I know you're there.

His footsteps crack across the floor as he accelerates toward my position. His left foot slams into the floor next to my right foot, bringing him to a complete stop. His body rotates at the hips. Employing the kinetic energy throughout his entire body—a fascinating human process known as kinetic-linking—his fist whistles through the air, delivering his full weight to my jaw.

Ow.

"Stop talking! Jesus, what they say about you freaks really *is* true. Stop fucking trying to get into my head!" He follows up with a strong right hook and an elbow to my temple.

Like being batted by a house-cat. Hilarious.

I can't help but snicker at his attempt to frighten me. His right knee lifts, striking my eye socket. If I were a mere human, my jaw would be shattered, and my retina dislocated. But I'm not human.

I sit there, smiling. Warm, thick fluid slowly streams down my face and drips from my dimples.

Huh … he drew blood. Looks like the house-cat has some spunk.

"I don't need to get into your head. I can hear your heart beating…" I mumble, spitting a mouthful of blood at his feet. A tooth bounces off the ground, landing in the puddle at my feet.

He's military for sure, but I was able to set him off that quickly? That was too easy. He must be new. Best to make an example of him.

He strikes me three more times, spewing my blood across the cell floor in scattered arcs.

"Oh yeah? What's my heart saying now?" he huffs, squatting next to me. He gets into my face and spits. "Huh freak?!"

A little too close.

Gotcha.

Sinking my teeth into his carotid artery, I give a minor flex of the jaw, and it tears. And it's heaven. His blood is warm, mild, and oaky, indicative of at least a pack-a-day smoker.

Standing guard over me all this time must have driven him mad with cravings.

As the sweet liquid flows down my throat, hints of apple and fennel come through on the back end. Sumptuous.

The kill is over before it begins as the weight of his limp body tears itself from my teeth.

Damn you, gravity.

From the short imprinting I receive before the interruption, I find him rather … complex, like a robust wine profile. His dark list of intimate desires, created in a perfect storm of a troubled childhood filled with beatings and molestation, makes him somewhat remarkable. These were mitigated by his strict moral code and his chosen identity as a protector. He was perfect for this job.

"Now it's silent, for you have *no* heartbeat," I say to his corpse lying on the floor.

Ha.

Thank my Maker for the blood; I can hear outside the cell now. I close my eyes and listen to the world around me.

Everything reverberating through the building's structure makes it very difficult to tell its overall size. Six, maybe seven floors above me? The hustle and bustle astound me. It must be the middle of the day. The two floors below me don't seem to have anywhere near the same number of people as the rest of the building. I sense only one person down there and something else … deeper.

This damn silver. I can't make out what it is, but it's something.

A set of footsteps plus one. They come from far past my cell, but still within the building, likely just inside the main entrance. What makes them stand out isn't the size eight heels clacking on the hard linoleum flooring, nor the gait, nor pace of their walk; all decent cues that this is most likely a woman. No … it's the tap.

A cane.

But not a cane for stability that moves on the opposing side. No, not at all. This is a very specific cane.

She's blind.

Based on her confident even gait, however, she'd be damned before letting anything slow her down.

Hello. Who might this be?

She's stopped. Maybe she's checking in with security. She cannot be just an errand girl sent by some corporate executive to do their bidding. First of all, it's the twenty-first century, not the 1940s. Secondly, and more importantly, I can feel the confidence, the determination in her steps. She's pissed. She may have high status here.

Down the hall roughly one hundred yards, the elevator track engages. *Ding!* The doors open. The mysterious woman's clicking heels enter the elevator and it begins making a slow descent. She taps her foot inside the steel box.

She's anxious, almost excited, rather than nervous. Curious.

She must not know what I am, or if she does, she's not intimidated in the slightest. The elevator stops on my floor. *Ding!* The tapping starts again, closer and closer. Just outside the cell door, she stops. An electronic device beeps, causing something within the door to unlatch.

A scanner of some sort? Retina? Fingerprint?

She opens the door and I can't help myself. "Come in, my dear. Come and see the animal in its cage." I chuckle a little as she gasps from the other side of the door. I catch a glimpse of cinder block walls making up a long hallway.

Fearlessly, she makes her way toward me, and a man dressed in an ABU—Airman Battle Uniform—follows closely behind with a padded folding chair. She stops three paces into the room allowing the man to pass her.

Unfolding the chair four feet from my toes, he taps the metal backing of the chair twice, saying, "Here you are, ma'am."

"Yes. Come. Sit. Please, do pardon the mess. I would have prepped for company, but I'm a little *tied up* at the moment."

Folding her cane, she rests her tote beside the chair on the floor, and assertively takes her seat, dismissing the man. "I do not want to be disturbed for any reason."

In the center of his chest is a patch with four lines and a star—Staff Sergeant. The badge on his right breast reads, Burr. Staff Sergeant Burr.

"Yes, ma'am."

I look at the Staff Sergeant. "Did they tell you what I am?"

Eyes trained on the dead body, he gulps and begins to stammer, but nothing comes out.

"That will be all." She waits for the man to exit, but he makes no sound. "What are you waiting for, Staff Sergeant?"

"Sorry, ma'am, but what would you like done with him?"

She gives him a puzzled look. "I would like him to remain shackled."

"No, ma'am, the dead guard lying at the prisoner's feet."

She pauses. Behind those glasses, it's impossible to tell what she's thinking. Then, with a slight nod, she says, "Can you safely retrieve the body without compromising your safety?"

"Yes."

"Then do so and notify Henry immediately."

Henry?

"Yes, ma'am."

"Thank you, Staff Sergeant."

He drags the body out of the room, closing the door tightly behind him. Silence settles into the room.

I'm intrigued they sent a female. Foolish, it won't make a difference. If anything, it'll be easier. She's no more than 130 pounds soaking wet and her neck will fit nicely in the palm of my hand. Fresh manicure and slim-fitting skirt … Administration? They should know better…

Sighing, I ask, "And you are?"

Give me the person in charge.

"Good morning," she says, smiling. She clicks a small device in her tote to RECORD. "I'm Dr. Jean Allicines, Principal Psychologist for beings labeled as: Paranormal. Falling under the subcategory: Apex. It is the morning of January 18th, 2019, and I'm here with…"

It's been hours, not days.

She pauses, waiting for a response.

"A man tied to a chair bleeding all over your floor."

Without a sigh or a shake of her head, she moves on. "Tell me about the guard? How were you able to kill him while restrained?"

She's bold, unfazed by anything other than the task at hand. I wonder what she tastes like. No, focus. I'm definitely in the right place.

Raising my head slowly to look her in the eye, I click my tongue. "Tsk, tsk, tsk. Don't you know how this goes? You answer my question, then I answer yours. You're Jodie Foster, and I, Anthony Hopkins."

How much do they know?

"I assume the guard grew arrogant and got too close, close enough for you to strike."

Licking my lips, I smile. "I would have gone for his liver, but I was short a bottle of Chianti and fava beans, so I went for the carotid."

"I believe it's my turn, if I've got the game correct."

Is she really blind? Is this a trick? Bottom line, she's crafty.

"Hmm, it seems it is, Dr. Allicines."

"Jean is fine. And you are?"

Cute.

"Sorin Harker."

"Okay, Mr. Harker. Yes, I know what you are. You have been called many things throughout history: *strigoi*, *upir*, or most commonly, *vampire*. Nevertheless, your species self-identifies as: Nocturnae," she says, adjusting her blacked-out spectacles. "The light of the sun or decapitation will kill you. Garlic, religious artifacts, and hallowed ground are utter bullshit. You *can* be photographed and you will appear in a mirror. How am I doing so far?"

So, she's not just a businesswoman. And her pronunciations were flawless.

"Very good."

Let's move this along.

I shift through near-infrared and ultraviolet wavelengths until I can see through her darkened lenses. Her eyes are erratic like they have a mind of their own because they've never been used before. Her milky pupils stare back into mine, and I have her now. The room glows crimson as I unleash the full, devastating power of my ability to compel her.

She blinks and shifts in the chair to a more comfortable position.

What?

I try again, more focused this time, and the room swirls in bands of red light growing brighter and brighter. She scratches her nose.

Why can't I compel her? Something is wrong.

And then it hits me. In all my years and all my paths, I've never compelled a blind person. Can I not? No, that wouldn't make any sense. That's not how it works anyways. Is it the glasses? Maybe, if they've figured out how to diffuse the compulsion, but I doubt it.

Occam's Razor—the simplest solution is almost always the best. Silver.

I'm too weak. Shit.

Let's ruffle your feathers…

I sniff the air and lick my lips. "You wear Clinique moisturizing lotion and sometimes Burberry *Brit*, but not today. Your manicured nails are chipped and uneven, not a good look for a professional. And you've stopped bleeding from your shaving accident this morning—ankles and knees can be *such* problem areas."

She looks on, cold and silent.

Where are you, Claret?

"You're ambitious, driven—only because you have something to prove—but what is it? You dress classy and are escorted by military personnel, so you're someone of importance. However, that Michigan accent you try so hard to hide says everything you're not saying. Am I wrong? No, don't answer that, that was rhetorical."

Mm, smells like A-negative. And she's a vegetarian. Iron deficient—she should add kale or spinach to her diet. Her blood will be drier on the back end of the palate, but beggars can't be choosers, I guess.

Unaffected by my goading, she smiles. "But it was a question all the same. I believe it's your turn to answer: Do you know where you are?"

Checking to see if I'm disoriented. She's good, for a human.

"I'm restrained by silver shackles confined to a silver chair, my bare feet in silver-laden puddles, in a room with no lights, sitting across from a human," I sputter. "At the bottom of a steep hill on the southwest side of the base there's a string of five hangars. I'm beneath the one you call THE RESTORATION HANGAR."

"Very observant."

"Honestly, Jean, what makes you so confident that I am Nocturnae?"

She cocks her head slightly.

Is she amused?

"Well Mr. Harker, you successfully infiltrated a United States Air Force Base, bypassed video and audio early warning systems, and broke into a secret facility everyone believes to be an aircraft restoration hangar, all without raising a single alarm. That is before you bled dry all of those people in a top-secret building eight stories below ground. I'd say it speaks for itself."

So, I'm eight floors underground. I was close.

"Oh, and you deduced the water under your feet has silver in it," she adds.

Shit. I hate being right.

I pop a fang over my lip and tongue it. "Did you find fang puncture marks on the victims?"

"No."

"Then they bled *out* and were not *bled dry*, as you put it." I smirk.

Words matter Dr. Allicines. And I always claim my kills. Always.

"You expect me to believe you killed those people without feeding on them at all?"

"That's not what I said… Killing people is a rather messy endeavor, blood squirts everywhere, and body parts fly about. I'd be lying if I said I didn't sample the accouterments or lick my fingers clean. After it all, that would have been rude."

She shifts her weight on the chair, uncrossing and crossing her legs. Clearing her throat, she winces, but says nothing.

That got to you, didn't it? The blood. The mess. The accouterments.

"If you're looking for an apology, you won't get one."

"I don't expect to."

Reaching into her tote she pulls out a small electronic note-taking device. It's similar to a keyboard, but it only has six large oblong keys. Setting the small device on her lap, she types. And it hits me.

Braille. The one language I don't know. It's not that I couldn't learn it … the opportunity just never presented itself, hunting the blind just isn't as much fun. You don't get to see that rush of fear in their eyes.

That's quite a gamble on their part; maybe they know more than I assumed.

"You're no different from the average murderer, and they aren't remorseful, so why would you be? But I'd like for you to think about the military police you ripped to pieces in the hallway. Had the service members not been carrying AP-shells, our losses could have been much, much greater."

"AP?"

"Anti-paranormal."

Coy. Translation: silver. Smart, don't want people knowing they're shooting jewelry at us. Shells: shotgun. Birdshot I bet. Buckshot would have gone through me. Explains why I can't move my head to the left, that arm is numb, and my ribs feel like hot coals have been stuffed in the cracks.

"How many did I get?"

"Seven. Seven people died. Let me ask you, Mr. Harker, does that affect you? Do you feel remorse of any kind?"

People? They stopped being people a long time ago. Tasty treats are more like it. But the second they joined this organization they became succulent fruit dipped in chocolate with caramel drizzle, ready for me to indulge in.

"When a bug hits the windshield of your car, does it affect you? Do you feel remorse? I think not."

"So, humans are insects to you?"

"You're missing the—"

"What if it had been your … coven? Is that the right term? Would you have cared then?"

Unable to contain myself I burst out laughing. "What is it with humans and their love of buzzword-bingo? *Coven*. One Twilight film and you think you know everything. Are you team-Jacob or team-Edward? You look like a Jacob fan." I take a couple deep breaths and lower my smile. "If you're waiting for an apology or a sign of guilt, you're wasting your time. Besides, they took the first shot…"

That fresh blood should speed up the healing process and expel this silver from my body. Could still take a couple of days though.

My only hope is to keep her talking and figure out a way to compel her, and I'll find you, Claret.

She uncrosses her legs. "So, had you not been shot at, you wouldn't have killed them?"

I scoff.

"What if it had been one of your birth parents? A brother? A sister?"

Cora.

Clearing my throat and adjusting myself as best I can in this ridiculously uncomfortable chair, I smile at her. "You look like a cat-person. Are you cat-person Jean?"

"Yes."

"Wonderful. Have you ever seen your cat—or any cat in general—tossing a bug or—better yet—a mouse around?"

"I don't see what that—"

"Shush. I'm not done. To me, you humans are mice, and I am a cat. If I want to play with my food before I kill it and eat it, I will."

Intelligent, sophisticated, and organized mice that have gotten very, very good at hunting and killing us over the centuries. So good in fact, that you're no longer scared of my kind.

We're … I'm, scared of you. I've been fighting and running from your kind since my new birth. Your kind took everything from me.

Jean types another note. "Okay, Sorin. Can I call you Sorin?" she asks, as a tuft of hair falls in her face.

"You can call me whatever you'd like, for what's in a name?"

Jean fakes a smile, unamused. "Why are you here, and how did you learn of this place?"

"You're changing the rules? That's two questions, my dear."

I'm here for Claret.

"Please answer."

So serious.

"I had a recent acquaintance in Washington, for supper—and yes, I do mean, I ate him. And although dry and rather acidic, his imprinting gave me some choice information. I am here for what is mine. No one had to get hurt, I was simply defending myself. No one else needs to be harmed. Simply give me what has been taken from me and we'll be on our way."

Silently, Jean's fingers glide across the keys as she logs another observation.

"And what is it that you believe we have?" Jean asks.

No conscious or subconscious responses. She's been trained.

"You're changing the rules again Jean. I answered both of yours. I find it only fair that you extend the same courtesy to me."

Jean pauses for an exceptionally long time before answering, "Fine."

"Hmm. What to ask? What to ask? What to ask? Why did they send you and not your boss?"

There's a response.

The hairs across her body stand on end as goosebumps form on her arms. Her heart rate increases. She swallows. She ignores all of it. "I am the boss. Your next question?"

"Oh no, no, no. No *lies* Jean," I sigh. "If you lie, then I have to lie, and I'm sure we don't want that now, do we? What good is that to anyone?" She doesn't move. "Let's try this again, shall we? Who is your boss? The one who goes out and gets the money for you and whomever else needs resources in this place. The one who does all the research. The person who's going to study your notes, compile them into a report, and send his report up the chain of command. The person in *charge*. Where is that person?"

I saw that: your hand quivered. You know you got caught.

"I apologize, I misunderstood you. I'm the head of my department. But my direct superior was pulled into a meeting and requested I perform the interview in his place."

"It's quite alright. You're only human after all."

She waits for me to call her out on her poor attempt at an excuse, but I don't. "How large is your coven?"

"I don't have one."—Anymore—"You're well-trained Jean, I can see that. You're exceptionally calm for a human whose body is nothing more than a thin bag filled with fluid waiting to be popped and spill its succulence onto the Earth. Which tells me you've been around my kind before, but I wonder, have you ever been *this* close? To where you can feel the heat radiate from me? To where you could simply reach out and touch me if you wanted? Or have you only watched from afar? Waiting in comfort while your boss does the talking?"

"That was five questions," she says, pushing her bangs behind her ear. "Which one would you like me to answer?"

"Pick one," I snap.

"This is the closest I've been to a Nocturnae." She adjusts her glasses. It's a tiny, nervous tick that I take as a small win. She sits silently for a moment, seemingly deep in thought. Then nods slowly. "Sorin … if you can tell me what was taken from you, perhaps I could have the object returned. How does that sound?"

You're lying but I will play along. As long as I'm here with you, then I'm not being sent to die. But why are they keeping me alive? I need more answers.

I need to buy time.

"I can tell you, but it'll take time for it all to make sense."

"I have time," she says, crossing her legs.

Does she care? Why would she? Her tone and unconscious body language is so different from other humans, but also so familiar. There's something there and I can't quite place it. I must know what it is and I must know why.

I contemplate where to start: Étretat, the mountains, or further back? "I will accept your offer on one condition. You allow me to tell my side of the story before making any rash conclusions about me or my kind. The entire story."

I watch her body language for anything. A twinge. A flick of the hair. A tapping of the foot. But there's nothing.

"Do we have a deal?"

Quickly, Jean adds a note on her writing device. "Yes."

"Where would you like me to begin?" I ask, tonguing the crown of the tooth regrowing.

Yes, the blood is working…

"What's preferable for you? Would you like to start with how you were turned?"

Manners. She sits before me and uses manners. I never thought I'd see the day when a human would use manners with a Nocturnae.

"Only if you tell me when you started here."

She gives a quick double nod. So, I begin.

# 4



MY SISTER AND I served the MacTíre family, the most prominent family in Dundalk, a small town in north-eastern Ireland. Mr. MacTíre, the town's alderman, treated nobles and peasants alike with respect and kindness.

Surrounded by the stillness of parchment and ledgers, I refilled an inkwell before copying entries for the day.

"Sorin, come quick!" a voice yelled from the hallway.

"Can it wait?" I sat with a stack of papers under one arm, ready to be checked and categorized. "Mr. MacTíre has guests coming this evening, and the ledgers need to be done before they arrive."

A red-headed servant peeked into the library, panting, deadly serious. "It's your sister. The lady of the house has been drinking since breakfast and something set her off."

I froze.

Mrs. MacTíre loved her wealth and power, but it was never enough, and she had become bitter and violent, retreating into her cups. In her darkest moments, she'd find solace in the bathhouse with a bottle of the finest Gaelic whiskey.

When I didn't move, he continued, "Your sister's taken quite a beating. You need to come now."

I dropped the books without hesitation and ran to the bathhouse. The servant followed.

Cora was sprawled face down, soaking wet, on the bathhouse tile. Blood ran from the side of her head, soaking her linen shirt. "Cora!" I ran over to her.

I scooped her into my arms, and then turned to the servant. "I can't—I need to—"

"Don't worry about it. Take care of your sister. I'll make sure everything is ready for the guests and cover for you tonight."

"Thank you."

I got us out of the bathhouse and into the garden. The high bushes and thick trees kept us out of sight as I scurried off the property. I never looked back to see if someone was following us. Not once.

Just outside the gate as I turned west through the fields, she began to rub her eyes. "Rin?"

"Shh, you had an accident. I'm taking you home."

"My head hurts." She moaned, rubbing the back of her head.

"I know. I know. We're almost there."

"Can we have stew tonight?"

I couldn't believe she was thinking about food after what she'd been through. To be honest, I was relieved. "Ugh—sure—I don't think that'll be a problem. We still have some carrots, turnips, and onions."

"Okay," she said. "How about a *rabbit* stew?"

I looked down at her, confused, for rabbit game was expensive.

"Oh, I don't think—"

She pulled out something from the folds of her dress. It was long and gilded—an ornate wooden spoon. I stopped in my tracks.

"Is that what she beat you with?"

"Yup." She gave me a proud smile.

"Cora," I gasped, "that's worth a fortune."

She flipped the wooden spoon in her hand. "Well, I figure if she's nearly killed me with it, it's only fair."

"You little minx. I don't know what I'd do without you."

"Together forever."

We traded the spoon for two rabbits from a traveling merchant on his way out of town. It both got rid of the damn thing and filled our bellies.

That night's meal was the best tasting stew I ever had.

Five months later, when Mr. MacTíre was first infected, it seemed like a mere cold. A day later, when his fingers blackened, I ran for the doctor. Despite our best efforts, a panic set in, for rumors had been swirling around the countryside of a deadly disease that knew no bounds. In less than a day it became clear the Black Plague had come to Dundalk, and it spread like wildfire.

Cora and I feared going to work, but we still needed wages, or we'd surely starve.

Four days later, I entered Mr. MacTíre's room with his breakfast.

"Who cares about that? You're needed here," he argued, speaking to the high back chair at the foot of his bed.

"Oh, I'm sorry. I didn't realize you had company. Shall I bring some tea for your guest?" I set his food down on the small table adjacent to the chair. But the chair was empty. I paused. "Who are you talking to sir?"

Mr. MacTíre remained fixated on the chair and never even looked at me. "Conor, you can't go. It isn't right, you leaving in this manner!"

I cautiously approached the bed. "Mr. MacTíre, it's Sorin … who's Conor?"

"Stop. Please, brother," he pleaded.

As his head turned, I noticed a large nodule on his neck that wasn't there the previous day. Alarmed, I backed away from the bed. "Sir? There's a sore on your neck. I'm-I'm going to check you for more of them, is that okay?"

"If it will keep you from leaving, Conor."

Looking at his desiccated hand, I said gently, "I'm not going anywhere." I pulled back the sheets and gasped. He was covered from head to toe in sores. While some had burst, others were still festering.

It smelled terrible, but I refocused. "Sir? Can you swing your leg over for me? We need to check your back and tend to your sores." There was no response. Holding his blackened hand in mine I continued, "Squeeze my hand sir."

It was faint, but he did squeeze my hand.

"Get away from him!" a woman yelled from the doorway.

I whipped my head around to find his wife standing in the doorway.

"I-I-I'm sorry ma'am. Your husband is … I'll fetch the doctor."

"Please—" Whatever she wanted to say was interrupted by a

ferocious, deep cough.

"Are you okay ma'am?" I poured her a glass of water from the pitcher beside her husband's bed.

"Fine."

"Here." I passed the water to her.

Taking the glass from me with a nod, she smiled through blood-stained teeth. Blood trickled from her nose.

I gasped, and forced myself to choke back my vomit. Horrified, I pushed past her and ran through the doorway.

I only had one thing on my mind: Find Cora and get the hell out of this house.

Rounding the corner of the kitchen, I found her pulling fresh bread from the hearth. By looking at her, you'd never know she was beaten the way she was by the lady of the house; but took harder jobs as to not be around the woman.

"Rin, what are you—"

"That's it! We're done!"

"What are you talking about?"

"Mr. MacTíre is covered in boils and sores. Mrs. MacTíre is too and she's spewing blood. We've *got* to go."

Grabbing her hand, I pulled, trying to force her out the door.

"But how will we buy food without money?"

"We can't buy food if we're dead."

Suddenly, she realized what I was saying and stopped resisting. "Together forever."

We smiled at each other and ran. Once we'd put some distance between us and the estate, we shortened our gait to a normal walk.

I glanced over. Her head hung low and her arms dangled limply by her sides. "Is everything alright?"

"Yeah…"

I put my arm around her shoulder. "You can tell me anything. You know that."

"I'm just thinking about Father."

Our father wasn't a good man. He blamed me for the death of my mother. The asshole never let me forget it either. He was a drunk and a thief. Then, he left us without a word during the hardest of times.

It wasn't until then that I realized the irony in it all. I was leaving my second family—the MacTíre's—to their fate, much like my father left us.

Cora paused for a moment and looked up at me with concern in her eyes. "Do you think he's okay?"

"I don't know, Mo Chroí."

"Family doesn't leave during hard times." Her tone betrayed both her bitterness toward our scoundrel father and her guilt over not helping Mr. MacTíre or his children. "That's why I'm your Mo Chroí!"

I bent down to pick a lavender flower poking out from under the snow. I sniffed it softly and turned to Cora. "Yes, because my heart is my family." I nestled the flower behind her ear.

The sun had just set when we got home. We shivered from the bitter cold and I hurried to get a fire started. After a few moments, the kindling crackled, but I hadn't heard a single peep from my sister.

"If you're still cold, take the blankets from my bed."

Cora didn't answer.

Peeking over my shoulder toward the door, I said, "Cora?"

Again, she didn't answer. She just stood in the doorway with her arms wrapped around herself.

"Come closer to the fire," I encouraged.

She wavered limply and let the wall prop her up.

"Rin… my arms hurt." Despite the chill, she lifted them up, and we both stood there in silence. There, on her upper arms, were two red welts.

COLD AIR BURNED the back of my throat as I gasped awake, startled by the screaming wind beating against our tiny window. My muscles creaked as I shifted under the weight of my blankets.

"Cora?" I called out.

I commanded my aching limbs to reach for my sister's body; I felt nothing but air. The weeks had not been kind to either of us, and now, fully afflicted, we clung to what little hope we could.

Gritting my teeth against the inevitable pain, I heaved myself to my elbow and scanned the dim, one-room cabin for her. Her chest rose and fell as she slept on the floor, huddled close to the dying embers of our meager fire.

I sighed in relief that she was still alive.

With a quick jerk I pulled myself to a seated position, swinging my legs over the edge of the bed. If I thought moving quickly would hurt less, I was sorely mistaken. My ribs strained against my chest, as if they wanted to break free from my body. I tried not to scream for fear of waking Cora. Stricken by coughing, I buried my face in my shoulder to keep flecks of blood from escaping. I forced my body to rise.

The fifteen steps to the fireplace took every ounce of my

concentration. Though I was a man of only twenty-eight, my body ached like that of an eighty-year-old. The sickness burrowed deep inside me now, waiting patiently for my certain end, and it was all I could do to put one foot in front of the other.

I collapsed between the fireplace and our small log pile, narrowly missing Cora's blackened toes. Toes that used to prance and jump around the peat bogs, dirtied but lively with curiosity and joy. Nothing like the wasted things festering next to me. Gently, I pulled the blankets over her exposed feet.

I moved her matted, sweaty hair from her flushed cheek. "I am here, little one. I'm not going anywhere."

At ten years old, she hadn't even lost all of her baby teeth. She tried to take a deep breath, but her lungs only managed stuttered inhales. Tucking the blankets tightly under her shoulders, I rested my arm on her back and watched her tiny body rise and fall. "I don't know what I would do without Mo Chroí…"

Cora coughed. "My arms hurt." She had been repeating this same refrain for days.

I pulled the blankets tightly under her mottled chin. The freezing winds wisping down the chimney blew out the flames.

Gripping the nearly empty pot of broth to place it on the embers of our fire, I heaved with all the strength I had left, but it wouldn't budge. Trying again with both hands, I still couldn't lift it. Instead, I grabbed a mostly empty cup of water, and brought it to my sister's mouth. I couldn't worry her by letting on that the sickness grew within me, too.

Her cracked lips reddened when the cold liquid touched them. She coughed as she tried to swallow, and the water erupted from her mouth and spilled onto the floor.

"Let's try again." I lifted the glass to her lips even slower, to no avail.

"It hurts." She groaned and looked up to meet my eyes.

"I know, Mo Chroí."

She blinked and winced. "Thank you for staying with me Rin."

"I'll never leave, Mo Chroí." I brushed her cheek with the back of my hand and forced a smile.

"I'm cold." She wheezed.

"I'll get the fire going again. Hold on."

It took both hands and every ounce of will I had to move just one of the logs onto the embers. The chunk of wood might have held the weight of an entire tree behind it. I forced myself to move another and then another. With each new log, the fire grew and so did my determination. Proud of my work, I arranged the logs to ensure an even burn. It took nearly twenty minutes to get the fire roaring again, but I did it.

"There we go." I dried my bloody, pus-ridden hands on a dirty rag. "How is that Mo Chroí? Better?"

She didn't respond.

"Mo Chroí?" Her little eyes remained closed, sealed, almost as if…

Panic washed over me. I gripped her by her shoulders and shook her as vigorously as my body would allow, "Cora! Wake up! Come on, wake up!" Bringing my cheek to her lips, I felt no breath escape her. I held my breath. There was nothing. "No, no, no, no, no!"

A lump formed in my throat. Hugging her with every ounce of strength I had, I willed her back to life. My freezing cold lips cracked as they curled under themselves. Through my tears, I coughed, releasing a bloody ooze onto my sister's chest. I whimpered softly. "Mo Chroí."

Hours passed.

I drifted in and out of sleep, adjusting my hold on her every time I awoke. The temperature slowly dropped. But I stayed there on the floor, curled around my sister's corpse until I couldn't hold her tightly anymore.

Her body had grown ridged, stiff … dead.

I knew I couldn't stay with her, but I couldn't bring myself to leave her. She was my best friend. My world. My Mo Chroí.

The memory of us rolling in the fields of her favorite purple flowers and just watching the clouds. Calling out the shapes we saw as they floated by. And the songs we'd sing as she played with the toys I made for her.

I smiled at the happy thoughts like they were warm blankets welcoming me into the next world. A place I was going to visit soon.

It took every ounce of strength, but I returned to my bed. Knowing I'd be joining Mo Chroí numbed the pain and took away my fear. An uncontrollable cough took over me, choking the air from me and forcing blood from my lungs. My head pounded and my throbbing joints swelled … then I passed out.

By the time I woke, the waxing gibbous moon hung high in the sky. The wind shuddered the window, giving me glimpses of the pasture and forest edge I loved.

A figure passed between the trunks of the trees, quickly followed by two others. I watched through the crack in the door as they made their way to my cabin's porch. I drew a labored breath.

Was someone coming to check on us? I tried to call out, but I gagged on the blood pooling in the back of my throat.

A hopeful fear came over me. That I wasn't hallucinating. That it wasn't just the wind. That something, or someone, was actually there. I tried to speak once again but I coughed instead.

Suddenly, the door whipped open and snowflakes and cold winter air burst into the cabin.

Blinking into the darkness, I took a shaky, shallow breath. "Hello?"

Moments passed without sound. I scanned the room. But I could not perceive a presence.

The door flew shut. I gurgled out a scream, curled myself into a ball, and pulled the covers up to my cheeks.

My eyes scanned the room over the blankets tucked high on my face, darting between the shadows dancing through the window and the darkest corners of the room.

A single branch tapped against my window, at the same frantic pace as my heart. And then, I felt the foot of my bed dip mere inches from my toes.

I opened my eyes and there, under the pale moonlight, sat a hooded figure with its back to me.

No breath escaped it. No twitch or movement overtook it. The moon's light ran from it.

I trembled. "Who are you?"

It didn't move.

"What … are … you?"

It didn't speak.

"Death?"

The figure finally stirred. "Of sorts."

I had the urge to beg Death to take me. To let me join Mo Chroí. To have a better afterlife than the human life I'd lived. But every breath took more and more effort than the last. Willing air through lungs that wouldn't fill, I mumbled my entreaty for mercy.

"Hush, you must save your strength." Death's monotone voice was soft and feminine, a comforting kind of cold. "We've been watching you Sorin. Ever since you were a small boy."

Every word seemed to have a specific purpose, like how I imagined it would be to talk with an omnipotent Goddess. Death turned toward me, pulling a cloth from her side and wiping the blood from my face. Two additional figures stepped into the moonlight from opposite corners of the room.

The man on the left sniffed at the air. An aged, dark-skinned giant with silver hair and hands large enough to crush a man's skull, he turned his head to one side like a rabbit who twists one ear, listening for danger.

"Maker. They are coming." His distinctly deep voice held an urgency that couldn't be ignored.

"I know, Fenix."

Death motioned to the other figure, a child of no more than fourteen, whose face was hidden behind golden locks under his hood. "Gaius, buy us some time. We'll meet you at camp."

Gaius nodded. The door opened and shut, and he was gone before I could blink.

"Who are … *they*?" I didn't know whether I merely thought it, or if the words had escaped my lips until she shushed me.

"You mustn't try to speak."

Fenix moved to the window, scouring the snowy wilderness. "Gaius is using himself as bait and has them moving West. If we're going to move him, we need to go now, my Maker."

In an instant, Death pressed her cheek firmly onto mine. She whispered something in my ear in a language I did not understand. She stared deeply into my eyes. I could not move, speak, or break from her gaze, and all my pain slipped away. I crept into something like a dream; with no more fear of death.

"My Maker." Fenix's tone held the sharp edge of warning.

She nodded without breaking her gaze, and softly said, "Sleep."

Against my will, my eyes closed, and I drifted into a dreamless night.


I AWOKE TO the scent of woodsmoke and the crackling of a fire just an arm's length away. The clean blankets nestled me tight and were topped with expensive furs. The festering aroma of my filth was gone.

I reached out from under the blankets and my hand found hard, moist, rocky ground. Risking a painful cough and a tight chest, I breathed deeply a thick, stale air. It had to be a burrow or a cave of sorts.

All of a sudden, a river of blood bubbled from deep in my lungs and spewed onto my chin and cheeks. Groaning loudly from the pain, I tried inconspicuously to raise my head and blink away my foggy eyesight. A dark figure began taking shape.

"You're awake," Death said, making her way to my side.

"Who are you?" I sputtered blood and saliva all over myself.

Kneeling beside me, she wiped my lips and face. "My human name was Claret Ivet Ingelehmann, but now it is just Claret." She peeled the hood away from her scarlet hair revealing pale gray, almost white skin, and smiled. "Or Maker."

I tried to speak—I had so many questions—but she raised a finger to her cerise lips. "Save your strength."

Just then, silhouetted by the moonlight, Fenix and Gaius appeared at the cave opening as if from nowhere.

"You crazy fool. You could have been killed!" Fenix patted Gaius on the back, nearly knocking him over. "You did well!"

Gaius quickly regained his balance and smiled.

Realizing their Maker was watching them, their faces hardened and their eyes glowed red. They seemed like two children silently scolded by their mother.

They sauntered over to her side. Their eyes remained fixed on hers and hers on theirs, like they communicated somehow. They flanked Claret, on either side, upright and stiff as if waiting for orders.

She seemed powerful. Respected. Cold.

"What *are* you?" I thought, careful not to say it aloud.

Looking back at me, her eyes glowed crimson, illuminating the darkness. "We are Nocturnae."

I gasped at the answer to a question I did not ask with a word I did not know. "What are—How did you—"

"In time, you will understand."

"We don't have time for this, my Maker," Fenix interrupted. "The Ceremony is in three days."

"Three days is plenty," Claret said with a face cold as stone, "and then time will never be an issue again."

"It won't be long before they realize they're off our trail and turn back," Fenix said, concerned.

"Then I guess we should get started."

Gaius and Claret exchanged looks.

A vision of Claret in a barn flashed in my mind. She sat opposite a woman who uttered a single word: prophecy.

Claret turned toward me. "Because if he dies … we will never find The Faceless King. It must be now."

Claret sternly addressed Gaius in their own language.

Gaius glared at me with his crimson eyes. "As you wish, my Maker."

Fenix followed suit. "Yes, my Maker."

"We will work quickly then." Claret stood and repositioned herself until she was cradling my head in her lap. Fenix and Gaius made their way to either side of me. Kneeling with their heads bowed, they began chanting in their mysterious language.

Fenix and Gaius gripped my hips and knees tightly, rendering me immobile. Laying there, helpless and terrified, I began to panic. I begged them to let me go. I had no idea what they were going to do to me, but I knew it couldn't be good.

Claret's hovering face overtook my vision as I fought to free myself. Our eyes locked once more.

Just like before, I heard a voice in my head. "Do not be afraid Sorin."

I wriggled one leg free, but Gaius quickly wrangled it.

"It will all be over soon," Claret said aloud.

Lunging upwards with all my effort and will, I tried freeing myself once more, but I couldn't move an inch. I couldn't overcome her physical and mental hold on me.

"Let the power come over you."

*"What do you mean power?"* I thought.

"Stay calm."

*"Please."*

"Breathe."

*"Just let me go."*

"You are far too important Sorin. I am sorry."

"Trust me," the voice said, just before the connection broke.

She centered her fang over the meatiest part of her lip and bit down, releasing a steady stream of blood down her chin. As painful as it looked, she never grimaced or flinched. She began kissing me, mixing her blood with my saliva, but it tasted sweet rather than metallic.

Suddenly, a strong pain pricked in my bottom lip as she pierced it, and our blood began to flow as one. In that moment fear and pain left me. I experienced the most euphoric, natural high, as I tasted my destiny.

My eyes shot open to experience the horror of the world around me changing. The darkness within the cave vanished. Crystals camouflaging themselves in the stones glowed green, and every insect became a beacon of light. The cave walls that held me in suddenly vanished, and I could see forests stretching out for miles that had not been there mere moments before.

My jaw popped, and a horrible pain like being force-fed hot ash wracked my face as my teeth began to move. I couldn't help but scream, violently kicking Claret and her two comrades away from me.

Claret hit the wall of the cave behind her, calling to the others. Somehow my mind translated the last bit of her sentence, "…him be."

A crippling churning began to fester in my stomach, growing so unbearable it forced me to curl into the fetal position.

A voice called out from the chaos within my mind, "Sorin. Sorin."

"*What?*" I screamed, grabbing my skull.

"You need to embrace the power, or it will kill you."

A searing heat wrapped around my knee and shot into my lower back, like someone pulled on a marionette string. "I don't feel power! Only pain!"

"*Embrace the pain.*"

Another string was pulled, but this time it connected my fingers to my ears and then to my eyes. "I can't. It hurts. I'm not strong enough."

Against my will, my own hands continued to force my eyes and ears closed. I thrashed wildly, but to no avail. I was dying.

"Focus on your strength."

"I-I-"

"FOCUS!"

And as my pulse weakened, I found it. My strength. *Mo Chroí.*

The warmth and the light from the fire blurred into darkness. "That's it. Now, envision a small room in your mind."

Darkness.

A light slowly illuminated the center of a room in my mind, revealing a wooden box just large enough for me to fit perfectly within.

"Make it whatever you like; it is yours."

All of a sudden, a heart burned its way into the center of the box, purple winter flowers appeared on the hinges, and an ornate wooden spoon grew where the handle would be.

*Cora.*

"Enter it."

Opening the creaky lid, I climbed inside.

"Wall off everything else."

Closing the lid tightly, I felt safe, whole.

"Use your pain to strengthen your foundation. Harden its extremities. Do that and you will be Nocturnae."

The pain that had been erupting in my gut calmed itself as steel lined the inside of my coffin sealing me away from the light. The tight, fiery pain in my knee and my back cooled itself. The piercing, electrical irritation in my fingers, ears, and eyes left me. My eyes shot open in the coolness of the cave.

That was the day I first felt my heart beat the way it would until my true death. I took a slow, deep breath and let out a horrifying scream of victory and rebirth.

# 5



A BURST OF loud clicking erupts from the braille device. I can't help but tease, "I hope you're writing good things about me."

"I'm sorry, what did you call your sister? Mo Crete? Crete like the Greek island?" She continues to type feverishly.

"Mo *Chroí*. It's Gaelic and means: my heart. You're close, but it's pronounced *mu cree.*"

Moving her lips ever so slightly, she logs the information. "Thank you."

She searches for the words to her next question.

"I believe it's my turn," I interrupt. "Who's Henry?"

But she's lost in a thought—or perhaps she's evaluating me—and doesn't respond.

She's either playing games again or distracted by something.

"Who is Henry?" I ask again. "You mentioned his name. He must be someone important if you wanted your escort to update him." My eyes fill with fury at the fact that a *human* dares to ignore me.

Oblivious to my irritation, she takes her time before offering a reply. "He's Dr. Shelley's apprentice."

"W-o-w." I roll my eyes as my frustration mounts. "Could you be any more ambiguous?"

She offers a measured grin. "You said, 'Claret bit her bottom lip, kissed you, bit your lip, and then your blood and saliva became one.' Am I correct in understanding that this is how you became Nocturnae?"

I look up at the ceiling. "Are you sure I said that? That doesn't seem right."

"Mr. Harker, please answer the question." She quickly types an irritated note.

"Yes. You are correct in your understanding."

But that's only half the equation dearie.

"Human-Nocturnae *relations* do exist then. It seems like that *one* Twilight movie gave me more information about human-Nocturnae relations than you'd thought." Her tone grates on my nerves and the corner of her mouth curls into a subtle smirk.

I bark out a laugh. "Unlike that glittering vivacious twink, we Nocturnae don't fuck our food. Imagine—if you will—the thought of conducting the act of coitus with a cow. Not a cow figuratively, but a literal cow … or I suppose a chicken … or pig."

In shock and disgust, Jean squeezes her eyes shut, crinkling her nose. "Mr. Harker, you refer to humans as nothing more than 'thin bags of fluid waiting to spill their succulence onto the ground,' correct?"

"In a manner of speaking." I run my tongue over my canine.

"Now," she continues, "tell me a little about your sister. Were you close?"

"Yes."

*Stop.*

"How old was she when she passed away?"

"Nearly eleven."

*Too young.*

"And that would have made you?" Jean asks in a soft tone.

"Twenty-eight."

She taps her finger twice like she's doing the math. "So that would make you seventeen years older than her… that seems a little odd. That would make your mother what, almost forty when she had Cora, if she had you in her early twenties?

Leave it alone.

"Unless…" Jean continues, "Cora wasn't your *sister*—"

I will drain you dry.

"—but your daughter."

Mo Chroí!

I lunge headfirst. My restraints tighten and the chair lurches forward. "Leave her OUT OF **THIS**!"

Smoke from my burning flesh fills the room as two silver bullet fragments fly from my side and onto the floor.

Flinching, Jean lets out an ear-piercing scream and hides her face behind her tablet for protection.

Between my trembling body, racing heart, and overwhelming desire to rip her spinal cord through her sternum, it takes everything in me to restrain myself.

Closing my eyes, I return to the dark room in my mind with the box in the center. Running my hand over the carved heart on its face, I open the box and step inside. I pull the lid closed and wall myself off from the world, shutting away both the pain and the power.

Slowly, my breathing returns to normal, and I open my eyes. "I apologize. That was rather primal of me."

Jean cautiously fixes her hair and adjusts the tablet on her lap. "I think that's enough for now Mr. Harker. I can see you're growing irritated. Let's take a break and pick this back up when I return shall we?"

"What about my question?"

"You shall have it," she says while flashing a smile, "once I return."

Curious.

With her cane in one hand and the braille device in the other, she leaves.

# 6

A SOFT CLICK echoed down the linoleum hallway as Dr. Jean Allicines closed the cell door behind her. From the doorknob, her hand floated up the edge of the Murphy door frame until it reached shoulder height. Her fingertips danced across the muralled wall until they found a large crack between two pieces of drywall.

Staff Sergeant Burr called out, "Oh ma'am. Can I take that from you?"

"This?" she asked, holding up her braille typewriter. "Please. Thank you, Tim."

He stood to take the device and noticed her arm shaking slightly. "Is everything alright?"

"Yes, everything is fine," Jean said, airily.

Taking the device, he stood near her fearing she'd faint. "Can I get you anything?"

"No, thank you. I'm just finding the center of the hallway," she said with a smile.

"Don't you just count your steps?"

Tapping her cane on the ground, she turned toward Tim, chuckling softly. "That's a common misconception. Imagine counting your steps on the way to your car, but you're stopped by a friend and have a five-minute conversation. By the time you're done talking you've forgotten what number you're on. Or what if there's construction somewhere on your typical route? Then what?"

"I guess I've never thought of that," Tim said, scratching his head. "I'm sorry, I meant no disrespect."

Jean shook her head. "I didn't find it disrespectful. In fact, I find it rather telling."

"What do you mean?" Tim said.

"You put yourself in my shoes for a moment and, even though inaccurate, you considered how I might work around my handicap." Jean looked at him. "That's kind."

"How *do* you work around it? I mean, sometimes, honestly, it's almost like you can see."

"Like you, I use landmarks but instead of seeing them, I feel them with my cane or hand, smell them, or hear them. For example, two hallways down, on the right, the radiator bangs every three seconds, and at one fifteen p.m. every day the hallway leading up to the Major's office smells like burnt popcorn."

"Wow. That's really cool," Tim said with a smile and nodded at the lead door. "Are you finished in there already?"

Jean glanced back. "No, just taking a break. The Subject needs a few moments to himself."

"Sure, I can't get you anything? It's nearly lunchtime."

Jean paused, considering. "You know, lunch would be nice. Who am I kidding, I'm famished. Is there a place I can sit and review my notes?"

"You can take my chair if you'd like," Tim said, gesturing to where he'd been sitting. "Or there's an empty conference room just down the hall."

"The conference room would be ideal, thank you," Jean said, and held out her arm.

"Right this way." Slinging his arm through hers, he escorted her to the empty conference room. Tim flipped the lights on, revealing a long conference table for sixteen with high back carpet-like chairs lining the edge of the table. Pulling the head chair away from the table, Tim set her writing device down and patted the head rest. "Here you are."

Jean held her cane perpendicular to the floor as she approached the seat to shield her from slamming her thigh into the table or its corner. "Thank you," she said, taking her seat.

"And what can I get you for lunch ma'am?"

"A big salad with a vinaigrette dressing would be wonderful."

Snapping his finger, he cautiously smiled. "Vegetarian, right?"

"Yup. And an iced tea. Maybe peach or raspberry, if they have it."

"Sure thing. I'll be back in a few minutes."

"Oh, Tim," Jean called, as the Staff Sergeant headed for the door.

"Yes?"

"Does this room have a white noise generator?"

"Oh, umm…" He reached his arm around the door frame to the

light switch and searched with his arm. "Yes! Yes, it does."

"Would you mind turning it on for me?"

"Sure thing," Tim said, flipping the switch and closing the door behind him.

Folding her cane with one hand, she swiveled herself under the table with the other. She placed the cane on the tabletop beside her note-taking device and ran her fingers across the braille tabs to review her notes:

Doctor Jean Allicines with Mr. Sorin Harker, Subject 076-7-46, on the morning of January 18, 2019. The Subject displays signs of antisocial personality disorder, specifically, malevolence. He exhibits parallels to Ted Bundy.

It isn't clear yet how he learned of this facility, but he may have knowledge of other facilities within The Company. We need to contact the Washington office and find out if anyone with the proper clearances is missing or dead. I have to assume he knows about either Subject 252-7-38 or 053-8-79.

He is far more talkative than our other Subject, or he is at least willing to talk if, in exchange, I talk. This breaks protocol, but we need this information. I must learn more.

It turns out the Nocturnae had been watching him for years and only turned him when he was knocking on death's door - why?

If he is as important to them as he
described, why did they not change him
sooner? What is the prophecy he mentioned
in the story? Does he even know?

I believe he has blindly given us the
missing piece to the PHANG program. The
Patient and the Subject must have their
blood and saliva mixed together before
being ingested and injected. This new
intelligence should secure continued
funding for the PHANG program under the
pretense that the procedure on Patient-XIV
is a success.

She pauses a moment before adding another note:

The Subject had a daughter, Cora, who died
from the plague in 1350. Bringing her up
infuriates him, sending him into a violent
rage. I recommend staying clear of this
subject unless absolutely necessary…

7



THE SEDATED PATIENT'S rusted bed wheels squeaked on the linoleum flooring as Henry made the final turn into the lab. His racoon eyes locked on the old clock hanging on the opposing wall.

"Twelve fifteen. But that clock is seventeen minutes fast so it's eleven fifty-seven. Wait … fifteen minus seventeen is … fuck, I don't know, I'm so freaking tired," he mumbled to himself.

"Hurry up," Dr. Shelley, goaded, refusing to look up from his clipboard. "Did you stop for dinner on the way?"

When Henry was halfway through the door frame, the thick metal clipboard holding the patient's chart fell from the bed and onto Henry's foot. "Jesus, Mary, and Joseph," he bellowed, and raised his throbbing foot as he picked up the chart. Catching Dr. Shelley's subtle glance at the loud commotion, Henry chuckled. "No, but I can go out if you'd like. I'm starving!"

"Smart-ass." Gifting him a smile, Dr. Shelley threw the clipboard onto the unconscious patient's lap. "Let's go."

Dr. Shelley's weathered hands gripped the cold steel bed frame, swinging it hard into the laboratory and nearly ripping it from Henry's hands.

"And I'm tired," Henry whined. No response. "We've been here for like a day and a half straight, Professor," Henry pleaded.

Together, the two men wheeled the bed into a small patient room, centering the bed under a series of medical lights. Locking the wheels down, they attached an array of electrodes, monitors, tubes, and wires to the patient.

"Once we finish this, we will call it a day."

A childish grin spread across Henry's face at the news. "Really?"

"Well, once *you* finish, I mean. My back has been killing me," Dr. Shelley said, walking away from the bed. "I need to lie down for a bit."

"You're not going to go *lie down*. You're going to go sit in that hideous, rusty tweed chair that's straight out of the 60s and watch me do all the work."

"Yes, exactly. And the chair may be god-awful to look at, but it cradles your ass in ways you would not believe. You should try sitting in it sometime. It will change your life."

"Nooo, thank you. But you are gonna get that checked out, right? Your back's been bothering you for months."

Ignoring the young man, Dr. Shelley groaned and flopped into the seat of his chair. "And, don't forget to give me a central line." He reached for an unwashed CIA mug, stained with forty years' worth of coffee grime, from the middle of his desk. Blowing into the mug to make sure it was 'clean,' he raised an eyebrow. "Did you hear me?"

"Yes Professor. I heard you. You go ahead and pour yourself a coffee, kick your feet up, and turn on *Gilmore Girls*."

Dr. Shelley smirked and poured three-hour-old sludge-like coffee into the mug. Black droplets splashed across a number of official reports pertaining to the patient. "I think I will."

"Do you even know what *Gilmore Girls* is?"

"No. But thank you for bringing it to my attention. What was the patient's drug of choice again?"

Henry applied a water-soluble lubricant to the tip of the catheter. "Hold on." Inserting a catheter into the eye of the patient's penis, he checked the patient's medical chart. "Umm…"

"Morphine?"

"No, oxy."

He made a note in his open research notebook. "Did they tell us where they found *this* one?"

Henry glanced back at the chart as he attached a pulse oximeter to the patient's index finger. "It says that he volunteered for the procedure."

Sighing, the old man ran his hand through where his hair used to be and fixed his eyes on the constellations of star-like holes that dotted the ceiling. "No one volunteers for this procedure."

"Do you think he was manipulated?" Picking up the chart, Henry began writing.

"No."

"Blackmail?"

"Worse."

Henry stopped quickly. "What's worse than blackmail?"

"Hope."

Henry paused, bewildered. "What do you mean?"

"I bet he lost something very important to him because of his addiction."

"Like what?"

"His house. His job. It could be anything."

"And you think The Company promised him he would get his old life back if he volunteered for this procedure? Fat chance of that."

"No … I think they told him they could cure his addiction, and he *assumed* the rest would come."

"And they let him think that. Preying on the weak … that's just messed up."

"That's science."

Shaking his head, Henry checked the patient's pupil response. "I hope you're wrong."

Dr. Shelley took a large gulp of his coffee, and swallowed hard. "How is the patient looking? Are we all hooked up?"

"Well, he's more machine than man now." Henry gestured at the patient.

Dr. Shelley breathed deeply into his cupped hands that covered his face in his best Darth Vader impression.

Henry yawned. "I see what you did there."

Heaving himself up to join his apprentice at the patient's bedside, Dr. Shelley checked the connections and monitors. "Well done. Well done indeed."

"Thank you, Professor."

"When we administer the Suboxone, I want vitals taken every

hour for the first four hours and then every three hours for the following twenty. I want blood draws every thirty minutes for twenty-four hours after administration. Keep his fluids up. I do not want his liver or kidneys failing during his semi-rapid detox. Oh," he added, snapping his fingers, "I'd like stool and urine samples as well."

"I will make a note of it for the nursing staff." Henry scribbled on the chart.

"We will begin the procedure at," Dr. Shelley studied his pocket watch before looking to the ceiling as if the constellations knew the level of generosity he wished to bestow upon Henry, "Nine a.m., Thursday morning. How does that sound?"

"Sounds good." Henry rubbed his eyes. "I'll see you tomorrow."

"Henry, that's in three days." Dr. Shelley patted the boy on the back. "Go home. Get some sleep. You need it."

"Thank you!" Henry peeled off his nitrile gloves, blindly tossing them into the waste bin, and grabbed his coat on the way out. As he neared the door, he heard Dr. Shelley softly flipping pages in the chart and mumbling to himself. "Don't sleep here again Professor. There's more to life than work."

"The paperwork won't fill itself out. See you Thursday."

A frigid gust of wind rifled through the room as Henry exited. Dr. Shelley returned to his desk.

"Alone at last." He downed the last bit of his cold, burnt coffee, and removed a bottle of Jameson from the bottom drawer, pouring four fingers into the mug.

The first sip caused him to grimace. It burned ever so slightly, clearing his palate. He smiled, leaned back in the chair everyone hated, and took a second sip. Vanilla with a subtle bit of honey flooded his senses. Holding the mug under his nose, he closed his eyes, breathed deeply, and began to drift off into a daydream.

The whiskey's light floral aroma, peppered with spiced wood and glazed nuts, lifted his soul. He tapped his wedding band against the ceramic mug to the beat of Elton John's *Your Song*, and spun the band with his thumb between clanks.

Visions of his beautiful wife's face flooded his mind. Her perfect ivory teeth sparkled under the dazzling sunlight, drawing contrast from her dark chocolate hair and malted eyes. A soft giggle floated up to him. Pink bows bound the little girl's ponytail that bounced around his wife's legs as she laughed. Her tiny, perfect hand reached for his, and she looked at him with her shimmering sapphire eyes.

Falling fully into the dream, his grip loosened, and he spilled whiskey all over his khakis.

"Shit." From amongst the papers on his desk, he grabbed an old napkin and dabbed at himself.

"I guess I better start going through this mess," he said to no one, picking up his thick, gray leather notebook.

In the center of the cover was the title:


```
Project:
Phylogenetic Human Alteration with
Nocturnae Genomics (PHANG)
Classification Level:
Top Secret/PII/Paranormal Intelligence/No
Foreign
```


Licking his fingers, Dr. Shelley opened the book to a

bookmarked page, and wrote:

```
Date: 14-May-2018
Patient: XIII
```

He paused, looked at the patient and guessed, "Late-twenties? Early-thirties?" He scanned the document to confirm. "Thirty-six. Huh, he's aged well for an addict. His addiction must be new."

Adding the information to his research notebook, he continued reading the documents, writing only what he deemed important.

```
European, Caucasian descent. Roughly 190 to
200    pounds.    Athletic,    likely    a
weightlifter, shoulders striated and back
well-defined. Out of the ordinary for an
addict.
```

"I need to confirm that," he thought, sifting through the papers until he located a document titled: EARLY LIFE. "German-American. Football. Wrestling."

Dr. Shelley removed his heavy glasses and rubbed the sleep from the crooks of his eyes. Removing the CAC—Common Access Card—from his lanyard, he accessed his encrypted emails on the unclassified network and read:

```
Gunnery Sergeant Roger T. Stephens DD-214:
Dishonorably discharged for rape, assault,
and battery. Blood type, AB-negative. Top
of  his  unit.  Multiple  deployments  to
Afghanistan, Iraq, Kuwait, and undisclosed
locations.
```

There were more than two dozen additional documents attached to the email.

Dr. Shelley opened the first document and rolled his eyes. "Why would they send me this? I don't care about his report cards." He opened the second document. "Redacted." He opened the third document. "Useless." Groaning to himself, he threw his hands up in the air. "This is going to be a long night."

The hours passed slowly as Dr. Shelley read through the documents, scribbling notes. Soon the notebook was filled with arrows joining a myriad of important facts in the ledger.

By the time Dr. Shelley found satisfaction with the story he'd pieced together, the sun crested the horizon and he wet his lips with whiskey for the last time. He flipped his mug over, placing it rim down atop his closed notebook, grabbed his jacket, and made his way out of the lab.

Pausing at the door, with a hand on the light switch, he looked back at his desk. A photo of his wife peered back at him, an anchor in a sea of chaos. Pulling a chain from under his collar, he caressed a small, studded wedding band.

"Good night, my love," he whispered and turned off the lights.

It was 8:45 A.M. Thursday morning when Henry arrived again at the lab. He turned the remaining lights on as he entered.

Making his way to the kitchenette to clean the pot, he noticed the redacted reports littering Dr. Shelley's desk. He cleaned the pot and quickly started the first pot of the day. Leaving the coffee to brew, he returned to Dr. Shelley's desk where he sifted through the documents Dr. Shelley had studied for hours.

Henry shuffled the pages in his hand, trying to make sense of them, he noticed Dr. Shelley's notebook between the loose papers. He looked over his shoulder at the lab's entrance to see if anyone was coming. Dropping the papers, he grabbed the gray leather-bound notebook and opened it to the bookmarked page.

From parsing through the seemingly little contents of the redacted documents here is what I have learned:

During Gunny's time in either Iraq or Kuwait, mid-90s to early-2000s, he was captured and tortured for an extended period of time—this could explain a number of scars across his body. This would mean he was one of the top elite special force's soldiers—at one time.

Jennifer, his ex-wife, filed for divorce in 2008, claiming domestic violence and endangerment. However, it's likely the patient was suffering from severe post-traumatic stress disorder (PTSD) or complex PTSD after being captured and tortured.

I wish I had a better idea of the time period he was a prisoner-of-war, allowing me to better diagnose him.

There was no mention of children, however, that could have played a role in the divorce as well. A mother runs, scared for her child's, or children's, safety. Worse yet, upon Gunny's return, they could have tried to have a child and lost it.

```
Resulting in Gunny, already afflicted by
PTSD, spiraling into depression and numbing
his pain with opiates.
```

"What the fuck," Henry said. "Sometimes the old man says some of the craziest things. Reminds me a lot of Gerard Parkes's portrayal of Doc in *Boondock Saints*." Laughing to himself, he did his best impression, "Why don't you make like a tree and … g-g-g-get the fuck outta here." Henry shook his head, smiling. "Great movie."

The coffee pot began to burp, pulling him back to the present for a moment; but Henry quickly returned to his reading.

```
Brazilian Jiu-jitsu, twelve years. Krav
Maga, five years. Multiple arrests for
disturbing the peace throughout his teenage
years. However, placed among the top eight
percent of his graduating class. Top of his
class at basic training. Excellent
marksman. Earliest acceptant into the
special forces in nearly a decade.
    He began using opioids…
```

"Good morning, Henry."

Startled by Dr. Shelley's greeting, Henry let out a quick gasp. He closed the notebook quickly and tossed it among the papers littering the desk. Scooping the CIA cup from the desk, he briskly made his way to the coffee pot while Dr. Shelley hung his cap and jacket on the coat rack adjacent to the door.

"How was your time off?" Dr. Shelley asked, making his way toward his desk.

"Very restful." After filling the cup, Henry met Dr. Shelley at his desk. "How was yours?"

"It was very nice." Dr. Shelley accepted the coffee with both hands.

"I did go for a few walks in the park, thought about our friend over there."

"Oh yeah? What about?" Dr. Shelley inquired.

"Mostly how awful it must have been for him to lose his family. I mean, understandable that his wife would file for divorce, it is still terrible to lose your family."

Pausing a moment, Dr. Shelley glanced at the photo on his desk. "I cannot imagine how terrifying it must have been for him. Fighting in wars. Being a POW. Watching his friends die. Being blown to pieces. He probably wanted nothing more than to cry in his wife's lap. And instead of comforting him, she left him."

"Maybe he wasn't the same man that she'd married before his deployments," Henry said.

"She gave up in his darkest hour … when things *really* got hard." Dr. Shelley's eyes glistened as he stared into the distance.

"Are you alright Professor?"

Turning his back to Henry, Dr. Shelley wiped his eyes. "Fine, just something in my eye. Is Gunny awake?"

Henry punched in his six-digit pin to log into the computer. "No. He could probably sleep through an explosion."

"Run through the chart once more. Make sure everything's in order."

"Yes, Professor." Henry relocked his computer and made his way over to the patient's bed. *Just What the Doctor Ordered* by Ted Nugent began to play, quietly, over the lab speakers. Henry looked over his shoulder. "Really?"

Dr. Shelley did nothing but crack a smile.

Henry couldn't help but smile himself. He picked up the chart hanging at the foot of the bed and began comparing the machines to the records, nodding his head while sipping his coffee. After a few minutes of silence, he looked up. "Everything looks good, Professor."

"Wonderful." Dr. Shelley pulled a stool up next to the bed and called out softly. "Gunnery-sergeant, it's Dr. Eugene Shelley."

The patient slowly opened his eyes and the heart-rate monitor began beeping more quickly.

"Heart rate is elevated," Henry said, watching the monitor.

Dr. Shelley gently grabbed the Marine's hand and slowly patted the top of it. "Everything is fine. You're in my lab. Calm down. Do you remember me?"

The patient's eyes fluttered open. "Good morning, Dr. Shelley. Henry," Gunny said.

"Heart rate is slowing," Henry said. He pulled a small flashlight from his breast pocket and checked Gunny's pupil response. "The medications we gave you the last few days can make you a little nauseous without food in your stomach. I'm sorry about that."

"Good morning, Gunny," Dr. Shelley chimed in. "Hopefully we didn't startle you while waking you. Detox seems to have gone well. How do you feel this morning?"

"I could use a drink of water."

"Sorry Gunny, no food or drink before the procedure; but you can have all the water and ice cream you want after. Will that work?"

"Sounds good to me doc."

"Before we begin, do you have any questions about the procedure?"

"As long as it's going to fix whatever's wrong in my head so I can move on with my life, I don't care what it is, how bad it hurts, or how long the recovery is. I just don't want to be broken anymore." Gunny's guilt-ridden eyes darted back and forth. "Hey Doc, do you think this could help me win Jen back?"

"Anything is possible," Dr. Shelley patted him on the shoulder before turning to Henry. "Prep our friend here for the procedure."

Henry nodded. "Yes, Professor."

"Lie back and relax." Dr. Shelley's tone was gentle "You are in good hands. Henry, get to it."

An hour passed before Henry had completed running through the list of questions, made sure all the necessary equipment was present, and sedated the patient.

Dr. Shelley, washed, gloved, and gowned, and stepped into a small-scale surgical room. He approached his instrument table. "Wonderful, let us begin. *Syringe*."

Henry passed a large needle and flipped a recording device to ON.

"We still start with fifty-nine milliliters and take a parasternal approach to inject the solution into the right ventricle. Although this method is no longer practiced, it will allow for the virus to reach the patient's heart and filter through the body much more rapidly."

Dr. Shelley spoke loudly for the audio recorder as he pierced the patient's skin.

"Pulling twenty milliliters of the patient's blood into the syringe, allowing for the two bloods to mix before injection. This should prevent a repeat of Patient-XII. Patient-XII died shortly after surgery from a pulmonary embolism and a cerebrovascular accident. We are doing everything in our power to prevent that from happening again. Are we not, Henry?"

"Yes, Professor," he answered, eyes glued to the monitors.

"Pushing the syringe now," Dr. Shelley said.

Suddenly, the heart-rate monitor spiked from fifty-three beats-per-minute to 179 beats-per-minute.

"Jesus Christ, he's tachycardic. Wait, now he's in V-fib!"

"Starting CPR. Push epinephrine," Dr. Shelley yelled, remembering their defibrillator was being serviced by PMEL— Precision Measurement Equipment Laboratory. Henry scrambled, but wasn't moving quick enough. "*Now*, damn it!"

Henry pushed the solution. The drug entered the man's blood stream, yielding no change to the monitors. His eyes rolled back in his head as foam formed in his mouth.

"Shit, he's seizing," Dr. Shelley muttered, looking at his pocket watch to time its length. "Suction."

Henry quickly grabbed the suction tube, placing it in the corner of the patient's mouth as he and Dr. Shelley turned the man onto his side.

Henry, focused on the patient and his monitors, gave a quick appreciative glance at Dr. Shelley. "Now what?"

"The poor man has to ride it out. Keep suctioning and push that instrument tray back." Twenty seconds or so later the seizing stopped, and so did the patient's heart. "Start compressions."

Henry interlocked his fingers and drove all his weight into the man's sternum. A rib broke on the third compression. He stopped and looked at Dr. Shelley with a terrified face.

"Keep going!" Dr. Shelley yelled as he retrieved a bag valve mask and began bagging.

The men continued performing CPR for forty-four minutes before Dr. Shelley looked at the clock. Removing his hands from the patient, he softly said, "That's it. Time of death: 10:58 a.m."

"What are we doing wrong?" Henry asked despairingly. "We've had 252-7-38 bite the patient before snapping their neck because we thought death might trigger the change. Failure. We tried not snapping the patient's neck. Failure. We've had the patient drink 252-7-38's blood from a vial. Failure. We had the patient drink the blood from the wrist. Failure! Then we added human blood. Repeated everything. All *failures*. All of them, dead. Why?!"

Henry had failed at very little throughout his life until now, a thirteenth failure in a row.

"Science, Henry. In the interest of science."

# 8



THE TAPPING OF Jean's cane returns to the main hallway and I straighten up in my seat as best I can. Slowly, the clicking of her heels, tapping of her stick, and the squeaking of her escort's shoes close in on my prison door.

They stop and the electronic device outside the room beeps, triggering a mechanical device to click, unlocking the door.

The door opens and a familiar red-tipped cane slides into view, pattering along the floor. "Well, it's about time," I say, annoyed. "When you said, 'let's take a break' I thought you meant a *break*, not I'll be back at the end of the workday."

"I've got it from here, Tim. Thank you." Jean says over her shoulder before closing the door behind her with the heel of her shoe.

Gliding across the floor she finds her seat effortlessly, like she's done this a million times even though she hasn't. Once again, she folds her cane, tucks it into her tote, and positions her note taking device on her lap.

She doesn't take her tote when she leaves … could that be my way out?

"Bravo Jean. Bravo indeed. If I were a betting Nocturnae I'd swear that you could see in the dark." Licking the corner of my lips, I crack a smile. "Wanna bite on it?"

Ha.

She ignores my antics. "Tell me a little more about the giant man and the blonde boy. Fenix and Gaius, was it? What happened to them?"

"No exchange of pleasantries? No apology for your extended absence?" I poke.

She folds her hands on her lap and cocks her head to one side. "I apologize for my extended leave Mr. Harker. I hope I wasn't keeping you from any appointment."

She's feisty … I like that.

A smile squeaks through her red lips but evaporates into a hardened demeanor. "Shall we—"

Sniffing the air, I cut her off, "A salad of romaine, arugula, and spinach topped with fresh strawberries, goat cheese and a raspberry vinaigrette. Oh, and," I sniff the air three more times, "candied walnuts … no, pecans. Candied pecans. You washed it down with a cup of blueberry green tea and a cucumber and lime seltzer water. Do you like those? They don't really do it for me. Gives me heartburn."

Taking a moment's pause, she picks a piece of greenery from her teeth with the edge of her nail. "That's very impressive."

"Tell me, as a vegetarian, do you think about the hundreds of furry little creatures mutilated in farmers' combines when harvesting your various kinds of green, leafy goodness?"

Ignoring my question, she runs her tongue over her teeth to make sure they're clean. "Let's continue. Can you tell me—"

"Not yet. It's my turn now." She agrees with a single nod. "When did you start working here? Not the number of years it's been, but rather, when in your life did you start?"

She's clever enough to answer only what I ask and nothing more.

"I started during my undergraduate program as an intern. Can you tell me more about Fenix and Gaius?"

Well then. She wants information from me but short-hands her responses. I'll play her game.

"In due time."

"O-o-okay … Do you remember where the cave was? Specifically?"

"No," I say, barely allowing her to finish her question.

"Mr. Harker, if you do not cooperate, I cannot guarantee that I can restore to you what was taken." She folds her hands over her note taking device.

"It is you that must cooperate dearie. I answered your initial question in great detail only to have you spit in my face with your pathetic attempt at an answer. If you want me to bless you with my knowledge, then it's only right for you to do the same."

She sits still, studying the air in my direction, as though somehow, she can see right into me. After a moment, she slowly nods. "I was in my third year of undergrad pursuing child psychology; specifically, helping kids deal with the loss of a loved one. I had never thought to do anything else, but my money was running low, and when I was offered an internship to study the criminally insane, I couldn't afford to turn it down. How was that?"

"Much better. Thank you."

She didn't come from money. She chose to spend her life with children of loss … did she lose someone close to her at a young age? She's intrigued and driven by knowledge. Specifically, puzzles. Obsessed with what makes a criminal, a murderer, a Nocturnae tick?

"Now, about Fenix and Gaius, could you be more specific with your question? What would you like to know about them?"

"Did they have any definitive markings? Did they have any scars or tattoos?"

Chuckling, I say, "Nocturnae are unable to have or maintain tattoos and scars after new birth." A half-truth to keep my secret a bit longer.

"New birth? As in the transition from being human to—"

"Nocturnae, correct."

Jean quickly types a short addition. "So, no tattoos, is that a law of your race? Or are you physically unable to sustain a tattoo?"

"Do you have any tattoos?"

"What does that have to do with anything?"

That sounds like a yes. "My turn."

"Yes."

Right again.

Rolling my hands in circles under the shackles, I try to coax more from her. "Of?"

"An ear with a slash through it."

"Huh, I assumed you were the type to get something tribal like a rose or a butterfly on your lower back."

"It's actually on the back of my shoulder," she says.

"It's not a very flattering sounding tattoo. What does it mean?"

"My mom was deaf."

A blind daughter and a deaf mother. That'd make communication difficult. "Ah, I see. Sentimental. Have you noticed that the ink has faded since you first got it done?"

"How would I notice that?" She stares blankly out of her sightless eyes.

How did I blunder that? Is there something other than silver in my system?

"I do apologize." Clearing my throat, a harsh metallic taste consumes my mouth. "I don't know how I could have forgotten that."

Something feels wrong. Something feels very wrong.

"You were saying. Tattoos and how they fade," she encourages, while making a note.

The silver, it's inside me. It feels like it's in my veins. Did they inject me with silver? Can I survive this? I can't let her know anything's wrong.

"Yes. Many people believe tattoos fade because of the sun. On the contrary, tattoos fade because cells die, and new ones are born to take their place. As an immortal, tattoos would eventually become nothing more than a memory and in time, forgotten altogether. Much like the inevitability of death for you and your counterparts."

"But they could exist for a period of time then, yes?"

"Yes. But to more definitively answer your initial question: No, I did not see any tattoos."

"Scars?"

"No." My voice is off, even to me. It's shaky. I have to give her something to look past it. "When it comes to scars, I'm the only one I know of with a scar."

"Really? Where is it? How did you get it?"

Good. It worked. I could really use some more blood to help flush whatever this is out of my system.

"Jumping ahead of ourselves a little, don't you think?"

"What do you mean?"

Filing my canine with the tip of my tongue, I drop my chin. "Aren't you going to let me have you for dinner first?"

"Hilarious. Now, the scar. Better yet, let's back up a bit. Could you describe yourself for a poor blind girl?" Her fingers dance softly over the keys waiting for my reply.

"Why don't you place your hands on my face and see for yourself."

She smiles. "Nice try."

It was worth a shot.

"I'm short for a male, not much taller than you actually. I have thick, dark brown hair, almost black, kept exceptionally short. Today you call it—what's the … long and tight? High and fade?"

"High and tight?"

I snap my fingers in their shackles. "High and tight! Thank you. My eyes are green, though they shift to hazel or brown when I view the world in the limited spectrum of infrared or ultraviolet. And I have a rather large nose relative to my mouth. My features produce a rather ominous appearance, I dare say. And of course, there's the facial hair. Nothing feels better or looks more sinister than blood dripping from your beard."

Repositioning herself in her seat, she crosses her legs toward me, squaring up her shoulders with mine in an attempt to distract me from her flushed cheeks. She softly clears her throat and tightens her messy bun, forcing back her coy smile.

"Attractive and arrogant," she says coldly, like I've struck a nerve. "Now tell me about the scar."

"Of course … how could I forget it? There is a deep scar that stretches from the hairline near my right ear, through my eye, cresting over my nose, and ending on the opposing cheek. For decades I hated it. I smashed every mirror I passed."

"And now?"

"After 400 years, I've grown rather accustomed to it. I do believe it is my turn to ask a question. I've been rather lenient on you, haven't I?"

Startled, she draws back her head. "What do you mean?"

"I haven't … rattled your cage—so to say."

"No," she says with relief in her voice. "Which I appreciate. What is your question?"

Let's change that. "Tell me Jean, when you were a child, did your parents read you stories of princesses being rescued by their prince?"

"Yes."

"What was your favorite story as a young girl?"

"I was particularly partial to the story of Cinderella."

"Why is that?"

Leaning back, she lets her guard down a touch. "I'd say … it's an underdog story. It illustrates how important it is to never give up on your dreams, even if everything and everyone in the world is against you."

An inspiring notion riddled with the arrogance of Freudian projection.

"What if I were to tell you, the stories you've grown to love were not made up. Not entirely at least. Elders told them to keep children safe from wolves, bears, and other monsters lurking in the shadows of the forest. Unfortunately, for humanity's sake, these stories have been romanticized. Creating a false sense of security for you and your children."

"It's a story. It's supposed to be fun. I've watched it numerous times with Dr. Shelley's niece," she says. "Well, she watched, I listened."

The boss. And he has a niece … that she's *met*. A little odd but not unheard of for long-term colleagues.

"The truth is Jean, Cinderella's fairy godmother isn't a fairy, or even a person. It's a tree that she planted on her mother's grave and watered with her tears. For her stepsisters to fit their feet into the glass slipper, one cuts off her big toe, while the other cuts off a piece of her heel. Their plan is only foiled when the prince notices blood covering the glass slipper."

"I know the story," she grimaces.

Huh, she's smart… for a human and much harder to rattle. This is going to be fun.

"Or, in Hansel and Gretel, one of the last lines in today's story reads, '…now all their cares were at an end, and they lived happily together,' but originally, the wicked witch consumed the children."

"Okay. What's your point?"

"Fairy tales are merely a series of lies to keep children oblivious to the horrors of the world. When they grow up, however, their world crumbles because they don't know how to handle trauma and hardship. You humans are doing a dangerous disservice to your youth, allowing them to grow up to be ignorant, feeble, brats who walk blindly and willingly to their deaths. It's not my fault your people weren't prepared for me. They only had 400 years to prepare. And still they failed."

"Okay Mr. Harker, that's enough," she interjects. "I'd like to get back on topic. What happened after you were turned in the cave?"

# 9



WAKING THE NEXT morning, I assumed everything had been a vivid dream. Blackness often surrounded me in our cottage, especially in winter. But when I reached out from under my warm blankets, my fingers found damp stones all around me. The stones proved I found myself in a new reality. One where Cora had died and I had been turned.

Slowly, the room brightened and shadows danced on the walls. Though I searched for the source of light, I found nothing. Pine filled my nose, but there were no conifers in sight. A fly landed on my hand and I could feel every hair on its body separately as it scurried about before taking off.

Panic began to overtake me when a voice entered my mind. *"Your eyes are adjusting to the lack of light."*

"Claret?"

Claret took a small step away from the cave wall opposite of me. "Yes."

"What do you mean exactly? My eyes are … what?"

"We Nocturnae can see more of the world than humans. For now, your body will adjust automatically, but in time you'll be able to control it and see the world in ways you never dreamed possible. Your sight isn't the only thing that has changed. Stand up, explore your new body."

When I brought myself to my feet, my body felt weightless. It moved with such ease that it felt foreign. The hair on my arms, hands, and even knuckles had darkened and thickened. My spindly arms and legs had reached the size of a well-fed soldier, my skin pulled tightly across the protruding muscles and veins.

Peeling my shirt from my torso, I found that it, too, had changed. My flat chest and sickly, sunken abdomen had been replaced with a thick pair of masculine pectorals and well-defined abs. Although I couldn't see my back, I sensed its broadness. In the darkness of the cave, I explored my alien body. I softly touched my face with the tips of my fingers. I ran my hands across my arms. My chest. My thighs. Yes, even my groin.

"What happened to me?"

"You have experienced new birth. Your body has taken its perfect form," Claret said. "Even now, as I speak at barely a whisper you can hear me from across the cave."

Startled, I stumbled backwards, tripping over a pile of rocks and landing on my backside. The small pebbles and stones tumbling over one another sounded like an avalanche now.

"Go on," she encouraged, "look into the furthest depths of this cave and tell me what you see."

The blackest parts of the cave came into focus, and that which was right in front of me blurred.

"I see insects flying on the walls and bats dropping from the ceiling to feed on them." Standing from my fallen position, I took a couple of steps toward the cave life. "Unbelievable."

"He is strong," Fenix said from somewhere behind me.

As I turned to look at him, Claret panicked, "Sorin. Don't!"

But it was too late. My eyes met the rising sun beaming into the cave entrance beyond Fenix's head. I screamed in intense pain, dropped to my knees, and shielded my eyes with my hands.

"What's happening?!" I wept.

"You are no longer limited to just one small section of the world's beauty. You're able to see flowers as bees do, penetrate the bottom of the deepest abyss, or even watch a family of chipmunks through a dense forest on a moonless night. Your eyes are adjusting to your environment," Claret said.

Claret closed the twenty-foot gap between us in a flash. She didn't give me a reassuring pat on the back or a gentle caress of the arm. Rather, she stood behind me with her hands behind her back like a shepherd would watch over his flock.

"I don't understand. How is this possible?"

"When you became Nocturnae, your mortality and its flaws were stripped from you. Rendering your physical form a blank canvas, capable of being rewritten."

I knelt there, staring at her, confused, questioning the choice that had been made for me. Was this really better than death?

"The Firstborn came into this world many millennia ago. We Nocturnae, their children, were designed to be the perfect hunters for a perfect prey. Nothing on this earth can match our strength, speed, or our stealth."

"Then why did you fear those men last night?"

"He's observant, my Maker," Gaius said softly.

Revealing a fang from the corner of her mouth, she closed her eyes. "I'd expect nothing less."

"Humans have evolved. Although we can hunt in the blackest night, recover from almost any injury, and scale mountains with ease, we can no longer underestimate them."

"They also have a strong ally and weapon," Fenix added.

"Who's their ally? What weapon?" I asked.

"The weapon and the ally are one in the same, and it is the sun," Gaius said, pointing at the morning sky.

"Daylight can kill us? How is that possible?"

"Direct sunlight will quickly burn your skin, forcing your healing factor to engage. As your healing factor fights your injuries from the sun, you will quickly lose energy until you are exhausted. Your body will shut down, crippling you to the ground and shackling you to your true death."

The cold chill of her bittersweet foreboding rested heavily upon me. I had to know. "And … what is the *true death*?"

"First, you need to understand what humans believe happens when you're turned because, while death and true death are different for us, death is all the same to them," Gaius calmly explained.

"The human race believes that when a human is turned, their physical body dies, releasing their soul and allowing it to move on," Claret said.

"This plane of existence has gone by many names throughout

history: Heaven, Hell, Valhalla, Elysium, Aaru, Nifhel, or simply the Afterlife," Fenix said.

Claret looked to Fenix, nodding. "Once the soul has left the body, humans believe a demon spirit can possess it, transforming it into Nocturnae. Rather than educate them, we decided to keep humans ignorant and exploit their oldest and strongest emotion."

They all fell silent, but their crimson eyes remained fixed on me. "Which is?"

"Fear," Gaius said, raising his chin and flashing his ghost-white fangs. "And fear of the unknown…"

"…is the oldest and the strongest…," continued Fenix.

"…kind of fear," finished Claret.

For a moment, a tremor ran through me. These three monsters understood so much about human fear.

"If humans *think* that when you're bitten, and turned, a demon spirit possesses your corpse, then what is true death?"

"The true death is when a Nocturnae experiences death. Although the loss of a fellow Nocturnae is felt throughout our kind, the pain to their coven is unfathomable by the humans," Claret said.

Fenix quietly stared out the cave opening for a moment, turned to me and leaned in. "The loss of a Maker, for example, drives some Nocturnae to decades of insanity or suicide."

"So, we first die when we lose our mortality and humanity, thus becoming Nocturnae. Then we experience the true death when we die as Nocturnae?" I asked.

"Correct," Claret said.

"So, I'm dead?"

"No," Gaius said.

"So, I'm alive?"

"Correct," Fenix said.

"But I died?"

Gaius cracked a smile at my fumbling over the subject. "Correct."

"Some things we cannot explain and must simply accept. For example, you accept that you are confined to the ground, yet a bird is not. Rather, it is able to move freely between the two planes and isn't shackled by gravity," Claret said. I looked at her confused by the word. "Gravity is what we call the invisible force shackling us to the ground."

Gaius added, "Neither we, nor the humans, have all the answers."

"The Faceless King does," Fenix muttered.

"…we believe." Claret clarifies, looking over her shoulder at Fenix.

Turning to me she continued, "Luckily, we are blessed with the ability to find the answers, no?"

My mouth opened and closed numerous times as I tried to find the words, but I had too many questions racing through my mind. In a brief second of clarity, I turned to Claret and asked, "When you were telling me about sunlight you mentioned a … a *something* factor. What were you talking about?"

"Yes, a healing factor."

"What is that?"

I felt my arm rip open and a smile spread across Fenix's face as he held out a bloodied fingernail. Looking down at my arm I found a two-inch-wide gaping wound spanning from my shoulder to my wrist, all the way down to the bone.

"WHY?!" I screamed, as pain suddenly hit me.

*"Breathe Sorin. Return to your room,"* Claret's voice echoed in my mind.

Calmness fell over me as my focused breathing began centering on my wound. My muscle fibers grew back together and my bones retreated behind them and my regrown skin.

I stuttered, "It … it … it's a … a miracle."

"No Sorin," Claret said, moving to my side and placing her hand on my back. "It is Nocturnae."

"We can heal from any injury," Gaius said.

I could do nothing more than nod my head, mouth ajar, and caress the fresh skin. I had no fatigue and my arm felt and responded like normal.

"Wait. How did you move from there,"—pointing across the cave—"to here?" I asked, pointing to her current location. "And how did I not see you move?"

"You have only been Nocturnae for a little more than a day. You are still coming into your new self. Your gifts will come in time."

"When will I be able to move like you?" I asked eagerly.

That's when it hit me. I'd never have to work or do chores again. I could plow a field in minutes and without needing a donkey or horse. Killing a deer would be easy. But I couldn't bring Cora back. I'd never again hear her laugh—see her smile—watch her dance in the field—hold her in my arms during a thunderstorm—celebrate Yule—nurse her back to health.

She was gone. Forever. And I was still here.

"You'll know, when you run face first into a wall and don't know how it happened," she said.

Her delivery remained so even that it gave me pause. But did I detect a smile? Her cold demeanor intrigued me. I wondered what happened to her to make her have such a hard exterior. A question I still ask today.

Claret asked Fenix and Gaius to pack and they complied, leaving us alone to talk.

She looked to me and then to the other side of the cave without any expression on her face, "Walk with me."

Slowly, we paced within the confines of the cave.

The surge of questions building up in my mind came bursting out of me like waves breaking on the beach. "You said 'gifts.' Are there even more?"

"No one knows what unique gift a new Nocturnae will wield, if any at all. What we do know is that all Nocturnae possess the three essential gifts: regenerative healing factor, heightened physical prowess, and super acute senses. The healing factor manifests first because it is vital to our survival."

"Why are my gums tender?"

"Another attribute. When you became Nocturnae you acquired retractable canine teeth, allowing you to blend in with humans."

More questions formed on my lips, such as the nature of my gifts and hers, but she shushed me and told me to sleep and that we'd hunt when I woke.

"But it's daytime."

"Yes, and you are Nocturnae." She walked deeper into the cave.

I called after her. "But it's—"

"Never again will the sun warm your face without searing your flesh," Fenix clarified, stuffing his pack.

Gaius rolled his eyes and solemnly added, "Never again will you watch the sunrise over gentle slopes of pasture and prairie or see the highlighted colors of thousands of flowers littering every basin and peak."

Speechless, I followed Claret into the depths of the cave where Gaius and Fenix had already packed up most of the camp except for four large blankets, one for each of us. We retired until sundown.

I AWOKE THAT evening feeling refreshed in a way I never felt as a human. I wasn't stiff or sore. I didn't even yawn.

To my surprise everyone else was already awake. Claret was speaking to Fenix and Gaius at the entrance of the cave. Sitting there watching them, I focused, trying to tap into these new *gifts* Claret spoke of. No matter how hard I tried, my ears would not cooperate, and I couldn't hear their conversation.

Fenix and Gaius took a step back from Claret, crossed their arms over their chests, and gave a slight bow to her. In the blink of an eye, they disappeared.

Slowly, I arose. Before I could stand entirely upright, Claret appeared next to me at the rear of the cave. "I hope you slept well."

"Gah! Why do you have to do that?" I flinched. Her sudden movement had caused me to nearly poke my eye out as I rubbed my face awake.

"I'm exposing you to my movements so you can learn to track them. I'm starting off slowly."

"Slowly? You're moving slowly? Compared to what?"

She ignored my question. "Are you ready for your first hunt?"

"My mouth tastes like copper," I said, rolling my tongue up and down my teeth and along my gums.

I ruminated on when I first had this taste in my mouth. A girl was being harassed by a group of boys—I was seven or eight. I tried to rescue her, but was quickly knocked out. I came to with a mouth full of blood and a crowd of kids laughing at me.

"The copper flavor in your mouth is our equivalent to a human's stomach growling or mouth salivating. Come," she said, pivoting on her heels. "We must move swiftly; you have much to learn."

I made my way toward the front of the cave with her. As I approached, the light from the moon became more prevalent and my vision began shifting again. The sensation was so strange. It didn't hurt. Nor was I in control of the transition. It was like breathing or blinking.

"Will you teach me to control what's going on with my sight?"

She stood at the edge of the cave, gazing out over trees. "Yes. Moreover, I am going to help you explore your new body, the gifts, and the curses that accompany this life. It will be easy for you, especially early on, to believe you're invincible and arrogantly consider yourself a god. A god you are not. Humans don't hunt gods, nor can they kill them. They hunt Nocturnae, and we can be killed. Some do it for fame, some fortune. Others simply do it for sport. In short, you're going to need to forget your humanity and learn how to be a Nocturnae if you're to survive."

She never looked at me once during her short speech. Nor did she offer any form of affection or empathy toward me to soften the overwhelming journey ahead.

Her bluntness terrified me.

Follow-up questions jostled in my mind, competing for me to ask them: What did she mean by forgetting your humanity? What is she going to teach me? Gifts? Curses? Besides the sun, what else can kill us? I waited for her to say something. Anything. But she simply stood in intense silence.

*"Okay, follow me," her voice said in my mind.*

Suddenly, she jumped from the cave with her feet together, toes pointed back at me, her head lifted toward the moon, her back arched, and her arms outstretched like wings. Somehow, she hovered in mid-air a moment before she dropped toward the earth, chest first.

"CLARET!" I yelled from the edge of the cave lip.

Looking down, I couldn't see the ground. Our cave was so high up a mountain, cloud cover obscured everything. Her feet fell under her body as she brought her arms in tight to her chest. She drifted farther away until the thick, puffy clouds swallowed her whole. I stepped back from the edge of the cave, and cradled the back of my head.

"Does she expect me to jump too?" Before I could contemplate further, Gaius appeared in front of me and threw me over the edge.

"NO!!" The plea flew from my lungs.

Everything around me blurred into browns, grays, and blacks. My eyes began to water and my lips stretched into a horrific smile. Weightless, I plummeted toward the treetops. I shut my eyes and prayed.

As I accelerated toward the ground, time seemed to slow to the point that I was one with the sky, and I flirted with the moon at horizon's tavern. I allowed my eyes to open. Beautiful doesn't even come close to expressing the awe-inspiring image I captured in that moment. As trees came into focus, quickly growing in size, my second thoughts, regrets, and my old life flashed before my eyes just before…

Impact.

Instinctively, my legs flipped toward the ground and my torso flew back to an erect position. I landed on the ball of my right foot first, and then my heel slammed into the earth, and I shattered every bone in my body.

My body miraculously repaired itself as quickly as it shattered. My right foot had completely regenerated by the time the left foot hit the ground. As my body worked tirelessly to repair my left lower limb, my right knee slammed down hard, forming a small crater beneath it.

The bone fragments of my knee and femur knitted themselves back together from grains of sand to their original form. My torso fell over my folded left knee and both hands ripped into the soil.

A shock wave echoed from my fingers, through my palms, and up my forearms into my biceps, triceps, and shoulders. The energy blazed up my spine, popping each vertebra like a beetle between two fingers.

The concussive forces all met at the base of my neck, bullying their way into my skull and out my eyes. My eyes burst open, gleaming a bright crimson, the color of blood, and the ground under my body trembled in a large cloud of dust. The soil I found myself crouched upon steamed. Every molecule in my body tingled as the cells finished their repair.

Slowly, I stood, stretching out my ligaments in wonder. My body had shattered and yet I had lived to tell the tale. I felt better than ever.

She was right, I felt like a god.

Claret stood before me, shaking her head. "Neophytes are so destructive. So loud."

A bright crimson aura radiated from her. I didn't question it until much later, when I realized it never happened again. What could it have meant? I may never know.

"I feel…" I said, fumbling to find a word. I looked down and became distracted by the involuntary zooming and focusing of my eyes. I could clearly see the outline of my arms, and the hairs that blanketed my skin. I could even distinguish the newly formed skin where my bones had broken through. The color difference between oxygenated and deoxygenated blood. Then I found the word that described the indescribable. "Nocturnae."

She stood there emotionlessly studying me. Not in a judgmental manner. No, this was more like the look a parent gives his child after they do something profound, but are too proud to show their excitement.

"Next, for your sight and reflexes." She turned to enter into the black forest.

Enamored by what had just transpired, I began running my hands over my body to reassure myself I wasn't hallucinating.

"Run." A soft, echoing whisper percolated through the forest.

*BLAM!* A fist landed right between my eyes.

Holding my bloodied nose, I looked around for the source but saw nothing. "What was that? Where'd she go?" I thought to myself and closed my eyes.

With that thought, my mind raced back to the moment just before, with Claret. She peered at me with her blank face.

Turning away, she said, "Come, the night is still young, and you still have much to learn," and walked into the black forest.

This time I focused on where Claret walked into the forest.

I kept my focus on her and felt the transitioning of my vision to stay focused on her. The blackness shifted into the greens and blues hidden from the human race, and her figure remained the only constant in my vision; everything else faded away. Claret walked about forty paces into the forest before turning around and staring right at me.

Gaius appeared just inside my periphery, leaning against the trunk of an old tree. He winked. Focusing back on where Claret had been, I only saw Fenix's hulking body hurling itself at me. Shaking my head and blinking repeatedly, I flashed back to the present.

"What just happened?" I asked myself, softly. Sprinting toward Claret, this time with slightly more control. I cried out, "Claret!"

*CRACK!* went the oak tree as I ran into it.

"What's happening to me?"

*CRACK!* I slammed into another.

When I finally reached her, she was still squatting down. "What did I just do? How did I relive what already happened?"

She stood slowly.

"We, Nocturnae, are aware of all that is happening around us even if we're not actively perceiving what is occurring. You began studying your arms and failed to listen to my instructions and, in turn, failed to see where I was walking in the forest. Your body naturally compensated for your confusion by reliving the events that have already transpired, showing you events that had taken place, yet were not consciously retained."

I stood there in silence—I did that a lot those first few weeks. "I can relive events that have taken place, which I failed to consciously observe," I repeated slowly.

Fenix and Gaius suddenly appeared on either side of Claret.

A familiar copper flavor suddenly filled my mouth again, overtaking any semblance of logical thought. "I need…."

"Before you can hunt, you must learn how to see the unseen. Once you have learned how to see the invisible, then we will move on," she said to me. As the last word left her lips, she was gone.

I blinked twice, looked to my left, then to my right, and after a moment, behind me.

"AH!" I screamed, staring directly into Claret's eyes—only inches from my face. "Why? Why? Why?" I yelled at her, still trying to catch my breath.

"Because you must learn," she replied, zipping back to my front side and flicking my nose.

"Ouch! What was that for?"

"Pay attention." She zipped back three tree lengths and took one step to my right.

"Concentrate."

Fenix and Gaius sped in and out of my field of view, distracting me and keeping me from seeing where Claret had moved to. "Don't try to see me … *see* me."

In an instant, she was standing shoulder to shoulder with me, so we were looking in opposite directions. Then, she was gone again.

"What the hell kind of an instruction is that? 'Don't try to see me, see me.' That doesn't help," I thought.

Instinctually, the palms of my hands slammed together so close to my face, the knuckles of my thumbs rested on the tip of my nose. I had caught a dagger, but immediately dropped it in shock. Confused, I questioned where the blade came from and how I caught something I never saw. It didn't take long for me to realize what Claret meant when she said *automatically*. By focusing on trying to see the blade, I was keeping my body from doing what it wanted to do naturally.

Suddenly, my head slipped to the left by an inch, like it had a mind of its own, and a second dagger zipped past my ear. "Are you guys trying to kill me? That almost hit my head."

"It would not have killed you because of our healing factor. More importantly, you needed to learn quickly how to see. Before the dagger left his hand, your eyes already saw it and were tracking it before it even moved—this is predictive tracking. Once it left Gaius's hand, you continued tracking it, and when you consciously didn't act, your subconscious took over."

"All subconsciously? How? Why?"

"By triggering your body's subconscious, I'm exposing you to your gifts at an accelerated pace."

"As opposed to…"

"Simply letting you—blindly—figure it out over the next decade or longer, which we don't have time for."

*CLAP!* My hands slammed shut again, catching another dagger.

Yet, Claret stood by my side but faced the opposite direction.

"Did I throw that one?" she asked.

Quickly looking between the dagger on the ground and the one between my palms, I attempted to logic my way through the scenario. But nothing made sense. "Do it again."

This time, I closed my eyes, focusing all my senses on the world around me. A vacuum of air pulled the hairs on my right arm. Claret had moved. Tree branches swayed and flower petals broke as she ran through the forest.

Astonishingly, through my closed lids, the world appeared before me. I painted a picture in my mind from the sounds of everything around me. The forest and the life within it. Changes in air pressure. Smells fluttering across the air currents. It was beautiful.

Focusing again, Claret's figure became clear to me. She was still running. Trying to dodge debris so as to not give her position away. She changed direction suddenly, running straight back at me.

Before I could react, everything went red followed by a loud boom.

My eyes bulged from my head, glowing crimson. I bent over, trying to breathe. Both knees drove into the ground and with my first breath, I let out a cry that shook the ground. Claret stood with her feet together only inches from where I knelt in silence.

Balling both fists into one, she brought them down into the middle of my back.

Everything went black.

I awoke on my back, staring up at the sky and Claret on top of me pummeling every square inch of my body. Fingers and toes shattered, femur and ulna protruded from my skin, and my blood soaked the earth.

Fenix and Gaius appeared from nowhere, standing on either side of Claret.

Looking at me intently, Gaius said, "You're going to kill him, my Maker."

Claret ignored him.

By this point, I'd had enough of the bitch and her toying with me the way a cat plays with a mouse before dinner. Bubbling from the pits of my being was a torrent of emotion I'd never felt. It trickled down my spine and filtered its way through my body from the tips of my fingers to the bottoms of my feet. It felt like ants crawling under my skin, freezing whatever they touched.

"I'm fine," I said from between my gritted teeth.

I exploded off of the ground and put everything I had into a single punch that landed square on Claret's jaw. The force catapulted her into the forest. She came to a sudden stop, splintering the trunk of an old redwood three miles away.

Laughing, Fenix leaned over to Gaius and whispered, "Big mistake."

"No, she's doing this on purpose," Gaius added, smiling.

Fenix turned to Gaius with wide eyes and an open mouth. "On purpose? Why?"

"She needs him to become more … quicker than we have time for. She needs his gifts to trigger."

It was at this point I realized I had made a critical error. I didn't understand what had just happened. I couldn't follow her with my eyes; I had to close them and use all my energy to focus on my hearing to even have a chance of tracking her movements.

Claret fell from the tree and landed on her feet. "Nice hit. Let's see if you can do it again."

"I can't see her, but I can *hear* her?" I thought.

In the blink of an eye she was gone, rattling the leaves with her wake. She closed the distance between us in an instant. She wrapped her fingers around my throat, lifting me from the ground, and continued to run. We were moving so fast the world around us was a blur of color. The power she possessed was both terrifying and breathtaking. She was able to manipulate and warp the world around us. She jumped, hurling us both into the air. Just as our bodies became weightless, she locked eyes with me and smiled.

BOOM!

My shoulders, neck, and head slammed into the ground while both feet pointed toward the moon. The impact split the earth around us as we fell deeper and deeper into the soil. By the time we came to a stop, we were nearly fifty feet below ground.

As we slowed, her torso rotated, and she slammed her knee firmly into my gut. I felt my strength returning and my organs rebuilding themselves. Healing was no less painful than breaking, as my bones and vertebrae snapped, popped, and scraped together until they'd been reconfigured to their original state.

My agonizing pain slowly, very slowly, mellowed. Claret twisted herself off of me and stood over me with a foot on the other side of my ribs. She said nothing as she made eye contact with me for only a second before hurling herself straight up and out of the hole.

Slowly, I turned onto my right side, pushing off the earth with my right forearm and stabilizing with my left. I felt like I was going to pass out and throw up simultaneously. But I forced myself to stand.

My strength was not returning as quickly as it had when this whole debacle began. I slowly climbed to the edge of what was now a small crater in the middle of the forest until I reached the ledge where Claret was sitting cross-legged, hands folded in her lap.

"You could have killed me," I said, pulling myself onto the flat forest ground.

"She nearly did," Fenix whispered to Gaius.

Whipping her head around, she flashed her crimson eyes. "I knew what I was doing. *Almost* killing him and killing him are very different."

Gaius leaned over to Fenix and whispered, "I told you."

Claret's gaze returned to me. "For me, my neophyte, killing you is nearly impossible," she said, in the same calm monotone voice she always used. "You did quite well for your first sparring session."

"Sparring session?" I asked, gasping for air. "This was all a game?"

Gaius stepped forward with his hands cupped behind him. "Quite the opposite. What our Maker was doing was forcing your new body to rapidly call upon your new gifts. Your speed, reflexes, eyesight, strength, and healing factor are all vital for survival in this world—especially with humans hunting us."

"Okay, so I *called* on them. So what? Did it have to be done in such a cruel way?"

"Yes. We become strong in two ways: growing older and being forced to."

"By force, you mean being beaten?"

Gaius opened his mouth to speak but Claret stopped him. "No Sorin, by putting you in real danger where your only option is to find the strength or die."

"I like the other option better. You know, the one where I'm not beaten to within an inch of my new life!"

Claret approached me. "If I had not pushed you, it could have taken months, years, or even decades for your abilities to manifest."

"Why…" Catching my breath, I was only just realizing how exhausted I was from the fight.

"You're tired from our session, but more so because you turned a day ago and still haven't eaten," she said.

Claret turned and began walking south east, "Come, we—"

"Wait," Fenix said, stopping. His eyes glazed white and he was gone for a moment before returning. "Maker, they're coming."

"How long?"

"They'll be here just after sunrise."

"We're not far from a human settlement and you must feed first, and quickly," Claret said.

They all turned and began walking again.

My heart sank in distress. I remembered the stories my father would tell me after Cora went to bed. Stories about creatures that could never die and feasted on humans. Until now, I'd always assumed the stories were just that—stories—and were meant to keep children from wandering away from home or into the forest late at night. I never imagined the stories to have any truth. Worse yet, now I was one of the creatures my father called…

"Stop," I cried.

She did and Fenix and Gaius followed suit. Turning only her head as far as it needed to for her to see me, she waited.

"What do humans call us?" I asked softly with words that

quivered in fear of the answer.

Her head dropped ever so slightly as she let the air out of her lungs. Her body language told me she knew why I asked the question. "Wait here boys."

Turning around she made her way back to me. When she reached me, she took me in her arms, and I laid my head on her shoulder. It was at this point I knew the answer before the words ever left her lips. I started to cry.

She held me for a few moments before saying, "They call us vampires."

My stomach sank and I began to sob harder, gripping her tightly in my arms. She stood there, holding me, for as long as I needed to find peace with my new fate. My new life.

# 10



Do Nocturnae believe in an afterlife?" Jean asks.

"Why do you ask?"

It's been so long since religion has even been a thought in my life, aside from being a useful tool for manipulation.

"Fenix gave examples of various heavenly paradises including the Egyptian *Aaru* and the Greek *Elysium*. Do Nocturnae have a paradise after experiencing the true death?"

I don't know. But I won't tell her that.

"This is our paradise."

"And by this you mean…"

"Here. Now. Earth. Us." My words hang in the air, and Jean nods with what appears to be, curiously, a soft smile. "And you? What do you believe? Humans have so many options to choose from these days."

"Afterlife or religion?"

"Aren't they one in the same?"

No.

"No," she says, quickly.

Interesting.

"Afterlife then. Do you believe there's a place, a heaven, a realm your being goes to, after death?"

Jean folds her hands over her device on her lap and looks me straight in the eye as if she *could* see me. "I believe there is a physical form and a spiritual form of every being. I believe there is something else—call it heaven or another dimension or even a realm—where our spirit lives on. Wrong or right, it's more comforting to me than a black void for all eternity."

An open-minded perspective to the unknown that ultimately terrifies her. I love it.

The thought of Cora just being gone in all of eternity is a reality I don't want to live in. "Yes, I too believe there is something after human life. Although I don't know what."

"And why were they following you that night?" she asks.

"Humans have wanted the same thing for nearly a thousand years. To kill—no, to exterminate—Nocturnae."

"Yes, but why you, specifically? Claret said she had to rush your transformation—why?"

Not today dearie. Maybe tomorrow.

"I'm growing tired Jean and rather hungry. May we continue this tomorrow?"

Jean studies the air in silence. Neither of us speaks, then, abruptly, she smiles. "If you so wish … yes, we may. I was planning on coming in this weekend anyway."

I nod, silently.

"Would you like to ask one last question before we call it for the day?" She's stalling. It's like she doesn't want to leave.

The discomfort from the silver scalding my body makes it difficult for me to think straight. My distracted mind wants to fixate on only one thing… Cora.

"What is your darkest secret?"

"My darkest secret?" She's dodging the question. "What do you mean?"

Licking my lips, I lowered my tone of voice, and slowed my speech. "It's been a very long time since I've shared Cora with anyone. If I'm set to die here anyway, there's no harm in telling me. What is your secret?"

Her breathing changed.

"I appreciate you sharing your story about Cora, but I can't think of a story of similar gravity."

Oh, your pulse quickened. Liar.

"Your lips tell one story, but your body says another. Don't tell me what you think I want to hear. Don't tell me what you've been groomed to tell me. I want to know the worst." Silence. "An act you've committed and lost sleep over for months, perhaps?" Silence. "Have you murdered someone? Oooh, I hope you have."

"That's a little morbid, don't you think?" she asks defensively. "Why not ask if I've been blind my entire life or if I'm an only child or how my parents died?"

"Because I don't care." Although, every one of those would be interesting. Tomorrow then? "I've asked my question. Answer it, and I'll see you tomorrow for another festive, story-filled day. Or don't answer it, and I stop talking."

Jean's palms moisten as she fidgets with her sleeve.

She's going to need some coaxing, but there's something here. Something real. If there wasn't she wouldn't be working this hard to keep it from me.

"You're a straight shooter Jean. You are confident, driven, motivated, and good at your job. You've been respectful, well-mannered, and, for the most part, calm. It's easy to conclude you're also a very compassionate person from the line of work you chose."

She turns her head away, obscuring my view of her pinched lips and reddened cheeks.

Look, the monster made her blush. A regular *Beauty and the Beast* we are; except, I drain her dry at the end.

I continue to prod her. "I've found that in my many years of life, people like you are hard to come by. Typically, people let their pain and envy fester within them until they explode. Someone to have come from your background and your callus tenacity, requires something truly terrible to happen in one's life to look at it in the truest sense, finite."

Her eyes race wildly around the room, focused only on finding a way to dodge the question.

"Answer the question, Jean. Answer the question or don't come back tomorrow."

"Then you'll never be connected to what was taken from you," she shoots back without hesitation.

"I don't care. All is lost anyways. If you *ever* want the answers you seek, then you need to play the game and answer the question. Otherwise, you lose the answers you're searching for, ruin any credit you hold, and embarrass yourself and your boss." Unable to help myself, a venomous sneer spread across my face. "I'm all you've got Jean. It's me, or nothing dearie."

Jean's heart rate increases as she takes a deep breath. It's a resolution.

"I…"

"Go on. It's not so hard. You, what?"

"I lost my daughter."

That… I didn't expect. Is this a ploy, a manipulation built on Cora's death? No, I don't think so. She worked too hard at hiding it. She's not lying either; her body would betray her without knowing it. She's telling the truth. Bearing her heart. This is raw, unrelenting anguish and regret and guilt, all wrapped into one. I know this. I know this well.

"Oh, I'm so sorry to hear that. How did she die?"

Fidgeting with her loose hair, her voice breaks, "I was working when I went into labor at twenty-five weeks."

"That's very early."

She nods, "When paramedics arrived at my office, I was bleeding, and they told me they were concerned for my baby's health, and my own, and would be taking me to the Air Force Medical Center here, on base. By the time we arrived at the hospital, I'd passed out."

"From blood loss?"

"I can't remember if it was from the pain, loss of blood, or some type of drug they gave me to decrease stress on the baby. I woke up a little more than fifteen hours later to a nurse checking my vitals. I remember asking her where my baby was. A doctor came in shortly after, I never even knew his name, and he told me they did everything they could. But the baby was stillborn.”

No one deserves to go through that.

Shaking my head, I ask, “how long did they keep you for observation before letting you go home?”

“I remained in the hospital for close to a week.”

That’s too long. Something happened.

“A week? Did something else happen? Complications?”

A softer touch is required here; otherwise, I risk losing her.

“No—well, kind of—I would have been released from the hospital the following morning, but I attempted to kill myself when a nurse accidentally left a bottle of little blue and yellow pills in my room.”

“Jean…”

“I was admitted to the psychiatric ward of the hospital for seventy-two hours of observation; apparently, it’s protocol. It was definitely for the best, but it wasn’t long enough because I tried again a week or two after they released me. The medical professionals talked to my family, who’d been keeping a close eye on me, and recommended I spend time in a psychiatric center under twenty-four-hour watch for the next three months.”

Suicidal, yet your bosses allowed you to keep your job?

“Once my time was up, they re-evaluated my mental state and assessed treatment options from there. I did not have to spend any additional time at the clinic, but have been seeing a grief counselor ever since.”

Maybe if those people existed when I lost Cora, things would have been easier.

The thought of losing Cora consumes me and I try to shake it off. "It never gets easier—"

You just live with the pain.

"—you just learn to live with it," she says.

Pity? Empathy? Me? For a human? This is … new. I don't like it.

"I'm so sorry you had to go through all of that in your short life." Subconsciously, I reach for her hand but the silver only burns my wrists deeper. "I would cradle your hand, if I could."

She cracks a smile at the thought, pulling her hands to her chest.

I smile at her reaction and continue, "I truly believe people don't develop the mindset you do, unless they've been through something as difficult. To be honest, I believe the majority of people would have ended up broken in every way."

No one should have to go through that.

"I would offer you a pocket square or a sleeve to dry your tears, but both seem to still be soaked in blood at the moment."

Chuckling, she pulls a tissue from her tote and blots her damp eyes. Stuffing the moistened tissue back into her bag, she gathers her things and makes her way to the door, "Until tomorrow?"

"Bonne nuit."

# 11



FOUR HOURS EARLIER...

Dr. Shelley removed the badge hanging from his neck and scanned the RFID reader. The door beeped, and the light on the reader turned green. Taking a deep breath, he opened the door of a noisy room. Two dozen highly ranked U.S. military and government personnel, senators, and directorate leadership sat at a large, round table.

Subtly he cleared his throat, and addressed the party. "Good morning, all."

The noise quickly dissipated as all eyes found the old man.

"I apologize for calling this meeting on such short notice, and for the tight quarters. It was the only SCIF available."

Although no one said anything, it was clear no one was happy.

"As stated in my email, there was a break-in here at the WPAFB facility, and this was a rather *unique* event. The culprit, who is in custody, is a Nocturnae. I believe he was trying to free Subject 252-7-38." Dr. Shelley could feel tension building. "In response to this event I wanted to be sure *everyone* is on the same page. Many of you—most actually—have never come to one of these briefings, but I know all of you are very busy so I will keep this as short as possible."

Dr. Shelley looked to the broad shouldered, gray-haired man with a square jaw sitting at the head of the table.

"Carry on Dr. Shelley," the gray-haired man said.

"Thank you, Director Ziegler." Dr. Shelley cleared his throat and straightened his well-worn, wrinkled oxford. "It is unclear how long the Nocturnae species has existed; however, it *is* known that they were present for the second Crusade. Due to their nearly immortal lifespan, it is highly probable they have extensive training with not only a vast array of weaponry from throughout the ages, but also with advanced hand-to-hand combat techniques. Nocturnae are theorized to be masters of virtually every fighting style from the time of their new birth."

"Excuse me, Professor," the Director interrupted. "Could you please briefly explain what you mean by 'new birth'?"

"That is an excellent question, Director," Dr. Shelley said and leaned over to the Senator of Ohio, whispering, "Thank you for being here." He stood, wet his lips, and addressed the group. "The term 'new birth' is in reference to the subject's transition from human, *Homo sapien*, to Nocturnae, *Homo profectus*. The subject's human body dies, but its consciousness lives on in the animated Nocturnae body."

"Are you saying these creatures are dead? Like, zombies?" asked the Senator.

"No, Senator, they are not zombies. A zombie is nothing more than an animated corpse. Its heart does not beat and without electrical or chemical stimulation, the lungs will not ventilate nor will the brain show any activity. Nocturnae, like us, have a pulse and breathe air but—"

The Senator nodded, rolling his wrist impatiently. "But the human body died."

"It is theorized that during new birth, the human body dies for a brief period of time. Upon waking from new birth, the human's consciousness and memories are intact; however, their body has been altered. For example, the typical adult human resting heart rate ranges from sixty to one hundred beats per minute, but the typical resting heart rate for a Nocturnae ranges from one hundred and thirty to one hundred and seventy beats per minute, similar to a fetal heart rate."

The Senator held up a finger in thought. "So, when you said the 'body dies' it wasn't literal; it stems from when the known transformation occurs?"

"Exactly!"

The Senator gave a shallow smile and whispered something to the Director before sitting back in his chair.

"Nocturnae possess the ability to regenerate damaged or destroyed areas of their cellular structure at a rate far greater than that of a human. This mutation, and how it's triggered in the Nocturnae transformation, is not completely understood. However, through testing and experimentation, we have concluded that the speed at which this healing factor works, varies in direct proportion to the severity of the damage suffered by the individual."

"What do you mean? So, the more severe the injury, the longer the recovery? Can you provide an example, or a laboratory experiment you've conducted?" asked a blonde Colonel.

"Of course, Colonel…" Dr. Shelley squinted, straining his eyes to read the name on her breast, "White?"

"Wyatt. I'm from Directorate 2," she corrected, tapping the purple frame around the CAC hanging from her neck.

"Ah, my apologies ma'am. My eyes aren't what they used to be, even with my cheaters." He tapped the frame of his glasses with his finger and smiled. "We drove a five-inch diameter steel beam into Subject 252-7-38's abdomen with a fully loaded eighteen-wheeler truck at eighty miles per hour. Head on."

"Jesus," gasped a brown-haired CIA agent. "How did you settle on these parameters? Was it a simulation of some kind?"

"Right you are. We were simulating the wounds likely inflicted by another Nocturnae in hand-to-hand combat."

The CIA agent mouthed the word *fuck*.

"It should also be mentioned that the Subject was only provided the amount of blood required to keep it alive. Thus, it is theorized a Nocturnae will heal substantially faster if satiated with fresh, human blood."

"How extensive is this *healing factor?*" asked General Grissom as he smoothed his large, white mustache with intrigue.

"The natural healing of Nocturnae affords them virtual immunity to poisons and drugs, as well as a highly enhanced resistance to disease. The healing factor, in addition to an unknown chemical compound found throughout the Nocturnae composition, provides them with an extended lifespan and retards the effects of the aging process. We theorize the aging process can be further slowed through an extended type of hibernation, called *generational hibernation*, where the Nocturnae sleep for decades to even centuries, allowing them to essentially leap-frog through time."

"They're immortal?" asked General Grissom, frustrated.

"That, we don't know. But in theory, I suspect their lifespan approaches immortality. If the injuries are extensive enough, especially if they result in the loss of multiple vital organs or organ systems, large amounts of blood, and/or loss of physical form, such as having flesh burned away by fire or acid, Nocturnae will be rendered incapacitated."

"But not dead," the brown-haired CIA agent added.

"Theoretically."

"Professor," Colonel Wyatt said, raising her hand. Dr. Shelley silently acknowledges her by lifting his chin.

"Would a Nocturnae die if it was decapitated?"

Dr. Shelley scratched his jaw, pondering the concept for a moment before answering. "I would think so; but it's never been tested due to the very limited number of Subjects we've had access to."

"The Company has existed for centuries and you're telling us there's nothing in the files?" asked the man in the blue suit with a condescending smile.

Dr. Shelley faked a smile and adjusted his tie. "The files vaguely make the claim that decapitation has been successful, but I cannot *definitively* say it would work. If there's one thing I've learned over the years while studying these creatures, it is: once you think you understand them, they surprise you. So, I cannot say definitively."

The Colonel nodded.

Dr. Shelley went on to explain Nocturnae healing factor.

The Director slammed his cup on the table. "Jesus! How do we kill one of these things?"

"I'm getting there, Director," Dr. Shelley said behind a surrendering hand. "Nocturnae possess an innate precognizant ability, an early warning detection system linked to their superior kinesthetic awareness. It allows them the ability to avoid almost any injury, provided the Nocturnae doesn't cognitively override their autonomic reflexes. The extent of their precognizant ability is unknown."

"Has this *ability* been tested?" asked the CIA agent.

Dr. Shelley shook his head. "We are in the process of developing techniques and experiments to not only test this ability but also measure the timeframe required to make the detection."

"What is the extent of the Nocturnae arsenal?" asked General Grissom.

"What do you mean, General?"

"How fast can they run? How strong are they?" General Grissom asked, counting on his fingers. "Have you quantified the extent of their abilities?"

"Umm," Dr. Shelley began with a cracked voice. He cleared his throat. "In testing, the Subject was able to lift and press an M1A2 tank with relative ease."

"And the patients in the PHANG Program? How are they

faring?" General Grissom tapped the back of his pen on his notepad.

"Unfortunately, we haven't yet been successful." General Grissom shook his head, disappointed, and scribbled on his notepad. "But," Dr. Shelley desperately blurted out, "we believe this new intruder holds the answer."

"And if it does?"

"We will immediately proceed with Patient-XIV, and have preliminary findings to you by the end of next week."

"Very good. Don't let me down." General Grissom pointed with his pen.

Dr. Shelley nodded, averting his eyes.

"Dr. Shelley," said the man in the blue suit, calmly placing his hands on the table. "Are the physical, cognitive, ocular, olfactory, all of this *data,* in your reports? Because right now all we're hearing is a lot of theory."

"Yes…"

Leaning forward in his chair the man brought his hands together and placed them on his chin. "Then tell us what we're here for: How do we kill them, the incident, and funding."

Clasping his hands together he nodded, "Right you are. I apologize, I'm not very good at public speaking. To your point, mister…"

"Glass. Gabriel Glass with Directorate 1."

Pivoting, Dr. Shelley resumed his slow pacing in the center of the room. "Mr. Glass, I believe—"

Mr. Glass slammed his hands on the table and stood. "General. Director. Senator. I urge you to reevaluate the funding for

Directorate 3. It's very clear they're doing research, but they have yet to produce any concrete results. Their directorate has only encountered *one* Omega Level threat in all of its years while Directorate's 1 and 2 have dealt with many."

Without pause or hesitation, Dr. Shelley stopped pacing and glared at Mr. Glass. "Let me finish…" The General gestured for him to proceed. "The most obvious way to kill a Nocturnae is to expose them to direct sunlight or high levels of ultraviolet radiation. The aforementioned decapitation is plausible; however, it's more likely the Nocturnae will smell you coming and rip out your throat only to drain you dry before you come within five kilometers. It has been found that they have negative reactions to certain metals. Specifically, silver or compounds containing silver, rendering the subject physically weakened when coming in contact with the substance."

The Director smirked from behind his coffee.

Colonel Wyatt and Mr. Glass looked at one another, nodded, and together said, "We've come to similar conclusions."

"Our Subjects show no serious decline from extended exposure, do yours?" Mr. Glass followed up.

"If exposed for long periods of time—like sitting in a silver-lined cage for twenty, or more, hours a day—the Subject's appetite is greatly suppressed. Cellular regeneration is retarded to that of a typical human. Ocular response within the Nocturnae's visible bands—which includes mid-wave infrared through the entire visible spectrum and the majority of the ultraviolet bands—slowly degrades to a human's ocular bandpass. In other words, the Nocturnae become temporarily blind in the ultraviolet and infrared regions of their visible spectrum. Thus, it is theoretically possible to kill them with a silver bullet or other projectile." Taking a second to further ponder the original question, he continued, "Allow me to elaborate. Let us assume the mission is to hunt down and kill a Nocturnae. The gut reaction would be to use existing bullet molds to fashion your forces with magazines filled with silver bullets. Correct?" Dr. Shelley looked out at a sea of bobbing heads. "All of your soldiers are dead."

A myriad of gasps, mutterings, and disbelief filled the room while he, the old man, stood silent with hands intertwined behind his back.

"You see, an overwhelming majority of the bullets fired will travel through the Nocturnae's body, rendering those bullets useless. Others will hit the limbs and be more of an irritation than debilitating or fatal. Some will be evaded completely thanks to their heightened reflexes and speed. The remaining sub-percentage that hit the body could be manually removed within a fraction of a second after impact."

Silence filled the room.

"Now, I would recommend a birdshot style of round where a barrage of particles penetrate the target simultaneously and are too small to be removed manually. Ideally, the counsel would fund a DARPA program to develop a capsule round. The bullet, or shell, would break apart upon impact, similar to an explosive- or hollow-point round, releasing liquid silver into the target's bloodstream. This *will* put the target down quickly. Eliminating the threat while keeping them alive. Prototype rounds, developed in my lab, were used to bring down yesterday's intruder and save human lives."

Smiles spread across the faces of those in military garb and former enlisted among the crowd.

One by one, the attendees stood in applause while Dr. Shelley made small bows to individuals, making eye contact with each one of them.

As many began leaving the SCIF—Secret Compartmentalized Information Facility—others broke off into smaller groups. The Director approached Dr. Shelley with an outreached hand and a smile stretched tightly from ear to ear. "Wonderful presentation, Professor."

"Thank you, Director. I appreciate you not making that sparkly vampire joke," Dr. Shelley said, recalling his last briefing where the joke didn't land well.

The Director laughed. "Oh, I wanted to but this wasn't the right audience. Plus, the suits could use a good laugh in the middle of all that doom and gloom. I was surprised to see that Henry wasn't with you."

"I felt it imperative that he stay at the lab and prepare for the arrival of our next Patient."

"For the PHANG program?"

"Yes." Dr. Shelley nodded. "I have a hunch that Jean will get the information we need for a successful transformation."

"Good, because I have it on record that if General Grissom doesn't start seeing results like Colonel Wyatt and Mr. Glass are, he's going to reallocate your funding."

Dr. Shelley's eyes widened. "What? He'd pull my funding on the PHANG Program?"

The Director gave a defeated smile. "And the Artifacts … and

Project Innocence."

"When did he say all of this?"

"Mm, two to three weeks ago via e-mail." The Director patted Dr. Shelley on the back. "But don't worry, based on your presentation and Jean's track record with interrogations, you're golden!"

Dr. Shelley faked a smile.

The Director laughed and pointed at him. "Just don't fuck up, or he *will* cut your funding."

"I look forward to the next presentation. You're doing some amazing work for this country, Professor. Oh, that reminds me … one last thing and I'll leave you be."

"What's that?" "When I visited your lab back in 2018, I couldn't help but notice you were outgrowing the space. I requested funding to begin upgrading a secure prison, near Edwards Air Force Base, and set up a lab for you, at Edwards, to continue your work. You'll grow, with easy access to …all of them."

"The Omega—"

Waving him off, the Director said, "Yes, the facility will be outfitted with all the best technology taxpayer money can buy from DARPA. Completely undetectable. I'm telling you, it's amazing what these tech-nerds can do these days. You could drive over the damn thing and never know it was there."

"It's underground?"

"You betcha. You wouldn't believe how difficult it is to build not only underground but without being detected by foreign, or domestic, satellites. Thank God for contractors, though. Give them higher pay-bands and hazard pay, and it's amazing what you can get done. Anyway, I'd really like for you to check it out. You're already in the system. Give me a call anytime," the Director said, handing a small key fob to Dr. Shelley, "day or night. Hell, we'll even come pick you up. We have teams posted twenty-four seven at every CONUS outpost of The Company. My superiors tell me that by 2023, we'll be global."

"How do I call you?" Dr. Shelley examined the small device. "There's no number pad on this thing.  Hell, there isn't even a button."

The Director chuckled. "Press your thumb on either of the larger, flat surfaces and hold it there for five seconds. The Mississippi kind. A red ring will appear around the key fob's edge. Once that ring appears, you'll have seven minutes before we arrive within one hundred meters of your location."

"It's amazing what you kids can do these days."

"Thank you for your time." He shook the old man's delicate hand. "Have a wonderful day, Professor. I look forward to seeing you again."

# 12



JEAN OPENS THE outside prison door, letting a gust of recirculated, stale air into the anteroom again; but there's something new this time. I lift my chin and take a deep breath through my nose: coffee, whiskey, menthol, cinnamon, musk.

A man that drinks coffee with his whiskey during the workday, but hides it by chewing a strongly scented gum and coats himself in pain relief cream for his arthritis. I like him already.

The mysterious man calls from down the hall. "Jeanie!"

"Ugh, don't call me that," Jean mumbles, closing the door behind her.

Why not Jeanie? Is it that she doesn't care for the nickname? Or is it that it infantilizes her and belittles her legitimacy? Does she simply not like it?

The door clicks shut behind her, and she searches for the crack in the wall as his footsteps grow closer.

I'm going to need to focus to hear through these walls. I need to know everything.

I take a deep breath, slowing my heart rate, my breathing, and my healing factor. I close my eyes and focus on every step, sounds, and flicker of hair on the other side of the wall.

"Eugene is that you?" she asks, loudly.

"Yes, Jeanie. Wait right there. We can walk together."

There it is again … Was 'Jeanie' a hypocorism from a past lover?

Eugene quickens his pace, exaggerating his subtle limp. As he approaches Jean, a man to his right stands and takes a breath, preparing to speak.

Staff Sergeant Burr I bet.

The air around Eugene whistles, and there's a faint snarl. "I've got her, Staff Sergeant. You're dismissed."

He blew the Staff Sergeant off. Did he even look at Burr?

"Eugene," Jean says, in a high pitch. "That was rather rude and uncalled for."

"He'll be fine," Eugene snaps.

They're colleagues, but there's more to it. It's not sexual, he's likely much older than her. No, it's almost … paternalistic. Maybe I can use this to my advantage somehow.

"It's fine ma'am," Burr cautiously interjects.

"See, he's fine," Eugene says.

Jean turns her head and says something—or possibly mouths it—but I can't quite make it out.

I'm sorry? Does she apologize to the man for Eugene?

"What's wrong Eugene? Did the meeting not go well?" Jean asks, folding up her cane.

"Those suits, they don't understand," Eugene snarls.

Dry flesh rubbing against cloth. He's likely taking her arm to escort her. How chivalrous.

Suits? Superiors.

"Have a good weekend," Burr says.

Metal hinges squeak. He's folding the chair he sat in.

"Thank you, you … are you available to help me tomorrow? If not, it's completely fine, I can get the front desk to assign someone else."

"I'd be happy to, Jean," Burr says eagerly.

Slow down killer. You're making it a little too obvious.

"Thank you. I'll see you tomorrow at eleven a.m.," Jean says softly.

There's a faint *tap-tap* of skin-to-skin like Jean pats Eugene's arm signaling she's ready to move. Together they make their way down the echoey hallway.

Shit, they're getting further and further away and they're whispering. I'm going to concentrate even harder now.

"What don't the suits understand?" Jean asks.

"That these things take time, the importance of multiple Subjects, and that my research cannot be rushed," Eugene says.

My eyes burst open, and I gasp for air like I'm suddenly suffocating. Those words that so effortlessly twirled off his tongue are choking me!

Subjects!

Research!

I'm not alone. She's still here. Somewhere.

"Um, I thought today's meeting was about the incident and," Jean pauses a moment but doesn't slow her gait, "*my* Subject."

"It started off that way, but you know how it goes … one thing leads to another and by the end, all fingers were pointing at me."

"Okay," Jean chuckles, softly, "so what happened?"

"Ohhh, that will take too long and you have had a tiring day. I have work still yet to do and I just want to see—"

"Eugene. Breathe."

They stop walking and Eugene takes three long, deep breaths. "Thank you my dear."

Their arms interlock again, and they continue walking further down the hallway.

"Now, tell me how I can help?"

Eugene doesn't answer right away. Slowly, he asks, "What have you learned?"

"Eugene, you wouldn't believe how—"

"Anything about the Artifacts?" Eugene asks, poorly hiding the panic is his voice.

Wait … Artifacts?

Jean stops, turns, and asks, "The Artifacts?"

"Yes Jean. The Artifacts. You *must* find out whatever you can about the Codex."

Codex?

"What's the Codex?"

Does he mean the book from the Étretat Cliffs?

"That's *Need-to-Know* but I'm working on getting you read in. Find out whatever you can about it. It's imperative!"

"Okay, I'll see what I can do," Jean agrees with a soft voice.

"Thank you. Anything that will help PHANG?"

Fang? It can't be a sharp tooth. It must be something else. I bet it's an acronym. What is it with humans and their fucking need to shorten every damn thing? What does it stand for?

"Yes! I'll send you what you need on the classified network before I leave tonight."

"Oh, that would be perfection! It sounds like the interview is going well then."

"It … is … but it's strange," Jean says, searching for the words.

"What is?"

"His willingness to talk. He's almost—"

"Some humans, in these situations, are talkative while others are quiet; we all have different reactions to stress. It would be foolish to think it wasn't the same for Nocturnae."

"No, no, you're right but it's almost like…"

"Like what Jeanie?" Eugene begs.

"…*he's* interviewing me."

"You're right *Jeanie* … I am interviewing you," I say to myself as their footsteps trail off until they become indistinguishable from the noise of the building.

Without the tapping of Jean's cane, I can't track them farther than the first stairwell.

"Fuck! I need to know where they went," I mutter.

Suddenly, the ventilation system kicks on and I begin to feel weak. Weaker than I was just a moment ago.

Silver?

Dizziness.

And I'm unable to form—let along keep—coherent thoughts.

This isn't merely silver.

This is something else … silver aerosol.

# 13



IN A WINDOWLESS lab at Wright-Patterson Air Force Base, Area B, Henry Ingvar sat, diligently sifting through the stack of papers on his desk.

The room reeked of the bitter scent of burnt coffee and the sweetness of pipe tobacco. The furnishings dated back at least a decade and a half. The once white and black checkered flooring looked a pale urine and gray. But none of that mattered to Henry, he cared about the science and helping people. When his thoughts wandered to something other than the task at hand, they landed on his father, who had just yesterday been diagnosed with Lou Gerig's Disease.

When Dr. Shelley entered the lab, Henry updated him on his father's condition and asked him how the meeting he'd missed had gone.

"Not good," Dr. Shelley said.

"Oh no," Henry's eyes widened. "How bad?"

"Well, the Director and our constituents from the other Directorates were there and not only did General Grissom have it out for me—"

Henry's ears perked up. "Gabriel Glass was there…?"

"Yup."

"Shit." Henry made a sour face. "I should have been there. I am so sor—"

"No Henry, your priorities were in the right place," Dr. Shelley said, shaking the mouse to wake up his computer.

Henry turned around in his chair and reoriented himself in front of his desk. "I've been going over the paperwork for Patient-XIV this morning and let me tell you, it makes such a difference when they send documents down more than a day in advance."

"Uh-huh," Dr. Shelley replied softly, looking off into the distance.

Rifling through the pages on his desk, Henry found the information he wanted to share with Dr. Shelley. "It says this girl is a … Shit where is it I just … Ah! There it is. She's a Major, medically discharged after taking an IED—Improvised Explosive Device— in the field. She's paralyzed."

"Uh-huh," Dr. Shelley said. "And now?"

Henry checked the paperwork. "She's a heroin addict and during her most recent hospitalization, she had to be narcan'd six times before she came back." He shook his head in disbelief. "I think we should do a moderately accelerated detox again. It seemed to work well on Patient-XIII."

"Uh-huh."

Henry stopped rifling. "Is everything okay Dr. Shelley?"

"Yes, yes, yes Henry. Everything is fine. I'm just a little distracted by the pressure from the General and Mr. Glass and this recent event with the Nocturnae." Eyeing the strange gap in the cinderblock wall, Dr. Shelley smiled ever so slightly. "I think I need to see her."

Henry shook his head, clocking the wall between two shelving units. "Sir you can't. She's on a very strict schedule and it can't be altered. Our research could be—"

"I don't care. I need to see her."

Getting up from his desk, Dr. Shelley pulled out his card for the RFID reader camouflaged against the secret door.

Henry stood. "But Sir, I—"

"Do *not* follow me," Dr. Shelley ordered. "I will be back momentarily."

Dr. Shelley triggered a secret door to open, revealing a hidden doorway that led down a long, narrow corridor. He slowly made his way down the dimly lit passage until he came to a metal spiral staircase.

He gripped the cold, damp handrail and descended into the darkness. He took it one step at a time until he reached the bottom.

Three prison cells with titanium doors coated in silver stared back at him, and the back of the guard on duty, Jimmy, in gray coveralls.

Each door had a three-by-six-inch sliding door at eye level and a small hatch at floor level to slide meals into the cells. In the center of each door, just above the locking mechanism, laid a six-digit number.

The center door read:

**053-8-79**
ATTENTION: Subject has been relocated to
The Sandbox.
POC: Director Ardisson Ziegler

It was clearly empty.

The door on the left read:

**252-7-38**
Gamma Level Subject
WARNING: Bloodthirsty, cunning subject
contained. Unknown age and origin. Do not
look into Subject's eyes. May cause loss
of inhibitions and may lead to death.
If Subject has escaped, call 727-2191.

The small window in the door was propped open, allowing a slit of light into the dark room with no overhead lights.

Dr. Shelley reprimanded the guard for leaving the window open and asked him to close it.

Jimmy stepped toward the door, and in doing so, caught a glimpse of a tiny pillow and a tattered, mossy green blanket resting in the center of the cell. Atop the blanket sat a figure with its back to the door. The darkness of the room made it impossible to make out anything more than what could have been a shoulder under wild hair.

The figure glanced over its shoulder at the door, revealing a pair of crimson eyes.

"Shit!" Jimmy gasped.

Quickly slamming the peephole closed, he flattened himself against the thick steel door, sliding down while holding his chest.

"Jimmy!" Dr. Shelley cried, and quickened his pace. Once at the man's side he gave him a once over. "Are you alright?"

"Yeah. Yeah. I'm alright. Just startled me a bit, that's all."

"It could have happened to anyone. That thing is rather … well, you saw." Dr. Shelley patted him on the back. "Is the empty cell clean and ready for a new guest?"

"Yessir."

"The nameplate?" Dr. Shelley pointed at the bucket on the floor. "Replace it after you see medical. 076-7-46. Got it?" Jimmy nodded. "Tell medical what happened and if there are any questions, have them call me."

"Alright." Jimmy swung into action.

Dr. Shelley turned around and approached the third and final door, that read:

**072-4-63**

Delta Level Subject
In case of emergency, call 727-0488.

Pulling open the door he revealed pale blue walls covered with posters of musicians, and drawings of landscapes, ponies, and other fantastic beasts. A pink comforter draped over the twin bed nestled in the corner, accented with paisley throw pillows, was home to numerous stuffed animals. Although the pearl white furniture highlighted the imperfections and scuffs on its surface, it was a beautiful backdrop for the unicorn figurines and dolls scattered across its landscape.

In the middle of the light-blue carpeted floor sat a young strawberry-blonde girl, no more than ten years old. Her legs were crossed as she played out a scene between Dr. Barbie and a makeshift patient Military Ken.

The young girl whipped her head around, and her piercing sapphire blue eyes connected with his. "Daddy!"

Excitedly, she threw the dolls down, thrusted herself off the floor, and bolted to the door like a child running to the tree on Christmas morning. Dr. Shelley dropped to his knees and her tiny arms wrapped around him, gripping his back as if to never let go.

"I'm glad you're home, Daddy. I missed you."

"I missed you too, sweetheart. How have you been? Has Henry been keeping you good company?"

She rushed back to her dolls. Gripping Dr. Barbie in both hands, she returned with the gift, arms outstretched, joy radiating from her every pore. "Yes! He brought me this. Isn't she pretty?"

Overwhelming happiness and admiration for this tiny, innocent creature washed over his psyche. Frustration with his work fell away.

"Oh, she's beautiful." Dr. Shelley accepted the doll in one hand and stroked its hair with the other. "What is her name?"

"Brenda."

"That's a pretty name," he cooed, wondering where she'd heard of or learned the name. "I will have to be sure I thank Henry for taking such good care of you whilst I was away."

"Did your meeting go well Daddy?"

"Oh, yes." Dr. Shelley gripped her around the waist, hoisted her up to his hip, and stood up. "Everyone was very pleased with my results and findings. We are still in business."

He put up his hand for a high-five. Her little hand smacked his, and they both giggled.

"The mean man was there again,"—her nose scrunched as he recounted for her—"but I think this time we impressed him with the breakthroughs we've had." Looking at his pocket watch, he kissed her on the forehead. "I have to get back to work, honey, but you have fun during school today."

Dr. Shelley returned her to the ground and admired her for a moment.

"Thanks, Daddy," she said, wrapping her arms around his waist. "You go help save lives."

"Okay," he said, smiling. "I love you."

"I love you, too."

A thin, old, white-haired lady turned the corner at the end of the hall. She stopped there, gripping a small red book at her waist. Dr. Shelley reluctantly ripped his gaze from his child to acknowledge the old lady. He nodded silently, agreeing to the unspoken words.

"Okay, sweetie, time for your lessons." He wrapped her in his arms one last time before parting and she kissed him on the cheek.

Dr. Shelley watched her every step, memorizing every detail as she sped down the hallway and slipped away behind a hidden panel within the wall with her teacher.

Closing the child's door, Dr. Shelley smiled to himself as he imagined her tiny arms wrapping around him again.

"She's coming of age, you know," a muffled, malicious voice

from the adjacent cell said. "She may no longer be your sweet little innocent girl."

Dr. Shelley rushed to the cell door and kicked it. "Quiet!" he snapped before apprehensively continuing, "I know." Shaking the weakness from his demeanor he sneered at the voice, opened the window, and peered into the cell "I can make the next series of experiments exceedingly more painful than they need to be."

Silence filled the air. His eyes darted around the room's abyss through the small opening in search of its occupant.

"Ah!" Dr. Shelley screamed, jumping back as a pair of crimson eyes appeared from nowhere.

"There is nothing you could do to me that is worse than what Heinrich Himmler, Dr. Isaac Nikude-Varna, or any other of your predecessors have done to me."

"Do not be so sure, demon," Dr. Shelley said, grinning hatefully.

They stare motionless into each other's eyes; both refusing to blink and submit. Just then a muted voice echoed from down the hall. Dr. Shelley strained to hear.

"Your lackey is calling for you," the creature whispered. "Don't want to keep him waiting. Professor."

Gritting his teeth, Dr. Shelley balled his hands into fists and prepared to fire back but stopped himself. He closed his eyes, took a deep breath, turned silently, and made his way down the corridor toward Henry's voice.

"I look forward to our next encounter," it called out, pressing its face against the metal door, searing its own flesh and melting its lips on the silver.

Unable to deal with the pain any longer, the creature ripped itself from the door, letting out a terrifying scream of pain and utter frustration in its hopelessly helpless situation.

UPON RE-ENTERING THE lab, Dr. Shelley was greeted by Henry. "Must you play the 'whose dick is bigger' game with it?"

"Yes, Henry. I must," Dr. Shelley snapped back. "That animal needs to recognize who its master is."

"I understand that, sir, but are you not concerned there could be another incident?"

"Absolutely not. I was foolish the first time, believing it could be trusted. The upgraded cells have proven to be quite successful in limiting its abilities, infuriatingly humanizing I'm sure,"—he smiled—"while keeping it in a constant state of mental and physical torment."

Henry rubbed the back of his neck and glanced back at the secret door. "It's awful what we're subjecting it to. Jesus, the weekly testing."

Dr. Shelley slammed his hand down on a nearby table and glared at Henry. "Awful? Nocturnae are the perfect weapon. We have never seen a beast with abilities such as these in all of human history. At least not in the literature we have been privy to, Henry."

"I—"

"Studying them, understanding them, and exterminating them are the *only* things that matter. At best, maybe we can weaponize them or their blood and develop countermeasures against their species. At worst is the death of the human race. So, I don't give a shit if it is pissed off or uncomfortable or suffering. It would snap your neck without thinking twice."

Horrified and beaten down, Henry replied, "Yes, Professor."

"Good. Now, where is my coffee?"

# 14



THE TIP OF a cane and rubber-soled shoes wake me from my slumber.

It's morning already? It feels like she just left. Fucking silver is still pulsing through my veins. It's less though … much less.

The lock clicks and the latches within the door slide open.

I need to buy more time to expel this silver and learn where, exactly, Claret is being kept. Let's try a different tactic today.

I smile broadly at the sight of her. "Good morning my darling, aren't you looking *ravishing* in those … well, what do you call those things you have attached to your feet?"

Pulling the tote from her shoulder, she finds her seat. "Good morning Mr. Harker, I must say that's quite an improvement from yesterday's greeting." She looks down at her feet. "And these are Ugg boots."

"They're hideous. Although,"—eyeing her over—"with those painted on jeans, the oversized cashmere cardigan draped atop that scant camisole, and your soft curled hair, I'm sure the men are just lining up."

She folds her cane and exchanges it for her note taking device and a small clear box.

"Flattery will get you everywhere Mr. Harker." She slowly folds her bangs behind her ear, hiding her smile. "I have something for you."

"A silver spike for my wrist?" I goad.

She shakes her head. "No. And it's nothing bad. I swear."

She's telling the truth.

Jean reveals the small box she'd been hiding behind her note taking device and I'm suddenly at a loss for words. "Oh…"

Centered in the box was a beautiful boutonniere made up of lavender and thistle filled in with baby's breath and chamomile. It was simple, yet elegant and reminded me of the bouquets of wildflowers I'd pick for Cora all those years ago.

"I hope you like it," Jean says, compassionately. "I told the guy at the flower shop it was for my grandfather and he didn't like flashy things."

For the first time in my Nocturnae life, a human has rendered me utterly speechless.

"I … I don't know what to say," I confess.

Jean smiles and doesn't even try to hide her blushing glee. "So, you like it then? I know it's probably not the same purple flower you tucked behind Cora's ear, but I hope it's close."

"No, it's perfect," I say, unable to take my eyes off the flowers. "No one's ever done something like this for me before. Thank you." Finding myself smiling and genuinely touched, I change the subject. "I believe you forgot your glasses this morning. Would you like to go grab them before we begin?"

"Thank you but I didn't forget them. I don't think I'll be needing them," Jean says, putting the box on the floor as she slides it as close to me as she can with her foot. "I'm going to leave this here, okay?"

She's confident that I won't or can't compel her. It's a shame she's right, at least for now. But she's not confident enough to pin the flower on my lapel.

"Thank you," I say, staring down at the small box.

Adjusting the device on her lap, she sits back in her seat. "How did you sleep last night?"

"Fine, I suppose. I was drugged, but I would expect nothing less from humans. You? I'm sure your night was more eventful than mine. Please, indulge me."

"Well actually, I was thinking about our conversations yesterday and," she reaches into her tote, again, pulling out a folded stack of papers, "I wanted to ask you about a few stories."

"Okay."

This should be interesting.

"Before I start, is there anything I can get for you?"

Huh, manners. She continues to surprise.

Coughing hard, I clear my throat, "A mug of hot water would be nice. I've had a tickle in the back of my throat since you walked in."

"Sure." She stands, turns around, and balances the writing device and papers on her tote. "I'll be right back."

Eyeing the crumpled pages, I decide to unsettle her. "And your tampon."

Horrified, she glares at me. "Excuse me?"

"I'd like a mug of hot water and your tampon; it's not quite due to be changed, but I'll take what I can get."

She swallows her emotion and settles back into her chair.

"I'm sorry Mr. Harker, we're out of water at the moment."

There she is.

Unfolding her papers, she runs her fingertips over one, reading the Braille. "Seventeen twenty-five in Kisiljevo, Serbia, Petar Blagojević died at sixty-two and three days later allegedly returned home for food. In the days to follow, more people in the town were found dead … was this Claret, Fenix, Gaius, or you?"

"It wasn't them nor was it me. I was in Habsburg Monarchy around that time."

Feeling through her papers, her fingers stop on one with very few braille cells. "November 1725, Habsburg Monarchy, Arnold Paole is allegedly plagued by a vampire, but cured himself by eating soil from its grave … that was you?"

Ha! I remember this fool.

"Yes, and if I remember the story, he died from a farming accident—broke his neck falling from his hay wagon, I believe. Shortly after, a handful of people claimed they were plagued by him."

"Yes," she confirmed.

Ha. That was fun.

"All me."

Shifting the papers on her lap, Jean types quickly before grabbing more pages.

She stops on a photocopied page with braille notes in the

margins. "Are you familiar with Francois-Marie Arouet?"

"Quite familiar actually, but by a different name. Voltaire. I think I know where you're going with this one Jean. In 1764 he wrote, '…these vampires were corpses, who went out of their graves at night to suck the blood of the living, either from their throats or stomachs, after which they returned to their cemeteries. The persons so sucked waned, grew pale, and fell into consumption…' it goes on, but to talk about the corpse and other locations but that's what you wanted to talk about, correct?"

"Yes, was that you?"

"No, that was Voltaire himself, at least to my knowledge."

"The village of Blow?"

"The Blow vampire you mean?"

"Yes."

"I wasn't Nocturnae then, but I heard the story from my father, who heard it from a traveler in the pub."

Confused, she runs her hand over the paper again. "Here it says it occurred in the early 1700's."

"This story can be confusing because it appeared in the work of Charles Schertz in 1704, but wasn't mentioned by Don Calmet until 1751. Nevertheless, they're both referencing the same story that took place in 1337 in the village of Blow near the town of Kadam, Bohemia." I pause a moment and watch her hand glide over the pages with such grace. "This is fun and all, but do you really want me to fact check stories, or is there something more … specific you'd like to ask me?"

Sifting through the papers, she narrows her brow as her fingers blitz across each page. Stopping on an old, tattered page with weathered and faded ink, Jean sighed in frustration. Turning the page over, her hand moved from right to left.

She's reading the impressions made by the quill. I will hand it to her, that's rather resourceful.

"Just one more, if you don't mind. This story has fascinated me ever since I first read it. Would you mind if I read it to you?"

Is it a story I've never heard before? I hope so… Could that 'story' be Claret? I can only hope.

A silver fragment, housed in a bead of sweat, scurries down my back.

"Of course," I say, forcing myself to sound enthusiastic.

You're just buying me more time to heal.

"Please forgive me if I misspeak, reading backwards—"

Reading backwards? She's reading the impressions in the paper that Dr. Shelley made while writing the entry. Impressive.

"Please, you've piqued my interest."

She begins:

```
I gazed out over my kingdom this evening,
like I did every night. However, this
evening I witnessed a man. No, it was more
devil than man outside my tower. He coaxed
a passerby to his side. It wasn't long
before the devil attacked, gripping the
innocent woman, and burrowing his face into
her neck.

    Eventually her body went limp, accepting
death. The devil ripped itself from her
with a terrifying growl that lifted the
hairs on my back, spraying what was left of
```

her blood on everything nearby.

I gasped at the sight.

Releasing the useless corpse from his grip, the body fell hard on the cold, moonlit ground. He wiped the blood from his face, licking his fingers clean, and returned to his nonchalant demeanor as quickly as he'd broken it.

The devil turned, directing his gaze at me. Our eyes locked. I tried to retreat into my chambers, but I was unable to move. A spell of sorts had been cast upon me, rendering me immobile.

A voice entered my mind, "You have three sunsets to pay a blood tribute to me, The Faceless King, or I claim your life and the lives of your entire kingdom as my own. Soak your lands in blood."

The connection broke and the figure was gone. Sliding down the wall until I stopped on the floor, I began to weep, coddling myself in my arms. I stayed there until morning. I didn't sleep that night.

I ordered my militiamen to invade a nearby Saxon village and to bring every man, woman, and child back to the kingdom before the sun was high the following day.

Many of the men were brought in cages, some unconscious. The children screamed while the women soothed them. For the greater good, I gave the most heinous of orders. I instructed half my men to go into the forest and find the tallest, sturdiest tree limbs no thicker than three inches and sharpen them at one end.

The fields that surrounded my kingdom were littered with corpses of my enemies on spikes, creating a moat of blood.

I paced within my chambers that third night, constantly checking the time on my Watch. It wasn't until that night I noticed the sapphire runes etched around its silver edge.

When the sun rose the next morning and the creature hadn't returned, I was relieved. The devil was satisfied and I'd never have to see those crimson eyes again.

The page grew heavy in her hand as she neared the end of the story.

"Whose journal did you say this came from?" I ask with sincere interest.

Jean folds the page and returns it to the stack. "It's from the personal journal of Vlad Tepes III."

Vlad the Impaler. Dracula.

"I've heard the name, but I never met him."

She straightens the pages and returns them to her tote. "Oh…" Disappointed, her fingers reveal her frustration as they bang against the keys. "…I thought that you may have been The Faceless King or knew something about it. Where were you then, if not in Romania in the mid-fifteenth century?"

Pausing, I contemplate her question. "That would be skipping ahead in the story."

She smiles a bit at that. "Yesterday you left off with Claret telling you humans refer to Nocturnae as vampires. Please continue."

"Ah yes. The Hunt."

"Your first time feeding on a human. What was it like? Was it a man, a woman, a child? Tell me everything about it."

As you wish.

# 15



IT WAS COLD that night, very cold. The snow was falling hard, but my Nocturnae eyes had no problem seeing through the snowstorm. Each time a snowflake landed on my clothing; it sounded like a cannon firing. As they dissolved on my skin, it sounded like a pot of boiling water. The air was sweet, like each snowflake was collecting the scents of the forests.

Amongst all the new sights, sounds, and smells, my father's voice echoed through my mind. "…Vampires are the children of Satan. They are creatures of pure evil, put in this world to tempt man, perform malicious acts, and gorge themselves on sinners…"

I slowly loosened my grip on Claret, stepped out of her embrace, and wiped the remnants of tears from my face.

My father's voice returned to the forefront of my mind. "…You mustn't go into the forest after twilight. If the moon is high, stay inside. And son, if you ever see a vampire, you must run and never look back…"

"What is wrong, Sorin?" Claret asked.

"I am a monster," I said with a trembling voice. "The monster my father warned me about when I was a child in bed."

Claret said nothing as she studied my every movement, my every tremor. It was like she expected me to react this way and was waiting it out.

Fenix took a breath to speak, but Gaius hushed him with a stiff hand and a slow shake of his head.

"I'm sorry. I'm sure this isn't very 'Nocturnae.'" I stared at my feet in shame.

Tilting her head to one side, Claret asked, "Why do you say that?"

"I don't know. The weakness of it all."

With a hand on either of my shoulders she turned my head to meet her eyes. "Do not be embarrassed, my young neophyte. You are growing much faster than any of us have and with that comes consequences. Your emotional outburst isn't the weakness you think it is."

"What do you mean?"

"Remember how I told you that Nocturnae have heightened senses?"

I nodded. "Like sight and sound."

"We also experience our emotions in a deeper, more amplified way than humans," Claret said. "Anger, guilt, sorrow, fear, and empathy are all heightened."

Gaius and Fenix listened to the north, then looked at one another with mild concern.

Fenix stepped forward, "Excuse me my Maker. We must keep

moving. The humans will be in Brasov by midday tomorrow."

Claret nodded without looking at him. "I'm aware, but we'll be fine. Are you ready Sorin?"

"Yes, my Maker," I said, still distracted by my father's haunting words. "What's next?"

Claret raised her left arm high into the sky and roared. "Now we hunt."

Fenix and Gaius joined Claret in the war cry of nightmares.

We began walking west, toward the town of Brasov. Our journey was slow and silent. Fenix and Gaius tracked the humans' movements and compared their observations with each other while planning our next move. Claret kept a close eye on them, ready to abandon the hunt at a moment's notice to keep us safe.

We walked for nearly an hour before reaching the tree line just outside the town. Claret said we were too near the town to move like Nocturnae and needed to blend in. I remember the desire to stop wasn't completely my own. It was like my entire being was told to *stop*. The eeriness of it was frightening.

"Fenix, you will hunt on the northwest side. Gaius, the southwest. I will watch the east from here."

"Maker, you must feed," Gaius pleaded.

"I will be fine," she barked. Turning her head, she watched me as the lenses of my vision flipped to penetrate the cracks, windows, and doors of houses, taverns, and barns. I saw babies sleeping, couples rutting, and friends drinking. Then she asked, "Have you made your decision? Who will be your first kill?"

"You say that like it's no big deal."

Fenix tightened his hand into a fist. "It's not."

My eyes darted between Fenix and Claret. "These people aren't slabs of beef—"

"They are, actually," Gaius interrupted.

"—waiting to be chosen for dinner at the butcher. They're people. They have lives, families. How can I choose which one to take that from for my first feed, hunt, meal … whatever?"

"Your prima vedere," Claret said, astutely.

"My what?"

"*Prima vedere* is Romanian," Claret explained, "for first sight."

"I don't understand."

"You will." Claret pointed into the town. Fenix and Gaius disappeared in the blink of an eye. "Remember, you are Nocturnae. You are the perfect hunter. But you must also be calm. If you are not calm, you are distracted."

Her enigmatic speech infuriated me. I balled my hand into a fist, wanting to punch her, but I knew it would be foolish.

"Calm yourself. Envision the box in your mind," Claret said.

The scent of oak filled my nose. I closed my eyes. The heart Cora drew, burned into the center of the box focused my mind. I slowed my breathing. The hinge squeaked as I opened it to climb inside. The world faded away.

Opening my eyes, I focused on the small dots in the town until they clearly became people bustling about under the night's sky.

Smiling uncontrollably, I whispered, "I'm doing it!"

"Stay focused," Claret said. "Find your target."

Three buildings into the town and four streets south of center was a tavern with an old man stumbling through its doorway. His tattered clothing clung to his filthy body. A disturbing stench of whiskey, urine, and vomit leaked from his core.

He awkwardly fell down the two stairs in front of the tavern while trying to stabilize himself in the doorway. Failing to catch himself he hit the frozen ground hard and narrowly missed a pile of horse manure with his face. He cursed and mumbled to himself as he came to his feet. Keeping one hand on the building at all times, he walked away from the tavern's entrance muttering inaudible nonsense to himself.

"I choose him."

Claret turned her head to look at me. "The drunken old man?"

"Yes," I said.

He was old and had already lived his life. A younger man would have so much yet to live for. I couldn't bring myself to fathom killing a woman or a child.

Claret gave two light pats on my back. "I will be here when it's done."

I made my way into the town at a slow pace so as not to draw attention to myself. I expected my hands to grow clammy from nervousness as I approached the man, but my heart fluttered with excitement instead.

I began to salivate. The muscles on my back flexed as my shoulders came forward. My weight shifted onto my toes. My prey was now within striking distance. The pathetic old man had barely made it a block from the tavern in the time it took me to close the distance of a quarter mile.

In one motion I wrapped my arms around the old man's torso, pinning his arms to his sides, and sank my teeth into his carotid artery. Blood squirted from the wound, running down his shoulder onto his chest and back, while droplets lay motionless in the corners of my mouth.

As his warm, metallic blood rushed onto my tongue, the world I knew faded away. This psychedelic drug plunged me into an altered state of reality. Various shapes and colors littered this euphoric parallel universe. Slowly, everything transitioned into a realistic dream world.

I couldn't see anything, but I could make out a woman screaming, "George!"

Echoing behind that voice screamed two other feminine voices. "Daddy!"

As a world formed and the words echoed from the abyss, I could feel George's fear rushing through his body as I actively fed on him. As quickly as the fear came on, I felt depression from a tragic event and nausea from a bottle's worth of whiskey sloshing around in his stomach. Curiosity drove me to focus on his depression, and as my focus intensified, the dream world changed.

It was daytime. The ground was damp from a light rain, but the air was thick with smoke and soot. When the wind blew, the stench of blood and shit enveloped my senses, bringing me to the brink of vomiting.

In the distance I heard the same three women screaming for their lives while other men laughed and joked with each other. I slowly made my way toward the commotion while searching for an opening in the thick smoke.

A village burned, but I could not perceive the snapping or cracking that should accompany burning. Although I felt the wind change directions, fanning the flames, silence reigned. The only sounds I heard were the three women's voices.

The figures came into perfect view, revealing George pinned to the ground by two large men with long hair and beards, and a third man stood towering nearby. His shoulders were so broad they engulfed his neck, and his hands could easily crush a man's skull.

George's eyes squinted under the heat of the flames as he flailed his limbs, trying to free himself from the crushing grip of the large invaders. He freed his right arm for a second and stretched it out in front of him toward the women. A man drove his elbow hard into George's shoulder before ratcheting the arm high onto his back. George screamed in pain.

The giant gripped a large clump of George's hair, forcing George to look into the sky. "Do that again and I'll make it so you never walk again. Blink if you understand me!"

George held a long blink and a fist greeted him when his eyes opened again. He clenched his eyes in pain, but the man refused to let him pass out. "Wake up. Wake up. Wake up," he yelled, lightly smacking George's face between words. George opened his swollen eyes. "Ah, there you are."

The man grabbed George's jaw, pivoting slightly so George could see past him. "You're going to watch every second of this, or we will kill them."

As I looked between George and his family, I noticed two bodies another five or six meters from the women. I could only assume these were the two young ladies' husbands.

The man holding George's face lurched for his youngest daughter, and a wave of energy flooded George. "No. Stop. Please!"

He screamed with such ferocity his voice cracked as he fought the grip of the two men holding him. Every few kicks or thrusts of an arm, a limb would break free just to be held in place again.

"Rebecca!"

A shadowy figure from behind the men ripped the child from the woman's arms. The men began to strip the women of their clothing.

The older daughter smacked the ogre-like man. She froze after doing so as her aggressor stared deeply into her eyes before headbutting her unconscious.

Lifting his fat sack of a stomach onto her back, he awkwardly slid himself between her cheeks. His stomach pulled on the skin of her back with every thrust making a gut-wrenching wet muffled slapping sound. He finished quickly, and flicked the remaining droplet or two of semen hanging from his tip at her before pulling his pants up. He laughed the entire walk back to the leader.

The girl brought her knees together, dropped her hips to her ankles, continuing to sob in the mud as their blended juices seeped from between her legs.

Rebecca trembled as she undressed herself.

I sprinted at George's captors, cocking my arm back in preparation of firing a blow that would turn the man's face into a mound of chitlins. I released the blow, my fist whistling through the air and right through the man's face. I had to catch myself from toppling over as my hand passed right through him, leaving him unscathed.

Then I realized this was all a dream, or a memory rather.

The leader turned to his comrades, his mind made up, and said something inaudible. Unanimously, the other men cheered, and terror fell across the women's faces as they began to scream.

Then one by one, the barbarians walked into the distance, with his grandchild in their arms, and were lost in the smoke and embers of the town.

I felt the old man's emotions rush through me, as if they were my own, blood pooling in my eyes—a droplet trickled like a tear. Returning from the dream-like state, my eyes burst open, ripping the old man from my clench, pushing him away like spoiled meat.

My eyes radiated in horror while he stared deep into my crimson eyes and smiled. "Thank you," he said.

Life left his body, quickly falling to the ground, ironically landing in a slumped position against a wooden barrel. Standing there, still trying to wrap my head around what the hell just happened, I closed the man's eyes. "Be with your family and leave the nightmares of this world behind."

I made my way out of town much slower than I entered it. Splinters of George's memories plagued my mind. I saw George— he was much younger—standing just outside the entrance of a cabin sipping warm mead as he watched his two daughters, seven and nine, playing in the open grasslands. I smelled the rich, braised duck with roasted carrots and onions his wife made for his birthday dinner in addition to sweet honey bread for dessert.

Distracted by the memories, I didn't realize Claret was near. When within speaking range, she said nothing. Rather—like always—she watched me, forming conclusions she never shared.

My eyes twitched randomly as I deciphered the sixty-some years of memories I acquired from my first meal.

"How did it go?" she asked.

"I think something went wrong. I was feeding and … this doesn't feel right."

"What do you mean?"

Although the memories were painful to think about, I began retelling my experience in excruciating detail; the memory I relived while feeding, how I had attacked George, and the memories continuing to unfurl.

Wiping droplets from my face, I interrupted myself, "What is this?" I held out my bloody fingers. "I'm bleeding … from my eyes."

"Nocturnae cry blood instead of tears. We don't know why exactly. I believe it's because we are more in sync with life and mortality than humanity. Thus, instead of crying saltwater, we cry life itself," she said.

I continued relaying my feelings and experience for nearly an hour. She stood silently studying every word and expression I made. A sigh of relief fell over me when I'd finished, like when a child tells the truth after lying.

Claret placed her hand on me. "Congratulations, you're truly one of the Nocturnae. The memories George gifted to you, you will carry until your true death."

"Will this happen to me every time?" I asked.

I shuddered when I thought of all the pain and suffering, I'd have to experience each time I fed from that day forward.

"Yes, but in time you will be able to guide it."

The memories pulled on the strings of my mind like it was a marionette, and my head violently twitched. "The pain … it's incredible." I gripped the sides of my head in agony

"But the amount of knowledge and number of skills you'll be able to accumulate from it over a lifetime is immeasurable," Claret explained. "You will master skills from every culture, speak the language of every land, and navigate the seas using the stars. What would take a human a lifetime of practice, repetition, and failure to achieve, you will have in mere minutes."

"Through tortuous memories that aren't mine."

She lifted my chin. "You must overcome it. The burden of coping with each victim's worst memories can drive even the strongest Nocturnae to depression, madness, or even suicide. You cannot—"

From out of nowhere Fenix appeared. "Maker, look!"

He pointed to the northernmost side of the town where two dozen men on horses bounded over the hillside.

"They're down wind of us, but how did we not hear them?" Scanning the horizon, she frantically searched. "Where's Gaius?"

"I'm here," Gaius said, halfway up the hill. Looking back over his shoulder at the cloud of dirt and snow left in the horses' wake, he ran to Claret. "What shall we do my Maker?"

She scanned the world around us, forming the most optimal strategy. Her lips moved at an incredible speed as she spoke to herself, making a number of complex calculations based on air temperature, wind current and direction, and altitude. Focusing on two different paths of dense forest, her eyes fluttered back and forth, as though she could see through the trees.

"Gaius, scout ahead southeast." She pointed. "Go, now."

Without a word or a gesture, Gaius was gone, leaving only a

single leaf shaking in his path.

"Fenix, you will—"

But he had already pulled two eight-inch curved daggers from his pelt and twirled them about with a knowing grin. "As you wish, my Maker."

Looking over his shoulder at me, our eyes met and a voice in my head said, *"Take care of our Maker, brother."*

Cocking his head from side to side, he grinned an evil grin I'd never seen before. His shoulders, back, and arms bulged and the ground beneath him cracked when he stomped his foot.

He let out a loud *ROAR!* And made for the tree line.

Slamming the palm of her hand hard into the middle of my back, Claret urged, "Sorin! What are you waiting for? Move!"

"But Fenix—"

"He's staying for *you*. He will hold them off. Now move! Follow Gaius's path."

I cycled my vision to see beyond the town for one final look at the remaining dozen men that circled Fenix's monstrous form. He swung wildly at a man, spilling his guts onto the snow.

He looked back at me, and his voice entered my mind, *"Go Sorin. Fulfill the prophecy. NOW!"*

Fenix palmed another man's face, slamming it into the earth, and let out a horrifying yell that shook the earth.

I turned, and I ran.

# 16



SILENCE FILLS THE room, tainting it, making it stale and awkward. But awkward is just fine. I've said more than enough at this point. It's her turn. What do they know? Where is Claret? Who *specifically* is holding her?

Her hand reaches out, as though she wants to comfort me, but she stops herself. Of course, she knows she cannot come near me.

Empathy? Again. That's … unexpected.

"I'm alright my dear, it was a long time ago, but thank you."

She clears her throat. "What happened to Fenix?"

My head hangs heavy hearing his name. "I don't know."

"You don't know?" she says, incredulously. After a brief pause, she leans back. "You don't know, or you don't want to tell me?"

"I don't know. I swear on my Maker."

"How can that be? Mr. Harker, you've had an answer in some way for every single question. 'I don't know' seems out of character, if I may."

There's a lot to unpack there.

"What you're asking is…" I take a deep breath. "…complicated."

"What's complicated about it? Did you or did you not go back to the town of … Brasov, and find Fenix?"

You're not going to let this go, are you?

"We did *but* it wasn't until three nights later, when we were sure it was safe."

Gently, she prods, "What happened to Fenix, Sorin?" Her face goes soft with concern.

She's getting it.

"There was no ash. No footprints. Nothing left but pools of frozen blood hidden beneath fresh snow. But the winds blew strong and when he hadn't joined us by the third day… I knew. He'd died his true death."

Jean adds a note to her ledger.

Ow. Another shard of silver exits my body.

I pull my legs together, catching the sliver between them.

Almost rid of it all. Mid-day or early evening, I should be clean.

"So," Jean says cautiously, "you formed a deep emotional connection with Fenix after only three days of knowing him … the bonds that forge during a … Transformation? Transition? Resurrection? Are they extremely strong then?"

"*Rebirth* is the word you're looking for and yes, you could say that I felt akin to him. I'm sure to you this seems odd, almost fictional but I assure you, everything changes after that transformation."

"How long does it take?" she asks quickly, in an almost

compassionate tone.

"How long does what take?"

She pauses and bites her lip, as if forming and reforming the question in her mind. "How long does it take for a Nocturnae to burn under the sun."

Why you little—

"Rather insensitive, don't you think? I tell you my friend likely died, and you ask me how long it took? You humans really have no regard for life beyond your species, do you?"

Quickly, she puts both hands up, "No, no, no… I'm sorry that I came off as insensitive, that wasn't my intention. Please—"

"It's fine," I say calmly, leaking a smile.

Fucking with you is so much fun. If only Fenix could see me now … he'd be so proud. Me, playing with my food.

I raise my head to stretch the middle of my back and allow the wound to heal from the silver fragment that just fell out. "Let me ask you, if you were stabbed in the stomach, would you die right away? It's the same with us and the sun."

"I assume that by *stomach* you mean *abdomen*. In which, the answer really depends. In the abdomen there's the liver, the pancreas, the spleen, and so on."

So many tasty snacks, so little time.

Nodding my head. "Keep going."

"If an artery is nicked, you'd die in minutes from blood loss. Hit the kidneys or liver, hours maybe. Bowels, death would come after several painful days of sepsis."

"Someone paid attention in anatomy class." A grin spreads widely across my face as I envision myself devouring her slowly …

organ by organ, as she bleeds out on the concrete flooring beneath me. "It's a lot like that. We burn at rates that are relative to how well fed we are, what physical state we're in, and the levels of humidity and ozone in the atmosphere."

She sits up from her slumped position, reaches for her writing device, but stops just shy of the keys and returns her hands to her lap.

What was that about?

Without hesitation, I ask, "Tell me about your family. How did your mother die?"

Her mouth hung open. "How—"

"Our conversation yesterday … your strange tattoo, an ear with a line through it. When you described the tattoo's significance you said your mother *was* deaf, rather than *is* deaf; thus, implying she's deceased. How did she die?"

"My parents … they…" She folds a hair behind her ear and the hairs on her arms perk up. "I'd prefer not to talk about them."

Something happened. Something she may hold herself responsible for. Better not to press it and have her clam up; but I need information. Where is Claret, exactly? If I can pry more information, I also buy time. Two birds, one stone.

Slowly, I nod. "Of course." I pause, studying her hands as they fold into one another, nervously picking at a cuticle on her pinky finger. "A different question then … siblings?"

She chuckles, twice, and blots under each eye with her forefinger. "I thought you didn't care?"

She remembers. Good.

"You're right, I don't but I would like to know if you've always been blind."

"No, I haven't been blind my entire life." She breathes deeply, sighs hard and slumps forward slightly. "It started when I was twelve. The doctors tried everything to figure it out. Some thought it was puberty-linked, others a virus, but it didn't matter in the end. It happened."

"How long before you were completely blind?"

"A year or so." She pauses for a moment and shows a half smile, "It's a blessing really, in hindsight."

"Going blind is a blessing?"

"No, losing my parents—well, my mother specifically—when I did."

Now you have my attention dearie.

"Why do you say that?"

"My mother was deaf." She looks down at her hands like the thought was painful and weighing on her. "It would have been nearly impossible for my mother and I to communicate. My father would have been the translator and the stress would have driven a bigger wedge between them."

I sat there in silence, unable to come up with anything to say.

Before an awkward silence could set in, she says, "Let's try something that's a little… lighter." Adjusting herself in her seat, a smile spreads across her face. "In all the years you've walked the Earth, if you could have anyone's memories imprinted upon you, whose would it be?"

She's actually enjoying this.

"Stephen Hawking," I say, quickly. "The wealth of knowledge and innovative thinking skills I'd have gained would have sustained my intellectual appetite for *decades* to come. Alas, even though I thought about it a number of times, I didn't want to carry his crosses for eternity. The terror of being stuck in one's body with no control over it must be utter torture."

She begins to type but stops to grab her stomach as it gurgles.

"Do you need a break?" I ask.

"Do *you* need a break?" she challenges.

I let loose a coy grin. "Not unless you're going to get me that hot water for your—"

She can't hold her composure and picks up her device. "You know what, you're right. We'll pick this up in five minutes."

Discreetly, she exchanges the story-filled pages for her cane and heads out.

Finally.

Flexing the muscles in my back and torso a few more bits of silver fly from me, *clinking* on the floor below.

It won't be long now.

# 17



THE DOOR CLICKED shut behind Jean, echoing down the empty hallways of the quiet building, temporarily abandoned for the weekend.

Jean flattened herself against the door and let out a heavy sigh. "Why did I reach for his hand? It's like I forgot he is Nocturnae. Stupid … I could have lost my arm."

She stood there, silent and motionless, for nearly a minute before searching for the crack in the wall. She found it quickly, centered herself, and began to slowly walk down the hall, tapping her cane twice between each step. She passed a hallway with a crash-bar door on her left and various wall hangings of aircrafts, servicemen from World-War II, and even a map of the building's floor plan.

Jean turned right at the next hallway, passing numerous cypher-locked blue-gray doors but stopped halfway down the hall. Holding her cane between her thumb and forefinger, she felt for a sign: WOMEN.

The bathroom was dark, and reeked of must, tart urine, and recycled stale air, but she didn't wince at the smell. She entered a stall and relieved herself in the quiet.

*Zzz zzz zzz*

Jean grabbed the pager from her tote as a monotone, robotic voice said, "9 – 1 – 1. Eugene."

"Shit," Jean muttered and finished up.

Quickly washing and drying her hands, she felt for the door.

Retrieving her folded cane from the tote, she snapped it straight. Suddenly, something crashed into her sending her cane and tote flying.

Stunned, Jean felt about as a young man gasped, "Oh my gosh. I am so, so sorry Dr. Allicines. Are you okay? I'm sorry. I looked back to make sure the door closed, and—"

"Tim?"

"…yeah. Sorry, good morning. Here let me help you," he said, holding out his hand.

Jean scoffed, "I don't know where your hand is. Could you snap your fingers?"

"Right." He winced his reddened face and snapped his fingers twice. "Sorry. Shit."

Jean grabbed his hand, stood, and found the wall with her other hand. "It's okay. Watch where you're going next time, okay?"

"Yes ma'am."

"Would you mind?" Jean asked, offering her hand.

"Of course, where are you headed now? Back to interrogation?"

"No, I got a page from Dr. Shelley and I need to call him back first. Can you…" she said, holding out her arm again.

"Conference room it is," he said, gently taking her arm.

Jean followed ever so slightly behind him, to feel the slight tug on her arm when he changed directions.

Tim broke the silence when they turned into the main hallway. "Does Dr. Shelley not like me? Well, he doesn't know me, so I guess ... did I do something?"

"What do you mean?"

"The end of the day yesterday, when he called down the hall at you," Tim explained, loosely.
"He didn't look at me. Not once."

"I wouldn't worry about it. He has a lot on his plate at the moment."

Tim opened the door to the conference room, released her arm, and tapped the door twice. "Okay, the phone is on the edge of the table nearest the door; three, maybe four steps from the edge of the door."

She nodded.

Tim awkwardly got out of her way. "That was just an ... interesting, first impression with Dr. Shelley."

Jean instinctively found his shoulder and gently placed her hand on it. "Don't take it personally." She patted his shoulder twice, stepped into the conference room, and turned her head. "Give me two minutes."

She shut the door behind her before Tim could say anything else, grabbed the secure phone, and dialed Eugene's office number.

*Ring! Ring! Ri—*

"Hello," Dr. Shelley answered.

"I'm with the Subject. You paged me '9 – 1 – 1' is everything okay?"

"Ah, no. You never sent me the email."

Jean snapped her fingers. "Shit. You're right."

"Can you tell me now? You're on a secure line," Dr. Shelley said.

"The PHANG Program. We need to mix the Patient's blood and saliva with the Subject's blood and saliva before the solution is ingested by the Patient."

The sound of a glass hitting a hard surface echoed through the phone.

"Well, I'll be damned … you did it Jeanie! Ha, ha! We won't know for sure until it's tested, but if this works, we'll never have to worry about funding again." Before Jean could say anything, he said, "The Codex … has the Subject said anything about the Codex?"

"No. Not yet, but I plan on staying all day if I need to."

"Good. Very good. The Director, General Grissom, and … it doesn't matter who else, everyone has been up my ass about this. We need to show them something they're not expecting. PHANG is good, but the Codex will secure us for years to come."

"I'll do everything I can."

"Wonderful. Okay, now get back in there!"

# 18



BARELY FIFTEEN MINUTES pass before the door locks begin their *clicking* and *beeping* and *churning* once more. Jean glides in, smoothly taking her seat.

She's enjoying this…

"Alright. Moving along, if we may."

"Well, someone's got their panties in a twist. Bad news on your break, or are the suits breathing down your neck?"

Jean fakes a smile and ignores my antics. "We left off with you fleeing the humans after your prima vedere. Did they catch up to you?"

"No, not for quite some time … but humans are persistent."

"Did they have a book with them?" she asks.

That's randomly specific.

"A book? No, not that I saw. What would it have looked like?"

You know that if you lie, I'll know. Ha.

Jean opens her mouth, preparing to speak but thinks better of it.

Smart girl. This book is of interest to you … this can play to my advantage.

"You know," I say, tapping my finger, "now that you mention it … yes."

"What?" she asks, her head snapping to attention.

"A book did cross my path once but…"

"But what?" Jean asks, eagerly.

"Do you know what *polar night* is?"

"No, I don't think so," she replies, scooting to the edge of her seat.

"It's roughly a four-to-ten-week period of complete darkness that occurs in certain parts of the world."

"Ideal for a Nocturnae," Jean says, studiously.

"When our planet's rotation around the sun and its own rotation on its axis are aligned in just the right way, the sun stays below the horizon, seemingly indefinitely."

Jean nods. "What does polar night have to do with the book?"

"I'm getting there … it was a cold morning on All Hallows' Eve in 1414 on the Lofoten Islands of Norway, and we were waiting for polar night."

# 19



THE SETTLEMENT WAS small, at the water's edge, and backed into the mountain's foot. The water, still as glass, reflected the moon back upon itself and glittered with gas lanterns from the dock. In the distance, just outside the town, elk whistled to one another and a reindeer softly grunted.

Seated in silence on the porch of our cabin, Claret, Gaius, and I enjoyed the night sky. A cup of tea clutched between my hands reminded me of my humanity as we breathed in the frigid air. At almost half-past the tenth hour, red and orange hues backlit the mountain, forcing us to turn in, as humanity's greatest ally spread its warm blanket over the land.

Claret and Gaius had retreated well into the shadows of the cabin when the sun's rays hit the cracks of our front door. I, on the other hand, held my ground as long as I could stand the searing pain.

"Sorin, you fool," Claret scolded, just above a whisper.

Fully blind, I retreated toward her voice in the darkness.

"I don't know why you are still so fascinated with the sun after all this time," Gaius sneered.

The scent of burnt flesh lingered in the room as my face regrew.

"The pain is worth a glimpse of the beauty, brother," I said softly as I found a seat.

Gaius smacked the cup of tea out of my hands. "You're gambling with your life brother. A life Fenix *sacrificed* himself for," he graveled.

"Gaius, that's enough." Claret's expression didn't reveal the disappointment I knew she felt … in both of us. "Fenix, our brave protector, sacrificed himself for *all* of us, not just for Sorin. He saved your life as well Gaius."

An ominous crimson glow emanated onto her cheekbones, her voice entered my mind, *"Once a year, always at this time, you flirt with your true death in order to catch a glimpse of the sun. Why?"*

Gaius caught Claret's eyes and scoffed, retreating to the corner.

I projected my thoughts into her mind. *"It's just … there is no logical reason that we, the most powerful creatures on the planet, cannot withstand something so simple as the sun. There* must *be a way!"*

Gaius rolled his eyes as Claret and I continued our private debate.

*"What happens to the bear when it is thrown into the sea? The bear drowns. No matter how fierce. Like the bear, we too are subject to the awesome power of the Earth."* Turning, she placed her hand upon my cheek. *"All creatures have weakness, Sorin, but that doesn't take away from their beauty or their awesome power. Nocturnae, whether we like it or not, are more like the bear than we would like to admit. Even after all the awesome gifts bestowed upon us and the pleasure of watching history unfold before our very eyes, we are*

*still mortal."*

She turned her back to look out a window.

My eyelids fluttered uncontrollably as her mind ripped itself from mine.

Gaius sat in the corner stewing in grief.

"What is it like?" I asked, changing the subject.

"What is what like?" She refused to turn her gaze from the shadowed landscape.

"The Polar Night. Being able to walk around at any time of day that you'd like? What is it like living in a world of complete darkness? Do any flowers bloom? What happens to the animals? Do they hibernate? Does it even affect them?"

"Quiet," she snapped, causing Gaius's ears to perk up.

"Hush!" Gaius demanded, his head snapping from left to right as he tried to zero in on his target.

Closing my eyes, I focused on the sounds around me. The wind beat on the cabin's outer walls. There were quick, shallow breaths from Claret. Gaius's licking of his lips. Ripples along the water's surface from life below. *Voices.* Three of them. Southwest of our cabin, just outside of the village pub.

"No, I haven't heard of anyone going missing," said the pub owner, in his uniquely haughty tone.

"Have you heard of anyone passing away recently? Specifically, strange deaths or those with bite marks somewhere on their body?" asked a raspy-voiced man, clearly a smoker.

"Old-man Bjørn died last week of consumption, but he'd been sick for weeks."

The conversation paused.

"He's thinking," I said aloud.

"Quiet," Gaius scolded.

Claret glared at us both.

The pub owner spit out his chew. "I think that's it. No one else comes to mind."

Relief spread over me as the two men began walking away.

The pub owner smacked the doorframe softly. "Well ... ah, but ... never mind. It's nothing."

Stiff leather, likely a belt, cracked in the cold air.

"What's nothing?"

"Found the remains of one of our fishermen last week. Torn to pieces by a wolfpack we tracked."

There was a long, ominous pause.

"Anyone come through town that week, or the week before? Someone new. A red-headed woman maybe? She would have been with two men."

"Mmm, nooooo ... well ... a gentleman, blonde, a boy really. I never got his name, first passed through the pub a fortnight ago. He stayed in town for a brief period before moving on."

The two men must have reacted to each other before the owner finished his thought.

"Thank you for your time, sir," the raspy man said.

"Now wait a minute," the pub owner said, stepping down the pub steps after the men as they turned away. "Do I have something to worry about? Am I, and my family, in danger?"

I heard fingers running through animal fur and a palm take a firm grip of old skin like a man giving a convincing supportive gesture to a comrade to hide an imminent lie. "No, you have nothing to worry about. You and your family are completely safe. Do you have akvavit?"

"Of course! It's the water of life."

"Perfect. We're going to take a look around, if you don't mind. We'll bring our men in for a drink."

"We have room here for your men, if you'd like to give them somewhere warm to sleep, too."

"That's very kind of you. Thank you." The men stomped through the snow, distancing themselves from the pub.

Once the pub door had closed firmly behind the old man, the travelers stopped and turned toward one another.

The raspy-voiced man asked, "What do you think?"

"They're here."

"I agree. I was skeptical, but the blonde boy…"

"Polar night is also upon us," he said, pulling out a small metal object with moving gears from his pocket. "They will be harder to track once the great night falls. We must find them quickly or we risk losing them."

"They can't be far," the raspy-voiced man said. "This town is no more than a fishing village."

"Yes, and they must know we're here. What do you suggest we do?"

He ran his fingers through his beard. "We sure as hell can't go breaking down doors or go house to house. That would take too long and could incite panic. The sun is up. We're safe … at least for a little while." He paused for a moment. "We should position the men throughout the town to watch as many houses as possible. The cabin that no one enters, or leaves, is the cabin that will house our vampires."

Claret snapped at Gaius. "I told you to be more careful!"

She explained to me the man with the raspy voice was Franklin Gilead, the youngest son of Sir Isaac Gilead, and current leader of the Night Hunters; a faction of The Company specializing in hunting, tracking, and killing Nocturnae. Without giving a second's pause, she told me The Company was a group of highly skilled and specialized people within the Roman Catholic Church—or funded by them, she wasn't sure—with the sole mission: To rid the world of Satan's demons.

Angrily, Gaius stepped in. "They were the ones that killed Fenix. They were the ones I led away from your cabin as you lay dying of plague. They were the ones—"

"You've made your point Gaius," Claret interrupted, softly placing her hand on his shoulder.

"But we're not demons," I said. "Nor are we the children of Satan."

Gaius began packing his flint and steel with a stack of blankets in a broken leather sack. "We know that, but humans make magic out of that which they do not understand."

"Gaius, where's the Pearl?" Claret asked.

He held out his closed fist. "Here."

"Give it to me." She wrapped both her hands around his, preventing me from seeing the Pearl. She tucked the mysterious object into a small pocket hidden within her belt. "Humanity labels all terrifying things in this world demons. Us and every other beast of myth and legend."

"The children of Encomiâ, the Lygos. The misunderstood

Meliāki. The thaumaturgy of the Penyihir," Gaius added. "All demons."

"What are those?" I asked.

"Not now brother. We've wasted too much time already." Turning to Claret, Gaius asked, "What is our plan, Maker?"

Without looking, she sped around the large cabin, in and out of rooms, ripping pieces of fabric and tying them together. "Lift up your arms," she ordered, fastening cloth over every gap in my cloak.

I didn't argue, I only looked at Gaius who seemed envious of something I couldn't understand. Examining myself in the patchwork clothing, I raised my arms. "What's this for? I can barely move."

Gaius began fabricating his own hooded cloak from the remaining curtains and discarded garb.

"We,"—she paused to wrap her face in extra cloth similar to mine—"are leaving."

"Why—"

Closing the distance between us quickly, she slid her arm through the sleeve of her cloak. "These men are more powerful than you think."

For the first time since my new birth, I felt her pulse change. The blood in her face surged from her eyes to her ear lobes. The seemingly emotionless and callused face didn't break, but a tear formed slowly in the corner of her eye. The tiny drop of blood clung to her eyelashes, threatening to fall. She looked me dead in the eye.

"They killed my Maker." Her lip quivered as the words sprung from her lips.

"These men killed your Maker?" I suddenly felt hot with anger.

Gaius continued dressing himself, but reverently.

"Their ancestors," she said. "I've kept an eye on The Company for more than a century now, since we first learned of their existence."

"Where did they come from?"

Gaius walked to the front door. "Maker, I will keep a lookout, but we can't linger. Hurry."

"Thank you, Gaius," Claret said.

Her face quickly became somber like a bad memory had come to the forefront of her mind. She shook it off and finished the wrapping of her tattered coverall. She examined me for places light could enter through my coverings. She tied her sack and threw it over her shoulders.

Poking his head through the ajar cabin door Gaius signaled for us to follow him. "We can talk more about this later, but right now we need to leave."

Claret flipped the scarf-like cloth across her face, around her head, and tucked it tightly into her breast. She gestured toward the cabin door. As I made my way, I focused on our pursuers' position, calculating the most probable of their movement patterns. Incredible how these abilities just started to happen seamlessly, the more I got used to them.

"Now," she said.

We exited the cabin at a human pace and headed toward the neighbor's hitching post. Horses drank from an iceberg-riddled trough under their warm blankets before their morning ride. We each approached a steed from the rear, ensuring we made no sound so as not to startle the gentle creatures.

When my mare was within reach, I placed my hand gently on her hindquarters. "Good morning, beautiful. It's a nice day for a ride, wouldn't you say?" I rubbed my hand up her side as I traversed the distance to her head. My eyes locked on to her one large brown eye, coaxing her into trusting me. "Good girl."

Once her body language shifted from caution to ease, I looked to Claret, who was having a harder time winning over the colt.

Gaius was already mounted.

"Maker, what's wrong?" I asked, inching my way toward her.

"Nothing."

The horse flared its nostrils and shied away. "Be gentle with him."

"I *am* being gentle."

But she wasn't. Something was wrong.

"Whoa there," I said softly, and approached with an open palm. "That's it, that's it."

Claret eyed me, a touch of anxiety in her face. We had to get going.

I stroked the colt's side and took a step forward. "There you go. Yeah, that's it." Glancing at Claret, I invited her over. "Use a calm voice. Calm yourself and the horse will calm."

She did, and so did the horse.

Once mounted, she looked at me with embarrassment and said, "Thank you. I ... after hundreds of years, we lose some of our humanity. Our empathy. Our compassion. Eventually, we can only compel."

Simultaneously, we all lifted our ears in the direction of our pursuers. The men were still organizing the troops and dealing out orders. This would be the only opportunity we had to escape unscathed, and we rode quickly toward a small hunting caravan moving up the mountain.

Forty-five minutes later we caught the caravan's tail. An hour later, we were fully integrated and spread far apart from one another.

Anxiety of the silence between us took over me, and I looked back toward Claret. Our eyes met and we stepped into each other's minds. *"How long shall we travel with them? We're well out of sight of the town, and no one is following us."*

*"We need to get to Étretat, France."*

*"Why?"* I asked.

*"Amicia's cabin is there. We will be safe there."*

*"Amicia, your Maker?"* I clarified.

*"Yes."*

I knew better than to question how we'd all get there, but France was nearly 2,000 kilometers away as the crow flies.

Once the sun had set and the caravan had camped for the night, Gaius appeared, holding my horse. "Come on," he whispered to me, passing the reins.

"Where are we going?" I asked.

"Moskenesøya."

Confused, I repeated the unfamiliar town as we found Claret mounted in the moonlight. She called out softly. "It's time we took to the sea."

GAIUS HAD BARTERED us passage to Bruges, Belgium. The ship

was due to leave port mid-day. Under the midnight moon, we made our way aboard and quickly went below deck in hopes of catching a few hours of sleep before the crew boarded and we'd have to stay alert.

At first, we kept ourselves hidden during the trip. There were far too many men to compel them all. Although disgusting, we fed on the vermin scurrying across our feet below deck in order to keep ourselves invisible. The ocean was no place for Nocturnae to be found.

Easily found. Easily killed.

It took two nights for me to gather the courage to ask Claret about her Maker and the men that killed her.

Claret sat with her back to the hull, her arms resting on her knees, and her head hung. "Back then, before my Maker was killed, Nocturnae proclaimed themselves gods, enslaving humanity. Not long after ... *the Incident* ... The Company was formed. My Maker, Amicia, was among the first to encounter the organization led by a man named Aeneas Gilead, the forefather of Franklin—the man with the raspy-voice at the pub."

"What happened? What *incident*?" I asked as compassionately as I could.

"The Twin Incident," Claret said. Gaius quickly moved to the other side of the ship, not wanting to be a part of the conversation. "Two sisters, twins, of the Encomiâ family ended the Nocturnae reign over the humans and drove our kind into the shadows."

"And they killed your Maker?"

"No," Claret said, lifting her head for the first time. "Nocturnae did that." Shocked, I instinctively raised a hand to my mouth. "A ripple effect of the Twin Incident was the splitting of the legion of Nocturnae into two factions—one led by Amicia, the other led by The Faceless King."

Her voice grew shaky with sorrow. I wanted to comfort her, but I knew better. Even though my intentions were good, Claret would have seen comfort as me calling her weak. And I never wanted her to feel that way.

"Amicia was slain quickly," she continued, "as were two others in our coven. Her dying words to me were: Run, Claret. I obeyed and am the only one of our coven who survived. Two dozen other covens fell before year's end. I'd like to say they all fell to The Company, but The Faceless King was ruthless."

"They killed everyone in your coven but you? That's awful."

Claret shook her head. "Covens back then were much larger. Each consisting of dozens of members and before then, thousands. However, since the inception of The Company, covens greater than two or three members have been driven into extinction. Larger covens are easier to track. They require more blood to satisfy their numbers, leaving higher death tolls in villages they pass through. The family dynamic within a large coven is also different. There's a constant power struggle among the children to be the alpha, and the favorite in the eyes of the Maker."

I began to ask another question, but Claret raised a silencing hand—she'd had enough. Although the story was hard for her to share, it seemed to bring us closer.

HALFWAY THROUGH OUR journey, none of us could stomach the sickly blood of rats any longer. Claret turned to us with a fouled face as she forced down the blood of another vermin. "That's it. Tonight, we must truly feed."

Gaius and I looked at each other with faces like children today have on Christmas Eve night. Overwhelmed with excitement and foaming at the mouth with hunger of human blood, we discarded our rats.

"But just this once," she said, raising a finger. "We cannot afford to take the risk with so few humans aboard. One can be claimed by the sea and it be believable, but two, three, or more … there's no way we'd stay hidden for long. We'll have to share."

We waited until all but a handful of the men had been in their bunks for hours. Quietly, we traversed the winding stairs from the lowest level of the ship to its deck. The ocean air was salty but eerily free of a breeze. The ship floated freely across the calm water under the moonless, star-filled night sky.

We stopped at the top of the stairs and Claret whispered, "Strike quickly. Feed but don't kill. We need him to scream when we throw him overboard."

Turning our heads toward the stern, the captivating sounds of two intoxicated men caused us to salivate. The shorter man tripped over his own feet only to catch himself on the railing, but then crashed forward into the oak pillar supporting the rail, which knocked him unconscious.

Our moment to strike had arrived.

We rushed the conscious man. The drunken ingrate must have seen us out of the corner of his eye as he fell, stricken with fear, and dropped his bottle. Claret caught the bottle inches below the man's hand as Gaius muted the man's speech with his palm.

Collectively, we sank our teeth into him. Claret sucked the alcohol-tainted blood from his femoral artery, impressively not spilling a drop. Gaius latched onto the man's underarm, choking on the man's odor. I sank my teeth into his carotid artery and euphoria overtook me. Scenes of the man's life rushed through my mind: playing with hand-carved wooden statues on the floor—pickpocketing—the brothel where his mother worked—the breaking of his arm—raping and killing a man—joining the crew to evade punishment for his crimes.

We drank him to within an inch of his life in less than a minute. Claret pulled the man close, slapped him, and flashed her reddened eyes. "Scream for me." And as he screamed, she tossed him overboard.

Gaius smashed the bottle on the deck.

The exploding glass bottle rattled the drunken sailor conscious. He looked up, rubbed his head, and looked around for his friend. When he saw the bottle shards, he rushed toward the sea, and extended his body over the banister screaming, "Bristol!"

He ran to the side of the rail and screamed louder for help. But it was too late, we had already returned into the shadows of the ship and made our way below deck. There we remained for the rest of the voyage with full—enough—bellies and the rats to keep us company and curb the cravings.

As the twenty-second night approached, we heard a man from the crow's nest cry out, "Land ho!"

The air on the shore reeked of rotting fish and seaweed sprinkled with hints of human feces and vomit—humans have always been a disgusting species.

Claret gave her instructions. "We need to get to Bruges before sunrise. From there, we'll take several nights to travel the 300 kilometers to the Cliffs of Étretat."

We made our way out of the small port that had become overrun with lust, infidelity, misogyny, and filth and into the calmness of nature. Into the heaven of nocturnal life.

Wild boars rummaged through the brush in the distance, killing and consuming everything in their path. A giant rabbit darted from its den, doing barrel rolls around tree trunks. The rabbit's heart raced as it puffed the air, pushing its muscles to their maximum capacity. But, like many before it, the rabbit ended up being dinner for the Lynx that chased it.

Inadvertently, I turned inward, as we made our way through the forests and fields to Bruges. Were we, Nocturnae, the Lynx and humanity is the rabbit? No, that didn't make sense. Humans had no evolutionary traits that would allow them to escape us—did they? On second thought, there was a small, organized group of them hunting us. They'd already killed Fenix. Had I underestimated them and their capabilities for nearly a century?

"We're here," Claret said.

Gaius sneered, "It's a dump. Barely a farming village out here. We'll be lucky to find enough food for all of us without going into the city."

"We can't risk it," Claret said, quickly.

It had been more than a week at this point since we'd fed on that drunken oaf on the boat. We were all thirsting for a taste of fresh, sweet, untainted blood. We did what we had to do to survive on the boat, but I was now ready for everything the land had to offer.

"We need to eat before the sun begins to rise. But without raising alarm. Make it look like an accident." Gaius pulled a long blade of grass and held it between his teeth. "When the human comes to, rub their back with one hand while telling them they passed out. Ask them if they're okay. They will pass away quietly later."

Claret gave us permission. "When you've had your fill, meet me back here. Be sure there are still a few hours before sunrise. Then, we'll make our way farther."

Taking different paths, we made our way into Bruges.

# 20



STOP, STOP, STOP," Jean says, abruptly. "Are you trying to trick me?"

"Whatever do you mean?"

"I asked you about a book and in return, you're telling me about a polar night. What's the connection?"

She's growing impatient. Something must have happened during her potty break.

Leaning forward as much as I can, I wet my lips, smacking them loudly for dramatic effect. "Now Jean, you wouldn't happen to be accusing me of malus intent … would you?"

"Malus? Mm, no. Malicious intent, yes. Trickery … manipulation … evil…"

"Tsk-tsk, shame on you Jean. I thought we were beyond all of this. I thought we'd … made a connection."

I still cannot compel you yet. Once I can compel you, I can find Claret. I need her here just a bit longer.

"What does it have to do with the book?"

"Everything," I snap, cold and quick. Nuzzling myself into the back of the chair. "Now, since you *rudely* interrupted me. Do you have any other questions? Has anything piqued your interest? I'd hate for you to leave here with 'food' still on the table."

She sat there, silently stewing over the writing device, lightly tapping the keys for quite some time—long enough for me to think of eighty-seven different ways to consume her.

"Halloween," Jean says, softly. "What is it about that day?"

"You know." I pause a moment, but she still hasn't connected the dots. "I'll give you a hint, All Saint's Day."

"Halloween…" Her thumbs twirl like she's searching for the right words before cautiously walking down this path. "…and All Saint's Day, are both celebrations of the dead. And many believe the dead are allowed to walk the earth at this time because the veil between our world and the next is at its thinnest."

"Back then," I say, looking down at the flowers Jean had bought me, "we called it Samhain. It was an old Gaelic festival that you now refer to as All Hallow's Eve. The midpoint between the autumn and winter equinox."

I wait for her to discover my reasoning on her own. It doesn't take her long.

"…Cora. You were risking your life, every year, for a chance to see Cora again."

I nod, knowing she could not see my reaction. "Yes."

She drops her head slightly, leans forward, and gently places her hand on my knee. She says nothing nor does her hand move, it just rests there softly sharing my pain.

I quietly clear my throat. "How old is The Company?"

"You just said they found you in early fifteenth century, so roughly 600 years old I guess."

Pay attention.

"No Jean, they're older than that. Who do you think Gaius and Fenix were keeping an eye out for when they found human me in my cabin? The Company."

"…and Claret had been tracking them from before then." She pauses a moment as if realizing something herself. "Hm, I don't know, to be honest." She types, briefly, on her writing device. "I will find out. What else can you tell me about Encomiâ?"

"Nothing."

"Mr. Harker, don't start this again."

"My knowledge of the twin sisters, the incident, and Encomiâ begins and ends there. Claret never brought up the subject again, and *I* wasn't about to bring up those painful feelings for her."

"I see. How about the cabin? It was Amicia's cabin, wasn't it?"

"Yes."

"What was the importance of her cabin? Why was Claret so adamant on going there, a place so far away, rather than going farther north where the two men, and their company, couldn't follow?"

"I'm getting there…"

# 21



BRUGES WAS QUIETER than other towns and villages that we'd visited over the years. The air was thick, saturated in a dense, low-hanging fog that blanketed the grass surrounding the homes. The buildings were dark and musty, but a nearby bakery sweetened the air with its sugars.

There was no pub with drunken idiots falling in and out of its doors or from between the legs of its women. Nor were there any passed-out half-wits in the pig pens who'd taken a beating over a card game, or from their wife who caught them in the brothels. No, this was going to be more complicated, and it would require both patience and finesse.

Silently making my way through the town, I kept to the darkest of shadows on the off chance that someone might see me. A door latch clicked open, and a wooden door creaked as someone stepped out into the night. My ears perked up as my animalistic senses prepared for the hunt. Small feet tipped-toed their way across the cold, damp wooden flooring of a porch.

"I've got you." My gums receded, and my canines descended.

As she walked, eddy currents formed around her in the humid air. The soft sound of the steps made it clear it was feet of a small child.

"Shit." My heart sank and my mouth went dry from even the inkling of feeding on a youngling.

Feeding on grown men was one thing. This … this was unthinkable. Horrifyingly barbaric. The unbelievable thought of compelling a child, a little girl, to feed on the life pumping through her veins.

I looked around for another soul on the street, but there was no one else awake, and I was growing weaker with every passing minute. I needed strength for the journey ahead. The need overtook me, and I focused on the task at hand: Blood.

The tiny footsteps came to a stop in the middle of a field across the dirt road. The girl sat and stared up at the vast open sky. My heart jumped with excitement and drool pooled in the corners of my mouth.

The brown hair atop her tiny head blew slightly in a soft breeze. Her clothes, dirty from a day's worth of playing, hung heavy on her.

She looked so much like Cora, *Mo Chroí.*

Silently, I traversed the grassy land, and the distance quickly closed between us. I moved slower than normal, studying every pore on her face and every hair on her head. Her likeness to Cora was unbelievable; they could have been sisters.

*Snap!* went a twig, hidden in the dense grass, under my foot.

The young girl gasped, whipping her head around quickly, and blinked at me. "Oh, hello."

She seemed almost relieved to see me. Then again, I suppose seeing another human is much less frightening than a small pack of wolves, a stalking lynx, or a lonely bear.

Smiling, she asked in French, "Did you have a nightmare too?"

I smiled, and switched to French, "No, I'm actually trying to find my friend Claret." I folded my hands in front of me. "Have you seen her?"

She shook her head.

"Can I sit with you?" I asked. She nodded, looking back up to the stars, and I sat down beside her. "I'm sorry you had a nightmare. Would you like to tell me about it? I find that it helps me to talk about bad dreams. That way we can get you back to bed. We don't want your mommy and daddy to wake up and find you missing."

She twirled a blade of grass between her fingers. "I'm Genevieve."

I cleared my throat. "Good evening, Genevieve, my name is Sorin. Would you like to tell me about this dream of yours?"

The artery in her neck pulsated melodically under the moonlight, causing my canines to descend farther and my lip to curl slightly. I breathed deeply, fighting the hunger, and turned my body to face her. My folded hands rested calmly in my lap.

"It was dark." Dropping the blade of grass, she pulled a large purple and blue paisley pig doll from under her arm and clutched it tightly against her chest. "The stars were out, and the moon was really big. I was walking through the fields Daddy planted, running my fingers over the sugar beets and chicory. The air was cold, so cold I could see my breath. I heard the howls of the wolf pack that patrols the outer part of our land. Daddy says I'm never to wander too far from the house at night and I'm never to go into the fields or forest after dark, but I wanted to know what was in there."

"Your daddy sounds like a smart man."

"The howls frightened me. I began to cry, calling for Mommy and Daddy, but no one came. Then the tall grasses moved, and the moonlight disappeared. Something moved toward me. I cried louder, screaming, 'Daddy, help,' over and over again. But, still, no one came. I was alone. I could smell its bad breath. I remember saying to it, 'please don't hurt me,' and I woke up."

By the end of her story, the child was shaking and white knuckling her doll.

Instinctively, I put an arm around her as if to protect her from her nightmare. "Oh, my goodness, that's dreadful. Well, that won't happen tonight because I am here to protect you." I forced my fangs to retreat and flashed her a smile. "Now, how about we get you back to bed before your parents wake up?"

She nodded in agreement.

We both came to our feet, turned and started to walk, and she grabbed my hand—a hand I did not offer to her. It was cold and *so* small. It pained me to think of what was to come.

Suddenly, Genevieve let out a cry of pain and fell to the ground, clutching her foot. Tears flowed down her cheeks.

"What happened?" I asked, kneeling beside her.

Lifting her foot, I found a large splinter.

I heard Claret's voice in my head say, *"This is your chance."*

"I'm going to have to remove this shard of wood for the pain to stop," I said with a compassionate hand on her tiny, wet cheek.

Before she could object, I pulled out the splinter. Blood ran quickly from the wound. My mouth moistened, my eyes dilated, and my heart quickened at the sight of the dark red river. Her blood simmered black under the moon's light. The metallic aroma filled my nose and I subtly licked at the air, begging for a taste.

"Shh, it's all over now my dear." I consoled her in my arms, I ran my callused hands through her fine silk hair. "The piece is out, see?" Holding up the bloodied piece of wood, I waited impatiently for her eyes to open.

Her eyes had barely peeked open when my eyes reddened and a crimson glow appeared. Her amber eyes quickly faded to an azure lace, and I allowed my hunger to consume me. I raised her unconscious body to the sky with one hand and brought her blood-soaked ankle to my lips with the other.

Suckling on the warm blood, like a child to a mother's teat, I felt my strength return and my senses peak. I entered the Void—the place between my mind and that of my victim. I hadn't given a thought to the potential memories that were to come. I was too busy torturing myself over the act of preying upon the child.

Colors swirled from the hues of red among the blackness into the bright colors of spring. Dandelion-rich land spread wide from the small steps to the cabin entrance. The world was much bigger from her stature, but although it was beautiful, fear of things unknown in nature loomed in the shadows of her mind.

The shadows dug their claws into my mind, pulling me deeper into her fears. I became Genevieve lying in her bed at night, nestled tightly under the covers. Her mother was sitting by her side, "Would you like a bedtime story, Gene?"

She excitedly squealed, "Yes, mother," in her native French. *"Red Riding Hood."*

The focus of the room began to shift, yet again, this time growing dark. As the figures took shape, I found myself in a forest, under the light of a full moon. The trees were lush and blocked much of the moonlight, leaving what lay beneath the canopy feeling eerie. Genevieve was nowhere to be found and I couldn't default to the Nocturnae gifts in this world.

I made my way deeper into the forest. I moved slowly but still blundered about like a blind fool in the forest's abyss. I kept both hands out in front of my face to deflect branches from spearing my face.

When the hairs on my neck and arms stood at attention, I abruptly stopped. Someone, or something, was watching me. My eyes darted across the blackness around me. I could feel my heartbeat in my ears. Panic—a primal, human emotion—washed over me for the first time in nearly a century.

Then, fifteen meters over my right shoulder near a weathered oak tree, was a pair of bright yellow eyes sunken deep behind a long snout. Pearl white fangs reflecting the moon's glow emerged from under the animal's nose; almost like it was smiling at me. Our eyes fixed on one another, it waited patiently for the perfect moment to strike.

Terrified, I saw the creature's eyes move up the trunk of the tree and its ears disappear into the shadows. The animal, I thought a wolf or a wild dog, was something else entirely.

"This is no dog, they show aggression by dropping their head and their ears will hug their skull," I thought to myself. "Could this be a bear?"

The resting forest erupted as the beast let out a roar like none I'd ever heard. The trees quivered under the weight of its cry and the animals ran. A hand three times the size of my own gripped a nearby tree, splintering it into thousands of pieces, leaving the rest of it to fall helplessly to the ground.

Reality wrapped its hands around my mind, wrenching me free from this unknown, hellish beast that plagued the dreams of this poor girl. The colors of the forest pinwheeled together, forming two distinct yellow lines originating where the beast stood, still crying out at me. The colors bled into darkness as the feeding came to an end.

Pulling my lips from her once blood-soaked ankle, I held up a clean canvas of flesh, now licked clean. Ashamed of drinking from the child, I diverted my gaze away from the tiny morsel in my grip. I must finish the ruse.

Lying her flat on the ground, I softly patted her cheek and gently shook her. "Genevieve. Genevieve, wake up!"

Her eyes fluttered, regaining consciousness. "Sorin, what happened?"

"You cut your ankle on this stick. The sight of blood must have caused you to pass out. Are you okay?"

I felt terrible lying to this little girl. I felt worse that her blood flowed through me and her memories would haunt me for eternity.

"Yes," she said, bringing herself to her feet, brushing the dirt and dew from her body. "I'm okay."

She smiled up at me, grabbed my hand, and together we walked back to her home. Her hand gripped my three smallest fingers tightly as we ventured through the darkness.

Questions raced through my mind. What was that creature? Genevieve was nowhere to be found in the forest when it found me. How did I see it then? Was it … protecting her?

We stopped four, maybe five, paces from her house.

Crouching down to her level, I placed my hands on her shoulders. "Thank you for letting me share this night with you Genevieve. You're a wonderful, beautiful little girl, and I have a feeling you're going to do great things." Moving my hands to her cheeks, I brought her forehead to my lips, kissing her just below the hairline. "Now, back to bed."

Quietly, she made her way up the two small steps, disappearing into the blackness of the house. Immediately after the door shut, a great weight of self-disgust and disdain fell over me. Those haunting yellow eyes flashed within my subconscious.

"Don't beat yourself up, Sorin," Gaius said reassuringly from behind a nearby home. "She's a human. She is your food. Nothing more."

Claret appeared an arm's length from Gaius and slowly made her way toward me, speaking below a human whisper, "You need to stop this incessant compassion and infatuation with the human world. You are Nocturnae."

Her harsh words hurt.

Raising a finger to my face, she continued, "You mourn over the acts you … we commit to sustain our lives. We live off the blood of humans. But humans are nothing but a breed of mammals intelligent enough to infest the planet like the virus they are."

Gaius followed in her wake. "We are here to cleanse the world of the human virus and their destructive nature."

I said nothing.

"They are born. They die." Claret slowly wrapped her fingers into a fist. "They feed on other living things to sustain life. Just as we do. Humans are *not* special. They are food. Any guilt looming over you for satiating your appetite on a human child is insulting to your own kind." Pausing to look at the girl's door, she wiped reddened spittle from her lips. "This child could grow up to be like one of those in The Company. Hunting us and plaguing the planet with their existence."

As quickly as her emotions took over her, they were gone. She placed her hand on my cheek as she walked by me, sliding her fingers across my chin and lips as she moved.

"Come on, we need to keep moving. There is a cave not far from here. We'll rest there for the day."

Discouraged and ashamed, I followed at a distance.

Neither Gaius nor Claret said another word to me that night.

# 22



My eyes open to find Jean not sitting back, but hunched over herself. She sits studiously wrapped in her cardigan, hanging on my every word.

"Still no mention of a book, but…" She pauses an unsettlingly long time, tilting her head slightly while puckering, pursing, and curling her lips in various combinations.

Something has her attention.

"Buuut?"

Jean calmly relaxes in the chair. "A lot happened in that bit of your story. I'm not sure where to begin."

"Hardly, dearie. I think you know exactly where you want to begin."

Her lips snuck a smile as she bows behind the curtains of her hair. "I want to go back a little bit to the gentleman in Norway, was that the first time you heard the name Gilead or The Company?"

"Correct."

"Really?" she asks in disbelief. She lifts her writing device to cross her legs. "I don't believe you."

"Why would I lie? What benefit does lying about *that* get for me?

"I just find it odd that in nearly a century of running from these people, Claret nor Gaius, or even Fenix for that matter, mentioned *once* who you all were hiding from. It's just a little inconceivable."

I say nothing. How could I? She was right; it was, in fact, an oddity.

Touché, doctor. Touché.

"Hm…" I begin, thinking back through the day and a half's worth of conversations for any way to even the score. When, out of nowhere, I remember, and couldn't help but let loose an evil grin. "With your family gone, what do you do for the holidays?"

She opens her mouth to answer but catches herself. "Nothing."

"Well, that was a rather *useless* question then. Let's try again, are you being courted? I don't see a ring on your finger or remnants of where a wedding band used to be, so you're not married or recently divorced. Is there a beau in your life?"

"No, but what does it matter? I thought you didn't care about such things."

"I'm simply trying to determine if it would be a multicourse meal or just an entrée when I have you for dinner." I chuckle to myself as Jean looks on, unamused. "I couldn't help myself, *Jeanie.*"

She gasps, subconsciously.

I win…

"You can stop the charade." I wave my hand from under its shackle. "I want to know what it is about *that* name that you don't like. As I said before, what's in a name?"

"How-how did you know I don't like being called that?"

"You recoiled when I used it. Your nose scrunched a bit and your nostrils flared. All subconscious signals your body betrayed you with when I called you… *Jeanie*." Her body gave the same automatic response and her face tightened like she'd just eaten a sour grape. "Now, what is it about *that* name you don't like?"

…I always win.

She looks toward the ceiling. "The only man I ever loved would call me that. He would tell me he'd dreamt of me his whole life."

He dreamed of Jeanie. Ha. Ah, the '60s. When everyone's minds seemed to be on the civil rights movement, the Vietnam War, and this show—it made feeding in that decade rather boring.

"See, that wasn't so bad." I enjoy watching her eyelids flutter as they fight back tears. "What happened to him?"

"Nope, my turn. The girl…" There it is. "…you said she reminded you of Cora. Did that make things harder for you?"

Rather than lunge from the chair to rip her throat out, like I tried to before, I pause and take a deep breath. Closing my eyes, I return to the box with the charred heart.

"No, but also yes."

Folding her hands, she cocks her head to one side with intrigue. "In what way?"

A subtle pain grows in my chest, and it becomes noticeably harder to breathe. "It was like she was still there, and no time had passed at all. Genevieve's likeness to Cora made it easier to sympathize with and talk to her. That night, I battled myself to not wrap my arms around her and hoist her into the sky, like I did so long ago."

"The story her mother told her, *Red Riding Hood,* wasn't written until the seventeenth century. This occurred barely into the fifteenth century. How could that be?"

Humans … they think thoughts have never been had before, until they have been written down and stamped with a date.

"You're correct. The story was published by a Frenchman, Charles Perrault, in 1697 but that doesn't mean the story didn't exist before it. Come on Jean, you don't care about a bedtime story, do you?"

She's got something brewing in there. She's too smart not to.

Jean smiles and tosses her hair. "The little girl's dream, had that ever happened to you before?"

"Hm, you mean being wrenched from the imprinting dream and placed somewhere different—without my victim? No, nor has it happened since." Catching myself in a white lie, I wetted my lips, "That's not entirely true. Something similar has happened since, but it was far from the same."

"Care to elaborate?"

"I'll get to it…"

"Okay," she says, making note of it on her writing device. "What do you think it was about Genevieve that caused it to happen?"

"I'm not exactly sure. I never brought it up to Claret or Gaius, fearing I was overreacting. It was very strange. I can only describe it as a silent protector waiting within her mind."

"Waiting for what?"

"Me?"

She pauses and looks at me, her gray eyes still for the first time, and leans in. "You're telling me this *thing* seemed to be waiting for a Nocturnae? Would you say it was stalking you?"

"I wouldn't say that it wasn't."

"Interesting," she exaggerates, elongating the word, and types once again. "That's very … you said 'ripped' from the … the … the place you go when you're imprinting, the—"

"Void."

"Yes," she says excitedly, snapping her finger. "You say 'ripped' but could you have been, maybe, pushed?"

How would she…

"It's hard to say."

She didn't react to my words. "May I ask another?"

"By all means."

"The pig doll is odd. Are you sure it was a pig?"

"Yes, but before I go any further, I should mention that *doll* was the only word that existed back then to describe it."

"Oh, what would you call it today?"

"A stuffed animal."

"So, it was cute?"

"Hardly, the thing was hideous. It would give today's children nightmares."

Jean chuckles but quickly regains her composure and readies herself to take notes on her keyboard. "What did it look like again?"

"Oh, let's see … it was about a foot in length, from snout to tail, and half that in the other two directions. It had a dark gray and deep purple—almost mulberry—paisley pattern that stretched across its surface with flecks of silver and sapphire blue woven throughout. Mm, and black-fabric buttons for eyes."

"That doesn't sound so bad," she says, still typing the last bit of the pig's description.

"Ghastly thing. The strangest part of it all is, I didn't see that pattern again until Scotland in the eighteenth century—maybe it was the nineteenth century."

She makes note of my comment, straightens up in her chair, and takes her hands off the writing device like a child preparing for a bedtime story.

"After you fed on the child, you three made your way to a cave?"

"Yes, it wasn't long after reaching the entrance of the cave, hidden with overgrowth, that the blackness of the night, sprinkled with luminescence of the cosmos, began retreating from the deep reds of sunrise."

"It sounds beautiful."

# 23



IT WAS HOURS before we exited the thick forest and stood on the Étretat Cliffs, high above the crashing ocean waves. The forest opened into a clearing of fifty acres and beyond it was at least another eighty acres with pockets of trees scattered throughout before the timberline.

Ten perches from the edge of the cliff, on the open acreage, stood a small cottage-sized structure. The home was unique: half-timbered and brick, with a tiled roof and a beautiful chimney running up either side, built atop the original remnants of something much older. It appeared well-maintained and I wondered how, when Claret hadn't been around in quite some time.

"This is where your whole coven lived?" I stared out past the cliff's edge at the beautiful sea. "It's breathtaking."

"Thank you." Claret gazed out over the sea. "Yes, this is where we lived."

Gaius hung back a pace with his arms crossed and his eyes closed. A wide grin spread across his face as the salty air filled his lungs.

Claret smiled for the first time in months. "We are safe here. Many years ago, I compelled a couple of families to keep the home for me. I instructed them to pass it down from generation to generation; and periodically, if I wasn't pleased with the work, I'd kill them all and pick a new family. It's a legend that's stuck." She gave me a wink.

Gaius snickered.

The flower beds and the grounds around the cottage looked amazing, like the home had been lived in this entire time.

Slowly, we approached the home when something stopped me. It wasn't that something caught my eye, nor was it a scent that was off. This was something else. It was a feeling so familiar and yet, so foreign. I'd felt it before … but where, I couldn't place it. I slowed my gait to a halt in hopes of placing the feeling.

Claret looked left, then back at me. Gaius too. We were being watched.

Claret called out in sheer terror. "Gaius, get Sorin to the cabin. Now!"

A party of ten armored men sprang from holes dug in the ground, covered by the thick lush grasses on either side of us. Twenty more came from the tree line.

*"How didn't we sense them?!"* I screamed in my mind.

We were surrounded.

Claret reared her head, subtly pulling a small object from her belt and passing it to Gaius. "RUN!"

"Sorin, with me." Gaius lunged, grabbing me by the wrist and pulled me to his side.

Pivoting toward the cliff, we pressed hard into the soft grass in an attempt to propel ourselves away from The Company; but before our feet could leave the ground a loud click came from the ground under our feet.

"Fuck," Gaius cursed.

A metallic noose hidden in the ground snapped shut around our ankles, pulling each of us off our feet and smashing our faces into the earth. I shrieked in pain as the noose tightened around me.

"Why does it hurt so much?" I cried.

Pulling the chains that bound us from the ground, Gaius cried out in pain and shook his smoldering hand in the air. "Silver!"

Gripping me around the hips he pulled me from my chain as if I weighed nothing, severing both my feet in the process, and sprinted toward the edge of the cliff. I screamed in pain, but Gaius took no notice as he ran.

The sound of metal came again, followed by an ear-piercing scream that shook me to my core. From under Gaius's arm, I looked back and saw Claret caught in a similar noose.

"Gaius, we have to go back!"

"She's fine." Without looking back, he pressed on.

Somehow, Claret was able to get most of one foot through the noose before it fully tightened. However, the noose severed all of her toes and the two fingers she used to free herself. Blood spilled out of her like a cracked barrel of ale, but she didn't turn and run.

The first of the men nearest her swung a broadsword at her midsection.

She pulled her hips back, leaving the sword to cut nothing but air. She countered the attack with a strike that pushed his ribs through his back. Grabbing the man by his head, she pressed her stumped leg into his chest and removed his head from his body. Turning the dismembered head over, she drank the blood of her enemy like a queen drinks wine from a goblet.

Metallic objects whizzed past Gaius and me. One after the other, Gaius evaded them until a silver-tipped arrow caught him in the shoulder and another in the calf.

"NO!" he cried, falling forward, bringing me down with him.

Quickly, I flipped to my stubbed feet and turned to see that Claret's fingers and foot had returned. A wave of three men rushed her in quick succession.

The first swung a silver mace wildly through the air. The spiked ball blasted around him like a cannonball. Claret caught the ball, its spikes driving through her hand, and she used the weapon's momentum to launch the man toward the forest. He flew through the air screaming and flailing his arms wildly, trying to slow himself before coming to a quick and sudden stop against the trunk of an old tree. The man's spine snapped as his body wrapped itself around the tree, snuffing out his voice.

Claret looked at her hand, fused to the mace, and then saw me staring at her. "Get to the cabin Sorin." Her face hardened. "Now!"

The second man held his sword high overhead as he ran at her, planning to split her in two with one easy stroke. When within striking distance, he brought the sword down with all his might but stopped short. With his eyes wide, he dropped his sword. Shocked, he turned his head.

There, just to the left of the man, was Claret holding his heart.

Smiling, she said, "Your body hasn't realized you're dead yet, but"—she held the heart in front of the man's face as she took a bite out of it—"this is your heart."

The man looked at his chest and brought his hands to the hole in terror.

Arrows whizzed past my head as I pulled myself to my new feet. "Come on!" Dodging the flying objects, I gripped Gaius hard by the shoulder. "Let's go! We need to help her!"

Ripping a silver tipped arrow from his leg, he flung my arm from him. "Get off me." He forced himself to his feet. "Listen to our Maker, Sorin. Get to the *fucking* cabin! NOOWWW!"

He palmed the back of my head in his hand and pushed hard.

Together, Gaius and I sprinted the rest of the way to the cabin, catching arrows in our backs. Two of them protruded from my chest and abdomen, and I ripped them free as my healing factor worked furiously.

Safely on the other side of the cabin, I peeked around the cabin's wall and saw the third man loose an arrow at Claret.

She attempted to dodge it, but the silver weaponry used against her had greatly slowed her reflexes. The arrow whistled through the air, coming to an abrupt stop in her right shoulder, burying itself deep in the socket.

Her arm hung limp and useless. Looking down at her flaccid arm, fury spread wildly across her face as she stepped toward the man.

Two more arrows, one after the other, pummeled her torso. The first punctured her soft belly, an inch above the navel. The second impacted her hip, splintering her pelvis and bringing her to her knees as she bellowed in agonizing pain.

"CLARET!" I turned to Gaius. "We have to help her. We can't leave her."

Opening the door of the cabin, Gaius grabbed my shoulder. "I'm sorry brother," he said, tightening the silver-lined rope wrapped around my ankle, "but you're staying here." He opened his hand, revealing a small silver and sapphire Pearl in the center. "You're too important."

He smashed the tiny object into my forehead and threw me into the cabin, amputating my new foot. I bounced off the back wall and landed awkwardly in the center of the floor.

"Gaius!" I cried out, but there was no sound. "Gaius!" I tried again, but nothing. I tried to stand, but I couldn't move a finger.

What happened next, I pieced together by what I could hear.

Claret, unwilling to surrender, swung her limp arm like a whip at the archer, ignoring the agonizing pain. Two arrows buried themselves in her back and another in her thigh. Her screams were deafening as she fell to the ground.

Gaius bounded around the cabin toward our Maker and inadvertently stepped into two silver snares, severing both his feet just above the ankles. He screamed but was quickly muted as four arrows buried themselves in his chest.

The men surrounding Gaius and Claret stood quiet for many minutes after the onslaught immobilized them as if waiting for something … or someone. Slowly, a horse trotted out of the forest, revealing Franklin Gilead outfitted in a suit of polished silver armor.

At the sight of him, Claret struggled with all her might to gain footing and charge him. She got to one knee before a silver noose was slung around her neck. Screaming incessantly into the air, her rage fell on deaf ears. The men paid no heed, waiting patiently for their instructions after taking down not one, but two mature Nocturnae.

Sir Gilead approached Claret, stately, but kept a safe distance from her. "Hello, Claret," he said, looking down from the back of his horse. "I've heard a lot about you."

"Franklin."

He laughed, once, nudged his horse closer, and brought his armored hand to his chest. "Oh, you've heard of me."

Choking on her bloodied spit, she leaned over and vomited a bloody mess. "You, only by name, but your family … we have history, don't we?"

"Yes, I'm aware. I grew up on bedtime stories about your Maker. The legend who my forefather beheaded. What was the name again?"

"Amicia," Claret muttered, staring into the grass in front of her as tears of blood fell from her face.

Smacking the horn of his saddle, the horse took another step closer, as he scoffed, "That's right, Amicia—I always liked that name. It's French, correct?" Claret stared coldly. Sir Gilead's eyes wandered past Claret, and he cried out, "What do we have here?"

He trotted over to Gaius's side and stopped just outside his reach. Dismounting his horse, Sir Gilead walked over to Gaius.

Studying the bloodied, crippled boy, he spoke softly, "Tsk-tsk, from you, I expected more." Sir Gilead lifted his silver-booted foot, driving it hard into the back of Gaius's skull. "You didn't land a single blow. Pathetic." Surveying the grounds, he called out to his men, "Where's the third one?" No one answered. "If one of you idiots doesn't answer me, I'm throwing *all* of you off the cliff. Now, where's the third one?"

The hunter next to Gaius pointed at him and said, "This one came out of the cabin."

Rolling his eyes, Gilead gestured toward the cabin. "Well… go check."

"Yes, sir."

I began to panic as the man's armor clinked closer and closer to the door. I shut my eyes, fearing the worst, when the door opened.

"Well," Gilead called out.

Scanning every inch of the room inside the door, the soldier shook his head. "Nothing here but one of our restraints and a foot. Maybe he jumped from the cliff."

My eyes shot open; I peered down the bridge of my nose at the black-bearded man in the doorway. He couldn't see me. How was this possible?

"Check it for the book," Gilead ordered.

The man stepped into the cabin, closing the door behind him and started rummaging through cupboards, drawers, and everywhere else he could think to look. Somehow the man never came near me. He always seemed to find a path around me, even if narrowly missing me.

He searched for what felt like an eternity before noticing a single board on the wall that was slightly different in color from the rest. Pulling the board from the studs, he revealed a brown leather-bound book with flecks of silver and sapphires scattered unevenly across its surface.

"Sir Gilead! I found it!"

"Bring it to me."

The man scurried out of the cabin, leaving the door slightly ajar. He handed the book to Gilead with both hands.

Smiling, Gilead gestured to Claret. "Go help them get her set for transport. When you're done, get this one here too." He pointed at Gaius. "We can't waste any of them."

The man nodded and left.

"Finally … the Codex is mine." He stared at the book in his large hands, a gleeful glint in his eye.

Nearly an hour passed before I heard a different man tell Sir Gilead the prisoners were secure.

If the men were silent when they ambushed us, they were just as silent leaving. I never heard a horse. I never heard the sound of wheels turning. I never heard men complaining or Gilead bark another order. I never heard the sound of armor scraping across other pieces of armor. The eerie silence left me very unsettled on the cottage floor.

I couldn't be seen or heard, and I couldn't move. But most importantly…

I was alone.

Staring up at the moldy damp wooden ceiling, question after question raced through my mind. Questions about Claret and Gaius: Were they still alive? If so, where were they taking them? Would I ever see them again? Questions about myself: How was I going to eat? What was I going to eat if I couldn't move? Will I die?

There, on the cold, damp floor I lay as the sun broke the horizon. Seagulls sang as the tide rolled in. Bugs zipped around the room, landing on different parts of my body, but they mostly focused on my exposed wounds and the stump where my foot had been.

It was strange, and extremely painful, this feeling of my body trying to rid itself of the silver arrow tips and flecks of silver left in my wounds. I couldn't tell if it was from the silver or from the Pearl embedded in my forehead, but my healing factor seemed to have almost stalled out, leaving my bloody stump to fester and rot.

It didn't take long, only a couple of hours, for the maggots and other creepy crawlies to go from feeding on me—alive—to reproducing on my flesh. I could feel them land on my skin and burrow themselves between my muscles, tasting my tendons to find the perfect spot for their larva to grow upon. And there was nothing I could do about it.

I can't be sure of the time, but it was past midday when the first ray of sunlight broke within an inch of my face. Even though it wasn't touching me, the brightness burned my retinas. An hour later, the beam of light touched my cheek, like a white-hot blade.

I cried out in pain, but the silver Pearl prevented me from moving or making a sound. It was like being paralyzed under what we now call anesthesia, but being fully awake mentally. I was able to hear and feel everything that was going on, but only I could hear my screams in my mind.

The smell of burning flesh filled my nostrils. The sight of my own skin igniting and searing off my frame horrified me. The agony. The torture. Unable to move. Unable to scream. Seconds passed that seemed like hours. Minutes, like days. By the time the sun moved up to my nose, I was begging for death.

Four hours later and nearly dusk, the beam finally moved off of my face to my opposite ear. It left a cauterized burn, roughly an inch thick, across my skin, stretching from the hairline on one side to my ear on the other. My nose was a pile of charred meat with two fissures leaking smoke. My right eye, a melted pool of butter.

With the searing pain over my face gone, I realized that was not the only part of my body that had fallen victim to the sun's cruelty. On my left hand I couldn't feel most of my pinky finger, half of my ring finger, or the tip of my middle finger. My right arm felt like a gaping canyon.

That night I pondered the question, "Why didn't I experience the true death?"

I should have perished within minutes of the sun carbonizing my face. I could lose a hand, an arm, and a foot to the power of the sun and live. But vital parts of the body? My brain? No Nocturnae could survive.

Why did I? Was this because of the Pearl? Or … was this my *gift*?

I should have been tired, but I wasn't. I thought of all the stories Claret and Gaius told me of Nocturnae experiencing their true deaths under the awesome power of the sun. Yet, I defied it.

Two weeks passed, and day after day, what little flesh had regenerated from the previous day was burned off again. The pain never subsided. The torture never got less treacherous. Rather, quite the opposite. I could feel my heart rate increase as the sun got higher in the sky and only felt relief under the cool night's sky. I was barely surviving on the adventurous insects that wandered too close to my mouth.

On the twenty-seventh night, after my daily charring, I heard two loud, hard thuds on the wooden flooring next to my arm. Unable to lift my head to investigate, I lay brainstorming what could have made the sound. Eventually I realized, the wooden arrow shafts in my legs had rotted away, and the silver arrow heads fell to the floor.

By the end of the year, I could feel my toes again. I'd also consumed more insects than I'd thought possible with the occasional rodent, bird, and lagomorph that ventured across my face.

The months turned into years. Years turned into decades. The routine was monotonous, painful, and utterly boring with only my thoughts and memories, and those I'd stolen over the years, to keep me company.

To keep some semblance of sanity, I dove deep into my mental archives, reflecting on what my human victims had endured in their short lives. Some things were sad. The loss of mothers, fathers, siblings, cousins, children. Others were out of their control entirely. Famine, plagues, and wars of the elite were fought over petty things that always resulted in exploiting the poor. But many were hilarious, especially those that came from the church. They put the fear of a benevolent God into all that would listen and killed those who refused. All the while, justifying it under the predisposition that Lucifer and his demon army would enslave them all, while God sat back and watched because homage wasn't paid to him in the appropriate manner.

As the years passed, I began to notice my daily cauterization wasn't hurting as much as it did the previous year, and I was able to regenerate more efficiently, even in my severely malnourished state.

By the end of the second decade, I believed I could wiggle a toe. I had no proof or any way to test it, but I was pretty sure I could.

By the end of the third decade, my eye could regenerate fully within the day. Although to many it might seem useless, the ability to see from my eye, if only for a few hours, was uplifting. I felt whole, if only for a brief period.

The fourth decade came and went with little change. I still couldn't really move, but I could make short groaning sounds. I was growing frustrated and downtrodden after such remedial improvements, but it was something.

One morning, in the fifth decade, between the crashing waves and the fighting gulls, I heard a sound I'd almost forgotten. It was subtle at first, but quickly grew as their little feet trampled the grounds outside my walls. Children.

My fascination with them and the sheer amount of joy I received from hearing something other than my own body and the insects around me was … well there's no word for what I felt. The word that best described it, in that moment, was "hope."

Those human children were adorable, open-minded blank slates filled with curiosity and imagination. Their little bodies bound across the grassy knoll chasing dragonflies and butterflies in the morning sea breeze. Prancing on their toes, they talked to invisible entities that lived in the fantasy world only they could see.

To me, this was a much-needed break from the never-ending torment I endured every day. An intermission to the haunting thought that this life on the floor eating insects might be my new eternity.

I asked myself: Why did it take fifty years for humans to return to the cabin?

Claret's plan to maintain the cabin, although good in theory, had many flaws. Humans are weak, and frail. Thus, plague, sickness, or other humans could have swept through the town, killing everyone. They also have free will. Eventually, the children of that generation would hear the stories of the demon and the cabin and claim them to be nothing more than a story to scare them. Thus, ending the cabin's upkeep.

It didn't matter why they were gone for so long though, it only mattered that they were back.

Curiosity got the best of a young boy, no more than six. His little feet raced across the porch as his sister counted: ten, eleven … the latch on the door lifted, letting in a huge beam of light that stopped far too close to me for comfort.

Slowly the child closed the door behind him, hoping it wouldn't make a noise—it didn't. He crouched low, just on the other side of the door frame. Covering his mouth, he muted a chuckle with a slight turn of his head. Just enough to notice something strange out of the corner of his eye, me.

The boy screamed and burst through the smallest opening of a door, slamming it shut behind him.

I can be seen? Shit, I can be seen…

His older sister—I assume—hushed his blabbering. She made her way to the door and opened it herself, peeking inside with just her head.

I shut my eyes waiting for a scream or cursing or for the sun to envelop me, but nothing happened. The door closed softly behind her, she returned to the boy, assured him nothing was there, and they left.

How did the younger child see me, but the older one did not?

I never heard either of them outside the cabin again. Nor can I explain what happened that day.

Time passed and decades turned into generations. Generations turned into a century—I think. It's hard to tell how much time passes when there's nothing new to use as reference. My only frame of reference was the slow decaying of the forgotten cottage, and the passing of the sun and moon.

# 24



JEAN'S EYES OPEN wide, and the skin on her arm is covered in goosebumps. Her mouth opens slightly, fluttering as excitement overtakes her.

Silver … is still in my hip. It must have been deep in the bone. But this … yes, this is it, the last of it.

"The Codex." Jean eagerly awaits more information.

"Yes, what about it?" Playing dumb is sometimes the most useful weapon.

Quickly, she scoots to the edge of her chair and leans over her writing device, stopping nearly within reach. I strain my fingers to reach her, but the silver bindings hold me at bay.

Ugh, not close enough.

"Tell me everything about it. What did it look like again? Brown leather? Silver? Blue?" she asks, waiting impatiently to type.

"Hm, let's see," I tease, resting the back of my head on the chair's top rail. "It was bound in brown leather, yes. Old, very old. Flecks of silver and sapphire were—"

"The visible sides of the pages, did you see them? What did they look like? Any discernible markings?"

I don't think she knows what she's looking for… I think she may have been given an instruction with no context.

"The outside edges of the pages were tanned and worn. The book was larger than your typical hardcover novel or even your average sheet of paper, and it was almost perfectly square but smaller on the edges of the spine. It was bound in a thick string."

"Cloth? Leather?" she asks, her fingers anxious to record my answer.

"Neither…"

"*What* then!?" she explodes, sitting back and throwing her arms up.

I smile and slowly say, "Braided black human hair."

Her nose registers disgust. "How can you be so sure it wasn't a horse or hair from another animal?"

"…I could smell it."

"What's written in it?" she asks, sitting upright in her chair. "Why did Gilead want it so badly?"

"I don't know. They never spoke of it or why we were going to Amicia's cabin. I have to assume the answer you're looking for is in that book."

She lets out a heavy sigh of frustration and closes her eyes. "You mean to tell me that you don't know what the book does?"

Does? That's an interesting word choice. Did she slip up, in her anger? Maybe she does know more about this book than she's letting on.

"The book?" I scoff, sarcastically. "Oh, I'm sorry. How silly of me. Well, the book is used to carry information, retell stories, and teach ideas of philosophy. You can use it to start a fire to keep warm or even level a table or—"

"STOP," she snaps. "That's not what I meant, and you know it." She pauses a moment with the face of someone at a crossroads, and shifts topics. "Can you tell me anything more about the Pearl? Specific, minute details about its appearance? Where is it now?"

"It was small, no larger than a grape but no smaller than a pea. It was shiny, silver and blue but beyond that, no, I can't." I wish I could. "The last I saw it was in that cabin. And you must remember, I'd been lying there motionless for more than a century. I wasn't thinking about the Pearl, or even rationally for that matter. I just wanted out. For all I know, it could still be there."

"You're telling me, that a magical item that kept you subdued for that long, and invisible from all but young children, is just lying on an old cliff somewhere?"

Magical? "I never said it was *magical.*"

She raises her chin. "How would you describe an object with abilities such as those?"

She has a point. I say nothing but remember something Gaius said, many years prior: "…thaumaturgy of the Penyihir."

"What I don't understand is how the young boy could see you, but his sister couldn't. Nor could Gilead's soldiers. And the bugs and small animals, how were they able to see you?"

The room falls awkwardly silent as Jean waits patiently for me to say something, anything. I don't.

Truth be told, I haven't thought about it. Ever. When I was in the cabin I only thought about Claret, Gaius, blood, and true death. I never gave the Pearl much thought. They used it to protect me. And that was that.

"I don't know what to tell you." I chuckle. "Those are good questions and I wish I had the answers to them."

"Spending that much time alone with your thoughts must have been treacherous," she says softly. "What did you think about— other than the obvious—if you don't mind me asking?"

She's invested now. To her, it's more than the book or the task she was sent to perform. She's a scientist and I'm the *hard puzzle* she has to solve … no, not solve … I'm the ever-elusive mystery that needs to be understood.

# 25



IN THE LATE spring of 1582, it happened.

As with every day prior, I stretched my toes and my fingers in every direction possible. I focused on my elbows more than my knees, which remained locked, refusing to give way.

I envisioned a rope in my grip connected to an immense boulder. I imagined pulling that boulder toward me using only my bicep. With my hand perpendicular to the floor, I called on every ounce of physical and mental strength to simply touch my nose. Clenching my eyes shut with such force that my cheeks nearly popped, I let out a deep groan.

I cautiously opened one eye. There in the shadows was the palm of my hand with two fingers lying flat on my nose. In one smooth motion, I flicked the Pearl from my forehead. The Pearl bounced across the floor before rolling to a stop near a tattered rocking chair.

As quickly as weakness fell over me all those years ago, my strength returned. The feeling and control flooded my body almost instantaneously. I sat up slowly, wide-eyed as my body returned to its functional state.

"Ha!" I screamed and started to laugh uncontrollably.

I had survived. I survived for more than a century on bottom-dwelling insects and flea-infested mammals. I sat there for close to an hour, just touching different parts of my body. In all honesty I'd forgotten what my body felt like. I was much thinner. Bony, almost desiccated. The majority of my muscles had atrophied to crippling levels and required an immense amount of mental fortitude to use.

I needed food … blood … fresh, warm, human blood more than anything at this point. But I was alive.

Beams of light radiated into the room from a low angle, the day had just begun. I debated just walking into the sun because for the last twenty years or so, the sun's rays hadn't seemed to burn me. Wouldn't it be ironic to wake up from an incalculably long slumber, just to become a pile of ash within seconds.

I decided against it.

With my newly regained freedom, I was able to scrounge up more food around the cottage than in the last hundred years. The family of mice I'd heard procreating in the walls served as my main course—disgusting little creatures. My dessert was even less pleasing to my palate: tenderized cockroach in an arthropod compote, braised mealworms topped with termite tartar, and a rhinoceros beetle reduction.

The concoction of textures swimming in my stomach nauseated me. The unpleasant flavors caused me to uncontrollably gag, an unfortunate side effect I'd become accustomed to with these so-called foods.

At this point, the sun was still high in the sky, and it would be hours still before nightfall. Rather than pace impatiently about the cabin, I took to the rocking chair in the corner and enjoyed a sense of movement I hadn't felt in ages.

The time gave me an opportunity to be thankful for my freedom and, more importantly, hypothesize where Claret and Gaius could be after all these years. They could be anywhere or nowhere. The Company could have moved a dozen or more times, experimented on them, tortured them, or killed them.

The sun dipped below the horizon, leaving a starless blanket to watch over me.

Exiting the cabin, I took in Étretat one last time. The sweet, salty ocean air. The waves crashing on the cliffs. The horizon as far as the eye could see.

I was free. I finally left the cottage, never to return.

The forest from which we walked into Sir Gilead's trap had been razed for agriculture. Low fences segmented the land, with sheep and goats scattered about.

Looking back at the cabin, I was surprised to find it looked exactly the way it had all those years ago. It was completely unchanged. Yet, no one ever came to repair it from insects and time, or keep moss from destroying the wood—even humans could clearly see the cabin on the cliff.

To this day, I don't understand why that cabin appeared completely immune to time; but rather than stand there and hypothesize all night, I opted to reacquaint myself with my body.

Blitzing up and down the shallow hills, not far from the cabin, I tested myself as I drove my feet harder and harder into the ground with each passing minute. It took ten minutes for me to remember how to accelerate, decelerate, stop on a dime, maneuver quickly, parry, slip, dip, dodge, weave, spin, and all the other actions Claret and Gaius had taught me.

"I will find you, my Maker." I walked to the edge of the cliff and admired its greatness. "I swear it."

Cycling through the light spectrum, I could discern differing animal and plant life at greater and greater depths. Nocturnal insects and flying predatory life flipped in and out of visibility as they played their game of cat-and-mouse over the vast ocean.

With my Nocturnae muscles flexed, I had only one thing on my mind: human blood.

I wandered over the grasslands and trudged through the Seine Eure for nearly three hours before the sweet, metallic scent of human blood filled the air. My fangs descended quickly, flexing my gums and pushing back the corners of my lips. Thick drool dripped from my lips and I didn't care. I was starving.

I bounded up a shallow hill and there, resting quietly under the night sky, was the town of Le Bec-Hellouin. Nearly every building in sight was made up of stone masonry on the first level while the upper levels were half-timbered.

People bustled about the town's festival and luckily, there wasn't a child in sight. Many of them walked in groups of three or five. There were couples walking hand-in-hand and loners with only their thoughts to keep them company.

I entered the town like a wolf in sheep's clothing.

A middle-aged man crossed my path, muttering to himself, "Fucking cunt got what she deserved."

He swung his cane out in hopes of countering his bum leg and gasped when I appeared in front of him, seemingly instantaneously.

"Move out of my way," he barked, poking my chest with his cane and dragging his foot.

I stepped to one side, allowing him to pass; but as he hobbled by, my hunger took over. Wrapping one arm under his, I held his torso while my other hand clamped his mouth shut. I ferociously tore into his carotid, breaking open the flood gates. Aroused by the warmth on my lips and tongue, I drank deeper, falling quickly into the walls of his mind.

I entered the Void—oh, how I missed the Void.

Quickly the blackness shifted, revealing a short, serrated knife being drug across a woman's throat as she screamed. Blood spilled onto the man's callused hands. Her breathless body fell to the ground, twitching in the growing pool of her blood. The man dropped his knife.

The man's cane fell lightly onto the dirt ground as I blinked rapidly, freeing myself from his neck. The weight of his limp corpse in my arms and the blood trickling down my neck felt euphoric after such an impetuous act.

I needed more. I tilted my head up at the night sky with closed eyes. I slowly looked to my right, eying a man, hyperventilating next to a drinking barrel of water that smelled tainted.

He whimpered, "No. Please—"

I muted the man's scream with my left hand, shoving his head hard into the wooden wall behind him, splitting it. In one smooth motion I ripped open his pants and his femoral artery, freeing the beautiful red fluid onto us and the ground. I dove into the blood, drinking in every ounce of it as I fell deeper into the Void.

This mind was unlike any other. I sensed four, no five, minds within one. The chaos disoriented me. I bounced from mind to mind: a midwife birthing a child, a slave being whipped for the hell of it, an Irishman with a drinking problem, a middle-aged man who'd been forced into battle at a very young age, a dim-witted man picking his nose.

Screaming in the warped world of our melded minds, I freed myself from the rancid meal. Ripping the man's throat out from his body, I let him slump lifelessly back onto the ground to bleed out.

Violently spitting the remnants of blood from my mouth, I turned my crimson eyes to my next victim. I had tasted human blood for the first time in more than a century, and nothing would stop me from drinking far more than my fill.

A young couple, no more than twenty years of age, innocently turned the corner only to find me standing over the lifeless man. The woman gasped. My hand gripped her throat before she could scream, and I caught her lover's throat in my teeth.

With a simple flick of my finger, I paralyzed her vocal cords. Panicking, she fell to her knees, gripping her throat with both hands as she tried to breathe.

Flashes of them holding hands as they walked through the forest and looking up at the clouds as they lay in the tall grass flooded my mind. Brisk air on my naked backside while making love. His fond memories of her and their life together became my own, for all of eternity.

I drank him dry in no time at all. But still, my powerful thirst remained. An insatiable thirst born from a century of longing.

Blood rivers ran from the corners of my mouth, pooling on my chin before inevitably falling to their eternal resting place on the cool, dark earth. Carelessly, I let his body fall limply next to hers as she attempted to breathe one last breath.

In her dying act, she mouthed the word, "Why?"

I continued my murder spree throughout the night. Taking life after life in the streets, in the bars, and in their beds. I didn't care who saw me or my crimson eyes. I had generations of built-up fury and anger that I needed to let out. I drank my fill from more than I could count, indulging in gluttony for the first time in my life.

Ecstasy came over me as I allowed my rage and bloodlust to consume me. It was primal and utterly animalistic. This feeling of ultimate power transcended any reservations. It was a bittersweet high—maybe this was what Claret and Gaius were alluding to.

Oblivious to the moon's position in the sky, I continued to feed like a man who has utterly lost his mind. But as the first peek of orange dusted the horizon, an old panic flared from deep within me. I searched everywhere but found no shelter. Realizing I couldn't escape my fate, I grimaced in preparation for my true death.

The sun broke the horizon in a blaze of heated glory. But I did not burn. The sun's rays merely warmed my skin. I turned, in awe, toward the light and smiled.

# 26



I HAVE BIDED my time long enough to expel the last of the silver.

Jean's hands move to make a note on her device.

My full strength returns, and I can barely rein myself in.

She stops typing as her eyes widen from an epiphany. "Did you say you became *immune* to sunlight?"

I won't answer this question. At least not before testing my abilities. I don't want to compel the girl and not be able to pull her out.

Her eyes dart uncontrollably across the room. I stare into her eyes, begging them to stall on mine just long enough to—

Gotcha.

Now I'll answer her question. "Yes."

My eyes glow red as I force myself into her mind. Breaking through her mental defenses is like pushing through a door made of tissue-paper. The mental projection of her psychic self stands before me motionless, terrified, seeing me for the first time.

She screams silently within the confines of her own mind while I contemplate my next move.

Where to bite first? Fiction would have me bite her breast but no, not me. It needs to last.

I could bite off the tip of her finger and drink her up as if I were using a straw.

No, I'm still shackled, I wouldn't be able to get out.

Do I have time for just a taste? Probably not.

I return to Jean. "When I say your name, you're going to wake up and have no recollection of this or that I can walk freely in the sunlight. You will also have a throbbing headache until you open the door. You'll try to fight through it but, eventually, you'll excuse yourself and forget your tote."

Quickly, I back out of her mind and watch her thin defenses heal as I exit.

"Jean," I say with panic in my voice. "Jean, are you alright?"

Her eyes flutter wildly as her consciousness returns to her control.

Shaking her head, she massages the back of her neck. "What happened?"

"I don't know. You kind of zoned out. Do you need a break?"

Oh, how I love playing with my food.

Nonchalantly, her fingers race over her keys.

Collecting herself, she brushes it off like nothing ever happened. "No, I'm fine. What did you do after you ravaged the town?"

"By the end of that year, 1582, I was in the village of Silesia, now Poland. One hundred and fifty years later, the vampire epidemic plagued the world."

Jean massages her temples while grimacing and ignoring me.

It won't be long now. If I speak louder, it should hasten the process.

I raise my voice. "I'm most proud of convincing humans that Catholic symbols and trinkets like the crucifix and holy water have some effect on me. To this day, I don't know where the claims pertaining to a branch of wild rose or mountain ash came from, but I welcomed as many faulty accounts as humanity would supply me."

Jean slumps over, burying her forehead in the palms of her hands.

She's a fighter.

I raise my voice another notch. "My all-time favorite *weakness* a human gave Nocturnae in fictional stories was the claim that we can't enter a house unless invited by the owner of the home. It's rather ironic how people these days have WELCOME mats outside."

"Well Mr. Harker, I think that is all for today," Jean interrupts, standing from her seat with her hand still on her forehead.

She quickly walks to the door, writing device in hand. She waves her badge in front of the ID scanner, the LED switches from red to green and a prolonged, loud *beep* erupts as the door unlocks.

The sound pierces my sensitive ears, causing me to shy away. The door clicks as she opens it, letting a breath of fresh air waft into the room.

Now.

"Dearie, you seem to have forgotten your tote."

She turns from the ajar door, removes her hand from her head as the headache I gave her leaves her, and she makes her way back to her seat. Reaching down to grab the tote, her shoulder falls in front of her, protecting her eyes from my gaze.

Foolishly, she turns toward me as she pivots back to the door and smiles at my chest. "Thank you."

Gotcha.

"Jean."

Her head lifts instinctively toward the sound, and her eyes, with a mind of their own, pass into the beam of my gaze. Her body stiffens upright.

Too easy.

Jean's world falls away until there's nothing left but blackness. The color drains from her face under the single flickering fluorescent light above me.

I have trapped her in my prison.

*"Jean,"* I say as I enter her mind, again. *"Release me. You will not be harmed."*

In a trance-like state, she walks to the far wall behind me. Pressing on a stone within the wall, it slides away, revealing what I can only assume is a control panel of sorts. With the press of a single button, my restraints open.

I stand and massage my wrists where the silver burned them. Turning around, I join Jean at the wall, examining every detail of her. Even though she is compelled, her conscious mind screams, terrified, in the darkness of her subconscious.

"Remember," I whisper with my hands on her shoulders. "I'm not here for you, dearie. I have a different agenda. Come,"—I tap her twice— "sit for a moment."

We make our way back to the chair where I take her seat, and she takes mine.

"This is the longest conversation I've had with a human in more than 600 years. You set aside your preconceived notions and listened to my story, even if you had ulterior motives. The story may come from the lips of a murderous monster that, until now, only lived in humanity's lore—but *you* know it." I smile and push a lock of hair behind her ear. "Most only know the truth on the dark day that the legend becomes all too real."

Leaning forward, I contemplate my next move. Shall I have her for dinner or dessert? She smells too good to be a main course. Too sweet… Oh, how do the French say it… Comme cela devrait être? Yes, that's right. As it should be.

"You wait here dearie. I won't be gone long." With both hands and great care, I remove the ID badge from her lapel. "I'm going to borrow this." I flip the badge effortlessly between my fingers. Turning toward the exit, I kick the boxed boutonniere. "Huh." I smile. "Well, I can't leave you here. That'd be rude." I remove the boutonniere and carefully put it in my pocket. "There."

A knock comes at the door. In a flash, I flatten myself against the wall.

"Hello? Dr. Allicines. It's Tim." He pokes his head around the door frame. "Is everything okay? The door—"

I snap his neck between my palms. Perfect timing. I need a new outfit.

Dragging his limp body into the interrogation room, I carefully close the door just enough so it's flush with the wall, but the locks don't engage.

I feed on him and strip Tim of his ABUs. His pants fit me well, but the boots are a size too big. The shirt and coat are slightly baggy in the waist, but beggars can't be choosers.

Looking down at the name patch stitched to the chest, I laugh internally. The poor boy's parents had a cruel sense of humor to name him Tim Burr.

I slide his body behind the door and walk out of the prison with SSgt. Burr's lanyard and badge around my neck and Jean's in my pocket.

The hallway goes on for a hypnotizingly long way, close to a quarter mile. A hand-painted mural of different military aircraft, vehicles, and technology marks the hall's abrupt end. I glance over my shoulder to find another mural with the faces of the greatest Presidents of the United States.

Clever. An interrogation room hidden in plain sight. With the door completely shut, a passerby would have never known to look for it.

Making my way down the opaque corridor, I assess the first of four hallways extending perpendicular to mine. I pause at the crossroad, looking both ways.

Where is the damn staircase?

The new hall appears to extend for eternity.

I don't have time to venture.

I look left, and then right, again. I notice a map bolted to the wall. The map is an exploded view of the building and, in the right-hand corner, reads:


NORTH: DIRECTORATE 1 (CELESTIAL)

EAST: DIRECTORATE 2 (ARCANE)

WEST: DIRECTORATE 3 (DARWINIAN)

I scan the map until I see a familiar name: DR. EUGENE F. SHELLEY, WEST SUB-BASEMENT 2.

Eugene told Jeanie about the Codex. That's who'll have my answers. He'll know where Claret is.

Laughter erupts to my left. Three women of various shapes, sizes, and ages appear out of nowhere. I glance around until I notice a faded STAIRS sign on one of the blue-gray doors. Calmly, so as to not alert the women, I turn and make my way over.

One of the girls looks up from the conversation and waves. "Good morning."

Eager to tear this one's throat out, smash the tall one into the cinderblock wall, and drink the fat one dry if I can't talk my way out of this, I smirk. "Good day, ladies."

"Hey," the tall lady says, eying me curiously.

"Yes?"

"Where's your badge?"

I feel my chest for the lanyard. "Damn it, I just…"—pulling the lanyard out from my collar—"ah, here it is. Silly me. Thank you."

She nods and continues walking.

Slamming my hands into the crossbar, I open the door, and escape.

One floor down, I pause to glance back up the stairs to confirm no one is following me and that I haven't set off an alarm. But no alarm goes off, and no MP—military police—or military members come rushing up or down the stairs. It is like I'm not even here.

Perfect.

Three floors down I find a steel door different from all the rest. It is red, seems to require a badge swipe to enter, and reads: DR.

EUGENE F. SHELLEY (PHANG PROGRAM).

With SSgt. Burr's badge in-hand, I swipe the reader. The sensor simply turns red. I reach into my pocket for Jean's badge, but I stop when I hear a door open in the stairwell above me.

A man hums Elton John's *Rocket Man* from one floor above as the door to the stairwell slams behind him. His leather-soled echo as he walks down the stairs toward me.

Guess this is going to get messy. He's halfway here. Five steps.

"Oh!" Startled by me, he nearly spills the cups of coffee in his hands. "Excuse me," he says, clearing his throat and removing one of his headphones. "Are you here to see Dr. Shelley?"

There's no way it's this easy.

"Yes, but my badge doesn't work for some reason." I flash him Tim's badge.

"The reader must be acting up again. Stupid thing," he says, finagling the cups into one hand. "Let me try mine."

I step to one side.

Holding his badge up to the sensor, the reader turns green. "Sometimes you have to hold the badge up to the sensor, rather than just swiping it." Shaking his head with a smile and chuckles. "Government equipment, am I right?"

"You said it."

He props the door open with his foot and points with his head, "After you."

"Why thank you."

Carefully, he follows me into the room. "Henry Ingvar," he says, extending his hand as the door slams behind him.

Ingvar? That name, Ingvar. Have I heard it before? No time to loiter.

"I'm Staff Sergeant Timothy Burr."

"What department or division do you work for Staff Sergeant Burr?"

"I'm not at liberty to divulge that information. I do a lot of work in eugenics, genetics, and the pseudo-sciences, also sociology, nonlinear mathematics, and psychology."

"You'll get along great with Dr. Shelley," he says, unfazed by the far-fetched list of specialties I rattled off or the inability to identify my employer. Making our way farther into the lab, he calls out, "Professor, there's a Staff Sergeant Timothy Burr here to see you."

An old man and a young nerd. I could drain them easily. And possibly sound an alarm only to hit another dead end. Best to play the long game.

"Staff Sergeant who?" Dr. Shelley peers over the rim of his glasses from behind his desk. Groaning, he puts down his pen and kicks himself back from the desk. "I will be right there, Henry," he says softly and uses the side of his desk to stabilize himself as he comes to his feet.

Henry escorts me to an old distressed wooden table, repurposed to be a conference table, with papers covering half of its surface. He gathers the scattered pages in no particular order, but I catch a glimpse of most of them: a Fiscal Year 2020 proposed Spend Plan addressed to Billing, ten articles on Genome Editing and DNA Sequencing, three stacks on Chimera Research, large construction plans for a new facility, handwritten notes on nonlinear and linear optics, and a draft report to General Grissom.

The report to Grissom is the only page with edits and notes in the margins in red. Everything else is done in black pen.

Henry shuffles the pages into a neatly arranged pile, smearing the ink on General Grissom's report, and proceeds to set the stack on a nearby shelving unit.

That ink is too fresh, and the notes look shaky. Almost panicked. You can see it in the curves of the Y's and R's. This one is important.

I choose a seat at the table's far end where I have the best visibility of the room.

I hate the long game.

"Can I get you something to drink?" Henry asks. "Water? Coffee? Tea?"

For being born in this century, the young Henry has rather chivalrous qualities.

"Water would be great. Thank you."

If only I had SSgt. Burr's finger to go with it or that tall lady's eyeball from upstairs.

I nearly choke on the stale air, and my eyes squint from the brightness of the lights. The laboratory walls are made of cinder block, and the open floor plan utilizes storage cabinets to create additional partitions.

Chaotic. Ordinary. Human.

Passing my hand over the cold, aged wood of the tabletop, I admire its weathered characteristics and feel a certain kinship with it. Beaten from years of hard dishes hitting its surface and stained with tea, coffee, and markers, it carries years and years of memories.

Henry places a mostly full glass of water in front of me. He takes a seat and whispers, "I'm sorry. Dr. Shelley tends to work at his own pace. It's something that can be rather infuriating about the man, even though he's absolutely brilliant."

Cupping the warm mug between my hands, I sit back in my chair. "It's no trouble at all."

"How do you know Dr. Shelley?"

"To be honest, I've never met him before." Noticing a briefing titled: NOCTURNAE 18-Jan-2019 0900, I point at it. "I missed yesterday's briefing and hoped Dr. Shelley could give me a quick run through."

Henry eyes the report. "Oh, so you were *just* read into the program."

Yes?

"Yes."

"He won't admit it, but Dr. Shelley loves talking about this stuff to new people."

"You're right, I won't admit it." Dr. Shelley makes his way to the table.

I stand to greet him.

"Sit, sit. No need to get up at my expense." Dr. Shelley groans ever so slightly as he falls into the chair. "Now, what can I help you with, young man?"

He's kinder than I expected.

"First off, please forgive my abrupt drop-in. I was unable to make yesterday's meeting. I got a flat on my way to base. I ran into Dr. Allicines later in the day and she said I should pop by the lab this evening."

Dr. Shelley leans in. "You know Jeanie?"

"We went out a few times, but quickly realized we were not each other's cup of tea." I chuckle.

Dr. Shelley's heart rate didn't change, but Henry's increased at the mention of Jean's name. He's smitten with her. Or envious?

"What organization are you with? N.S.A.? D.I.A.? C.I.A.?" Dr. Shelley folds his hands.

Humans and their acronyms. Better to not specify.

"I work for a black organization, an affiliate of The Company. General Grissom has tasked me with gathering as much intelligence as I can on Nocturnae."

Henry gives Dr. Shelley an incredulous look and nods a shallow, subtle nod.

"Mmhmm." Dr. Shelley, glances over at the stack of papers Henry had moved off the table, then back at me. "I assume…"—he looks at the ceiling lights intently—"you've read the documents provided to you after being read in?"

That was a tell. He's bluffing to test me.

"There were no documents provided."

He pauses a moment. "No, there were not."

Maybe this will be more interesting than I thought.

Dr. Shelley strokes the patches of his two-day old scruff. "With you *just* being read in, we're going to need to start from the beginning."

"The beginning of…"

"Yes," Dr. Shelley says, nodding to himself. "What do you know about *vampires?*"

Oh dear, this could be a long meeting. What if someone finds compelled Jean and dead Tim? Hmm… I passed a handful of people on my way down here, but no one has interrupted Jean thus far and the door is well camouflaged. I should be fine. Unless there are cameras.

I didn't see any, but that doesn't mean they're not there. However, if there are cameras anywhere in the facility, wouldn't the alarm already be raised? Rent-a-cop could be sleeping on the job—that'd be convenient.

At this point I don't really have an option. If I'd stayed in the cell, they could kill me or worse, make it impossible for me to escape. Stick to the plan: Find Claret and get out. Alive.

"We call them vampires, but they are Nocturnae," I say. Dr. Shelley and Henry exchange an impressed glance. "Sunlight or decapitation kills them…" Best to leave out silver, that may not be common knowledge. "…they need human blood to survive…" A lie. "…they're unable to walk on hallowed ground—" Also, a lie.

"Why do you think that is?" Dr. Shelley asks.

I make a show of contemplating his question carefully. "They must be animated, dead, or demonic in some way, the children of Satan."

Thanks dad.

Dr. Shelley nods approvingly. "Very good. You know a fair bit. But,"—he raises his finger—"what if I were to tell you that Nocturnae are the next stage in human evolution?"

I'd call you an idiot.

"That would be incredible," I say, feigning wonder.

Henry gently interjects, "It's far too soon for us to know that for any certainty, I think, is what Dr. Shelley means. That's merely a hypothesis at this point. It could also be a virus or something unknown that causes the Nocturnae transformation."

And you are *not* an idiot.

Over the bridge of his horn-rimmed glasses Dr. Shelley looks inquisitively at Henry for a good three seconds before asking, "What do you think about sharing our more recent finding with Staff Sergeant Burr? He is here after all; we might as well give him a first-hand account of what it is we do here."

Henry closes his eyes. "I can't think of any reason not to give him a tour of the lab. He's read in; thus, he has the Need-to-Know. Knowing General Grissom is overseeing our work is classified at the Special Access Program level."

"Wonderful!" Dr. Shelley winks and stands up from the table. "Do you mind if we walk and talk Staff Sergeant Burr? My legs tend to lock up on me if I sit for too long."

"I don't mind at all." I stand. "Lead the way. I'll be sure to tell my Section Chief, and General Grissom, you were so accommodating."

Henry and I follow Dr. Shelley through the lab as he points things out.

"I have been studying this subject for—oh, I don't know—twenty-five? No, more than that. A little more than thirty years now," Dr. Shelley brags.

His head turns to an old oak desk piled high with papers and books.

I follow his gaze to a faded photo of a woman holding her stomach. The photo is too old to be of his daughter. His wife then? Pregnant.

Dr. Shelley continues, "You are correct about the sun. Although depicted in fiction and fun to think about, the hallowed ground thing is nothing more than an old wives' tale. They are not dead, blood still pumps through their veins, nor are they any more demonic than you or me."

Humans are pretty demonic, Doctor. Have you studied the crusades?

An aggressive cough shakes Dr. Shelley, causing him to bend over until it passes, and he regains his breath. "Excuse me and these shitty lungs. Too many years of smoking." Clearing his throat, he continues our walk. "Although human blood is preferred by Nocturnae, for reasons still not entirely understood, other mammals are sufficient to sustain them."

"What are the side effects of consuming non-human blood for an extended period of time?" I think of my century of insect meals and shudder.

Henry chimes in with an exhaustive list including irrational thought, weakness, exhaustion, hallucinations, decreased vision, and hearing voices.

I gasp for effect. "Sounds like you guys have a good amount of research to back this up. How did you get that? Live Subjects?" The thought of what they must have done to Claret fills me with rage.

"We've conducted many experiments, both physical and psychological." Henry seems pleased to convey this information.

Who runs this lab, the kid or the old man? In any case, the kid didn't answer my question.

"Never underestimate a Nocturnae," Dr. Shelley adds. "Even in a degraded state, a Nocturnae would have no problem overpowering a well-trained human." Ironic that he should say that.

Turning to Henry I ask, "Hypothetically, could they survive on non-mammal blood? Such as the blood of birds, reptiles, or even insects?"

"I don't see why not." Dr. Shelley strokes his chin. "We've never thought to try running that experiment. Insects, I suspect, would be a bit of a stretch. However, the Nocturnae species has never ceased to surprise me." Dr. Shelley turns to Henry. "Make note of that. We should run an experiment on the Subject once the current tests have been completed and it has recovered. We should also write it up as a White Paper or even a Proposal for additional funding."

Run another experiment? To what end? Does she ever get a break? *Cruel* is an oversimplification for these two humans.

"You have access to a Nocturnae?" I keep my tone even.

Dr. Shelley admits, "Yes. I have built my career studying this Nocturnae who has been in The Company's control for nearly a century according to my superiors, and the documentation was handed down to me when I took over the work."

Only a century? Claret was taken more than 600 years ago. Did they lose control of her somewhere along the way? Is this *not* Claret after all?

"We've also recently acquired a male Nocturnae," Henry adds.

Me.

Dr. Shelley raises his eyebrows. "Dr. Allicines, is interviewing him now in an attempt to get a baseline regarding his mental abilities. Once she has performed a complete psychological profile on him, we will admit him to the cell that will house him, indefinitely."

I think not.

"What has she determined thus far?" I ask.

"I have not seen her official report yet." Dr. Shelley raises a finger. "But she did get confirmation that the Nocturnae experience, which they call the *new birth*, is when their human life ends and their Nocturnae life begins. It is during the new birth that they are changed at a genetic and—more importantly—a molecular level."

Henry sighs. "Therefore, Nocturnae are *not* the next stage in human evolution. Supported by your point that they change at genetic and molecular levels. Otherwise, you could say a dolphin and a human are the same, which they're not. Nocturnae have all the same organs as us but many have no function, like our gallbladder. This explains why a seemingly fatal blow or injury to a primary organ system has zero effect on the Subject."

Oh good, I didn't evolve from creatures like you—I'm something else entirely.

"What organ systems are still the same?" I ask.

"The Nocturnae female, for example, doesn't experience a menstruation cycle like a human female," Dr. Shelley says. "But during exploratory surgery we found eggs still residing in her ovaries. Which begs the question: How do Nocturnae reproduce if the females do not menstruate?"

"Reproduce—"

"Yes," Henry says with an eager nod. "We hope, with the newly acquired male Nocturnae, we can answer this question."

"Do you really think that's possible?" I cross my arms.

What they're proposing sounds like more torture to me.

Dr. Shelley shrugs. "I believe so, but I can't be certain. That's why it's called research."

"Dr. Shelley," Henry goads, "why don't you share your more recent discovery?".

"My belief in Nocturnae reproduction," Dr. Shelley says, "stems from the fact that a Nocturnae appendix secretes an enzyme that we've begun calling *acetase* that converts lactic acid into energy."

"What does that have to do with reproduction?" I ask.

Dr. Shelley holds up a finger. "Nothing, but it provides evidence that we understand how their body works." He holds up a second finger. "And move ever closer to answering the question of reproduction."

This human is smart. Dangerously, smart.

Dr. Shelley turns a corner and Henry and I follow. "First," Dr. Shelley says, leaving only one finger up, "Nocturnae energy output increases as lactic acid increases and, as you are aware, lactic acid increases due to a lack of oxygen within its system. In order to keep its body more basic, it has to have a higher respiration rate. This is further supported by a Nocturnae resting heart rate normalizing close to that of a human infant. Additionally, the muscle fascia that would reside around the muscles of a human, is nonexistent in Nocturnae."

Do they mean reproduce biologically or artificially?

Holding up my hands, I look at both of them with a puzzled look. "I'm sorry, could we back up … when you say 'reproduce,' do you mean reproduction at its truest, biological sense or are you including the act of turning a human into a Nocturnae?"

"Both," Henry replies.

With a subtly aggressive clearing of his throat, Dr. Shelley holds up a second finger. "And two, our most recent experiments have helped us better understand *how* a human is turned. For a long time, I believed it was a chemical that caused the transformation, and it was transferred through the teeth like a viper's fangs secrete venom. However, upon removing all of Subject 252-7-38's teeth and analyzing them, we found no evidence that a fluid could be transferred through them."

I knew that wasn't right, or at least, that's not how it happened to me. "And now?"

"Once Henry started working with me, he theorized it was an exchanging of blood between the two parties. This may occur when the Nocturnae and the human orally ingest the other's blood or by allowing blood to transfer between them, like a transfusion. This concept seemed far-fetched. We still explored it, resulting in rather horrific experiments." He says the last part without a shred of remorse.

Experimentation on your own kind and no sign of guilt. That's cold, even if the humans did deserve it. Neither of these men show signs they have any morals. I am Nocturnae, and even I have a code: No kids.

"Our new hypothesis is that Nocturnae secrete a chemical through their salivary glands, similar to vampire bats," Henry added.

"That's a little cliché, don't you think?" I attempt to keep the scoff out of my tone.

"I thought the same thing at first." Dr. Shelley removes his glasses to clean them. "But let us look at the overall picture. Nocturnae feed on blood. Thus, it would benefit them to inhibit blood clotting, prolong bleeding, and paralyze the blood vessels near the wound to prevent them from constricting."

"Have you confirmed this theory?"

"No," Dr. Shelley says quickly and looks to Henry, "we have not. We have made a number of other surprising advancements in better understanding Nocturnae, which were compiled into a report and summarized in a recent briefing I gave to my superiors to secure future funding."

"And what of the biological reproduction? What progress has been made there, if any?"

After checking his glasses in the light, Dr. Shelley returns them to his face. "We haven't started that research yet because we didn't have a viable male for the process. Until now."

Henry steps toward Dr. Shelley and addresses him. "I know this isn't customary, but under the circumstances, what do you think about showing him the Subject? He's read in. He has the Need-to-Know. He's here. This could open up a door to additional funding."

"Hm," Dr. Shelley says, glancing at me. "I like where your head is at Henry but—"

This is not progressing fast enough. I'll be here for hours at this rate. I need to make a move. Something subtle, that could provoke them into showing their hand.

"I should be going," I say in an underwhelming tone. "Thank you for your time and hospitality. I'll let leadership know of the great work you're doing here. I'll put in a good word for additional funding."

I hold out my hand for Henry to shake when Dr. Shelley interrupts. "Staff Sergeant. Do you have time for a tour of the bastille?"

Well, that worked quite well. A subtle hint of disappointment and boredom in my voice and presto.

I look at Henry in hopes of gaining some insight as to why his mentor used an old-aged French term for prison that hadn't been used since the eighteenth century.

Henry gives a small smile of agreement like the bastille was a last resort.

Dr. Shelley's gait hastens. He seems excited to give someone new the opportunity to look a *real* monster in the eye.

I follow the old man through the labyrinth of his lab while Henry trails me from the rear. At the end of the laboratory, hidden beside an overly large storage cabinet, is a secret door. There is no window nor is there a handle of any kind, just a button-sized circle on the adjacent wall that could have been anything.

Dr. Shelley reaches into his pocket and pulls out a small silver Watch with flecks of sapphire blue and quickly checks the time.

It can't be, can it? It looks just like…

He removes a lanyard from inside his shirt with an ID at the end and runs it over a blank spot on the wall. The door pops open about an inch from the wall before a motor takes control and slowly opens it, revealing a long, narrow hallway illuminated along the floor. The walls remind me of sections of the Paris catacombs with the natural, rough textures and a thin layer of moisture covering every surface.

Once through the doorway, Henry presses a stone on the wall and the door quickly closes behind us. Henry's leather-soled loafers click, while Dr. Shelley's rubber sneakers squeak, on the dew-laden floor.

Thirty paces or so down, we come to a spiral staircase. For ten long minutes, we descend into the abyss and exit into another hall deep within the building.

Moving at a human's pace is torturous. I could have been down there seconds after we stepped through the doorway. Is Claret down here? The anticipation is killing me.

At the end of the hall, four dim lamps separate three steel vault doors. We walk down the passage until we're in front of the doors and can clearly read them. Two of the three doors each have a six-digit numeric in the center. The far-left door reads, 252-7-38, while the far-right door reads, 072-4-63.

Stepping in front of the center door, Dr. Shelley pivots toward me, gesturing to the door on his right. "Here is our Subject."

My heart races. Here, in the middle of boring, flat Ohio. This whole time. After all these years, will I finally be reunited with my Maker?

I look at these two foolish mortals with rising rage. It would take no effort at all to rip the throats from their soft bodies and run like hell from this prison. As they bleed out, gasping for air, Claret and I could be crossing into Indiana or Kentucky.

The thought briefly intoxicates me, but my rational mind takes over. I need to be strategic.

"May I?" I point at the door.

"Absolutely. It would be cruel of me to have brought you all this way to only have you set your sights on a door." Dr. Shelley follows up with a laugh that makes me want to cut out his tongue and force it down his own throat.

I take three-and-a-half steps toward the door.

"The viewing window door slides to the right. You might need to give it a little *oomph*, it tends to stick from the condensation down here," Dr. Shelley says.

I slide open the small steel window. The pungent aroma of necrotic tissue, body excrement, and general filth pours from within, causing us all to cover our noses.

Humanity's cruelty and creative ingenuity frightens me more and more with each passing century.

It takes nearly a minute for my senses to become accustomed to the harshness proliferating from the cell. Slowly, I inch my way closer and closer to the door. My eyes shift to another spectrum and I gasp a short, shallow puff.

There, in the middle of the floor, lay a humanoid creature curled tightly on top of something.

"Is that a towel it's lying on?" I ask.

The creature's head lifts ever so slightly at the sound of my voice.

An evil, proud grin spreads across Henry's face. "Yes. Every surface in her cell is made of silver. Which confines her to that four-by-five-foot towel in the center of the room."

Making a childhood favorite game, *The Floor is Lava*, into a real scenario. Barbaric.

"Why?" I ask, knowing full well the answer.

"It keeps the Subject in a constant state of psychological trauma and makes it easier for us to control her," Henry says.

Causing her to engage in the decision to stay safe in her small section of the prison or venture outside and experience excruciating pain as her feet melt away slowly into the silver flooring. You fucking … monsters!

Dr. Shelley closes his eyes and nods. "This was one of Henry's first tasks when he first came to work for me."

"Isn't it a little—"

"You think this is overkill?" Dr. Shelley interrupts.

"I was going to say inhumane." I force down my anger. "But yes."

"No," Dr. Shelley looks at the center door and pauses. "Imagine if the Subject got out. The number of people who would be killed. The cost in damages to the building, equipment, and research. The threat to national security and the general population. No, this isn't overkill. This is barely the minimum of what we need—in my opinion."

Turning my attention back to the imprisoned creature, I rifle back through my vision bands. Starting in the visible spectrum, I move through the longer infrared wavelengths, back to visible and through the ultraviolet and return to the visible and near infrared, where I prefer to observe the world, hoping to catch a glimpse of anything to tell me it's my Maker. I need to see her face, damn it.

I close my eyes, to hide their crimson glow, and try to push my mind into hers, but I can't penetrate her mental defenses in the Void.

There's been too much trauma for too long. Fuck.

In an attempt to get the Nocturnae to move, I click my tongue against my cheek. But it doesn't work.

I turn my head far enough to bring Henry and Dr. Shelley into my periphery. They're having their own conversation now. Football, really? Not securing funding or speculating on what my thoughts or questions will be. Oh no, their arrogance is so great they're talking about the typical American males' favorite pastime—sorry baseball, you're so last century.

Now's my shot. I have to do it now.

Using their conversation as cover and at a volume lower than theirs I say through the window, "Maker."

At the sound of my voice her heart rate changes. She rolls over, revealing long hair, and flashes her crimson corneas. "Sorin?"

"Maker? I'm here to free you."

In the blink of an eye, she sits erect atop bent knees with her hands clasped over her heart. "Not now. There is more at stake than just you and me. I have endured this for centuries. I will be fine."

I look over my shoulder to check on the humans. These two are unbelievable. The egotism. They're comparing fantasy football scores, good.

"But I'm here," I beg. "I can—"

"The prophecy." Claret drops her mental defenses and enters my mind, *"Tomorrow."*

Before I can respond, Dr. Shelley breaks our connection with a firm grip of my shoulder. "I have something else to show you."

I smile at Dr. Shelley and nod, and ask Claret, *"What do you mean tomorrow?"*

*"The prophecy."*

Slowly, we make our way to the last door where he stops, smiles at me, and grips the handle. A loud *clang* erupts as he opens the door.

Light floods the hallway as the door opens, along with sounds about something living in a pineapple under the sea. There, sitting in the middle of the soft blue carpeted floor, atop a unicorn rug, is a small female child singing the song coming from the television about a man named Bob who wears square pants.

Strange.

"This is Rahne," Dr. Shelley proudly introduces.

Why would a child's bedroom be behind a silver door and right next to a Nocturnae?

Either Rahne didn't hear Dr. Shelley or she was ignoring him like pre-teens and early adolescents so often do their elders.

"Rahne," he repeats sternly, breaking the television's grasp on her reality.

Her head whips around with a confused look on her face and a curious tone she says, "Huh?" Her eyes touch Henry's and mine, but become lost in Dr. Shelley's, as a wide smile reveals her high dimples. "Daddy!" she proclaims, jumping to her feet to wrap her tiny arms around his waist, burying the side of her face in his belly with a smile spread from ear to ear.

Daddy?

Dr. Shelley let out a large puff of air the moment Rahne hugs him, but he pays no mind. Instead, he places one hand on her mid-back and the other on the other side of her head; sharing in her embrace.

Suddenly, a fast-thumping sound catches my attention. I turn my head toward Dr. Shelley, ever so slightly, and listen to his heart rate. His heart rate nearly doubled in an instant. He's either on the verge of tachycardia or … he loves her. She may be the only thing in the world that he truly cares for.

Rahne enjoys Dr. Shelley's hand as it brushes through her hair before stepping back.

"Hi, Henry," she says, flapping her little hand so fast she almost floats off the ground.

Slowly, Dr. Shelley drops to one knee beside her. "Rahne, I would like you to meet a new friend of mine. This is Staff Sergeant Burr."

"It's nice to meet you, Mr. Burr," Rahne says with her little hand outstretched.

Humbled by her polite gesture, I accept her hand and stare into her eyes.

She's adorable.

Still holding her hand, I lower myself until we're eye level. "It's lovely to meet you, Rahne. What is it that you're watching?"

"SpongeBob."

"Well, it looks like the commercials just ended, better run along so you don't miss anything."

With a hop and skip in her step, her gleaming face turns, and she runs back to her spot on the floor to do what kids do: watch, play, and imagine.

"I will be back shortly to play," Dr. Shelley says. She nods. "I love you."

"I love you too, Daddy. Bye, Mr. Burr. Bye, Henry," she says, refusing to tear her eyes from the screen.

I smile and wave. "Goodbye little one."

I stop mid-wave when a drawing by her bed catches my eye. It's a childish drawing done in crayon and the corners of the page are curled. In the center is a pink stick figure of a girl holding the hand of a larger stick figure in a lab coat. Above the two people, it reads: TUGETER FUREVR.

Cora.

Slowly, Dr. Shelley closes the door, trying to make as little noise as possible.

As Dr. Shelley turns around, Henry asks, "Back to the conference table for some cake?"

Dr. Shelley hums with a nod. "Cake sounds nice." He turns to me. "Do you have time for cake? What is your schedule like?" he follows up, preventing me from answering his initial question.

Claret said tomorrow. I need to buy more time.

"I am available for as long as you and Henry will have me, Dr. Shelley. And cake would be splendid."

Sounds disgusting.

"Lovely," he says as we begin our journey back up to his lab. A sense of unease grows within me the farther we draw from the cells.

I hate leaving her.

"Dr. Shelley," I say, breaking the silence. "I don't mean to be rude, so please don't take offense, but why is your daughter…"— *Imprisoned. Incarcerated. Locked up*—"…Confined?"

Dr. Shelley pauses and looks back down the stairs at me. "Because we believe she is a Lygos."

# 27



DARKNESS WAS A commodity that Jean had become well-acquainted with but this … this place … was a different *kind* of dark.

Everyone experiences darkness when they're trying to fall asleep. Jean had, before she went blind, and she remembered it well. It has shape and a kind-of gray aura emanating from its center. It's calming, welcoming, familiar even. This was not.

The darkness of the Void was the kind of darkness you only accidentally walk into as a child when you're playing hide-and-seek at night, in an old house, with the power out, and you decide to hide in the far back corner of a closet with the door closed and your hands cupping your shut eyes.

Jean could hear her heart in her ears.

"Where am I," she called out into the infinite blackness. "This isn't Sorin's cell."

Violently reaching with her hands in every direction, she searched for a doorway, a window, anything. In a fit of panic, she threw herself off balance and onto the floor.

Flattening her hands onto the ground, she found that it was neither warm nor cold, hard nor soft. On all fours, she used her hands to explore the world around her as she crawled deeper into the abyss.

But she found nothing.

She crawled … and crawled … and crawled … until she thought she had crawled long enough for her knees to bleed. She stopped, repositioned herself with both legs out in front of her, and checked her knees. Not only did they not bleed, they weren't even sore.

Frightened and alone, Jean pulled her knees to her chest and wrapped her arms around her legs. Slowly she rocked, back and forth, muttering inaudible nonsense as her eyes searched the infinite blackness.

Something like light originated from the crack between her knees and she was shocked to see a clouded wraith-like figure swimming through the black air. How could she see?

She stopped rocking, scrambled to her knees, and leaned forward, hoping to catch a clearer image of the figure. The last image she saw had been her grandparents' faces.

The shadow danced back and forth in the sea of darkness and then suddenly stopped. The figure tilted to one side and then the other, as it eerily studied Jean.

Her curiosity overpowered her fear. She brought herself to her feet and walked toward it.

The figure mirrored Jean and made its way toward her, matching her speed. It wasn't long before, what could only be presumed to be the figure's head, appeared from behind its hooded cloak. Deep within the hooded darkness was a pair of unique eyes glowing a lavender color, reminiscent of flowers on the Chaste Tree.

Floating closer to Jean, the figure inspected her from every angle.

She cowered when it tousled and sniffed her hair. Quickly, she collected her hair over one shoulder and mindlessly stroked it, comforting herself. She flinched and pulled her arm to her chest when it grabbed her wrist. Slowly, and with caution, Jean loosened her arm, allowing the figure to examine between each finger and under her arm with its mist-like hands.

It floated around her three times, at varying heights and stopped near her back side. Suddenly, it forced her legs apart and flew between them.

Jean shrieked, bringing her knees together and pulling the bottom of her sweater as low as it could go. In a fit of freight and embarrassment, she accidently caught a better view of the figure's face. It was smooth and bone-like with two holes where a nose would be.

The figure floated in front of Jean's face and repeatedly sniffed, like a dog catching a scent.

Squeezing her eyes shut she pulled her lips inward, hoping it couldn't enter her somehow. Her eyes flew open when she felt something wet and rough running from her chin and up her nose … a tongue.

"Agghh!" Jean screamed, throwing herself backwards.

The distance between them didn't seem to offend nor intrigue the eldritch figure as it floated before her in the black nightmare of the Void.

Captivated by the figure's eyes, Jean took a half-step toward it and whispered, "What is this place?"

Silence continued to fill the Void.

Jean took another half-step and stopped.

The figure's eyes disappeared as its head turned.

*BOOOM!*

Jean flinched at an explosion far off in the distance. Echoing through the blackness, the sound was quickly followed by trillions of indiscernible objects whizzing past Jean and the figure. She screamed, shutting her eyes for a second when she realized her hair wasn't blowing in the wind as the objects passed her.

There was no wind. If there was no wind, there was no air. If there was no air, this was a dream. Or something like a dream.

The objects stopped with a large painting displayed in front of her.

The figure floated beside the image and hissed, "No dream. Real."

Jean's eyes widened and her stomach dropped. Gulping, she stepped toward the image on her left and placed her hands on either side of her face in a poor attempt of keeping her emotions contained.

Centered in the image on the painting was an unconscious, bloodied woman lying in a hospital bed with her feet in stirrups. Jean gasped as she recognized herself. Behind her stood a doctor, holding a hairless, maroon infant.

Whipping her head around, Jean held back her tears. "Why are you showing me this?"

The figure didn't answer, but lifted what appeared to be an arm from under its tattered cloak.

Turning back to the painting, Jean watched as it morphed into the child crying. Jean, stunned, walked up to the image. Placing the tips of her fingers on the child's forehead, she looked back at the figure.

"She's alive?" Jean asked as she fell to her knees.

Again, the figure didn't answer as the image morphed once more to reveal an old cabin nestled deep in a forest of cottonwoods.

"I know this place." Jean stood there and studied the image from every angle as she slowly approached it, trying to place it in her memories.

The ground beneath her feet shook like something hard had hit it.

"What was that?!" Jean cried, searching the darkness and stopping on the figure.

Three more tremors. Jean quickly realized these were footsteps from something very large.

A pair of purple eyes looked through her and hissed, "Prophecy."

The figure pointed to the image of the cabin and vanished.

The sound of large feet racing across the ground echoed throughout the Void.

Jean stared into the painting at a pair of yellow eyes that appeared deep in the forest. The eyes grew closer and closer until the large, shadowy figure was next to the cabin. Steam vented from its mouth and nostrils. Its eyes screamed fury and rage.

"Oh, God," Jean gasped.

# 28



ONE BY ONE we emerge from the catacombs. The door hisses as it seals off the lab from the crypt. The humans scoff, shielding their eyes from the blinding overhead lights while I do the same to keep up appearances.

Henry doesn't miss a beat and makes his way to the kitchen, preparing forks and plates for cake.

My Maker, once the strongest living thing I'd ever set eyes upon, now struggles to stay safe atop a small, ragged towel while these despicable men justify it in the name of science.

Dr. Shelley places his spindly, spider-like fingers in the middle of my back and gestures with his other hand back toward the large wooden table.

Oh, how easy it would be to grab him at the wrist and elbow and break his arm for all the horrifying acts he has committed.

He groans as he descends into the chair, his back sore from many years of standing and sitting with poor posture. I'm glad I will never age like him.

Slouched in the chair, Dr. Shelley fixes his glasses that have slid down his nose. "What did you think? Pretty cool, right?"

Lygos. What is a Lygos? Why did I feel akin with the word when it was uttered? Why was the sweet little girl in a cage next to Claret? Why is Dr. Shelley looking at me like he's waiting for a reply…?

"I'm sorry, what was the question?" I ask, catching his gaze.

"The Nocturnae," Dr. Shelley urges, "what did you think of her?"

I abhor his hubris. The callous nature, regaling the torturing and imprisonment of my Maker for hundreds of years. The unabated twitching, fidgeting, and tapping of his spindly appendages on the nearest surface as he impatiently waits for my praise.

"It is more than I ever dreamed possible." His skull meeting this table … that, would be a dream come true. And is quite possible.

"Do you have any questions?"

Would you like to die slowly or quickly? "No."

Henry arrives with the desserts. Dr. Shelley accepts a plate of spice cake and a small fork from Henry. He cuts off a large piece, shovels it into his face, and chews.

"There must be something the experience stirred up in your mind," Dr. Shelley says with a wad of cake stuffed in his cheek.

Henry hands me a plate and I thank him. My poor attempt of ignoring the freshly spewed cake particles on the table, I cringe slightly and take a bite.

This cake is disgusting, but then all cakes are disgusting to me. "How was the Nocturnae captured?" I ask, forcing the cake down my gullet. "It seems like it would be quite a feat."

"When I came on to the program, roughly thirty years ago, the prisoner was already here, with a collar made of silver around her neck—"

Silver. Did he say anything about silver yet? Clearly, they know about silver, but would SSgt. Burr know? Probably not.

"—connected to a silver leash tethered—"

I hold up a finger. "I'm sorry to interrupt but I thought werewolves were weakened by silver, not vampires."

Henry perks up from behind his nearly-empty plate. "Right you are, according to folklore, but it also is incredibly useful when subduing Nocturnae."—looking at Dr. Shelley he gestures with his hand—"Please continue Dr. Shelley."

"Um, where was I?" Dr. Shelley asks, munching on another bite of cake. "It doesn't matter. The silver used to keep her at bay, back then, was putting her in a compromised state and skewing results. We argued for better living conditions in hopes they would yield more accurate and promising results. We were right."

That's nothing more than torture masquerading as its own salvation.

"Has she ever escaped?"

Henry stops with a small piece of cake halfway in his mouth and looks at Dr. Shelley.

What was that? Press again.

Having swallowed his food, Henry smacks his lips and wipes his face. "She did get free at some point in 1943—March, I think."

I look at both of them and put my finger firmly on the table. "From here?"

"No, in a facility near Ravensbrück," Henry says.

"Germany?"

"Nazis," Dr. Shelley affirms. "Just before we acquired her here at Wright-Patt."

"Why would the Nazis—"

"Jesus Christ, boy, these things are the perfect weapon! These fucking things could kill you before you even knew it. If they weren't condemned to the darkness of night, I can't even imagine the carnage that would follow. That's why we have these lights," Dr. Shelley says, pointing to the lab's overhead lighting."

My jaw opens and my lips quiver slightly. The lights and his glance up at the ceiling when I first arrived were a tell. I look up at the ceiling and gaze into the bright lights above. The lights are persistent defensive weapons. Shit.

"Don't worry, Staff Sergeant," Henry pats the table. "The light is harmless to humans."

Henry begins spouting off details of the experiments performed on Claret in order to determine the most effective wavelength to weaponize against Nocturnae.

Thank my Maker I didn't free Claret just now. His words morph into a mumbled concoction of sounds and syllables in the background as I fixate on the fact that humans have weaponized the sun to use against us at any time. An overhead persistent anti-Nocturnae weapon.

Creative little monkeys these ones are. If it wasn't for my mutation and immunity to the sun, then I would have begun incinerating slowly since I walked into the building two days ago.

I point to the overhead lighting. "You have these throughout the whole building?"

Henry and Dr. Shelley laugh.

"Oh God, no," Dr. Shelley says. "Do you have any idea how expensive that would be? No, they're just in this laboratory because that"—he points to the catacomb door—"is the only door the Nocturnae and Lygos could escape through."

One way in. One way out. Good to know.

The lights only being down here means they probably don't know I'm immune to sunlight and my human disguise is still working. Does sunlight hurt Lygos as well? I need to know more.

"Not to overstep my boundaries gentlemen, but could you explain what *Lygos* means?" I ask. "You mentioned it as we reentered the lab. Also, why in the world is your daughter imprisoned?"

Rubbing the crest of his nose, Dr. Shelley puts his glasses on and chuckles.

Getting up from the table with his plate, Henry checks his watch. "Please excuse me, I need to get to my father. Tim, it was nice meeting you."

Dr. Shelley dismisses Henry, leaving him and me to talk further. "Rahne is not my biological daughter even though she regards me as such. My wife died many years ago with my unborn child. Cancer."

I didn't ask. "I'm so sorry." But I'm really not. You deserve every horrible thing that comes to you for what you've done to my Maker.

Dr. Shelley accepts my condolences with a nod. "I never remarried, nor did I ever have any children of my own. However, a little more than ten years ago, a woman in the building had a problem with her pregnancy. The Company had taken a special interest in her for reasons I'll explain in a moment. In any case, we brought her in, she had delivery issues which caused her to pass out, but the baby, Rahne, arrived safely. However, we told the mother the baby had died. We showed her a dead fetus while we brought Rahne to another room."

I know I'm a monster, but this man acts more like one than I do. And The Company … The Company is something else entirely. I nod to keep him talking.

"I was a man in his fifties who had never had a child of his own. I didn't know the first thing about raising a child. Hell, I didn't even know how to change a damn diaper." Dr. Shelley looks at his hand with a big smile. "Then, her little, tiny fingers wrapped around my pinky, and it all went away. All of the doubt. All of the fear. All of the worries. All of it."

I bite back my disgust. "What happened to the mother?"

"Nurses consoled her. A psychological team was briefed to council and help work her through the trauma and depression. A team was placed at her home and another followed her at all times the years following," he says quickly, like the mother wasn't even a thought. "She's fine now."

My head begins to shake slowly. No, she's not. How could she be? Jean, I'm so sorry. These men you call colleagues, and most likely friends, are nothing more than Judas'—betrayers for a bag of gold.

"The entire experience still haunts me today," Dr. Shelley says, likely trying to save face. "But do I regret it? Not in the slightest. That little girl is absolutely perfect and has given me hope for this world. But I am terrified with every cell in my body for what comes next. The date, the time, and the alignment of all the celestial bodies at the time of her first menstrual cycle haunts my thoughts."

"What do you mean?"

"The Company became interested in the mother after learning she may be Lygos," Dr. Shelley says. "Legend says the first Lygos were twin sisters who lived between the eighth and tenth millennia BCE."

"That's twelve thousand years ago," I say, unnecessarily.

He nods. "Yes, a very different time. A time when Nocturnae ruled the world and enslaved humanity like cattle to feed their blood-sucking masters."

That doesn't sound so bad to me.

"Legend says an angel visited the young girls and gave them the ability to overthrow the Nocturnae, freeing their people from slavery."

"An angel just so happened to show up and magically grant these children their wish?" I snicker internally, but some of my derision must have leaked out.

Dr. Shelley throws up his hands, as if he realizes how silly he sounds. "I know. I know. But if vampires are real … is it really so far-fetched to believe in the Lygos?"

And I, a Nocturnae, can walk during the daytime. He has a point, but he's still a monster.

I lean forward and place my elbows on the table and my chin on my tented hands. "Why are you afraid of Rahne becoming a woman?"

"I believe all Lygos are female—"

Because Twin Sisters started it? It's thin but okay.

"—and the curse only triggers when they enter womanhood at

the apex of a *very* special moon."

"One like the one tomorrow night?" A Super Wolf Blood Moon.

Dr. Shelley snaps his finger and sits back, hard into his chair. "Precisely."

"Is it really a curse?"

Dr. Shelley makes a strange face. "How should I know? All I know is I'm convinced a small group of people, likely sharing a bloodline, evolved to hunt and kill Nocturnae."

My heart rate quickens. "Hunt Nocturnae?"

"What did you think overthrow meant?" he scoffs. "That the Lygos were going to nicely ask the Nocturnae to leave?"

"A new apex predator, are you sure?" I ask as my voice squeaks.

"I don't have a clue. Only legends. For all I know they made a deal with the devil, not an angel." He shrugs. "Or maybe a witch, if such a thing exists."

Is this what Claret meant when she mentioned the thaumaturgy of the Penyihir? Magic? Claret might know the answers to my questions around the Lygos, magic, and possibly the Penyihir. But have the centuries of torture buried them or destroyed her mind too much?

Since my new birth, I have seen civilizations rise and fall over spilt wine. And today, I learned of a mythological creature born to hunt my species, as real as I am. If the transformation is based in magic, there must be a cost.

"Staff Sergeant Burr, I apologize," Dr. Shelley says, standing from his seat. "I have quite a bit yet to do to prepare the cell for the recently apprehended Nocturnae."

He's talking about me. I should get back to Jean anyway. I've never left a human compelled this long; Maker only knows what this could have done to her.

I thank him for his time and we shake hands. Dr. Shelley never glances in my direction again, and the door slams behind me.

# 29



MY FEET ECHO down empty halls as I exit the stairs and walk briskly back to my cell.

How much truth is there in what the old man was saying? If there is magic, was the Pearl magic? Is that how the younger child could see me, but the older one couldn't? Is it magic, or is that what humans call it, and we call it something else?

Noticing a janitorial closet in the empty hall, I move SSgt. Burr's body and wrap it in plastic bags—bodies start to smell much more quickly than people think. I close the door and turn the knob hard in the wrong direction, jamming it. For safe measure, I bend the lowest door hinge ensuring the door cannot be opened.

Once back in my holding area, my eyes adjust quickly, revealing Jean still sitting where I'd left her. I move her back to her seat, reclaim mine, and loosely rest the unshackled restraints over my wrists.

Sitting in front of her, I can't help but admire her stoic face. A wave of pity washes over me as I envision the life she could have had, before Rahne was stolen from her. Jean rocking her baby to sleep at night. Playing peek-a-boo in the high-chair. Crawling for the first time. Her first words. Standing upright. Walking. Running. Skipping. Jumping. Reading bedtime stories from cardboard pages.

Mo Chroí.

I shake myself and focus.

It's been too long. I've never compelled someone for this long. Hopefully there's no cognitive damage—or worse. I need to pull her out now.

Leaning forward, I return her badge to its home and re-affix my restraints.

I'm not putting that destroyed suit back on. She'll never know I had a wardrobe change.

*"Jean,"* I say as I enter her mind, once more. *"You will see me as I was."* I free my mind from hers and whisper, "Jean."

"What happened?" Grabbing the side of her head, she winces at the annoying pain in her head.

Good, no brain damage. "I'm not sure. You came back for your tote."

Her eyes dance from the tote, to me, back to the tote, and back to me.

Shit, she suspects something. "Did you have another question?"

Still confused, she takes a moment before answering. "I'm sorry. No, I think I've heard more than enough for today. I may be back tomorrow evening."

"Oh?"

"I have to write up my findings, and if I have any further

questions or need something clarified I will be back. Otherwise, thank you Mr. Harker. Goodbye."

I say nothing.

Jean makes her way out of the dark room, tapping her cane on the flooring in front of her as she carefully walks out. The heavy steel door closes effortlessly behind her, sealing shut without making a sound.

"I'll see you tomorrow, dearie."

# 30



A BLACK RAM truck turned into a quaint neighborhood, on a dimly lit street not far from Wright-Patterson Air Force Base. It arrived at a mid-sized split-level home that sat quietly beneath the stars, waiting for Jean's return.

Jean pulled her tote from the floor of the passenger seat and a water bottle from her cup holder. She opened the door, and her driver and roommate, Gabriel Glass, cut the engine.

She stepped down from the cab. She paused as her foot hit the ground and sighed, "What a day…"

"Sounds like it. You alright?" Gabriel asked.

"Yeah GG, I'm just tired." She closed the truck door and made her way to the front door, unlocked it, and entered the home with GG behind her.

"Hey, I could have gotten that for you." GG closed and locked the door behind them.

"I can manage. That is unless you've moved things around

today."

Chuckling, he slid off his shoes. "After nearly fourteen years as your roommate, I know better."

Jean headed straight for her office and turned on her desk lamp, dropping her tote on the edge of the desk. She grabbed a stack of her notes and sat down.

GG poked his head into the doorway. "You're not going to bed? You know it's after one a.m., right?"

Cupping her hands over her mouth, she gasped. "I should have Uber'd home. I had no idea it was that late."

"It's no problem. You actually saved me from a rather mediocre date. If it hadn't been for the cute bartender and his fabulous drinks I probably would have left earlier," GG said.

"Oh yea? Wanna tell me about him? I could use a good laugh after the day I've had."

"How about tomorrow? We can do brunch at that new bistro downtown. Bottomless mimosas?"

Slouching in her desk chair, she sighed, "Oh, that sounds divine."

"I left chicken cacciatore in the fridge if you're hungry before then."

Jean placed a grateful hand over her heart. "What would I do without you?"

"You'd have to find yourself a man." GG laughed, smacking his leg.

"Ha ha ha, very funny GG."

"Night."

She set her note taking device in front of her and ran her fingers over the braille tabs, reviewing her notes:

Doctor Jean Allicines with Mr. Sorin Harker, Subject, on the 18th and 19th days of January in the year 2019. The Subject grows agitated at answers that I purposefully keep short.

For many years now, Dr. Eugene Shelley, Henry Ingvar, and I have speculated the term 'new birth,' used by a past Subject, is used to describe the transformation from Homo sapiens to Homo profectus. This has been confirmed by the Subject, Mr. Sorin Harker.

He loves to talk about himself. A quality I will not argue with at this point, as it's making my job much easier to be honest. It's unclear if this is his personality or a side effect of the cocktail of benzodiazepines, anticonvulsants, and sodium pentothal circulating in his veins. Either way, we're achieving the desired effect.

His passion and yearning for human blood are reminiscent of an addict's need for their drug. Is this a Nocturnae trait, or is this a side effect? Or a coping mechanism for the guilt he feels toward a specific event in his past? Perhaps the loss of his coven and Maker.

He denies being, or knowing of, The Faceless King even after I read part of

Vlad Tepes III's journal. This was later supported when he informed me that he was confined by 'the Pearl' on the Étretat Cliffs in France.

The Pearl is an interesting artifact. Its ability to render the Subject invisible to all but children is both unbelievable and fascinating. To my knowledge, no technology today has this ability which leads me to believe the only possible answer, no matter how illogical, is magic. Are there other artifacts like this? The stuffed animal maybe? They seem to share the same markings. Where's the Codex now? Is there anything in the records? Consult Dr. Shelley, and maybe even Henry, on this one. Also, contact Colonel Wyatt in Directorate 2.

Something happened over the century and a half where the Subject was confined to the cabin floor. Maybe it was just the Pearl or just the relentless burning of the sun's ray's day in and day out, or maybe it's a combination of them and the silver flecks that, no doubt, were floating through his veins. In any case, the sun seems to have a diminished effect, if any effect at all, on this Subject. We must study this further.

He seems to feel some empathy toward humans.

"That's only half true," Jean thought to herself. "Sorin has empathy for a select few humans. Those with dark pasts like his own or his first kill, George's, and children, specifically female children. And…"

Jean sat back in her chair and tilted her head back with her eyes closed. She returned her hands to the keys and continued reading:

```
Empathy is a trait not seen in any previous
Subject or documented anywhere in the
records. He informed me of a time he talked
himself out of feeding on a human because
he, '...couldn't bear to burden the
individual with yet another cross...' He also
told me of a girl, Genevieve, and how it
pained him to feed on her, but he had no
other option. I believe he still carries
this guilt.
```

Jean stopped, turned her head, and scratched her neck in thought. "He… trusts me."

Returning to her keys, she wrote:

```
The Subject may have just compelled me.
Review the tapes in the morning to confirm.
```

"As strange as it is," Jean mumbled to herself, "even if he *did* compel me, I feel like he wouldn't hurt me."

# 31



THE FAMILIAR TAPS of a cane slowly find my ears. I smile, until I hear a large number of feet trampling the ground around the cane.

The seal on the door breaks, letting the fluorescent light from outside flood the room. A large hand flips the light switch filling the room with red light.

Gah! Glad that wasn't on this entire time. The light isn't painful, it's just annoying. A band of light not naturally found that is bound to give me a headache. It's interesting, I haven't experienced this before now. Could it be another persistent defensive weapon? There's an interesting thought.

Five well-built men enter the room, followed quickly by Jean who floats gracefully across the floor.

Clearly, she knows she has been fooled. It's time for my great escape.

They file around, encircling me, and Jean stops directly in front.

"Good morning, Jean," I say, flashing a smile. "I see you've brought *The Fellowship of the Ring* with you."

I first heard of *The Hobbit* and *The Lord of the Rings* in the late 1940s when a Mr. Johnathan K. Etolin of Pembroke College joined me for dinner. He didn't eat much, but I left quite satisfied and quite intrigued by this epic fantasy.

"Mr. Harker, I have to say,"—she shakes her head—"I am disappointed."

"With what? The gang's all here!" I proclaim, spreading a smile tightly across my face. "You have Aragorn and Boromir to my left, Legolas behind me holding hands with Gandalf, and Jesus Christ, you even brought Gimli! Now,"—I look left and right—"where are the halflings?"

A gentleman behind me snickers.

She drives the tip of her cane into the top of my foot. "You compelled me last evening and left me for over an hour! Where'd you go?"

Ow. That is quite an unpleasant feeling, that cane. My Maker, that's quite an impressive amount of pressure she's applying for someone so small.

"You forgot the garlic, didn't you? I compelled you to bring me garlic!"

Jeanie doesn't laugh at my joke. "Mr. Harker. You are being charged with crimes against the United States of America. You have engaged in terrorist activities by breaking into a military base, attacking and killing federal, military, and state police, and civil servants."

"They shot first."

She ignores me. "As a Nocturnae, you are not privy to the same formalities as human terrorists under state, federal, or global law."

Clearly, I've kept the stupidity part of my humanity since I let Jean walk out of here last night when I should have dragged her tiny body down to Claret's cell and offered it up as a meal!

Bending at the waist, Jean looks me square in the eyes. But this move, intimidating as it may be to mortals, is a stupid thing to do a Nocturnae, especially one who has just compelled you.

I can feel the hairs on the tips of our noses dance under the red light. "Where do we go from here then?" I ask.

"Mr. Harker, from this point forward you are now considered property of the United States."

I wasn't already? "Here we go again, the hypocritical United States laying claim to a bipedal hominid as their property after abolishing slavery."

"Take the property into custody of the United States Air Force, Dr. Eugene Shelley, laboratory Sub-Basement 2," she commands.

Boromir's doppelganger reveals a pair of bright silver, reinforced handcuffs.

If those get onto my wrists, my chances of escape lessen.

The man approaches and reaches out to put the cuffs on me as Jean continues her speech, "After transport, make sure Patient-XIV is ready for Phylogenetic Human Alteration with Nocturnae Genomics."

Odd she wouldn't just say: PHANG. Is she warning me or taunting me?

The man opens the cuff, and I slowly turn my wrists over, revealing the open shackles on my chair.

Gazing blankly, unaware of my action, Jean steps back for the man to take me into custody. "Dr. Shelley has requested the property be placed in the cell labeled *076-7-46*."

The man gasps and looks at me, wide-eyed in fear. "Dr. Allicines!"

The man smells of basil and … garlic. Huh, I guess she did bring me garlic after all. I lick my lips.

"Just attach the damn cuffs." Jean seems to have dismissed me as a minor threat. That's a mistake.

"He … he … he…" the man stammers.

"He. He. He, IS HUNGRY!" I taunt, flashing my crimson eyes.

The room stands still. The man drops the cuffs in the panic of his hands trying to find his face.

Jean reaches out into the darkness. "Someone talk to me! What's happening?!"

Effortlessly, I rise from my prison seat. The open shackles clank against the metal chair. I rub my wrists, enjoying my freedom.

From behind me, another man's breathing quickens and his heart races as fear consumes him. "Lights! Lights! Someone hit him with the *fucking* AP-lights!"

"It's not very fun when your nightmares are real, is it?" I sneer.

The dwarven-like man stands dumbfounded and motionless.

The man with the cuffs screams and pisses himself. He jerks, likely uncontrollably, and snaps back to reality. Immediately, he smashed a button hanging from his keychain. Glaring white lights blast on, momentarily blinding me. I throw my hands up to shield my eyes, but it radiates through my hand like it's not there.

"Weaponized sunlight," I say, squinting. "Can't say I'm surprised."

In utter disbelief, the man incessantly clicks the button, glancing from the lights, to me, and back again.

Jean abruptly finds the wall lets out an airy, "Oomph."

Each of the men take a step back and reach for their guns.

"What's the matter, gentlemen?" I ask, glancing up at the lights. "Was that supposed to hurt me?"

"Sunlight doesn't work on him!" Jean calls out frantically.

Clapping my hands slowly, I goad her, "I must say, Dr. Allicines, you've surprised me the last few days. You're intriguing, smart, strong. I like that"—licking my lips—"I pegged you for something much … less. As for the rest of you, I give you this opportunity to kneel before me and swear your service to me. Otherwise, well, you know the rest. You have until the count of three." I pause. "Three."

The man in front of me gasps, steps back again, and loses his footing. I pounce on him, grabbing his wrist and the top of his head, I stretch him, and sink my teeth into his neck. My lips quiver as his rich, warm blood flows into my mouth. I gulp down two huge mouthfuls, jerk him forward, and slam his face into the silver-lined, steel arm of my chair.

The blunt object caves his nose, cheek bones, and mandible in on themselves before coming to a sudden stop near the ear canal. Blood and brain matter splatter across the chair like a bug on the windshield.

I whip my head around and set my sights on the Aragorn-like fellow. Grabbing him by the hips, I lift and drive him into the ground, headfirst. His vertebrae explode like firecrackers on the Fourth of July.

The two men that stood behind me, Legolas and Gandalf, are

two full steps away with guns pointed at me.

I raise my hand and suck the blood off each finger and grin. "Bang!"

The men squeeze the trigger of their gun, but I've already palmed their faces. In one quick movement, I force their skulls together until they're an intermingled soup of blood, hair, and bone.

The dwarven-like man drops his gun and pivots for the door. With his back to me I grab his spine and pull hard, severing his sacrum. He watches from the top of my spinal trophy as his headless body falls to the floor.

Carelessly, I drop the trophy beside my chair and return to my seat, centered in the blood circle. Jean blindly stares back at me, fury raging across her face.

"Don't test me, dearie," I scold without raising my voice. "Although I have shared a brief history of my life with you, there is much you don't know. Much you won't know. I told you that I wasn't here for *you* dearie. You're still alive, *only* because I allow it."

"I know you won't hurt me," she shutters, quivering in fear.

Her body doesn't believe her lips, but she's right, I won't hurt her. However, she cannot truly know that.

I step to within a hair of our noses touching, so that she can feel my breath as I speak. "Now, I'm going to get what is mine. Do *not* intervene, because if you do, I'll come back for you just so I can slowly peel the skin off your body and tediously suck the blood from each strip while you wiggle and writhe in agonizing pain. Nod if you understand."

She nods, aggressively.

I could compel her to stay, but I think I've made my point. Jean's a smart girl, she knows I'm a man of my word. But what about Rahne? That's not my fight. That's not why I'm here. Claret is my only concern now.

"I bid you *au revoir*."

She stands silently and motionless as I calmly leave the room and make my way back to Dr. Shelley's laboratory. I hurry down the stairs until I come to the door. I try using SSgt. Burr's badge, but the door doesn't open. I should've kept Jean's.

I press my ear against the door to have a better idea of what's on the other side. I'd hate to get a face full of silver.

Silence. It's safe. But locked.

I flatten myself as evenly across the door as I can. As I drive my entire body into its cold, hard surface, the door slowly begins to creak within the clutches of the door frame. The walls surrounding the door begin to bow as the steel supports and cinder blocks crack under the pressure. The door-hinge pins splinter, popping from their tight, cold home. Bending, the door quickly and suddenly pops from its frame, slamming hard onto the floor.

I step through the battered walls and run through the lab, stopping in front of the secret door Dr. Shelley and Henry had shown me earlier. The Bastille.

Something's wrong.

I place the palm of my hand flat on the door, plug my ear with the other hand, close my eyes, and feel. A steady march of feet stampeding through the hallways clutters my auditory vision. The aperiodic march of feet makes it impossible to make an educated guess at the number of soldiers on the move to intercept me below.

Shit. I'm running out of time.

Using the heel of my foot, I kick the center of the locked door blocking my passage. The solid steel door lets out a painfully loud *clang* from the impact. The pins snap, but the door—oddly enough—stays shackled to its hinges. The door swings open, slamming into the opposing wall.

I carefully and quickly make my way through the corridor, down the spiral staircase, and into the final dark, damp arched hallway leading to the three steel doors. It takes me less than a minute with access to my Nocturnae abilities.

This is it. The moment I have been waiting for.

Nervously, I approach the door marked 252-7-38 and wrap my fingers around the cold, damp handle. The hinges echo through the halls as the door swings open. The pungent aroma of decaying flesh invades my nostrils, blitzing my lungs as the air pressure in the hallway and the prison room equalize, causing me to cough uncontrollably. Heat radiates from the prison room onto my face.

Disgusting.

There on the floor, in the very same position she'd been in earlier that day, atop a small, ragged piece of cloth, is Claret.

My Maker.

Slowly, I make my way toward her, my eyes never venturing from her. Her eyes study me, retreating to the far corner of her island.

What's going on? She recognized me last night. Was that a lucid moment, like an Alzheimer's patient would have?

"It's okay Claret."

Only six feet separate us.

How long has she been in this state?

"It's Sorin," I plead.

She neither moves nor acknowledges my voice. She only glares at me from the small corners of her eyes as if she expects the worst.

Three feet…

How feral is she? What is the overall extent of the psychological damage? Is there any coming back from this or is true death merciful?

"I'm here to take you home." My foot rests at the edge of the towel. "I'm going to take you somewhere safe, where they can't hurt you anymore," I beg with an outstretched hand.

She doesn't move.

What can I say to—

"Claret, Amicia sent me. I'm going to take you to her cabin," I lie, stretching my hand out just a little further than before.

Someone's on the staircase.

In a swift motion, Claret grips my palm in her thin bony fingers, wrapping them tightly around my wrist.

Suddenly, the sound of soldiers sweeping through Dr. Shelley's lab echoes through the passage. Claret drops my hand and retreats to her frightened state.

No! We have two minutes at best before The Company's military is upon us! Shit!

I look to my right, remembering the tiny thing who lives next door.

Wrapping my arms under hers, I wrangle Claret upright as she claws at my back, kicking my stomach and legs, biting my ears, face, and lips. I tighten my grip on her, ignore the pain, and drag her out of the cell.

Once safely in the hallway, I set her withered body on the hard, cool ground as gently as possible. Instinctively, she begins screaming and doing everything in her power to stay off the ground; terrified the ground will begin searing her in place.

She's out of the cell. Now, blood. There's no other option, it must be the child. Claret is more important than her.

Turning around with hatred for Dr. Shelley beaming from my eyes, I pry the door to Rahne's prison away from the wall. The door is thicker, denser, and sturdier than any of the other doors. It doesn't bend or break easily, but does eventually give way as I fold it into the wall.

Dog-like, Claret sniffs at the air, as an enticing aroma wafts into her senses. She rears her head in the direction of the sound of the screaming child. A devilish grin spreads across her face, and her bright crimson eyes latch onto the terrified youngling.

"Go on," I yell, gesturing to the open doorway.

She sprints to the meat.

Behind us, feet race down the last few steps.

Who's there? The military can't be here already.

A man sighs at the bottom of the stairs. I turn around to find Dr. Shelley breathing heavily and still holding onto the railing. His footsteps were covered by the thunderous rumblings of the MP making their way down hallways, stairs, and the lab.

The soldiers grow closer and closer.

Now the horrible man can watch in horror.

Dr. Shelley looks up at me. I smile at him and gesture toward Claret and Rahne. He gasps and tightens his grip on the railing as his legs go limp. His heart skips a beat as he watches my Maker move closer and closer to the closest thing he's ever had to a daughter.

I turn back to watch my Maker feed for the first time in almost 600 years. The girl tries to scurry up the wall behind her bed, but there is no escape. An intense silence washes over her as her eyes gape with horror. Her fists clench with ashen knuckles, and her nails drive deep into the palms of her soft little hands.

She is going to die.

**POP!**

What was that?

"Daddy!" she screams, and grips her chest with both hands.

Claret takes her leap.

A second *POP!*

Claret opens her mouth widely, mid-air. Saliva flies across her face like a rabid dog. She wraps herself around Rahne's body, forcing the air from the child's lungs. Their bodies impact the wall, causing it to splinter.

Violently, Claret tries to rip into the girl's throat with her sharp Nocturnae teeth, but the skin does not tear or perforate under her bite. Ferociously, she tries repeatedly to tear the thin, fleshy membrane from the screaming child to access the deep maroon, life-giving blood with no success.

Why isn't the skin tearing? The child should be minced meat by now.

Concern washes over my face as my jaw drops. "Claret! Get out of there! Now!"

Claret ignores me. Crimson fire burns from her eyes as bloodlust consumes her. She's become erratic and illogical. Only capable of thinking about the hunt and the sweet metallic taste of freshly squeezed blood at a perfect ninety-eight point six degrees Fahrenheit.

It is too late. The troops are here.

293

# 32

RAHNE'S COOL BLUE eyes flash a warm yellow and return to normal.

*What was that? Where have I seen this before?*

I watch Dr. Shelley. He remains rooted by the chaos while he battles his most basic of human instincts: fight or flight. On the one hand, he could grab a gun, risk his life, and help the soldiers in subduing Rahne, Claret and myself. On the other hand, he could sacrifice Rahne to the beast he's experimented on for decades to save his own life.

It doesn't take long for the old man to turn around and quickly hobble back up the stairs. He hugs the rail, holding on tightly as a seemingly endless line of armed men rush down the steps.

*Pathetic.*

Turning back, I see Rahne's young, flawless body limp in Claret's grip. Still fixated on acquiring her first good meal in years, Claret doubles down, feverishly trying to pierce the child's soft outer shell without success.

"Move away from the girl," a soldier yells as he makes his way down the dark hallway.

Claret stops and turns her head to the humans.

Shit! This hallway somehow distorts my hearing. How many are there, seven? Eighteen? I can't tell.

"You," another soldier barks, "freeze! Hands up!"

"Is it freeze or hands up?" I snap. "You can't have it both—"

**Bang!**

Instantly, my shoulder fills with a searing pain only caused by silver entering my body. The heat of the liquid silver moves to my chest and quickly into my arms and the rest of my body.

Falling to one knee, I scream, "How dare you!?" Fuck, this hurts!

From the ground I pucker my lips, curl my tongue, and blow hard. Outside the normal auditory range of a human, an infrasonic tone echoes through the hall, causing the small group of soldiers to keel over in extreme nausea.

Huh, I guess brown note isn't hypothetical after all.

Claret turns to the soldiers, Rahne's ragged body dangling unconscious in her hand, and smiles. She tosses the child's body into the corner of the room and sprints toward the crowd of armed men.

Rahne's head cracks hard against the cinder block wall, and she crashes into her bed, tumbling hard onto the floor. Her body folds in half while her limbs lie disheveled beside her.

How long will it take for this silver to pass? Damn it!

The humans look up and fumble for their guns.

"Oh SHIIIIITTT!" yells one of the soldiers.

Claret drops her hips, preparing to pounce.

Suddenly, from her hunched over position, Rahne's head shoots toward the ceiling as she lets out a blood curdling scream.

All living things in the corridor freeze.

It's a scream unlike any other scream I'd heard before. It's the sound of an ancient threat, long forgotten. The humans behind me allow their guns to fall off target as they stand awestruck. The entire room watches her.

Breathlessly, Rahne screams at the heavens. A moment later, the sound of breaking bones echoes in the hall. Her body convulses as it breaks from within.

How hasn't the child passed out from this pain yet?

"Claret!" I scream, begging for her consciousness to return and help me.

She ignores my plea and remains fixated on the child.

I fall to all fours. The silver has circulated throughout my entire body.

Not now. I'm so close. So close to getting Claret out of here.

I vomit.

Rahne's voice grows hoarse, almost animal-like and into a low, deep growl. Foam collects in the corners of her mouth. Her hips shoot toward the wall in front of her, as her neck is thrust back, forcing her chest toward the ceiling and her body weight onto her hamstrings.

Her white camisole starts to rip at the seams. One after another, her ribs erupt from her chest, cracking like the legs of a crustacean before dunking the soft meat into melted butter. As her screams continue and her growl deepens, boils form across her body. Dark black fur sprouts from every bulbous pore.

The child's camisole is now speckled with the hues of blood and pus as her skin continues to stretch to new limits. Aware of her body changing, the girl raises her hands, staring at her flawless palms just as something begins moving under the skin, within the muscles and between the bones.

Crying as her fingernails fall from their resting places, the tips of her fingers sprout dark, razor-like claws. Blood runs down her forearms. The joints in her fingers swell as the tiny bones between them elongate and widen. Rags of flesh and skin stretched tightly across two large paws are all that remain of her once petite, soft hands.

Rahne's feet and limbs grow to monstrous proportions, pushing the bridge of her back into the seven-foot ceiling. Her childish head rests awkwardly atop her hulking, black-haired body as she peers over her shoulder at us.

Her sad blue eyes fill with pain, confusion, and fear. A fear that echoes through her soul, as her eyes fade completely into a pale yellow.

This is what I saw. In Genevieve's dream. The figure in the trees was a Lygos.

The yellowness of her eyes intensifies, growing radiant. The bones in her face and skull splinter and move under the skin tearing from within, leaving her face bloody, wretched, and unrecognizable.

Her head hangs heavy from the brilliance of the jet-black mane that flows from her mid-back to the back of the head. At the nape of her neck is an island of snowy fur in the shape of a diamond.

Thick, heavy drool flows from Claret's open mouth, pooling on the floor. She blinks wildly and licks her lips, overwhelmed by the scent of so much blood.

A deafening scream intensifies as the towering monster grows into her final form.

Dear Maker almighty...

She staggers off the bed, losing her balance and falling hard against the wall. Taking the full brunt of the impact with her head, she quickly cradles her grisly skull within the horrific hand-like claws. The monster falls frighteningly silent on the floor.

The room is too small for the creature to lie flat, forcing her to land on her knees as if praying to whatever god she hopes will save her. The hair from her upper and lower arms meets cumbersomely at the elbow, forming a dagger-like pelt of fur protruding from her powerful forearm.

I can't move. The silver, it's too much.

"Claret, get out of here!"

She ignores me and silence echoes through the hall with all parties waiting in angst, staring at the hulking creature.

Is she dead?

Discomfort and fear emanate from the meat snacks to my right; they know their armor won't save them from the beast's claws.

No one moves. Everyone stares at the beast. She looks dead.

After four, very long, seconds, the beast breaks the silence with a large inhale.

"It's still alive! FIRE! FIRE! FIRE! WEAPONS HOT! WEAPONS HOT! I repeat, OPEN FIRE," a soldier yells, breaking the silence.

The soldiers unleash a fury of metal through the air, narrowly missing Claret's left shoulder. She grimaces as bullets whistle past her head and she throws herself to the floor.

Seconds later, the empty rifles softly click in succession. The room goes quiet, and the creature doesn't move.

The commander lifts his gun and smiles. "That's it boys," he says as the others lower their weapons.

"Damn that was crazy!" one shouts, relieved, as the others laugh.

*PLINK!*

A bullet fragment pops out of the creature's back and onto the ground, but the creature remains still.

*PLINK!*

Another fragment.

Silently, the creature rises from her folded state.

Mid-high-five, a soldier's eyes widen at the sight of the creature. "LOOK!"

It's too late.

"WEREWOLF," a couple of the soldiers yell before dropping their weapons and running down the hallway.

The creature cries out, long and hard. She flashes her long fangs, spraying saliva from her jowls. Her yellow eyes soullessly fill with the rage from being locked away for so long and looks at us all, hostile.

Reality sweeps over all of us. We are outmatched. We are all likely going to die in the next few moments.

Suddenly, I catch a whiff of a familiar scent. Whiskey and tobacco from the breath of a saddened, pathetic, narcissistic man … Dr. Shelley. Standing there, far at the other end of the hallway at the foot of the spiral staircase, still clutching the railing in one hand.

I'd thought he'd made his way back up to his lab before the first shot was ever fired.

Dr. Shelley squints, straining his old eyes to see into the abyss. His eyes widen and he gasps, shuttering at the sight of the hulking black humanoid wolf creature.

"Rahne," he says under his breath, falling over in grief and remorse as his face and eyes swell. "My poor sweet Rahne."

The creature raises her snout and sniffs twice.

Dr. Shelley's hand falls heavy from the railing and he takes a small step toward the creature. "Rahne. Come on, sweetheart, wake up," he pleads, taking another half-step.

Wake up? Is that even right?

Crippled and unable to move, I watch Dr. Shelley.

"When Michelle, my wife, died with our unborn child I never thought…" he sniffles and takes another step. "I never thought I'd ever love again or hear a child call me *daddy*."

I look to the creature as her head tilts to one side, studying the old man.

Is he getting through to her?

For a second, I have perfect clarity of the creature: the potential speed, her mass, the plague-wielding claws. The tainted breath and tormenting voice cloud the beautiful, golden eyes of ice.

Claret turns to me from over her shoulder, pushing her thoughts into my own.

Like a time-lapse film of how the forest is born and dies only to be reborn again the following year, she shows me a litany of potential futures she's compiled from our current situation. In the two or three seconds that pass, I watch her die in countless horrific ways at the hands of the beast that stands before her.

No.

Claret blinks, breaking the bridge between our minds, allowing time to regain its grip on our reality.

"Claret, don't—" I cry from the floor.

The creature focuses on the nearest potential threat, Claret.

Claret smiles and flinches at the creature.

With fear radiating from her eyes, the creature lashes out with her large claws.

"RAHNE! DON'T!" Dr. Shelley shouts from behind Claret, covering himself with his arm.

Claret jerks back, narrowly escaping the creature's claw. She stumbles backwards, trying to regain her footing and knocks Dr. Shelley into the wall. He falls to the ground unconscious.

The creature comes at Claret with a quick jab and a ferocious cross, unifying all of her energy into a single, quick blow.

Claret screams, unable to dodge the attack and takes the full force to her skull, hurling her through the air. Her head cracks hard against the stone ground, bouncing four times before skidding to a stop just outside my reach. Slowly, her face begins to resemble its true structure as the bones and muscles in her face reconfigure, stalling partway through the process due to her weakened state.

The creature roars and sets her sights on the soldiers.

I've got to act fast.

Although my entire body feels like it is burning on the inside from the silver circulating through my veins, I have to do something. Forcing myself to one knee, I gasp for air.

I need to flush this tainted blood.

I turn my sights to the distracted humans who've become statues at the sight of the creature.

I've got one shot at this.

In one fell swoop, I pounce on two nearby men. I tear out the first man's carotid and send him spiraling through the air. He lands a foot from Claret.

"DRINK!" I yell. Turning back to the man under my palm, I quickly sink my teeth into his neck.

I smile coming up from the body, but instantly scream in pain as boiling liquid silver spills from my pores and into the bloody mess around me.

A little better.

Leaping at his comrades as they fumble to change out their magazines, I smack the first one across his face. His head spins around—quite literally—spraying his teeth like chiclets along the way. The second pisses himself at the sight of his friend.

A gift for my Maker.

The man's eyes snap to mine and quickly dilate, allowing me access to his mind. I push the idea for him to go lie next to Claret on the floor. Breaking the link, I move on to the next soldier while he walks fearlessly over to Claret and lies down.

Claret gulps the man's blood without a thought.

I look over my shoulder and stop.

The creature, standing on the remains of five men, sways her head, licking the air. Her golden yellow eyes dilate whenever Claret is centered in her field of view.

Claret whips her head around at the beast and roars, sprinting toward it.

A ferocious battle cry echoes from the creature's monstrous jaw as she slams her upper limbs into the ground, catapulting herself forward.

She moves like nothing I've ever seen.

Claret's head jerks as she tries to track the creature.

Impossible.

The creature bounds from floor to wall to ceiling, and back to floor effortlessly. Never slowing.

In a flash of blood, spit, and fur, the creature grabs Claret and slams her into the ground fifty feet back, almost to the staircase. Pinned under one of the creature's massive hind feet, Claret screams in pain as the creature's claws tear into her ribs while pummeling her face.

The bones in Claret's face shatter only to mend in time for the next blow, restarting the cycle.

The remaining soldiers make a mad dash for Claret's prison cell, slamming the door shut behind them and locking it.

Uncontrollably, I keel over and vomit a bloody mercury-like pile of fluid onto the stone floor.

Finally, the silver's out … most of it anyway.

Without a second thought, I charge the beast from behind. I can hear the soldiers pushing at one another so they can see through the small opening in the door.

Almost in striking distance, I cock my arm to deliver a hard blow to Rahne's kidney.

The creature's arm snaps back faster than I can see, and she palms my face like a basketball. My feet fly forward, still moving, turning my body into a bullwhip. Every joint is pulled from its socket, as every vertebra slips, straining muscles, and ligaments.

I try to scream from the pain, but I can't open my mouth under the creature's grip.

Panicking from the lack of oxygen, my limbs flail wildly under the creature's crushing grip. Kicking Rahne's stomach and hitting her forearm, I frantically try to free myself but fail, miserably. Although she stares at me through her golden eyes from over her shoulder, Rahne batters Claret's skull into the ground with a hammer fist.

My quick movements distract the creature long enough for Claret to regain consciousness and react.

The beast throws another punch. The fist slips through the air, Claret rotates her body on the floor, staying out of the fist's path. She grips the monstrous wrist, pulling it into her chest, rotating her body again, this time to the opposite side of the creature's arm. Kicking her legs back and raising her hips, she locks them behind the creature's head and back.

Quickly the monster drops me, recruiting the other arm to defend against Claret's counterattack, but it is too late. Claret has Rahne locked in an armbar. Driving her hips forward into Rahne's elbow, the beast cries out in agony as she claws at Claret, trying to free her arm.

In a final attempt to save the arm from being broken, the creature raises it high before slamming Claret into the floor, forcing the air from her lungs.

All the effort in the world isn't enough to prevent Claret from loosening her grip, allowing the creature to break free.

The beast's crushing jaws slowly turn toward me.

I look on in horror, examining the beast in her beautiful terror. Fear overtakes me as I stare into the eyes of death. I imagine this is what the hundreds of thousands of humans felt before I killed them.

She brings my face close. The top of my head is right under her nose. She sniffs me intently, searching for something. A large tongue reveals itself from behind dagger-like teeth and it slowly runs over my face.

I hit and kick and try to scream in hopes of freeing myself, but the creature persists.

This is it.

This is my true death.

As the creature's tongue retreats and she lets out a skin-flapping roar, I close my eyes in preparation for the end.

Claret punches the monster.

I open my eyes, only to find the creature's hairy back staring back at me as I fall to the ground.

The creature dropped me. No, threw me to the ground.

Claret circles the hulking beast so she is Rahne's only target.

My heart sinks as I gasp for air under the weight of the thought that I'll never be able to see her again. To touch her. To smell her. To learn from her.

The creature grips Claret's torso and brings her body up to her face. Meticulously, the beast inspects her, sniffing and licking her. The monster grimaces, exhaling quickly, spewing snot throughout the room. Her scent seems to disgust the creature, reigniting Rahne's fiery rage.

Claret screams as the beast digs sharp claws into her back, pulling her ribs from her spine. I helplessly stare up at the imminent massacre.

Claret looks at me.

Our eyes meet.

My mind floods with the memories we shared. From the night we met all those years ago, where she gazed down upon my sickened body, to the forest where she first showed a neophyte his potential, to my first feeding where she watched me from atop the hill outside the town; she was there, encouraging me. And she was proud.

My head throbs under the pressure as she pushes every memory of hers into my mind. I now see the one thing she had kept locked away in her shattered, traumatized mind that gave her the smallest bit of joy: me.

She breaks the connection with a blink and a smile. "I love you. Mo Chroí."

In one quick motion Claret's body tears between the towering beast's hands. Blood pours onto the floor, thickly flowing from her hanging entrails.

# 33



I SPENT THE better part of my existence searching for her, only to have her taken from me at our moment of reunion. To witness my Maker's gruesome true death as she's ripped apart by the hands of this colossal horror of biology.

The creature rears her head. In her strong, bony claws, she holds what remains of Claret. The beast rolls her back, repositioning herself into a crouch and gnaws on what's left of my Maker's left side.

Frozen, I stare on in terror as Rahne consumes my beloved Maker. As I look on, I grow ever more fearful the creature might drop her snack at any moment, in search of a juicier, fresher morsel to cleanse her palate.

Me.

The monster's powerful jaws crush Claret's bones with ease, slurping flesh, organs, and entrails like they are noodles covered in sauce.

Bringing myself to my feet, my heart races. My mind only has one thought: *vengeance*. I lunge, forcing my compromised limbs to do my bidding, and kick the beast squarely in the groin.

The creature's skin ripples as the energy transfers from my body into her fur. Shockingly, the monster doesn't move. She doesn't even seem to notice what should have been a crippling blow. Instead, she remains focused on the meal in her hands.

I lunge again, pounding my fists into her ribs, until I realize I've caused more damage to myself than to the beast.

Swallowing the last of Claret's foot, the creature turns and backhands me out of the way.

The world goes black.


MY VISION RETURNS, leaving me confused by the world I see. It is dark, yes, but I'm looking straight at the stone floor and also at my crotch. It takes a moment for me to realize the impact caused one of my eyeballs to pop out of its socket. I carefully cup the eye, popping it back in.

My body always heals faster than my mind in situations like this. I don't know if that's a me thing or if that's a Nocturnae thing. Nor does it really matter. However, it's unsettling when you—an apex predator of legend—are fine, physically, but have the mental acuity of a lobotomy patient.

As my mind returns to a state of equilibrium, I realize the hall is silent and absent of the scent of wet dog.

The creature is gone. Dr. Shelley is gone.

I hobble up the stairs, growing steadier with every step until I reach the landing.

Logically… Who am I kidding, this is no creature of logic.

I sprint down the hall.

This is a creature of chaos. Of emotion.

I bolt up the stairs.

A creature that brutally murders all living things in her path seemingly uncontrollably…

I run blindly into the lab and abruptly stop.

…Except for me. The beast, she didn't kill me.

The lab has been completely destroyed. Papers are scattered everywhere. Equipment broken. Pens, pencils, books, and glass create a collage of chaos on the off-white tile flooring. Decades of research destroyed.

"Well, that solves that problem," I say to the empty room.

Why me? Why didn't Rahne kill me? She tore Claret in half. She slaughtered the humans. But when it came to me, she only swatted me away like I was an annoying gnat buzzing in her ears, even after I attacked her…

The dead silence of the room is broken as a woman's scream echoes from a staircase.

Who's screaming? Jean? Could be. Sounds like it's coming from my old cell. Shit, the beast has Jean.

Leaping over the rubble, I hurriedly make my way up the spiraling staircase to the floor where I'd been imprisoned for three days.

I exit the closed stairwell and emergency lights flash nearly blinding me with their intensity. Blinded by a spotlight shining on the stairway door, I trip on the tattered remains of George Washington's painted face. From the debris pattern, it is clear the creature had entered my previous prison through one side of the wall and exited farther down.

Jean is not here, but neither is her blood.

Water trickles down the walls and onto the floor. Cables and wiring dangle from the ceiling. A power cord sparks between the wet linoleum floor and the cinder block wall.

The impact of the creature's large feet on the floors above reverberates through the ceiling.

The beast has her.

I turn and jog toward the elevator shaft, keeping an ear out for the creature's movements. Two nerdy-looking engineers come racing out of an adjoining room and into the wide, long hallway. They stop suddenly at the sight of me. Terror spreads across their faces.

"Back inside," I say, gesturing at the room.

Their shoes screech on the floor as they scramble to their feet and run back down the hallway.

I look to my left and see the elevator shaft. Half of the door is missing, and the other half is crooked in the doorway.

Jean screams. She's alive. Good.

I jump into the shaft and grab onto the thick metal cabling. I pull myself up, stopping at an opening that couldn't be made by anything other than that creature. Except maybe a M1-A tank.

The hallway I pull myself into looks exactly like the one I've just come from. Most likely an architectural deterrent, designed to disorient potential enemy combatants, prisoners, or creatures like me in the building.

I run toward the destruction, down the halls in ruins, into a shattered stairwell and find a gaping hole in the middle of the staircase wall blanketed in the light of the full moon.

The creature's outside.

The path of annihilation continues, through the base and the fence surrounding its border. I follow the path into the forest until I come to a vast, open clearing in the wilderness.

The tops of the trees form a crease in the speckled midnight sky. There, in the middle of the clearing the monster stands, with her back to me, staring up, mesmerized by the moon's awesome glow.

Not far to the right of the creature, on the ground, lies Jean. She has her arms wrapped tightly around her legs and her eyes are wide with fear. Scared of where she is. Scared of what is going to happen next. Scared that no one will find her.

"Jean," I call out over the snow-covered glade.

Her head perks up like a rabbit listening for an incoming predator. Cautiously, I make my way toward the middle of the field.

The hulking beast doesn't flinch a muscle as I grow closer. Her breathing doesn't even change. She doesn't fear me or anything else in this world.

I keep my eyes on the creature as I walk to Jean and kneel beside her to check for wounds. "Are you okay?"

"Sorin?" she asks, loosening her grip on her legs.

"Yes, Jean, I am here," I say, touching her shoulder. "I need to get you out of here."

"No," she says sharply.

"What do you mean *no*? This creature just ripped my Maker in half!"

With trembling hands, she blindly reaches for the creature. "I can't explain it, but I know for a fact it won't hurt me. I couldn't see the creature, but when it picked me up, I felt safe. It was like I knew the creature. Like we were one…"

"Jean."

"Yes?"

Passionately, I wrap her hands in mine. "I cannot be certain, but I think I know why you feel so comfortable around her." I stare up in wonder at the night sky, awestruck by the giant red moon, and continue, "I think this…"

The hulking black-haired monster lets out a blood-curdling, howling, scream into the silence of the night. The same sound it made when it … she … Rahne completed her transformation.

I watch in horror from only a few yards away as the monster beats the earth under her feet, screaming uncontrollably like it is burning from the inside. The creature drops to all fours and digs her claws into the snowy earth, grunting heavily.

Extending her back to the heavens, Rahne's howl changes to agony as chunks of her flesh fall from her once monstrous body. Her bones pop and shrink. Astonishingly, the transformation begins to reverse much more quickly, but seems to be equally as painful. The terrifying roar of unbearable pain turns into a horrified scream as the monster returns back to the bloody, naked body of a young girl, barely ten years of age.

Jean looks at me and her eyes flash yellow. "She's my…"

# 34



MID-AFTERNOON ON Monday, roughly 2,000 miles away, a CH-47 Chinook helicopter, escorted by two AH-64 Apaches, descended to the ocean of sand.

The helicopter blades kicked up more and more sand the closer it got to the ground. The rear cargo door folded down as it hovered inches from the desert floor. Dr. Shelley made his way down the ramp with a denim satchel slung across his body, squinting into the blinding sun.

Dr. Shelley distanced himself from the ramp, stopped, and turned to watch the helicopters lift off and speed away, leaving him alone in the empty, barren wasteland. He scanned the sand dunes that ripple on for eternity in every direction and stopped when he noticed a small shadow in the center of a dune. He squinted at it, and then started walking to the tiny shadow.

"There it is," he said to himself, smiling.

Carefully he walked through the sand, watching as the shadow became more and more door-like. Thirty feet from the door he could tell the dimensions of the concrete entrance: one meter wide, one meter deep, and a little more than two meters high.

Once at the smooth steel door, he looked around for a doorknob or handle or anything to open it. Suddenly, he remembered the key fob the Director gave him after their meeting. Pulling it from a side pocket of his satchel, he slowly ran it along the edge of the door.

The door hissed as fresh air rushed in, and its internal latches released.

Dr. Shelley returned the key fob to his pocket and slid the door open. A single light illuminated the ground just inside the door, revealing a three-by-three-foot landing.

Carefully, he stepped onto the landing and peered into the dark depths of the large cylindrical room. He gasped, unable to see the bottom and set his sights on the unending spiral stone staircase running along the cylindrical chamber's walls like the thread of a screw.

Making his way to the first step, he began the long, tiring process of walking to the bottom. Three steps into his journey he found a six-inch-long metal rod sticking out of the wall with a sign to the right of it: IF UP, PULL DOWN.

The old man grabbed the handle and, with all his strength, pulled the handle down. The sound of granite rubbing together resonated through the cylindrical chamber as the single light above the entrance flickered out.

From far below, the chamber began to brighten as can lights hidden in the walls flick ON. With the room fully illuminated, Dr. Shelley noticed lettering on the wall that read:

Nearly an hour passed by the time Dr. Shelley reached the bottom of the staircase.

He studied a seal painted on the floor; unlike anything he'd seen before. Six circles, one large and five small, overlapped one another and were connected through intersecting lines. Each of the smaller circles encapsulated a unique symbol.

Dr. Shelley bent down. "Nordic runes?" he asked himself, but as he ran his fingers over the symbols, he realized the curvature of the symbols were reminiscent of alchemical symbols. "Strange," he mused.

The double door entrance that stood behind the seal was massive. It was nearly five meters high and four meters across and covered in a strange texture with alluring colors. Flecks of silver and gold twinkled across the doors' iron surface.

A number pad sat off to the right, safeguarding the secrets contained behind the door. Dr. Shelley walked over to the keypad and noticed the twenty-one blank spaces above it and quickly entered the access code: 642-4235-83-77-2623-427-84-6.

The instant the final digit was entered, the wall behind the number pad let out a thunderous rumble and shook as gears moved the large doors. The doors opened to reveal a dark hallway, lit by a single emergency light.

The door stopped abruptly, leaving a three-meter-wide opening. More than enough room for Dr. Shelley to mosey on through.

Once inside, Dr. Shelley whispered, "Lights."

The lights snapped ON, revealing a massive warehouse filled with medical and other scientific laboratory equipment, computers, and filing cabinets. The two opposing walls were lined with prison doors of various shapes and sizes. Each door had a name plate, similar to the prison doors in Dr. Shelley's lab.

Making his way down the wall to his left, he passed two doors: 944-84-569 and 736-94-447.

### 944-84-569

```
WARNING: Malevolent, cannibalistic
Subject contained. Gaunt skeleton-like
figure with incredible physical strength.
Do not open this door or the window under
any circumstances. The cries of the
Subject may be fatal.
If Subject has escaped, call 727-0323.
```

### 736-94-447

```
WARNING: Charming and exquisitely horrid
Subject contained. True physical form is
unknown. Do not speak to Subject.
Exchanging words with the Subject may
lead to hallucinations, early onset of
terminal diseases, and/or infertility.
If Subject has escaped, call 727-0239.
```

He stopped at a door labeled: 053-8-79.

### 053-8-79

```
WARNING: Bloodthirsty, cunning Subject
```

> contained. Tall, slender male of unknown
> age and origin. Do not look into
> Subject's eyes. May cause loss of
> inhibitions and may lead to death.
> If Subject has escaped, call 727-2191.

Dr. Shelley slid open the small window at eye level and whispered, "Hello," into the darkness. He backed away from the door, allowing light to fill a small section of the cell.

A tall, swarthy man walked out of a corner of darkness and into the light. He was slender but well-muscled, reminiscent of an Ancient Egyptian pharaoh. His long, well-worn cloak trailed behind him. He eyed Dr. Shelley.

"How is my favorite Subject today?"

"It's been many years since someone of your kind descended here. It's been even longer since one of you dared to look upon my face."

"You will be seeing much more of me now…"

The cloaked man said nothing.

Dr. Shelley paced slowly in front of the door with one hand in the small pocket of his satchel. "My most recent Subject, has been… relocated, and I have to continue my research; but the last time you were in my care you made quite a mess of things."

"And that's why you're here?"

"Correct. I can't risk another incident when I'm so close," Dr. Shelley said, fumbling for the vials of blood in his satchel.

Pulling his hand from the bag he, for a second, cupped an Italian sapphire blue pocket Watch with a series of runes etched around the edges.

A deep blue glint quickly ran around the edge of the cloaked man's eyes, and Dr. Shelley's head snapped forward like something suddenly took control of him.

The mysterious man stepped back into the darkness of his prison, interlocking his arms behind him. "What has happened? What new information would be of interest to me?"

Dr. Shelley was unable to move his body, his eyes, or even blink. A force had taken over him, compelling him to answer. "A child of Encomiâ has been born."

"A child of the sisters is born every day. Why should I care about this one in particular?"

Dr. Shelley cleared his throat. "Not born, as in birthed from a mother. Born, as in born anew. Born *again* under the Super Wolf Blood Moon. Born Lygos."

Stepping back into the light revealing a crimson flash in his eyes, the cloaked man grinned. "Tell me everything."

# PART II: LYGOS

# 35



JEAN ALLICINES LIES awake thinking of all the ways she could kill herself.

With concerted effort, she rolled over in her bed, knocking an empty pizza box into a cascade of tissues, old take-out boxes, and a pill bottle stamped: Lexapro. Her anti-depressant. Prescribed for postpartum depression.

The drapes were mostly drawn. The room and its only occupant were suspended in a perpetual darkness interrupted only by a single beam of sunlight during the day or a passing car at night.

She slid her head out from under the covers and clicked the button on her talking alarm clock to get the time: *The time is twelve a.m.*

Still so much time until dawn…

She reached past the pill bottle for her phone when her sightless eyes landed on a bassinet. Although she couldn't see it, she knew it was there. Soft and white. It stood near a dresser with folded onesies, diapers, and cute little outfits piled on top. Wipes sat beside the changing pad and a frame on the wall read: I LOVE YOU LITTLE ONE.

It was a corner filled to the brim with all things a mother would need for her newborn child.

Her *first* child.

The alarm on her clock beeped, tearing her empty gaze from the corner of cuteness to the half-empty bottle of vodka beside her clock. She grabbed the bottle and popped the cork with her teeth. She took a swig and silenced the alarm with the bottom of the bottle.

Jean groaned and threw her legs over the edge of her bed. After a minute, she slid her feet into the purple bunny slippers beside the bed and shuffled to the bathroom door with the vodka bottle dangling in one hand.

Without turning on the light, she sat on the cold toilet seat to relieve herself. She reached for a mechanical device lying between the toilet and the tub. The device had two long, clear cords extending from its base to suction cups with bottles distending beneath—a breast pump.

Flipping the machine's power button to ON, the room was bathed in a red glow and quickly filled with an awful sucking sound. One at a time, she covered each of her nipples with a cup, grimacing when it latched.

She took another swig of vodka and slouched back on the toilet seat with her pants around her ankles, listening to the pulsating slurps emanating from the machine as tears ran down her face.

This irrational cycle continued for thirteen days.

A knock on the bedroom door woke her suddenly, and she clicked her clock: *The time is eight fifteen a.m.* Jean was tired of these knocks. The rapping on her door came at roughly the same time each day, delivered in precisely the same manner. And in a sickeningly gentle fashion.

"Good morning sweetie. There's breakfast right outside your door if you're hungry. I'm heading to class. But I'll come home for dinner. Love you."

She always groaned and rolled over, cocooning herself in the blankets. She'd hated mornings, even before her world fell apart.

The man paused, then placed his forehead on the door. "I'm here for you. To talk. To listen. To cry with. Whatever you need. I worry about you. I just…"

She heard the despair in his voice, but couldn't bring herself to speak to him. Not yet.

"I'll see you when I get back," the man called up the stairs, and closed the front door.

One day, in the early afternoon, an out of cycle knock on the door. "Jean?" Silence. He tried again. "Jean. Come on sweetie." Silence. "Jean, it's been weeks."

"Go away," she said, muffled by the pillow.

*Knock! Knock! Knock!*

"Jean. Come on."

Lifting her head, Jean yelled, "Go away GG!"

"I'm coming in, in three, two—"

She pressed her face into her pillow. "Please. No." Twisting herself deeper into her blankets she buried herself in bed.

"One."

The door opened quickly, flooding the room with light. GG recoiled at the sight of the landfill that surrounded her bed. The scent of body odor, vodka, and rotting food hit him in the face like a fist.

He regained his composure and carefully made his way to her bedside. Slowly he reached his hand into the blanket, searching for an opening in the covers.

"There you are," he said, laying his hand softly against her cheek. "You've got to be hungry. Let's get something in your belly."

The covers rustled as Jean shook her head. "No." Her stomach gurgled.

"Liar." GG patted the bed. "How about grilled cheese?"

Slowly, Jean revealed her head from the den of blankets. "I like grilled cheese."

"Okay. And then," GG sniffed the air and covered his nose, "we're going to *try* and get this smell out of here. If we can."

"This is stupid." Jean placed her head on GG's lap.

"What is, sweetie?"

"I can't even cry anymore. It's like I'm all out of tears." She looked up at him. "How is that even possible?"

"Sweetie," he said, pointing at her. "I want to know how it's possible your boob is hanging out of the neck of your hoodie. Hanging out of an over-sized sleeve or the bottom of a shirt, sure. But the neck of a hoodie … that, that is impressive."

"Shut up. You like it."

"Uh-uh girl. Only dick for this fella. Boobs are fun to play with though," he joked, bouncing her breast in the palm of his hand.

"Stop it," she laughed, covering herself.

Pushing the wispy hair out of her face, she closed her eyes as he caressed her head. Fresh tears sprung free and ran down her cheeks as they sat in silence.

Eventually she turned her head and said, "I'm glad you're here."

"I wouldn't be anywhere else." Looking around the room, he grimaced, "Okay, that's a lie … I'd *like* to be at Target getting cleaning supplies, trash bags, and candles for this nasty, nasty room that you've destroyed." Playfully, he jerked toward the dresser. "Oh gawd, I think I saw a rat!"

"Stop it," Jean laughed, swatting his leg. "You did not."

GG turned up his nose. "It smells like a straight boys' locker room in here."

# 36



A BLOOD SUCKER, a blind woman, and an ancient horror masked as a ten-year-old girl walk into a bar…

All joking aside, that's *exactly* how it feels as I stare at the image in front of me. A Nocturnae and once again, the *last* Nocturnae, standing in the middle of a dew-ridden glade between two of the most unlikely of creatures.

I look right: Jean. A mother. *The* mother. She kneels in the snow holding her chest, softly gasping for air, eyes wide.

I look left: Rahne. The once hulking Lygos lies naked on the ground in her human form. She's nestled in a pool of black fur and the biogenic ooze that was her Lygos self. Her once beautiful strawberry-blonde hair clings to her body like it's soaked in oil. She lets out a heavy sigh and falls onto her side.

Jean's head whips toward the sound, and she quickly scrambles toward the child.

The steaming furry wet soup surrounding Rahne doesn't faze

Jean as she crawls through it and wraps Rahne's limp body in her arms. A mother holding her child at last.

"I've got you," Jean whispers.

Cue the stereotypical slow cello music.

Slowly, as to not startle Jean, I walk toward her. "Is she alright?"

"Yes, she's asleep." Jean pulls back from Rahne's steaming body and combs the sticky hair from the child's brow. "Exhausted, but she appears to be fine."

Exhausted is likely an understatement. She grew roughly ten-times her human size in the matter of a minute, destroyed the facility, and fought off me, my feral Maker, and roughly twenty highly-armed Company members in less than an hour. But yeah. Sure. She's *fine*.

"We need to leave." I gently place my hand on Jean's shoulder, prodding her. "Now."

Jerking away, she glares back at me. "*We?* We're a *'we'* now? An hour ago, you killed my men—like actually killed them, not in self-defense because they shot first. Then, you left me for dead in a room of carnage. And now, *now* you wanna leave together?"

"Yes."

"This whole time you've said you came for what was yours. Well now you have her! Go run off with Claret and leave me alone."

I hesitate, glancing over at the sleeping child. How do you tell a mother her daughter murdered the thing you love? "She's dead." You don't. "We need to go. Now."

Jean's mouth falls open. "I'm … I'm so sorry Sorin. She meant so much to you." She rolls a handful of the wolf-ooze in her hand. "Why are you helping us?"

I shouldn't be.

"The Company wants all of us now." I carefully stuff my hand into my pocket. "You. Me. And especially, her. If we want to live, our best bet is to stick together." I hold the delicate boutonniere Jean gave me in my hand—reliving her kind gesture.

"The enemy of my enemy is my friend," Jean mumbles under her breath.

Enemy. A gross oversimplification. Former boss tries to kill her, while the Nocturnae she helped to torture doesn't.

Humans.

"Let's go."

# 37



RAHNE'S EYES FLUTTER open. "Mr. Burr?"

Mr. Burr? Oh, that's right, I was impersonating SSgt. Timothy Burr when I met her. "Sorin is fine." I smile and take my stolen ABU coat off, wrapping it around her. "Hello again little one. You've had quite a day."

Jean relents and pulls the coat around Rahne's shoulders.

"Thank you, Mr. Sorin," Rahne says.

So polite for someone so young. "You're quite welcome. Can you stand?" I ask, placing a hand on either side of her in case she loses balance.

Rahne nods and slowly stands.

Jean pushes herself to her feet. "We need to go to my cabin."

That's awfully specific … What's at the cabin? I hate cabins. "Why?"

"We'll be safe there."

I shake my finger. "We could go to any cabin and be just as safe, but you said *my cabin*. Why?"

"After you compelled me, I went somewhere." She closes her eyes like she's forcing herself to see the memory. "A dark, floating shadow with purple eyes told me to go there when I was in the—…shit, what did you call it?" She snaps her fingers four times. "The Void."

There are creatures in the Void? Why haven't I ever seen them? Do only blind people see them? "What did the creature look like?"

Could she have seen the creature because she was compelled for so long?

"Its face was hidden within the hood of its cloak. But it showed me the moment that,"—she places her hand on Rahne's head—"my baby was stolen from me. Then the creature revealed my old cabin tucked deep in the woods."

"And it told you to go there?"

"No." Jean shakes her head. "But it showed me a truth from the past, and I just feel like they're somehow connected."

"Did it say anything to you?"

"Only one word: Prophecy," Jean says.

Could this be the same prophecy Claret and the others spoke of? "Where's your cabin?"

"Harrisville, Michigan."

The middle of fucking nowhere, but spitting distance to the Canadian border. I can't imagine a better place to go.

I tilt my ear east and zero in on the sound of a turbine engine and blades slowly cutting through the air. No doubt it's a helicopter preparing to take off. And it's far away, for a human.

"Fine, but we need to leave now," I say urgently as a series of sirens sound across the base. "We have to put some distance between us and those soldiers."

I wince in pain from the long, drawn-out tones of the alarms blanketing the area. They wreak havoc on my heightened senses. My vision blurs.

Vertigo. Not good.

"Mr. Sorin, I'm hungry," Rahne softly whines.

I'm sure you are.

I squat down in front of her and zip up the jacket. "We'll get you some food in a little bit, okay?" I wrap my arm under her backside and lift her onto my hip.

She tucks her head deep into the side of my neck.

Been a long time since I've held a little girl like this. A very, very long time.

Mo Chroí.

"Where's your car?" Jean asks.

Two miles away, the helicopter's rotary wings hit terminal velocity and an ammunition belt is locked into the gun's housing.

"I don't have a car." I reach for Jean's hand.

Great, they've got an M134 minigun mounted to the helicopter. Just what every Nocturnae dreams of: AP-rounds coming at you 6,000 rounds per second.

"What do you mean you don't have a car?" Jean asks, panicking. "How did you get here?"

"I walked. C'mon."

Jean crosses her arms. "There's no way I'm walking to the cabin! That's like, 400 miles from here. Also, in case you've forgotten,"

Jean erupts, "I'm FUCKING BLIND!"

This is a different side of her. She was so calm, formal … professional these last four days. Humans and their emotions. No wonder Claret hated that I held onto that trait.

"I don't expect you to walk." I scoop her up with my other arm, before she can protest, and run out of the clearing back into the forest.

"SHHHIIIIIT!" Jean screams into my ear. In a fright, she wraps her legs tightly around my waist and buries her face in my other shoulder.

My, how far I've fallen. A Nocturnae helping … no, *protecting* a human. Claret would be ashamed of me.

The forest grows thick and spills open into a narrow river with thick brush on either side. I look back over my shoulder, listening for sirens, footsteps, and engines. They're faint, but they're there. Searching frantically and in every direction, like they don't know what they're looking for.

I listen to Jean's heart. It's slowed and so has her breathing. She's asleep, a side effect of a human moving at Nocturnae speed—the air is thinner. This is a blessing. I tighten my grip on the girls and run north. I'm slower than I should be, but that's more likely from fighting the Lygos and expelling silver bullets from my body than from the weight of the girls.

Rahne's grip on me goes slack and I almost lose my grip on her, but I quickly reposition my arm around her and keep her from hitting the ground. Her eyes open from the jerking on her body. "You're okay. I've got you. Go back to sleep little one."

We travel through the forests under the protection of its high, thick branches until we get to I-70 and are forced out into the open.

"Shit." I look over my shoulder, then back at the highway. "A mile a minute should have been fast enough for them not to follow."

Standing at the edge of the forest, I close my eyes and focus my senses on the sound of sirens, troops, and the helicopters. Five miles back, the helos are circling the perimeter of the base and emergency sirens are localized to the base.

"We're in the clear." I look up at the early morning sky and quickly cross the highway.

Gonna need to find a place to crash for the day. They need some sleep.

I take us another thirty-five miles north, until I find the Great Miami River. In the densest part of the forest near the river's edge, I lay the sleeping mother and daughter near the trunk of a large black walnut tree.

Again, my ears listen for any sign we were followed or imminent danger—nothing.

With more than forty-miles of distance between us and the base, we're safe … for now. And right now, the girls need warmth. Near the base of the tree, I stack four logs in a crisscross fashion and fill the center with kindling—small pieces of dry wood, leaves, and pine needles. Using friction, I start the fire.

Rahne stirs at the first *POP* from the fire. Smiling, she pulls herself closer to the fire and softly says, "Thank you."

"You're welcome." I smile. "But we can't make the fire much bigger than this. Just to be safe."

Jean opens her eyes, yawns, and props herself up with one arm.

"How long have I been asleep?"

"About an hour." I keep my eyes on Rahne and the fire.

"Where are we?" Jean asks.

"We passed a sign that said Tawawa Park about a mile back."

"That's in Sidney," Jean gasps in disbelief. "You ran forty miles in a couple hours?"

I need to be patient with her, she's been through a lot. In three days, she's been face-to-face with a Nocturnae, discovered her colleagues were lying to her for a decade, and her child was alive this whole time. Oh, and her colleagues—and presumable *friends*—had been experimenting on her daughter the entire time.

Okay, I'll cut her some slack.

"*One* hour, actually. And the run was more of a light jog. Can you keep an eye on her?" I nod, indicating Rahne.

"An eye?" Jean says, irritated. "No, but I'll keep an ear out."

Okay, not in the joking mood. Got it. "I'm going to get some more firewood and find you two some food. I'll be back before sunrise."

"You're leaving us? What if Rahne wanders off and I can't find her?" Jean pulls her hands tightly into her chest. "I don't know where I am and I—"

"It'll be okay Jean. I won't be far. Just stay put and if anything happens just say my name. You don't have to yell. I'll hear you even if it's a whisper."

"What if they find us?"

"They won't."

"But the fire, it—"

"The smoke will travel up the trunk of the tree and disperse evenly through its branches. Don't worry, it won't be thick enough for them to see. I won't let the fire get much bigger than that or they *will* be able to see it."

She nods once, scoots herself to the fire, and strokes Rahne's head.

I RETURN TO camp twenty minutes later with a stack of kindling and logs tucked under one arm and two rabbits in the other. Rahne is out cold where I left her. Jean, also asleep, is still sitting up and unknowingly let the fire burn to its coals.

Trying not to wake them, I cover the rabbits in snow, and add kindling and a single log to the fire. I skin the rabbits and flatten them on a long thin rock.

A cupped hand smacks the ground. Rahne pulls her hands to her chest and flattens them revealing a beetle on a pedestal.

Interesting. I wasn't alerted when her heartbeat changed or when she positioned herself over the bug.

The beetle walks off the edge of her hands and plops back into the bed of pine needles and leaves on the ground, narrowly missing the dusting of snow. Rather than picking the mulch up, she lowers her head to the ground as if she's trying to see how the pieces of fallen debris fit together on the ground.

Sitting up, she places her hand squarely on the green moss covering the large tree roots surrounding her. As her hand glides over the fluffy green organism, a smile quickly grows across her face and she giggles like it's tickling her.

She's acting like she's never seen an insect before or felt cloud-like moss. Has she never been outside? Never once felt the wind upon her face or the snow melt in her hands? The poor child, she has no idea what she's been missing. How dare the humans keep her from the wonders of the world?

"Rahne." I pat the ground beside me. "Would you like to come help me make dinner?"

She yawns a large yawn and nods. The leaves don't move or crack beneath her as she crawls on all fours to my side. "What are we having?" She sits beside me with her hands folded in her lap.

As curious as a child experiencing things for the first time, she seems … normal. As if she doesn't recall what happened while in Lygos form. What's more concerning, is if she does remember and isn't letting it faze her.

"My favorite, rabbit." I pick up the stone and place it halfway inside the fire. "The stone acts as a skillet and will cook the meat more evenly without burning it."

She says nothing while staring at the rabbit's flesh, mesmerized by its popping and sizzling.

I keep silent as the child watches meat cook, likely for the first time. Her curiosity and fearlessness remind me so much of you, Cora. Mo Chroí.

Jean's eyes flutter open just as I pull the rabbit from the fire. "Mm, that smells good. What did you make?"

"Rabbit." I smile.

Rahne snatches a rabbit from the stone and bites off a large chunk before I can react. Immediately, blisters form on her hands as steam sears them. She chews quickly, moving the scalding hot meat around her mouth with her tongue.

"Oh no—" Jean and I say together.

But the blisters and sores on Rahne's hands, lips, and mouth heal as quickly as they appeared. She swallows and her skin is as flawless as the moment before she burned it.

I look at Jean with amazement, but she's unaware of what just happened.

The child maintains at least some level of her Lygos gifts even in human form.

I push the rock with the other rabbit to Jean. "You should eat."

"I don't eat meat."

She'll torture Nocturnae, but Thumper gets to live? Hypocrite.

"Okay, Jean," I say, annoyed, and pass the plate to Rahne. "More for you!"

Without a thought, Rahne bites another piece off the rabbit and chews. "OKAY!" Saliva flows from the corners of her hungry smile.

"Slow down," I chuckle. "I don't want you to choke."

She looks at me like a child behind a giant chocolate birthday cake, and snatches the rabbit from the plate.

Will it happen again?

I watch as her hand bubbles and burns under the incredible heat and quickly heals.

Fascinating.

"This is soooo good," Rahne shouts, shaking the rabbits in her hands.

Jean giggles and covers her mouth.

"Rahne, when you finish your food, you need to get some rest. You too, Jean. We have a long journey tonight."

"We should travel at night because humans don't see as well

then," Jean says. "And they now know sunlight doesn't affect you, so they'll expect us to keep moving during the day."

Look who's got her wits about her again. Welcome back, Jean.

Jean looks in my direction. "And you're going to be keeping watch while we sleep?"

"That is the plan, yes," I say, coldly.

"Of course, it is," Jean says with sarcasm in her voice. "Little like falling asleep next to Ed Gein, don't ya think?"

"Comparing me to the inspiration for *Silence of the Lambs*? I'm touched." She merely rolls her eyes in response. "Might I remind you it was only yesterday that I told you, 'I'm not here for you?'"

"Yes, I also remember you saying that I was still alive, *only* because you allow it," Jean snaps, ignoring the jolt of fear pulsing through her body as her heartrate quickens.

Oh yeah … I did say that. "Trying times, Dr. Allicines. Trying times. The circumstances have changed since then. I mean neither you, nor the child, any harm. Please, trust me. Get some sleep. You will need it."

Jean throws up her arms. "We don't have time to sit around."

"What do you suggest then?" I fold my hands in my lap.

"I need answers." Jean buries her forehead in her hands.

"The Company isn't going to give them to you," I say, refusing to sugar coat the hard truth. "They have their own questions, and they'll extract the answers from you one way or another."

"I know." Slowly, Jean runs her fingers through her hair.

"We're only going to find answers by putting distance between us and them, and finding the answers ourselves."

"But how will we find out what that thing was I ran into in the

Void?"

"I don't know," I say, awkwardly. "But never fear, humans label all terrifying things in this world. It's bound to be rooted in a myth or legend."

With a furrowed brow, Jean shallowly points like the memory is floating in front of her. "You said that the other day."

"Mm, I don't think I did," I say. "I think I'd remember."

"No, you're right," Jean says, deep in thought. "It wasn't you … it was Gaius … Gaius added it to something Claret said—it was very close to your words just now." I watch her intently as her mind works. "Gaius said, 'The children of Encomiâ, the Lygos. The misunderstood Meliāki. And the thaumaturgy of Penyihir.'"

Rahne swallows her rabbit and asks, "What is thauma … thauma—"

"Thaumaturgy," I say. "Think of it as how a magician can work magic. Like Merlin in the *Sword and the Stone*." I look back at Jean. "I honestly have no idea what the creature was because I didn't see it."

"No, I know."

My eyes flash crimson. "I could compel you and—"

"Absolutely not!"

Figured, but I couldn't help myself.

Running my hand through Rahne's hair, I smile. "Finish up. You only got a couple hours rest and we have a long journey ahead of us." I throw a log on the fire. "I'll keep the fire hot."

"And keep us safe, right?" Rahne asks, stuffing the last piece of rabbit in her mouth.

Jean scoffs, mumbling, "Will he?"

I ignore Jean. "I heard a family of deer while I was out. How about venison when you wake up? How's that sound?"

"I don't know what deer is or venison, but if it's anything like rabbit, then sign me up!"

I chuckle and glance over at Jean. "You too, Jean."

She doesn't move.

Rahne positions her head on my thigh and tucks her hands into her armpits for warmth. "Goodnight Mr. Sorin."

"Goodnight, little one," I say softly and look at Jean. "Get some rest Jean."

Reluctantly, Jean turns away and settles in to sleep.

Minutes pass. Their heartbeats slow. Their breathing changes. They fall asleep.

Images of Rahne in her hulking Lygos form flash in my mind. The howling roars echoing in the catacombs and the smell of blood submerges my memory and it's like I'm back there. Watching from the floor as Claret sacrifices herself for me once again.

"I'm sorry my Maker. I'm sorry I didn't find you until now. I'm sorry I lost you forever just as we were reunited." I wipe the bloody tears from my face. "Rest in true death Claret Ivet Ingelehmann, my Maker."

Leaning back against a tree, I look up at the stars.

What a long couple of days. With The Company tracking us, I'm going to need my wits about me. Not to mention my strength—humans and their fucking silver. This cool air feels nice. I'll just close my eyes for a little bit.

My heartbeat slows. My breathing changes. I fall asleep.

# 38



THREE UNMARKED BLACK SUVs raced down the runway in a single file line toward an old run-down aircraft hangar. Six men stood at attention in front of the hangar's large doors in black suits sporting white oxfords, black ties, ear wicks, and Glock 19s on their hips.

Their leader grabbed his lapel and whispered, "Agamemnon approaches."

The hangar doors squealed, opening just enough for one person to slide through. A man in a tan suit and brown wingtips stepped into the morning air. He took three steps out of the hangar and stopped to tighten the Eldredge knot of his maroon tie and check the middle button of his suit jacket.

A gleeful smile spread across the man's face as the SUVs howled to a stop roughly one hundred feet in front of him.

Four agents exited the first and third vehicles, spacing themselves evenly around the caravan of cars.

The man in the tan suit looked to the agents on either side of him and nodded.

Returning the nod, the lead agent said, "Escorting Homer to Agamemnon. Begin approach."

Two single file lines of three men formed on either side of the tan suited man. Slowly, they walked toward the center SUV, keeping an eye on their surroundings. They stopped thirty feet from the vehicle.

From the center vehicle, a female blonde agent exited the front passenger seat and opened the rear door. Everyone stood motionless, waiting.

Carefully, in one coordinated and unforgiving motion, Dr. Eugene Shelley lowered his delicate old frame to the pavement. The sand that clung to the back of his sweat-stained clothing shook free as he brushed the seat.

"Are you okay sir?" the female agent asked.

"I'm alright my dear," he looked up and winked. "Never get old. You're much too pretty for it."

Turning around, he leaned over the backseat and grabbed an old, tattered gray messenger bag and fedora. He slung the bag over his shoulder, smiled at the agent, and flicked the brim of his hat. "In my younger years, you could have mistaken me for *Indiana Jones.*"

"I can see the resemblance." She tried not to laugh. "Good day, sir."

"You as well," he said and quickly walked to meet the man in the tan suit.

The man in the tan suit smiled excitedly, nearly bouncing on the balls of his feet.

"What's with the grin, Director Ziegler?" Dr. Shelley called out.

"So formal. Life-long friends call me Ardisson or Ardie." He extended his hand. "And what about my grin? Can't I just be excited to see a friend?"

"I'm not *that* exciting." Dr. Shelley shook his hand, and pulled him in for a hug. "It's good to see you."

"You too."

Dr. Shelley stepped back to take in the vastness of the facility. "It's been quite a while since I've been to Directorate 2's headquarters."

"The Arcane Division, or the Arcanus Arcane, you might say. So, what did you think of our Sandbox?"

"Well, it's definitely a serious improvement from what I had in my lab at Wright-Patt."

"Was the elevator in yet?"

"No, I had—"

"You walked *all* those steps," Ardie said in disbelief. "I'm so sorry about that, the elevator should have already been installed. I'll figure out what's going on and make sure it's in before you get out there again."

"I appreciate it, but that's a huge undertaking even for an unclassified facility. I can't imagine what it would—"

"Throw enough money at something and it's amazing what you can accomplish." Ardie laughed, and patted Dr. Shelley's shoulder. "Should we head inside? Talk about what happened?"

Reluctantly Dr. Shelley agreed. "I'm in the dog house, aren't I?"

The six agents escorted Dr. Shelley and Ardie back to the hangar doors.

"Yes," Ardie said, patting Dr. Shelley on the shoulder. "But not as much as you might think." Dr. Shelley looked up with hope in his eyes. "We learned quite a lot about the Lygos from that event and the incident raised a lot of new questions we'd like answered. Let's go inside, where we can talk candidly."

The men stepped through the hangar doors. The doors closed loudly behind them, while the three SUVs sped off as the sun began to rise.

Ardie led Dr. Shelley through the empty hangar bay to a door and badged them in using his CAC. They walked down four more hallways before coming to a large steel door with a combination dial.

Pointing to a small table beside the door, Ardie instructed, "Leave your cell phone, computer, and any other electronic devices here."

Dr. Shelley rolled his eyes and agreed. "I know the drill, Ardie. I've been doing this for what, thirty years now?"

"Just a friendly reminder. You don't need any more security infractions."

Ardie spun the dial until the door unlocked, and gestured for Dr. Shelley to enter first. As the door slammed shut behind them, a series of clicks echoed, and the door locks resealed automatically.

"No turning back now," Dr. Shelley thought.

Dr. Shelley walked to an eight-person conference table and set his bag on the floor. "What are we cleared up to?"

"The room is cleared up to TS/PI."

Dr. Shelley whipped around. "TOP SECRET/PARANORMAL INTELLIGENCE? The whole umbrella?"

"Yup, anything spanning Darwinian, Arcane, and Celestial Divisions of The Company," Ardie said. Looking around the room, he raised his arms in emphasis. "The room we're in, this SCIF is the last of its kind. We can even talk about the Omega Level threats housed at the Sandbox."

"Because of the ... *my* incident?"

"SCIFs costs too much to build and accredit and it's a security risk no one's willing to take, so they're allowing them to fall out of compliance one by one." Ardie took a slow deep breath. "And then there's the rest of it, money. Between budget cuts and everyone competing for the same pot of money, things are already tight and then add in priority changes with each election cycle and ... ugh, it's a mess."

"Don't bullshit me, Ardie. They're not renewing accreditation of SCIFs spanning the whole umbrella because of the incident, right?"

"The most recent one, no," Ardie said, coldly. "But the first one, yeah. Sorry Eugene." Dr. Shelley turned back to the table without a word and slid into the first chair. "Anything to drink, Professor?"

"Whiskey. Jameson."

"It's barely seven a.m. Eugene. How about a coffee?"

"Fine. Black. In a real mug. None of that Styrofoam or cardboard shit."

Ardie smirked as he poured the coffee and gently put a cardboard cup on the table. "Like I said, budget cuts." Dr. Shelley shook his head, but took the cup. "How's that apprentice of yours?" Ardie unbuttoned his jacket, sat in the chair next to Dr. Shelley, opened his water, and took a sip. "Henry, wasn't it?"

"Ugh, yeah." Dr. Shelley patted his pants and jacket pockets.

"Where is it?" He reached into his satchel and pulled out a leather-bound book and a weathered copy of *Fevre Dream* by George R. R. Martin and set them beside his bag. "Oh, come on."

"Is everything okay?"

"Fine. One moment." Dr. Shelley returned to the bag and retrieved an Italian sapphire blue pocket Watch. He placed it atop the stack of books and let out a heavy sigh of relief.

"Henry wasn't near the base when everything happened, was he?" Ardie asked, staring at the Watch as he tried to hide his momentary shock by clocking the pocket Watch coolly.

"No … damn it where is it…," Dr. Shelley huffed, blindly digging around in his bag. "Ah, there you are," he proclaimed, pulling out a small steel flask.

"Seriously Eugene?"

"What?" Dr. Shelley snapped, glaring at the Director. "My lab was just destroyed. All my research is gone. Rahne is in the wind as a—"

"A, confirmed, werewolf."

Ignoring Ardie's spite, Dr. Shelley continued, "The male Nocturnae is gone. The female Nocturnae was torn to pieces by Rahne. And to top it all off, I had to go see *him*."

Ardie leaned over the table, eagerly, and interlocked his fingers. "So, he spoke with you."

"No."

"Oh." Ardie sat back in his chair. "What happened?"

Dr. Shelley gulped down half of the coffee in the cup and replaced it with the contents of his flask. "At the Sandbox with him? Nothing. I stood on the other side of the door, asked my question, and never got an answer." Dr. Shelley sipped his cocktail. "Why so much interest in Henry?"

"The boy's been through a lot in his life for someone his age. Henry lost his mother as a child. Then, he and his father had a falling out not long after. And more recently everything with his brother back when *he* worked for you. *Before* you found Henry."

Dr. Shelley pulled the cup from his mouth. "Physically, Henry is fine. He was visiting his father in Ohio when everything happened. I called him and told him to meet me here. He'll arrive by tomorrow morning."

"Perfect. What did you think of the Sandbox? Pretty cool, isn't it?" Ardie asked with a big smile.

"The facility was very impressive. You said construction was recently finished?"

Ardie's hand hovered over the table, teetering back and forth. "Mostly. As you saw, the elevator still hasn't been installed. Then there are the mundane things that still need to go in, like a receptionist counter, security kiosks, and a hallway or two."

"Sounds like there's still a lot to do."

"You saw the front of the facility; the back is where all the magic is."

Dr. Shelley raised an eyebrow. "I'm sorry Ardie, but I don't buy it."

"What do you mean you 'don't buy it?' There's nothing to *buy*."

Leaning over the table, Dr. Shelley stared through Ardie's eyes with flared nostrils. "I mean there's no way *we*—the United States—built that entire facility. Sure, we gave it a facelift, but there's no way we did all of that. Not there. Not without someone seeing and posting it on social media."

"I don't know what you're—"

"Cut the shit Ardie," Dr. Shelley said sternly without raising his voice. "I don't give a shit about the *Need-to-Know* or the read-ins I don't have, or if it's above my goddamn pay grade. There was a lot down there I'd never seen or even fucking heard of." Dr. Shelley closed his eyes and took two long, deep breaths as he sat back into his chair. In a calm, mellow tone, he continued, "Stop talking to me with your politician hat on and start talking to me like the life-long friends and colleagues we are."

They kept unwavering eye contact for a long second until Ardie relented. "Fine. It was just after we bombed Japan in '45, and we were searching for a new testing range for the next generation of cutting-edge weaponry and WMDs."

"Tensions were still high from WWII and many speculated another threat was on the horizon."

"They were right." Dr. Shelley gave a shallow nod. "The Cold War started in '47."

Ardie pointed. "Precisely."

"Hold on." Dr. Shelley raised a finger. "This new testing range … it wouldn't happen to be part of the NTTR—Nevada Test and Training Range—would it?"

"Correct again." Ardie pointed, again.

"And that's how you found the Sandbox out in the Mojave Desert…"

"Yes. During a series of site surveys conducted using Ground Penetrating Radar, a structure was found below the Earth's surface. It was massive. Estimated to be at least the same size as the Great

Pyramid of Giza."

Dr. Shelley gave a short chuckle. "I'm sure that went well in Washington."

"Right," Ardie said, rolling his eyes. "After unknown substances were found in the soil, no one wanted their name attached to an order that could erupt into something catastrophic. We didn't know what it was or who built it or how long it had been down there."

"How far up the chain of command did it go?" Dr. Shelley said.

"The top. All the way to Harry S. Truman. He ordered a two-phase mission. Phase one was a team of what would eventually become the Special Forces—off the books of course, couldn't let the public know they existed until 1952. Anyway, they were sent in to investigate the structure with the objectives: infiltrate, observe, and clear any hostiles. Phase two was the nerds. They were to collect samples, explore, and begin analysis of the structure and its contents."

"Okay, so what did they find?" Dr. Shelley asked.

Ardie scoffed and ran his hand uneasily over the table. "I couldn't say. Most of the records are heavily redacted, and those that weren't seem to have been destroyed."

"Fucking government. I love this country," Dr. Shelley sneered, sipping his cocktail. "Okay, so what *do* we know?"

"The team of soldiers opened the giant doors and entered a larger, darker room. On all sides of the room were metal doors of varying sizes and shapes. Some had small viewing windows while others had none. Some had door handles, others had knobs, others had none. All had some form of a lock on them. Pad locks, combination locks, and some so obscure they're impossible to describe. A handful of doors were reinforced with wooden or metal beams stretched across them."

"You're talking about the main cell block, aren't you? The one where we keep *him*." The Director nodded. "But all the doors in there were the same size and shape with electronic keypads and security networked throughout."

"We built the facility around the existing one. It was discovered some of the cells were empty and those were completely modernized, the others—those with occupants—just got a face lift."

"Was there any writing on or around the original doors? Symbols? Runes?"

"Some doors had languages that matched, or were similar to, those written on other doors. Others had unique languages. One door in particular had a language unlike any seen before in recorded history."

"What made them so different?"

"I don't know." Ardie shook his head and took a sip of water. "Everything went to Directorate 1."

Eugene sat up, his interest fully piqued. "Celestial Division, why?"

"No idea, but it's locked away and above my clearance level. And yours, for that matter."

Dr. Shelley bit his lip and wondered if Mr. Glass knew anything. "Why not modernize all of them? Why leave those with … inmates … free of improvements and modernization?"

"We couldn't risk another anomaly like the one in '48. There's also the old adage: *If it ain't broke, don't fix it.*"

Dr. Shelley ignored the boredom in Ardie's voice and pressed him anyway. "What anomaly?"

"We ordered the initial team to proceed into the room. Almost immediately, every soldier claimed something called to them."

"What did it sound like?" Dr. Shelley asked with a narrowed brow.

"Not verbally calling to them. Telepathically calling to them, coercing them … compelling them closer and closer to the door. Ordering them to open it."

"Which door was it?"

"That information is redacted."

"Of course," Dr. Shelley scoffed.

"Something large crashed into the other side of a nearby door and broke them of whatever had a hold of their psyches. The door was windowless and easily fifteen feet high and eight feet wide and reeked of decaying flesh. The men stepped back. But as they cleared the main door to the room, a strange sound, like a bugle, echoed from within."

Dr. Shelley leaned over the table. "Bugle? Like a horn? Is that a word you chose or is that the word used in the files?"

"That was the word *explicitly* used in the report," Ardie said. Dr. Shelley silently questioned him. "*Bugle* is a very strange, and oddly specific, descriptive word because it's only associated with hoofed ruminants."

"You lost me," Dr. Shelley said, shaking his head.

"Cervidae, Eugene." Dr. Shelley looked at him blankly. "Deer. Elk. Moose. They're all hoofed ruminants and part of the Cervidae family of mammals." Ardie pursed his lips with a head shake and sat back in his chair. "The haunting tone was long and hard and quickly joined by incessant banging on the door in clusters of three."

"Jesus." Dr. Shelley ran his hands through his hair with a heavy breath. "Is that it?"

"That's it. That's all that was in the reports. Everything after that is redacted."

"Well, that's utter bullshit!" Dr. Shelley erupted, smacking the table with the palm of his hand. "Why didn't the soldiers notice the smell upon first entering the room of … prison cells—for lack of a better term?"

"We don't know. Perhaps the answer is in the redacted sections. Our working theory is that whatever had hold of their minds was pressuring them closer to a specific door. To this day we don't know which one was calling to them or which door they were being *pushed* toward."

"Didn't anyone ask them?"

"Eugene … No one survived."

"What?!" Dr. Shelley exclaimed.

"Each of the men had a camera on their lapel, microphones, and ear wicks. It's all recorded. Until it … ended. It seems the Commanding Officer sent a second team down to investigate, but they never returned either."

"Shit…" Dr. Shelley softly tapped his finger on the table.

"What is it?"

Dr. Shelley closed his hand and looked at Ardie. "Why are you telling me all this? I should be fired after what happened at Wright-Patt … again!"

"I told you outside you weren't in as much trouble as you might think." Ardie leaned forward in his chair and steepled a hand under his chin.

"Come on Ardie. I fucked up. Actions have consequences."

"Do you want me to stop funding your work at Langley?"

Dr. Shelley's eyes widened and his lower lip began to quiver. "No. Please. Not that."

"Then stop asking for more punishment than you've already received." Ardie popped the phalanges in two of his fingers. "Or I will terminate the agreement we made all those years ago."

"Okay, but I haven't received any punishment."

Ardie flattened his hand on the table and leaned over. "Eugene, your laboratory is gone. All of your personal possessions were—"

"Michelle," Dr. Shelley gasped.

"—destroyed."

The room fell silent and Ardie watched the weight of what was lost sink into his friend.

Dr. Shelley took a long-staggered breath and said, "What do you need from me now?"

"I need you to study the child." Ardie stood and buttoned his jacket. "And I need you to continue the PHANG Program with the information we gained from Jean's interrogation at Wright-Patt."

"Awful lot for one man to do."

Ardie tossed the water bottle in the trash and smiled. "That's why you have Henry. Divide and conquer."

# 39



My eye lids flutter as I squint into the morning rays shining through holes in the forest canopy. Yawning, I rub my face with a dew-soaked hand as I quickly realize—

Shit! I fell asleep!

Suddenly on full alert, I scan the camp.

There's Jean, still sleeping beside the smoldering coals of the nearly dead fire. Rahne…?

I sit up quickly. Rahne is nowhere to be found.

Did they get her?

A gust of air rushes over my shoulder as the wind picks up. I flair my nostrils, sniffing the air. And relax.

There she is.

Laughing to myself, I remember, this is likely her very first time outside. I flatten myself back against the tree trunk and close my eyes, watching her with my ears.

Rahne cheerfully gasps as the forest grows brighter—perhaps a sunbeam hit her face. She sounds joyous, inspired, and I can't help but feel something like compassion as her laughter reminds me of my daughter, Cora.

"You're so funny," Rahne laughs. "I'm glad we're friends."

Who's she talking to? Does she have an imaginary friend?

Rahne sits in a small clearing with a stream running between two large, old, black walnut trees. I sniff the air curiously and pause, only to sniff once more. Now she smells like she did before changing into the Lygos—

"No, he didn't do it…" Jean mumbles in her sleep and rolls over.

Is Jean dreaming … or reliving a memory? I hush her back to sleep, pondering if Rahne will retain any of her Lygos abilities while human and why she didn't kill me in the catacombs like she did everyone else. Was it the silver coursing through my body or something else?

"Mr. Sorin?" Rahne asks, hesitantly.

I guess now's as good a time as any to put the question to the test.

"I'm here little one," I say, well below a human whisper.

"Will you come play with me?"

Well, I'll be damned. "Of course, little one. One moment."

Stirring the coals until they redden, I add kindling and two logs to keep Jean warm. But when I turn to find Rahne, I immediately stop. Thrown off by the ABU jacket lying on the ground beside her and the cool air streaming off of her tiny naked body like a block of dry ice on display. I take a moment to collect myself.

I've only seen Nocturnae do that when sedentary—our bodies being so much warmer than a human's. Is this part of her Lygos mutation? It has to be latent abilities leaking out through her human form.

I slowly walk toward Rahne, studying her every conscious and unconscious movement. Her breathing. The way she scratches the nape of her neck and smiles into the still water like something's there. Even the way she watches the birds soar through the air in front of squirrels darting from branch to branch on the limbs above her.

I make noise as I approach, so as not to frighten her by a sudden appearance.

Could she hear me, in this human-looking state, if I stalked her like my prey? Maybe. She heard me whisper from a great distance after all.

"Hello little one," I say, clocking the jacket. "Are you warm?"

"Yes," Rahne says softly, without turning around.

"Well, we can't have you walking around naked."

"Why not?" she asks, innocently.

That's a question I never thought I'd have to answer. How do I answer in a way she'll understand? What would Dora the Explorer say? Or Moana? Or your friendly neighborhood Spider-Man?

"It's not something a *princess* would do," I say with a shallow smile, and remove my tan t-shirt. "Arms up."

I send a silent thanks to Staff Sergeant Burr. His clothing has been more useful than anyone could have imagined.

I fit her arms through the sleeves and let the shirt fall around her. "There we go. Much better." The shirt hangs off her like a dress. She looks like Dobby the house-elf, but less Smeagol-like of course. Eying the clump of sticks in each of her hands fashioned to look like stick-figures, I ask, "What are we playing?"

"This is Fred," she says, shaking the figure in her left hand as I sit. "And this is ... well I don't know his name, but he's the handsome man with the crooked smile. We're playing jailbreak."

"And that small pile of pine needles over there?" I point to the ground by her knee.

"Oh, that's the cat named after a bird."

A cat named after a bird? Woody the Woodpecker? Donald Duck? Zazu?

I point to action figures made of sticks and leaves. "Can I play too?"

Rahne gives a sad nod and hands me Fred. "I can't go home, can I?"

A prison called home. Sounds like the premise for an M. Night Shyamalan movie. "No," I say, marveling at the creativity of using a leaf as a cape for her homemade toy.

"What about daddy?"

The monster she calls father? The psychopath that abducted her, kept her in a cage, and experimented on her? Dead ... I hope. But I doubt it.

"I don't know sweetheart, but I will help you find him." Just so I can rip out his intestines and shove them down his throat.

"No, that's okay. I don't like being in my room all the time." She turns her face up to the sun. "It's so much prettier out here."

An uncontrollable warmth seeps into my heart for the first time in centuries. "Yes, it is. The world is a beautiful place even though the humans have destroyed so much of it." I turn to her and wait for her to look at me.

"The world was more beautiful than it is now? What did they do to make it less pretty?"

How much time do we have? "They killed many of the animals for their pelts and furs. They cut down the forests of trees and wildlife for fast fields of corn and soy. They plundered the planet for all of her natural resources, burned them, and polluted the air and water to the point that it can no longer be drunk, and the air is carcinogenic."

"What's carcinogenic?"

"It means that it can make you really sick."

Rahne turns away in disgust. "I don't like being sick."

"Nor do I." The Black Death.

"When was the world more beautiful than it is today?" She pets the rough and smooth sides of the acorn cap in her hands.

"Not that long ago, actually. It was before humanity built towers of steel, concrete, and glass that blotted out the sun. Before they disassociated the lives being lost from their plastic-wrapped food at their local grocery store. Before they cut down the trees, turned them into paper, and printed SAVE THE TREES on each page." Rahne watched me wash the air with my hands like it was paint and I was rubbing the varnish of time off the world. "Back before technologies were invented to distract humanity from their mortality. Back when monsters—like us—were real, living under their beds and deep in the forest. Before we became creatures of myth and legend."

Rahne stops playing with the acorn cap and looks up at me. "Monsters ... like us? Are you *like* me?"

She's aware to some degree at least.

"A so-called *monster*, yes,"—the image of Claret being ripped in half by the hulking creature Rahne flashes in my mind—"but I am different from you."

We sit in silence and watch the world come to life under the morning sun.

Rahne loosely tosses the acorn cap in front of her and sighs. "I don't like what I am."

She may be more aware than I expected. "Why not?"

"It hurts," Rahne says, rubbing her arm.

"What does?" I ask.

"Changing into … it."

I'd hoped she was unaware of the change or at least couldn't remember the pain. "Can you show me where it hurts?"

Running her hands over every inch of her body Rahne looks up at me with tears in her eyes. My heart breaks for her.

I pull her into my arms and hold her like I did Cora all those centuries ago. "I am so sorry Rahne. Sometimes I don't like what I am either." Most of the time, actually, if I'm honest. A flood of my victims' memories strobe through my mind like a rolodex. "It'll be alright, little one." I comfort her as she begins to cry. This child has been through so much and her innocence was stolen before her first cries of life. Yes, she killed my Maker; but she's just a child. "Do you remember what happened after you changed?"

Rahne wipes her tears and scratches the nape of her neck where the white diamond of fur showed itself in her Lygos form. "No, everything just went black."

In that case, she's not going to know why she didn't kill me too. Damnit.

"That must have been scary." I stand the stick-figure, Fred, up in the dirt.

"No, it wasn't scary." She tries to stand her stick-figure man up, but it falls over. "When it's bedtime and the lights go out in my room, that's scary."

"Yes, darkness can be *very* scary, and it's okay to be scared of it." More people should be.

"But when I'm asleep, it's not scary. It was like when I was asleep."

She's aware of the transformation, but has no recollection of anything that occurs once the mutation is complete. Almost as if a second person, or being, steps into the light as the consciousness of her child persona rests.

Distracted by two squirrels playing at the trunk of a nearby tree, Rahne says nothing else.

Sensing her shift, I decide not to press the child further and instead I offer my hand. "How about we go see if Ms. Jean is awake?"

"She's not," Rahne says, snapping a small twig with her thumbs.

"How do you know?"

"She's snoring."

I tilt my head slightly and listen.

Damn it, Jean is indeed snoring. Rahne possesses latent Lygos abilities even in human form. This isn't good. If the humans learn of this, they'll hunt her down and cage her until they can subdue her and sell her genetic material—DNA is one thing, but her eggs are another—to the highest bidder… or use her themselves to advance their political agenda. The Company wants to weaponize

Nocturnae. It's not a far leap to assume they'd do the same for a Lygos. Hell, they'd probably favor the Lygos. Lygos are bigger, stronger, and faster than Nocturnae.

"Well, I'm sure she'll be up shortly. How about we head back, then I'll get you some breakfast and you keep an eye on Ms. Jean. How does that sound?"

She smiles with big blue eyes and outstretches an arm toward me, seeming to trust completely. Even to me, that's pretty cute.

I can't let what happened to Claret happen to Rahne and Jean. I won't let it. We need to get out of here. We need to keep moving

Lifting Rahne, I hold her on my side. She wraps her legs around my waist like a koala bear and slings her arms loosely around my neck. Resting her head on my shoulder, she pops a thumb in her mouth. Even though she's ten years old, Rahne still has a few toddler tendencies, likely from her isolated upbringing thus far.

I make the short walk back to our camp and put Rahne down. I notice I'm struggling with a very strange, very new sensation.

Rahne's neck was *right there,* and I wasn't drawn to it at all. Her blood didn't smell sweet or appetizing, nor was it appalling, it just was. It's been a very long time since I've felt a hand so soft and so small in mine. The joy I feel, it's almost human.

Jean sits up as we walk up to the camp. Clearing the sleep from her eyes, she yawns. "How thoughtful of you to leave the *blind girl* alone in the woods." So dramatic.

"When are we eating? I'm hungry." Rahne thumps her fists on the ground beside her.

The tip of my ear twitches at the sound of a leaf crumpling under a hoof. "I hear a doe rustling in the brush a half mile from here." I point and smile at Rahne. "How about you start gathering firewood and I'll get the doe when I'm finished here."

Elated, Rahne dashes off to pick up twigs.

"You're really good with her," Jean says. "Believe it or not, I think your Maker would be proud of you."

"Rahne makes me remember what it was like, all those years ago." I half smile quickly and turn away, even though I know she can't see me.

"From what you told me it sounds like Cora had a wonderful father." The air between us suddenly felt awkward and unsettling as the compliment rang in my mind. I can only assume Jean felt it too. She changes the subject. "Can you try to find something that's not meat? I know it's winter in Ohio and it's unlikely, but—"

I've never understood why some humans willingly sacrifice such a succulent cuisine. If a human wanted to deter a Nocturnae from feeding on them, Veganism would be the way. "Lion's Mane mushrooms grow in this region, but it's too cold for anything else to grow."

Jean folds her hands around her knees and turns her head away. "Thank you."

"I thought you didn't trust me." I tongue my fang.

Jean rolls her eyes. "Hard to trust something that eats human blood."

"Humans eat animals. Yet, they also keep them as pets."

"So I'm your pet now?" Jean looks back at me.

Got me there. "Not what I—"

"When an owner is threatened by their pet," Jean says, frustrated. "They put it down. They don't sit around the campfire telling ghost stories with it."

"So, now I'm the pet?" It's not often I'm bested by a human, but you Jean … you're full of surprises. "I'm confused."

"Yes. You're the pet." She hums a little and rocks side-to-side. "Prey. Prey is actually more accurate—as you originally insinuated."

"Are you going to use the *we're all prey to something and predators to another* argument?"

She smiles. "I am."

"It's a little ironic for the prey to be using that argument." I tilt my nose to the wind and sniff for Rahne's scent. She's a quarter mile from the doe and on her way to cross paths with the animal. "Don't you think?" I'm impressed little one.

"Humans hunted your kind to the brink of extinction. Therefore, humanity could classify vampires"—she holds up a hand, blocking me from correcting her—"and werewolves and all the other things that go bump in the night as myths or legends or whatever term you want to use because they're extinct."

I don't like being wrong. I like it even less when a human makes a good point. "Huh…"

"But I don't think they did it alone," Jean says with a heavy exhale.

"What do you mean?" I ask and turn my head in the direction of Rahne. Dropping my voice to below a whisper, I say, "Too far. Come back this way."

"Okay," Rahne whispers back.

Jean fidgets with her hands as she works through her theory. "I don't think humans were technologically advanced enough to go up against a Nocturnae coven of any size." She points at me. "You took down seven well-armed, well-trained people all equipped with silver bullets that can travel at around 1,100 feet per second."

"I wasn't fast enough to not get captured and detained by silver."

Jean claps her hands once. "Exactly! When you were made Nocturnae, Nocturnae numbers were likely already way down and humans had what…? Primitive gunpowder technology? That's not enough to take down your kind."

"Therefore, the human revolution would have had to have started centuries earlier." I look up at the sky and sigh. "Maybe even millennia earlier."

Jean making good points is already getting annoying.

"Yup." Jean lies back on her elbows. "And I think Lygos were that ally, or, more likely, the enemy of my enemy."

"Your colleague had the same theory."

Quickly, Jean sits up. "My colleague? What colleague?"

"Dr. Eugene Shelley," I say, arrogantly.

"When did you—" Jean said, filing through the previous few days' events. Raising a hand, she waved herself off. "You went to the lab after you compelled me. That's how you met Dr. Shelley. I'd be willing to bet you met Henry too. And that's how you found Claret. Isn't it?" She grins. "Dr. Shelley wanted to showboat his work and took you down there, didn't he?"

"Yes."

Rahne strolls through the thick brush and huffs.

"What's wrong?" Jean and I ask in unison.

"Are you finished yet?" Rahne's stomach gurgles. "I'm hungry."

"Yup, all done. I'm going to get breakfast."

Jean clears her throat. "Umm, before you go. Is there a safe area nearby where I can relieve myself?"

Rahne spins around and looks up at me with a puzzled look on her face.

I whisper, "She means she has to pee."

Rahne giggles, puts down the sticks and skips over to Jean. "I'll help you." She grabs Jean by the hand and slowly guides her into the forest.

Sniffing the wind, I locate the doe and head in that direction.

WHEN RAHNE SEES me exit the brush with the deer slung over my shoulder, she jumps to her feet. "Mr. Sorin's back!"

I toss a small drawstring bag by the fire. "I stopped by a nearby house and picked up a few things. Don't worry, no one was home. And no, I didn't kill anyone. There's a pair of pants, a coat, and boots that should fit Rahne. And a pair of wool socks and tennis shoes for you. Sorry, checked the pantry but only tuna. Didn't think you'd eat something that once had a face."

Jean scoots closer to the fire, rubbing her shoulders. "Thanks."

"Rahne, could you go grab that jacket you were wearing and give it to Ms. Jean?" I ask, pulling the game from my shoulder.

"I'm fine," Jean says, retreating.

Rahne runs off to get the jacket.

"I don't know why you're in such a bad mood. And you're *not* fine. You're human. Humans are weak, hairless apes who lack the ability to properly thermoregulate in harsh environments."

"That's so sweet." Jean rolls her eyes. "And you wonder why I'm in a bad mood."

I shake my head silently and slowly count to ten. "I have to ask

… When are you going to tell her to call you *mother?*"

"Here you are Ms. Jean," Rahne says, before Jean can counter me—seemingly unaware of my last question.

"Uh … thank you," Jean says hesitantly, raising her hands to her shoulders.

Rahne gently drapes the coat over Jean's shoulders and smiles. "How's that?"

"Very nice," Jean says quietly.

"Okay Mr. Sorin, I'm ready!" Rahne shouts, sprinting over to me. She plops herself down beside the fire, crosses her legs, and waits as patiently as children can who are dancing with excitement.

"You know," I chuckle, "you can just call me Sorin. There's no need for formalities." She nods. "What we're going to do first is remove the skin from the meat—"

"Isn't she a little young to be doing this?" Jean asks.

"How to clean and cook an animal?" I look up from the animal. "No, it's a basic skill that should have been learned years ago."

"Maybe back in 1350, but nowadays we have Kroger."

If humans keep pushing the world in the direction they have been, it's going to become a basic skill again. Rather than respond to Jean, I explain the anatomy of the animal to Rahne. I grab a sharp, flat stone and show her how to skin the animal. I quarter the animal and use another flat stone as a cooking surface by stuffing a third of it into the fire.

Jean, deep in thought, sits silently as the animal cooks, and Rahne watches in wonder as the meat changes colors and bubbles next to the fire.

A human, a Nocturnae, and a Lygos sit comfortably around the fire, waiting for their dinner. What would Claret think?

The meat cooks quickly and, once again, Rahne doesn't wait for it to cool, scarfing it down as soon as I remove it from the stone.

"Are you sure you don't want any?" I ask Jean, holding up a large piece of the rump toward her so she can breathe in the scent.

"I'm fine." However, Jean's stomach makes noises that say otherwise. "I thought Nocturnae drank blood. Human blood."

"It's preferred, but you'll recall I discovered that wasn't the case while lying on my back in the cabin in Étretat for more than a century."

Jean's too smart to have forgotten that detail in two days. She's still in shock. Or she's distracted, lost in her own mind.

Jean blows into her cupped hands to warm them and stretches them over the fire. "So, what's the plan?"

"What do you mean?" Rahne asks, with a mouth full of venison.

"Last I checked we were going to your cabin in Michigan." Taking a small bite of my food, I chew slowly while sculpting my next statement before I swallow. "But if that's no longer the case, I'm all ears. Although, I must insist we don't split up."

Jean pushes her bangs behind her ear and says nothing.

Rahne looks from me to Jean and back to me. "Why not?"

"Well, Ms. Jean will need our help getting through the forest," I say, putting down my food. "And we'll be safer together with the people she works for looking for us."

"I don't think I work for them anymore," Jean says under her breath.

Right she is. She's a Subject like Rahne, Claret, and myself. Maybe she always was.

Jean's suddenly sits upright. "I just wanted to make sure things hadn't changed."

"What's Michigan?" Rahne asks.

I smile and rub the top of Rahne's head. "A state north of here." I look to Jean. "What's at your cabin?"

"Safety. It's in the small town of Harrisville. There's no more than five to 600 people in the town at a time. It's surrounded by dense forests. It's close to the Canadian border."

She's lying … a lie by omission. That all may be true, but there's something else.

I glance at Rahne as she stuffs another piece of meat in her mouth.

"We need a car," Jean says.

"We don't need or want a car," I say, shaking my head. "The Company will be expecting that. We will walk, that's what the new clothes are for. But it'll be two maybe two and a half days at the most, depending upon weather and a few other factors."

"What about Rahne?" Jean asks.

"She'll be fine. She'll set the pace."

"What do you mean by *other factors*?" Jean asks like my words just resonated with her.

"Never mind that." I pass Rahne the rest of the meat. "Finish up. Then get changed, we have a long walk ahead of us."

# 40



FOOTSTEPS ECHOED DOWN dimly lit and empty halls, painted in a yellow that was faintly reminiscent of urine. Steel office doors with rusty cypher locks reflected the echoes under the watch of a moldy, corrugated drop-ceiling. The footsteps slowly came to a stop outside door number fifteen.

A young man tapped on the steel door frame and poked his head inside. "Good morning, Professor."

Dr. Shelley looked up from his first edition copy of *Fevre Dream* by George R. R. Martin and smiled. "Henry,"—he closed the book around his thumb—"come in, come in. Sit, sit."

"Fifteen huh." Henry pointed at the door and stepped into the room with a blue canvas duffle bag slung over one shoulder and backpack over the other.

"I know. Fifteen letters in John Wilkes Booth. And Lee Harvey Oswald." Dr. Shelley leaned back in his chair and bookmarked his page with a well-worn ultrasound of a tiny fetus. "Booth shot

Lincoln in a theatre and fled to a warehouse."

Henry set his bags in the corner of the room. "And Oswald shot Kennedy from a warehouse and ran to a theatre." He pulled out the chair from the adjoining desk and took a seat.

"Everything's connected," they said together, chuckling.

"Oh, I missed you, my boy." Dr. Shelley poured a mug of coffee from the carafe in the corner of his desk and handed it to Henry.

"Thank you," Henry said, accepting the coffee and looking around the room. "I understand now why they told me there was no available housing per diem."

Dr. Shelley looked over his shoulder at the twin beds on either side of the back wall, separated only by a small nightstand. "Don't get me started. I gave Ardie an earful already. I expect we'll be getting new accommodations in the coming days."

"Ardie?"

"Director Ziegler," Dr. Shelley said. Henry nodded. "How's your father doing? I'm so sorry we had to pull you away."

Henry sighed heavily and stared blankly at the dark liquid in his mug. "His hands are getting worse and are—basically—worthless at this point. Watching him fumble and contort them to open the door to his house is just heartbreaking. How he cleans himself is troubling to think about, but he still does it. For now."

"That's terrible." Dr. Shelley discarded the book on the empty chair beside him.

"I'd rather not talk about it. It's been a rough couple of days and I'd kind of like to distract myself from it all for the time being."

"Of course." Dr. Shelley pushed his glasses higher on his nose. "Did you read the file I sent you on Monday?"

Henry shook his head. "Got a blank email from you and a cryptic call."

Dr. Shelley complained to Henry that NIPRNET—Non-classified Internet Protocol Router Network—was stripping emails again, something he always found annoying and unnecessary.

"And the cryptic call?" Dr. Shelley inquired. "What did they say?"

"Not much. The MP on the phone said there was an incident in Dayton, and the lab was closed until further notice due to a natural gas leak that caused an explosion." Henry reached into his pocket and pulled out a letter. "Later that day, I received couriered mail with instructions from Director Ziegler to report to Edwards AFB as soon as possible for debriefing; but I don't see how I can be debriefed when I don't even know what happened."

Dr. Shelley eyed the letter in Henry's hand. "It's a cover story. It's the same thing as 'during a recent training exercise blah blah blah' or 'systems are down for maintenance' or blaming gas prices on foreign countries."

"So, what happened?"

"Top off your cup," Dr. Shelley said, gesturing at Henry's mug and then to the coffee pot. "We're going to be a while. You missed a lot in that one day."

Dr. Shelley reached into his bottom drawer and pulled out a large white envelope. Sliding the thick, letter-sized envelope across his desk, five words in red ink came into focus: TOP SECRET DARWINIAN PARANORMAL INTELLIGENCE.

"JESUS," HENRY GASPED and slid the pages back into the envelope after reading them. "Is Jean alright?"

Dr. Shelley shrugged. "I don't know, but she's with the Nocturnae and the Lygos."

"How can you know who she's with, but not if she's alright?"

"Our friends at NASIC right down the road from Wright-Patt were nice enough to provide us with imagery of their location using OPIR systems in GEO." Dr. Shelley reached into his lap drawer and pulled out two pictures.

Henry shook his head. "I don't know any of those acronyms."

"National Air and Space Intelligence Center is where the Intelligence Community does the bulk of their processing and analysis." Dr. Shelley handed Henry the photos. "Overhead Persistent Infrared satellite systems sitting in Geosynchronous Earth Orbit."

"We have infrared cameras watching the surface from space?" Henry asked, looking up from the pictures.

"Mmhmm," Dr. Shelley said. "Hollywood actually gets it right sometimes."

Squinting at the images, Henry examined them for something useful. "What's the resolution?"

"Classified … I asked. The only thing they'd tell me was to trust them that the Subjects were heading north."

"What's north? Wapakoneta? Michigan? Canada?" Henry handed the photos back to Dr. Shelley.

"I don't know. Ardie was with me when I got the call from NASIC. He's tracking them, and you and I will be preparing."

Henry scooted forward in his seat. "Lay it on me."

"I think it's best we divide and conquer on this." Dr. Shelley laid his hands on the desk and bounced the left one twice. "I'm going to focus on the Nocturnae and will oversee the transfer of the male Nocturnae into the Sandbox." He bounced his right hand twice and ran it up and down his desk. "I'd like you to focus on the Lygos, oversee the transfer of Rahne and Jean, and perform the initial interrogation of Jean while I'm at the Sandbox."

"I'll start by replaying the tapes of that night and cross examine them with our records to try and identify what *exactly* caused Rahne to transform." Henry's leg began to bounce. "Was there a singular component or multiple? Was it proximity to the Nocturnae or the moon that night or her getting her period? Whatever the trigger was, is it the same every time or have the rules changed now that she's transformed once?"

"Good," Dr. Shelley said with a nod. "We've recovered the majority of Jean's notes from her computer and braille device; there was some damage to the hard drives. Cameras throughout the facility were severely damaged and looks like we lost everything after I paged Jean on Saturday, the nineteenth. I'll make sure you get a copy of everything."

"The male Nocturnae interrogation?" Henry asked. Dr. Shelley acknowledged. "The Subject that tried breaking in?" Henry's leg stopped bouncing.

"The same." Dr. Shelley took a deep breath and slid his hands to the edge of his desk. "Sorin Harker, according to Jean's notes. Because of the incident, we're treating him as an Omega Level threat, and upon capture will be transferred directly to the Sandbox."

Henry crossed his leg and tapped his chin with his finger while staring into the corner of the room. "We also need to determine why—more importantly, *how*—Sorin was unaffected by our passive deterrents. He never should have been able to get out of that cell."

"Read the transcribed notes. You'll be amazed at the answer." Dr. Shelley reached for the bottom drawer of his desk. He pulled the messenger bag from inside and placed it on his lap. Reaching inside, he retrieved a brown leather-bound book with flecks of silver and sapphire scattered unevenly over its surface, wrapped tightly in a long, strand of braided black hair. "Here take this. Oh!" He reached back inside the bag, pulled out a thick file, and placed it on the table in front of Henry. "And this."

Dr. Shelley handed Henry the brown leather-bound book from his lap.

Henry quickly examined the outside of the leather book and thumbed through the pages. "It's really flimsy for how thick it is. The texture of the pages is strange too. And it's almost square, but smaller on the spine."

"No author," Dr. Shelley said, slowly and taking a slight pause after each statement. "No title. No classification markings. Nothing but these faded odd rune-like markings."

"What is this?" Henry asked as he thumbed through the manuscript. "And why is there no writing on any of the pages?"

Dr. Shelley said nothing while tapping the cover of the folder.

Henry set down the book and opened the file folder in front of him. An inch thick stack of papers of different sizes, ages, and colors lay inside. He flipped through the stack, his brow wrinkling more and more with each turn of the page.

"What is this Professor?" Henry asked, quickly glancing up and then back down at the pages. "There are at least six different languages in here, and some of these pages are burned." He flipped the page and gasped. "Jesus! There's a Nazi Eagle on this page. What *is* this, Professor?"

"This is the Codex," Dr. Shelley said pointing at the book. Henry looked up from the pages in the folder and stared at Dr. Shelley with confusion littered across his face. "This book is very old. It's older than the Epic of Gilgamesh."

"But there's nothing written on its pages," Henry argued, quickly thumbing through the book again.

"Everything The Company has learned about the Codex over the years is in that folder but in short, the book is … I hate this word … magic."

"Magic? This?" Henry held up the book. "Like *Harry Potter* magic or more like Dr. Stephen Strange magic? Is it merely technology we don't understand?"

"I have no idea who Dr. Stephen whoever is, but *Harry Potter*—possibly. But it could also be technology we don't understand, yes. In either case, Directorate 2 refers to this item as one of the six Artifacts."

Henry cocked his head to one side as Dr. Shelley's voice trailed off with his last word. "But you don't think there are six Artifacts like there are six Pillars of Faith, you think there are seven … like the Seven Deadly Sins or the Seven Sacraments of Christianity."

"Yes, I believe there are seven."

Henry flipped over the book and examined it further. "What's the catch?"

"What do you mean?" Dr. Shelley interlocked his fingers and placed them under his chin.

"With magic there's always something." Henry abandoned the book and focused on Dr. Shelley. "A catch. A cost. A side-effect. Magic is never something for nothing. In *Harry Potter*, for example, you had to say the words just right with the correct inflection. In Brandon Sanderson's *Mistborn*, you needed a certain metal to do specific magic. Both are over-simplifications, but you get the idea."

Dr. Shelley raised his finger and nodded. "Ah, yes. Right you are. The cost is blood. More specifically, your life force. Directorate 2 calls the act of using the Artifact, *anchoring*. They say it answers any question with the truth. And the cost is dependent upon the complexity of the question or answer; but since there's no telling how the Codex measures complexity, you can't know if your question will kill you or not. Directorate 2 could have used you on their team because they assumed they could measure the complexity of a question. In their eyes, asking for the sum of two and two is much less complicated than asking for the proof of String Theory."

Running his hand over the page, Henry said, "The Codex killed the anchor, didn't it?"

"Mmhmm," Dr. Shelley said, "they claimed it was a heart attack. Called it a widow-maker."

"Big surprise." Henry smirked. "I'll look through the files. See if there's anything in there that can be used to better understand the Lygos. And don't worry,"—Henry slammed the book shut—"I'll be careful not to bleed on the book."

"Sounds good. Any questions?"

Henry thought a moment with his eyes fixated on the Codex's cover. "Yes, do all of the Artifacts have this silver and sapphire look to them with these odd-looking runes?"

"I don't know." Dr. Shelley leaned over the desk, aligned his glasses on his nose, and studied the cover of the Codex. "Could be. Why do you ask?"

"Your Watch has the same markings and coloring."

"My Watch?" Dr. Shelley reached into his pocket. "This Watch?" But before he could pull out his Watch, the phone rang. Dr. Shelley answered. "Already? Impressive. I will be there."

"Who was that?" Henry asked when Dr. Shelley hung up.

"They've been found. Just outside Harrisville, Michigan, and they're heading for Jean's cottage. A team is waiting there to bring them in."

"Oh wow, that was fast."

"The Nocturnae should arrive at the Sandbox by tomorrow morning which puts Jean and Rahne here the day after." Dr. Shelley stood from his chair.

He slung his bag over his shoulder and picked up his coffee. Walking around the desk, he placed his hand on Henry's shoulder. "You'll be fine. Research the Codex. Take Jean to interrogation, and make sure Rahne is secured in her cell. Then interview Jean, she should be the most forthcoming and willing to make a deal."

"I'll do my best."

"You'll do great Henry," Dr. Shelley encouraged, patting his shoulder. "I'll call you after we transfer the Nocturnae—"

"Sorin?"

"Subjects don't have names, they're just numbers. I'll call you with an update. That should also give you a better timeline. I probably won't be back until Monday, so I expect you to have some answers by then." Dr. Shelley walked off toward the exit.

Henry slumped back into the chair with his coffee in hand and stared at the thick folder beside the Codex. "For the safety of the human race."

# 41



An Akhal-Teke stallion neighs as an ebony woman in a metallic-looking auburn coat brushes him. She calms him with a smile and a gentle pat on the neck. He flips his jet-black tail and returns to his hay. The woman pulls her long box braids back into a long, red cloth and begins singing to him in a language I do not know.

I don't remember walking into a barn or even seeing one, is this a dream? No, I don't think so. I can smell the hay, the horse's scent, and the familiar aroma of a barn. This is no dream; this is a memory, but not one of mine.

From the far end of the barn, a hooded figure appears making their way toward the woman and her horse. Without revealing their face, the figure places a gloved hand on the stallion's withers and moves up his mane to his forelock and down the bridge of his nose.

A large man, whose face I cannot see, rushes to the hooded figure's side. He says something to her, but it's muted by the parade of footsteps closing in on the barn.

"Amicia," a woman's voice screams in my mind. Claret? Is this Claret's memory? It must be.

"RUN," a man yells in a deep, familiar voice. "RUN CLARET! RUN!"

Before I can place the second voice, a pungent puff of air hits me in the face. I shake my head violently and grimace. "Do you smell that?"

"Mmm…?" Jean sniffs the air from her cradled position in my arms and looks up at me. "No, should I?"

"It smells like horse manure and burning flesh." Pestilence. Brimstone. Fire. Blood.

Jean's face wrinkles in disgust. "Gross. No, I absolutely do *not* smell that."

Rahne walks a hundred paces ahead of me. "Rahne, how are we doing up there?" I call after her.

"It's amazing she can hear you from here," Jean says, but when Rahne doesn't respond, Jean chuckles. "Kid's already ignoring you. Guess that means she likes you."

Not hard to be pseudo-adopted father of the year when the last one kept her in a cage and experimented on her. I don't respond to Jean and call ahead without raising my voice. "Are you hungry? Do you need to take a break?"

"No, I'm okay Mr. Sorin." To any human, Rahne's voice would be nothing more than a whisper in the wind, but to me, it's like she's standing right next to me. "The sign up ahead says HARRISVILLE 1-MILE."

"So … seems like Lygos retain some latent abilities while in human form," Jean says, picking at her fingernails and refusing to look up at me.

"Seems like it." I keep my eyes on the road ahead. "What do you know of the Lygos?"

"Nothing."

"Your parents never talked to you about it or your heritage? The Company—"

"No, my family never said anything about it and The Company stole my…" Jean pauses like she's unable to say the word, *daughter.* "Rahne, and told me she died. They must have known about me somehow, and that's why they recruited me. They wouldn't want to jeopardize their sinister plan by telling me classified information about something that was dormant in my blood."

All fair points. "Do you know anyone that might? Someone that we can trust."

"The cabin belonged to my grandparents. They're gone now, but they might have left clues there." She bites her lip. "V would've known something."

"Who's V?"

"My ex. Victor."

Ah … the ever-elusive *ex*-boyfriend. "And what makes you think he might know something?"

"He was working for Eugene when we met and he always seemed to know things no one else knew."

The plot thickens. "Where is he now?"

"Dead." She lowers her head. "There was an accident where we were working."

I tilt my ear south-east at the faint sound of helicopter blades whipping through the air. "I'm thinking we need to get to your cabin and out of sight. Then, we'll figure out our next move."

Rahne leads us through the town and up East Main Street. We follow US-23 a few miles beyond the town until we exit the forest and come to an old dirt road hidden in the snow brush and overgrowth.

"I think we're here." I search the hidden entrance from the road. "But I don't see an address. Just an old, rusted blue mailbox with a red door."

Closing my eyes so I can better hone my Nocturnae senses, I take a deep breath. The air is astringent from the dense forests and is complimented by the refreshing sweetness of Lake Huron. However, no matter how hard I try, I cannot pick out gun oil or body odor.

Slowly turning my head in all directions, I confirm my conclusion with my ears. No heartbeats. No ringing of an open communications line. No shallow breathing.

We're alone. We're safe.

"We're here." Jean pats my chest with the palm of her hand. "Please put me down."

"There's snow."

Jean slips off the tennis shoes and wool socks, stuffing them in the shoes to keep dry. "I know."

I set Jean in the snow, sinking her bare feet into the fresh powder. Rahne steps beside Jean and grabs her hand. Jean flinches, but Rahne guides Jean down the snowy overgrown path, hand-in-hand, while I follow behind.

"What do you think?" Jean asks, just inside the clearing. "Beautiful, isn't it?"

Rahne lets out a cry of excitement, "It's wonderful!"

Of course she thinks it's wonderful. It's the first house she's seen in person. House? Cottage? Cabin? Dump? …Dump. That's the correct word. My cabin back in Ireland was better than this, and it was 1350.

The home appeared to have once been a double wide but somewhere along the line someone decided to jerry-rig a three-season room off the back door and cut a massive hole out of the middle of the home for a fireplace. Redneck engineering at its finest. It's hard to say for certain, but the original siding may have been white or gray, or maybe even a slate blue. I can't tell with the vines climbing every surface in all directions like they are trying to pull the cottage into the deep recesses of the earth.

"Is it safe?" I ask Jean as Rahne runs to the door.

Jean brushes the snow from her feet. "What's *that* supposed to mean?" she snaps, putting her socks and shoes back on.

It's cockeyed, structurally unsound, and likely infested. "Is it safe … to assume you haven't been up here recently?"

"It's been a little while."

"No kidding." I chuckle and extend my hand for Jean. "Shall we?"

She holds up her hand and I gently escort her to the front door.

"It's locked," Rahne says, wiggling the door knob.

Super strength isn't retained in human form. That's a blessing.

Suddenly the door snaps off its hinges. Rahne quickly releases the handle, allowing the door to fall loudly on the small porch.

Jean jumps and lets out a short scream. "What was that?"

There goes that theory. "Rahne ripped the front door off your cabin."

"She can do that?"

"Apparently."

Panic quickly fills Rahne's face as she pleads, "I'm sorry. I'm sorry. I'm sorry. Please don't send me to the chamber."

Chamber? Must be some place they'd take her as punishment. Must have been terrible if she's this scared.

Quickly, Jean walks up to Rahne, stepping just to the side of a hole in the porch. "It's fine Rahne." She drops to her knees and embraces the child. "It's just a door. Don't worry about it. It was probably rotted anyway."

Jean evaded the hole with ease. Is it coincidence, can she see, or has the hole been there so long she knows to avoid it?

Rahne pulls back from Jean and wipes the tears from her eyes. "I'm really sorry. I didn't mean to."

"I know sweetheart. It's okay," Jean says with a smile. "Why don't you go on inside, I think there are some toys in the bedroom with two twin beds."

Rahne runs inside, disappearing into the darkness.

"Chamber?" I ask.

"I don't know." Jean wipes her hands on her pants as she stands. "I've never heard that before."

"You didn't know about a chamber?"

"No, Sorin," Jean snaps, turning toward me. She drops her voice. "Remember, I was kept in the dark on a lot of things."

"But you knew she was kept prisoner in a small cell beneath Eugene's lab. You met her, played with her, even read to her but you didn't know—"

"NO!"—she throws up her hands—"OH MY GOD SORIN,

NO! I didn't know about the cell or her prison or her conditions. I thought he was just bringing her into the office for a little bit. If I'd known, I—"

Heartbeats don't lie. She's telling the truth.

"You would have done nothing," I say. Jean opens her mouth to speak, but nothing comes out. She drops her head in shame. Gently, I place a comforting hand on her shoulder. "…and that's okay."

Jean takes a shuttered breath. "Is it?"

"You would have been in quite the dilemma." I grab her hand, holding it between both of mine. "But you didn't know Jean. And that's okay. The Company hid her and the *truth* from you for more than a decade. To you, she was a happy little girl playing in her *daddy's* lab and drinking tea with his beautiful colleague."

"Not knowing any better doesn't make it okay."

"Then show her how much better it is when she's with her mother." I release her hand and walk into the house. The sooner she rips that Band-Aid off, the better they'll both be; but I don't see that happening.

To my surprise, the cabin is in much better condition than the outside would leave a passerby to believe. The carpet is relatively clean, the paint isn't peeling off the walls, nor is there any yellowing on the ceiling from water damage. But it's musty. There's a layer of dust covering everything and cobwebs stitching together books and decorations.

I peek my head into the washroom, even though I haven't had to relieve myself in centuries. It's almost too bad, as modern plumbing probably improves the experience greatly. I can still enjoy showers, but this one stood too cramped next to a sink with tarnished knobs and a rust ring in the bottom of the basin.

"Come out, come out wherever you are," I say into the dark home with a smile.

It's been a long time, a very long time, since I've felt this...

I hear Rahne giggle from one of the rooms further into the house to my right.

...fun.

"Gotcha!" I jump into the large bedroom at the end of the hallway.

Two twin beds sit opposite a large bay window nearly the full length of the wall, but no Rahne.

Twin beds?

Jean stands just outside the door. "Jean," I say just above a whisper.

She steps toward my voice, walking confidently through the doorway with her hands at her sides.

"Do you have a sister?" I ask Jean as she walks past me and into the kitchen.

Jean shakes her head. "No, why?"

"I saw the twin beds and—"

"That was my grandparent's room," Jean says.

"When did they pass?"

"Early in my pregnancy." She looks off like the thought of her grandparents is painful for her. "When I came up here to settle the estate, I was still having terrible morning sickness."

"You came all this way alone?" I ask, and stomp loudly into the kitchen. "I'm gonna *find* you!" I call out, playfully.

"No, my roommate, Gabriel, came with me."

The name sticks out in my memory. On the stacks of papers on Dr. Shelley and Henry's conference table. A page with the name Gabriel Glass circled in blue ink.

"Gabriel ... Glass?"

"Yes," she says cautiously. "How do you know that name?"

Son of a bitch. They *were* watching her before she was pregnant. Were they watching her parents too? Her grandparents? I no longer feel safe in the cabin.

"Oh, you mentioned him while you were interviewing me," I lie. I don't want to freak her out by letting her know the extent of the conversations I had with Dr. Shelley and Henry.

I step into the kitchen and stop next to a refrigerator littered with yellowed pictures, aged coupons, and magnetic clothes for Michelangelo's David. But the cheap alphabet magnets on the side of the fridge catch my eye. I stare at the collage of colors trying to talk myself out of what I was seeing: R – I – H – I – Y – N – E – P.

PENYIHIR.

Jean walks into a bedroom at the far side of the kitchen. Shortly after, Rahne darts past the door to the three seasons room.

Smiling, I point at Rahne. "I see you!"

"Aww, man," Rahne huffs.

"Rahne," I say, calling her with my finger.

She shuffles back into the doorway. "Yeah?"

"Did you spell this out?" I point to the letters on the refrigerator.

She shakes her head. "Fred did."

Ah ... Fred, the imaginary friend. Or, is Fred a little *more* than imaginary? "Would you mind seeing if there's any wood in the three-seasons room we could use to make a fire?" I ask, gesturing at the fireplace centered in the living room.

Rahne nods and walks out of the living room. I head into the bedroom and find Jean sitting on the bed holding a thin chained necklace with a small round charm at the end.

"What's that you have there?" I ask, noticing the framed photo sitting on the nightstand of a younger Jean with a man.

"It was my mother's," Jean says, without raising her head. "She was wearing it the day of the car crash." I walk over to the table and pick up the picture. "Oh, the picture,"—she chuckles—"I thought you were asking about the necklace."

"I was," I say, admiring the photo, "but who is the man in this photo with you?"

"You're going to have to be more specific. What's he wearing? Hair color?"

Blind, right. "He's wearing a flannel shirt, brown almost black hair, and—"

"And a scruffy face with a mole under his left eye." Jean tries to hide her pain in a smile, but I see through it. "That's Victor."

I look up at her and quietly ask, "Rahne's…"

"Yes."

I look back down at the photo.

There's a large commotion from the living room like dry logs being dropped on brick.

"Mr. Sorin, I found some wood," Rahne yells.

I set the photo back on the nightstand and join Rahne in the other room. The bed squeaks as Jean stands and slowly follows behind me.

"Thank you, Rahne. Place them next to the fireplace, if you would, so I can get started on the fire." I join Rahne in front of the stone hearth. "Then, if you'd help Ms. Jean to one of these chairs—"

"I know where the chairs are Sorin, I grew up here." Jean takes a seat behind me.

"Rahne, have you ever made a fire before?" I ask.

"No." Rahne kneels beside me.

I clean the ash from the fireplace and set the first log. Stepping back, I let Rahne do the rest. Guiding her only when necessary. She's a smart girl. She lights the fire and sits on the floor in front of it, mesmerized by its dangerous beauty.

Mm, that fire feels nice. Smells good too … pine was always my favorite, even if it does cause a mess in the flue.

I sit behind Rahne, in the high-back button chair next to Jean and study the dusty unfinished game of chess on the small table between Jean and me. I move the white knight from F4 to E6, taking the rook but sacrificing it to the adjacent pawn on F7.

Jean's heart rate has slowed and I notice her still holding the necklace in her hand. "You're very attached to that thing."

"Yeah." Jean silently rolls the charm between her fingers like she's memorizing every curve and fold of the metal. "I thought I'd lost it."

Rahne turns to Jean and asks, "Do you have any crayons?"

"I don't know about crayons," Jean says and looks over her shoulder, "but how about a pencil and some paper?"

"May I see the charm?" I ask as Jean stands.

"Sure." With the charm centered in her open hand, Jean hands it to me but knocks over three pawns, a bishop, and the queen in the process. "Oops."

"Not a big deal," I say, taking the necklace by the chain. "Do you need any help with the pencils and paper?"

"No, I know where everything is," Jean says and heads for the kitchen. "But thank you."

I place the charm in my other hand and immediately feel a rush of heat in my palm. Unable to move, I watch a puddle of black liquid and blood pool in the palm of my hand. I force myself from the charm's grasp, pulling it from my hand by the chain before my blood can touch it.

"SHIT," I shout, bursting to my feet.

Rahne and Jean jump and turn to me.

"Are you okay? What happened?" Jean asks standing in the kitchen with a stack of white paper in one hand and pulling a pencil from a drawer with the other.

I dangle the charm from my fist. "Where did you get this?"

Walking back to Rahne with the drawing supplies, Jean says, "I told you; it was my mother's…"

"Where did she get it?"

"I don't know, her mother…?" Jean retakes her seat on the other side of the chess board. "It's been in my family for generations. Why?"

Jean hands the supplies to Rahne who, without pause, starts drawing under the fire light.

I stare at the charm and notice the part that touched my hand is sparkling. Placing my hand between it and the fire, the shimmer disappears. I hold it above my head so I can see its underside.

Silver. Sapphire.

I can feel my heart beating in my eyes. "Do you know your family's ancestry?"

"Umm, my mom said her family is from England." The English Channel.

"Your father then, does he come from France? Or your father's father?" Le Havre. Rouen. Amiens. Anywhere in northwestern France I'll accept.

"My dad said he had French in his blood … What does—"

Holding the charm by the chain, I examine it for any clue that it is what I think it is. When suddenly, on the very bottom of the charm where the black coating had worn off, an opalescent sapphire shimmers.

"This necklace is no mere charm. It is the Pearl that kept me hostage in Amicia's cabin on the Cliffs of Étretat."

"No way, you're—"

*SNAP!*

My ears zero in on a branch roughly fifty yards away as it breaks in half under a man's boot.

"Quiet," I whisper.

Rahne looks up from her partial drawing of a unicorn. Dry leaves break under another boot, thirty-eight yards from the back door.

"What is it?" Jean asks, pulling her head back.

"There's someone outside," Rahne says innocently and stands holding her pencil.

"It's The Company," I say as Rahne climbs onto Jean's lap. "They've found us." They did it the same way they did it on the beach of the Étretat Cliffs. Shit. How did I miss them, again? How are they doing this? Not the time. Think. "Jean," I say hurriedly, holding out the necklace. "Put the necklace around your neck."

Merely touching or holding the item doesn't make you invisible. Otherwise, I'd be invisible and unable to move; but I'm not. There must be a way to activate it, but that's a problem for another day.

She takes the chain from my hand and clasps it around her neck. "But if they capture us, they'll have the necklace."

"It's a risk we have to take, but I doubt they'll even suspect it." I look at Rahne and then back to Jean. "Jean, look at me." She does. I'm sorry Jean but to protect you and Rahne, I have to… *"Jean,"* I say as I compel her mind. *"You have no memory or idea of who Rahne's biological father is and the necklace is nothing more than a keepsake from your mother."* I free my mind from hers and whisper, "Jean, do whatever they say."

"Wh—"

*CRASH!*

Two small canisters, the size of soda cans, break through the cabin windows.

Jean screams and pulls Rahne into her chest.

An invisible force rips me from my chair and hurls me into the kitchen. I slam into the refrigerator knocking the magnets onto the floor. *"Save the child,"* a voice says in my mind. *"Save the child at all costs. Save the child."*

"What?" I mutter, holding the back of my head.

*"Save the child!"* the mysterious voice says.

Five men in tactical gear pour in through the back door. Clambering to my feet, I grab the barrel of the first man's gun and slam it into his face. The next two men are standing side-by-side and I smash their heads together like Stone-Cold's beer cans. The fourth man, covered in blood and brain matter, is paralyzed by his fear.

Ripping the fourth man's heart out, I hold it up for him to see. "You've got about nine seconds before you actually die. Spend it with your friends."

I kick the heartless body down the hall knocking over the next wave of men like bowling pins.

"RIN!!" Rahne screams in an ear-splitting shrill. Mo Chroí. "HELP ME—"

I step to run back into the living room, but trip over my feet as the world spins around me. I feel the bullet stinging in my back. Then another. And another.

No. No. Nonono. Not ... FUCKING ... sil-ver.

*"Save the child,"* the mysterious voice says once again, as everything fades to blackness.

# 42



Dr. Shelley exited the elevator into a newly renovated entrance. The black granite flooring now sported The Company's seal in the center: An eagle embracing the Earth and shielding it from the moon.

He quickly walked up to the long reception desk and smiled at the guard holding a donut. "Good morning. I'm here to see—"

"Sign in here," the man interrupted in a bored tone. He handed Dr. Shelley a clipboard.

While he signed in, Dr. Shelley eyed the men in tactical gear on either side of the single door to the right of the reception desk. The Glock 19s strapped to their thighs were fine, but he didn't like the look of the M4s slung over their shoulders.

"The system has been running a little slow today, I apologize but…"—the guard reached into his desk and pulled out an envelope—"Director Ziegler left this for you." He handed Dr. Shelley a large manila envelope with E. F. Shelley scratched on the front.

Dr. Shelley stepped away from the counter, opened the envelope, and pulled out a stack of papers. The top page read:

```
Eugene,
  I hope you like the improvements made to
the facility since your last visit—it's
amazing what you can do with a little
money.
  I was in the facility when Subject 076-
7-46, Sorin Harker, arrived. I signed the
necessary acceptance and transfer paperwork,
see attached.
  I'm off to Washington to secure more
funding but should be back at Edwards AFB
within the next six weeks for an update on
the mother and daughter, and Project PHANG.
  Keep up the great work!
        -Ardie
P.S. If you need anything from China let me
know. I'm headed to Wuhan next month.
```

The guard called Dr. Shelley over, gave him his badge, and pointed to the entrance on his right.

Dr. Shelley held his breath as he passed through the door, fearing the damn thing might go off, but it didn't. The door shut behind him and Dr. Shelley found himself in a long white-walled hallway with construction lighting and doors on both sides. The card readers beside each door weren't a surprise, but the Greek letters centered on each door were.

Taking particular notice to the missing Greek letters, he paused between doorways; but stopped the longest between the *Nu* and *Omicron* doors. At the end of the hallway was the *Omega* door, guarded by a young Asian woman sitting behind a desk and two more MP.

The woman looked up from behind a worn-out paperback. "Hello, sir. I need you to sign in to access this door." Dr. Shelley quickly filled out the sign-in sheet and dropped the pen. "Okay, you're going to go through that door. Only after the door closes behind you will the lights turn on—stupid construction. In order to enter the cell block, you'll need to type in your eight-digit pin."

"The guard out front only gave me a four-digit pin," Dr. Shelley said, confused. "Was I supposed to set up an eight-digit one?"

"Director Ziegler set up your pin. He said you'd know it," the Asian woman said.

Dr. Shelley scratched the back of his head and gave an unconvincing smile. "Oookay. And after the pin?"

"After you type in the pin, the door will open with a single light over the doorway. The rest of the lights will turn ON by voice command, but only after the door is closed and has locked behind you."

"Can't be too careful," Dr. Shelley said, jokingly.

"Right," the woman said with a smile. "Have a good day!"

"You too." Dr. Shelley stepped to the door but stopped midstep. "One more question, if you don't mind."

"How can I help?" She folded her hands, leaning over the table.

"Can I access the other wings from this level? I'm trying to get to the *Xi* door," Dr. Shelley confessed.

"Yes. Certain doors, like *Xi*, are only accessible through the Omega Level door." The woman scooted forward in her seat and used her hands to help show the path. "If you go through the main room, all the way to the back, you'll find another door. Take the stairs up one level for *Xi*."

He gave her a thumbs up, walked past the table, and through the door. The door closed behind him, and the room erupted in a blinding light. Once he could see again, he found himself in a six-by-eight-foot room and a large steel door in front of him with a backlit number pad to the left of the door.

"Eight digits huh…" Stroking the stubble on his face he cocked his head to one side. "Month, date, and year could be six or eight digits. I wonder…"

He quickly typed the keys with his thumb: $1 - 0 - 2 - 6 - 1 - 9 - 8 - 5$

The seal on the door released with a *POP!* and a swift gush of air flowed into the small room as the door pulled away from the frame ever so slightly. "Clever Ardie, choosing my wedding day," Dr. Shelley said as he pushed the door open. He stepped into the blackest of rooms. Letting the door close and lock behind him, he barked, "Lights!"

His voice echoed through the large stone room as the fluorescents turned on, one by one. He scanned for the door: 053-8-79.

With each step he took, an unimaginable stench grew ever more present, forcing him to cover his nose and mouth with the sleeve of his shirt. Cautiously, he approached the first door. The paint on the door seemed to morph and ooze, moving almost, and he stopped. Inching up to the door, he squinted his old eyes; but it didn't help. With a sigh of frustration, he moved closer and leaned in for a closer look.

"Jesus!" Dr. Shelley shouted, jumping back from the door.

Thousands of tiny insects moved over the door. Dr. Shelley eyed the name plate, but could only make out three numbers: 9 – 8 – 5 –

A fly jumped from the door to his hand revealing white wiggling maggots beneath the thousands of creepy-crawlies on the door.

Dr. Shelley turned away from the door as he coughed and gagged. "Oh my God that smell. It's unbearable … it … it's…"—he sniffed the air and turned back to the door, only to sniff again—"…it's spicy, like cinnamon and nutmeg. Yet, sweet like honey. And it's, familiar. What is that?"—he sniffed the air and kept huffing, inching closer with each breath until his nose was floating just above the insects—"I know that smell. It's my wife's strawberry-rhubarb pie."

"Hello?" a woman's voice called out softly from the other side of the door.

"Hello?" Dr. Shelley echoed in a fright and flexed his clammy hands. "Ma'am?"

"Eugene, is that you?"

His heart sank and his mouth went dry. "Michelle?"

"EUGENE!"

"Oh, Jesus fuck! Michelle! HELP! SOMEBODY HELP ME!" Throwing himself on the door, Dr. Shelley ignored the insects. Clawing at the door, he fought to find a way inside. The woman's voice screamed with him, mirroring his panic. "MY WIFE! SHE NEEDS HELP! SOMEBODYFUCKINGHELPMEGODDAMNIT!"

In Dr. Shelley's frantic movements, his Watch popped out of his pocket. Swinging from the tether tied to his belt loop, it slammed into the steel door with a muffled *tink* and gently grazed his hand.

*"Stop Eugene,"* a voice said in his mind.

Dr. Shelley ignored the voice.

As the Watch swung back at the door, the chain wrapped around his finger forcing the Watch into his hand like it had a mind of its own.

*"None of this is real,"* the voice said. *"Nothing more than a trick to lure you into its embrace, like a spider does to a moth."*

"She's there! I can hear her! Please help me," Dr. Shelley sobbed with eyes gaping, unable to blink.

*"No Professor, your wife is dead. She has been for many years now."*

Dr. Shelley clawed at the door until his nail broke, but he didn't stop. He didn't slow. He didn't even wince at the pain. "But how—"

*"The creature behind that door is a malevolent, supernatural being of immense power and trickery. To free yourself from this illusion, you must renounce it."*

"Renounce it?" Dr. Shelley questioned as blood dropped from where his fingernail had been.

*"You must admit to yourself that it … that she, is not real."*

"But, my wife—"

*"Is not real. That is not your wife."*

Dr. Shelley stepped away from the door and slowed his breathing. He wiped his tears and cleared his throat. "I love you, Michelle…"

"I love you too, Eugene," the voice said from behind the door.

"…but you, you are not my wife."

The scent of strawberry-rhubarb pie vanished in an instant and was replaced by the distinct smell of a decomposing human body. Dr. Shelley covered his nose and mouth. Gagged. And vomited.

*"Very good. I know that was hard and you want to remember her voice but you will forget the interaction you just had with the voice behind the door, the pleasant smells, and me. When I tell you, return the Watch to your pocket and clutch your bloodied finger; there was a burr on the door and you cut yourself on it. Now."*

Dr. Shelley shook his head while blinking rapidly and picking at his ear like a mosquito buzzed beside it. "Ah, fuck," he gasped at his bloody finger. "Damnit!"

He searched his pockets for anything to use as a makeshift bandage. He wrapped his finger in an old napkin and looked up at the door in front of him. Slowly, the insects blanketing the door peeled back enough for him to make out the plaque in the center.

**944-84-569**

WARNING: Malevolent, cannibalistic
Subject contained. Gaunt skeleton-like
figure with incredible physical strength.
Do not open this door or the window under
any circumstances. The cries of the
Subject may be fatal.
If Subject has escaped, call 727-0323.

Dr. Shelley took three steps back. He looked at the door one more time before moving on and paused at the next door. Unlike the other door, it was clean … oddly clean, as if not a speck of dust had ever landed upon it. There was no rust, no bubbling or peeling of the paint, and no wear of any kind.

### 736-94-447

```
WARNING: Charming and exquisitely horrid
Subject contained. True physical form is
    unknown. Do not speak to Subject.
 Exchanging words with the Subject may
  lead to hallucinations, early onset of
   terminal diseases, and/or infertility.
   If Subject has escaped, call 727-0239.
```

"…unknown physical form…" Dr. Shelley muttered, raising his glasses higher on his nose. "How can something be 'charming and exquisitely horrid' when its physical form is unknown?'"

Dr. Shelley shook his head and moved on to a newly built cell door. He removed his glasses to clean them and cast his raw, deteriorating eyes on the label below the small viewing window.

### 076-7-46

```
WARNING: Bloodthirsty, cunning Subject
contained. Short, built male, born in the
  14th century in Western Eurasia. Do not
  look into Subject's eyes; may cause loss
    of inhibitions and may lead to death.
   If Subject has escaped, call 727-2191.
```

Fury and rage quickly built within Dr. Shelley, and he stormed up to the window. "Hello again, Staff Sergeant Timothy Burr. Or should I say, Mr. Sorin Harker."

"Where did you take them?" Sorin asked coldly.

"You'd be wise to concern yourself with your own predicament." Dr. Shelley paused a moment, letting his warning sink in.

"Ah," Sorin said with a single-clicking sound from the corner of his mouth. "You found Jean's writing device and notes."

Dr. Shelley took a breath and flattened his hand on the door. "Right you are, Mr. Harker of Ireland. Born human in 1322. You experienced your new birth in 1350. You've seen quite a few things in your time on Earth, haven't you?"

"I've seen the unchanging and unwaning cruelty of man, yes."

"Only to ensure the safety and existence of our race against threats." Dr. Shelley chuckled to himself. "Such as you and your kind."

Sorin suddenly erupted into aggressive and uncontrollable laughter. "'Ensuring the safety of your race' what a fucking joke! And a lie. Humans have committed genocide time and time again throughout history: The Crusades, the concentration camps of your second world war, and the Gonohotta."

"Those were different times—"

"You humans," Sorin interrupted, "will always be the greatest threat to your own existence."

"—humans have evolved since then."

"Yes." Sorin's eyes flashed crimson. "Into us."

Dr. Shelley swallowed his pride, knowing Nocturnae manipulate. "It's strange Mr. Harker."

"What is?"

"With Jean you were smug, crude, and sarcastic—in the beginning—and by the end of your third day with her you'd become trusting, honest and sincere."

"Yes, well she was sweet for someone so dry. But you," Sorin sneered, sniffing the air. "You're acetous, sour … medicinal. Your blood, it's old, turning—like spoiled wine smells of wet dog when its tainted. You reek of something foul."

"What does that have to do with you trusting her or being honest and sincere with her?"

"Nothing." Sorin pressed his face into the small window. He ignored the pain and the sound of his flesh bubbling, as it melted into the silver on the door. "I just don't like men who cage children and torture them like they're animals."

Unable to withstand the pain any longer, Sorin ripped himself from the door, burying his face in his hands with a scream, and retreated to the far wall of his cell.

Dr. Shelley laughed, placing his hand on the door. He stared through the window a moment, enjoying Sorin's obvious pain. "You know what I think? I think you have feelings for her, and her dog."

Sorin looked up from the darkest corner of his cell, but said nothing.

"Ta-ta Mr. Harker," Dr. Shelley said, sliding the window closed. Walking toward the door on the far wall, opposite the one he entered through, he shouted, "We're going to have so much fun together."

Pushing the crash bar on the door, Dr. Shelley opened the door, and climbed the stairs to Xi-Level.


DR. SHELLEY GRABBED the handle of Xi-Level and opened the

door, revealing a nurse's station lined with monitors and meds on one side, and a single steel door on the other.

"May I help you?" a male nurse asked sternly, standing from behind his desk.

Dr. Shelley quickly scanned the patient charts on the nurse's station. "Yes, I'm here to see a former colleague." He pulled a chart. Laying the chart on the counter, he tapped it twice. "Him."

The nurse typed something into the computer and shook his head. "He's sedated."

"Oh," Dr. Shelley said and took a step toward the door ringing his hands. "I was just hoping to see him again. The way we left things wasn't the greatest."

"I mean … I can let you in to say your peace," the nurse said walking out from behind the counter. "But he won't be able to say much."

"That's quite alright."

Dr. Shelley followed the nurse to the second door and looked through the long plexiglass window that stretched down one side of the door. In the center of the padded room sat a young, bearded man with long hair wrapped in a straitjacket.

The nurse looked at Dr. Shelley and said, "One minute. That's all you get."

Agreeing with a nod, Dr. Shelley stepped out of the way and reached for a chair.

"Sorry, no chair," the nurse said, shaking his head. "Can't risk it."

"I understand."

"Keep your back against the wall or the door," the nurse warned.

"Do not approach him." The nurse opened the door.

Dr. Shelley gave a hard blink. "I know the drill."

"One minute. No more." The nurse slammed the door shut and locked it behind him.

Dr. Shelley flattened himself against the padded wall and slid down onto his bottom. He didn't say anything at first. He just sat there, enjoying the bound man's presence. In silence.

"Hello, old friend." Dr. Shelley looked around the room at the images on the walls, ceiling, and floor. "I see you're still painting."

The man groaned.

"Ah." Dr. Shelley bobbed his head, eyeing the dried dark red fluid smattering the room. "I thought so. You used blood because it was the only thing you had. Is that what landed you in the jacket?"

The man blinked once.

Dr. Shelley looked at each drawing in the room, taking his time. "The Gaelic triquetra. The Eye of Horus." He sat up from against the wall to reveal a slightly smeared painting behind him. One very similar mirrored on the other side of the doorway. "Okinawan Shisa dogs,"—he paused and eyed around the room again—"they're all for protection." Concerned, he looked to the man in the center of the room. "What's wrong? Why do you need this much protection?"

The man closed his eyes and did not answer.

The door opened beside Dr. Shelley, startling him.

"Alright doctor, times up," the nurse said, waving his hand in a *come-on* motion. "Let's go."

Slowly, Dr. Shelley stood and followed the nurse through the doorway.

"Goodbye, old friend," Dr. Shelley said with a wink, and grabbed the doorknob.

The restrained man's eyes widened and he thrashed about in his cell and the door slammed shut behind Dr. Shelley.

# 43



THE OLD MAN'S footsteps grow quieter and quieter as he walks away from my cell.

Possible exit to my right or another level in this prison … or maybe it's just a bathroom. Ugh, my head. I guess aerosolized silver's lingering effects are nausea and a headache that would drive humans mad, noted. Without blood, the residual effects of the silver are going to be present for a while.

Fan-fucking-tastic.

A heavy door opens, and the man's footsteps disappear when the door slams shut.

Noise-reducing walls and flooring. Thank you, Maker. And the Clinton administration, for lowest price technically acceptable rules and regulations. I may not be able to know everything about this awful place, but I'll know enough for a strawman drawing.

Stuffing my hands in my pockets, I find them empty. The boutonniere Jean got me is gone. I can't say I'm surprised. Damn it.

I pace in my ten-by-ten-foot cell with a steel feeding trough in the back corner and a thin camping mattress against the wall adjacent to the door. Playing out every possible scenario the girls might be in right now in my mind when all of the sudden, a muffled voice catches my attention.

"Is it true?" asks a mysterious guttural, masculine voice.

I stop in the center of my cell and look around. My cell is empty, but maybe there are other cells. I woke up in here. I close my eyes and listen. A heartbeat like mine thumps faintly from a distance. I don't believe it. It can't be.

"Is what true?" I ask, below a whisper.

"No need to test it, neophyte. I'm Nocturnae like you."

I'm not the only one?! I gasp. Alert, I square myself up with the door. "I thought I was the last."

"No, there are more of us but, I digress—is it true?"

I take a step toward the voice. "Is what true?"

"That you have *feelings* for an Ubiet," the mysterious Nocturnae says with a coy tone.

I don't know what he's referring to. "*Ubiet?*"

He pauses for a long moment before speaking again. "Your Maker didn't educate you, I see. *Ubiet* is the term we Nocturnae use for humans."

"Why not just call them humans?"

The man wheezed a painful cough and cleared his throat. "*Ubiet* is Bulgarian for *will kill.* We use it as a scathing insult toward them. Humans are arrogant, cowardly creatures whose unending spree of murders has brought our kind to our knees, begging for survival. They slaughtered our women, cutting off our ability to turn humans and replenish our ranks by spawning our neophyte children."

Well, that was a long-winded, hypocritical speech. I don't answer.

"Do you have feelings for the Ubiet?" he asks again.

Depends on how 'feelings' is defined. This man should be an ally, but something in his tone and manner is putting me off. "No, I don't have feelings for her. Who are you?"

The sound of skin crackling into an evil grin up one side of a face puts a lingering image in my head. "I've been called *many* things over the years," he says in a haughty tone, "but most recently I've gone by Phaeton LéTry."

Sounds Créole. Maybe French Créole. But that first name is almost, mythological. "That's an interesting name, Phaeton. Where's it from?"

"The Greeks, it was the name for the son of Helios—Phaeton, the 'Shining One.'"

Right again, mostly. Go me. "And before that, what did they call you?"

"I wouldn't concern myself with any of that right now."

Too quick a response not to be dodging something. "How long have you been here? What *is* this place?"

"Think of it as a super-max prison for the supernatural. The Ubiets call it the Sandbox—Supernatural Anomalies something, something. We are on the level of the prison known as, Omega."

"Omega," I scoff. The end.

"Things that can bring about the end of the Ubiet. Things like you and me."

What did Jean call me in that cell? An existential threat? "What else is down here? What was that thing that—"

"Manipulated the mind of the Ubiet? A creature of Algonquin-lore known as the Wihtikow."

"The Wendigo? That's real?"

"Are we not real?" Phaeton asks quickly and in a callused tone.

He makes a point. "What's on the other floors?" I ask. Maybe he knows enough to help me get my bearings.

"I suspect each floor above us becomes progressively less dangerous—as dangerous things go." He coughs violently, straining to catch his breath.

I mumble to myself, "Less dangerous. Means lower security. Means easier to escape from."

"Exactly." Gasping for air, he spirals into a frenzy of coughs.

"Are you okay?" I take another step forward. "I've never heard a Nocturnae cough like that before."

"This?" Phaeton heaves a single, hard cough. "A side effect from prolonged exposure."

"To silver?"

"No—not exactly anyway—an item much older. An Atrocity…" He coughs again and then asks, "How did they capture you?"

Best follow his lead, don't want to ward him off. I could be down here a while, and it'd be nice to have someone to talk to. "Aerosolized silver took me out. Jean and I were…"

"Jean?" Phaeton steps forward in his cell. "The Ubiet?"

Shit. Stupid. Can I turn this around? Don't lie, he'll know. "Yes. What are the Atrocities?"

Phaeton slowly paces his cell, gathering his thoughts. Then he stops suddenly, as if he's decided something. "The Atrocities look innocent enough. If you saw them on the street, you'd think nothing of them. They're magical items which can only be used when an individual anchors themselves to the item by spilling their blood over it. The bond remains until the anchor dies or a new anchor is made."

"Dies?"

"They're *Atrocities*, not greeting cards," Phaeton scoffs, chuckling to a punchline only he finds funny—okay, it's a little funny. "Yes, dies. Every time an Atrocity is used, it pulls a little more of the anchor's life force. The amount taken is dependent upon the power needed by the Atrocity to do what the anchor asks."

That's why he sounds sick. "You're an anchor."

"Yes," Phaeton says and quickly coughs hard into his hands. He kicks the feeding trough of blood in the corner of his cell. "And this liquid the Ubiets call blood is just enough to sustain our kind, but insufficient if anchored to an Atrocity."

Blood is the key to using the Atrocities and that's why I didn't turn invisible when I held the Pearl at Jean's cabin. I hope Jean doesn't accidently become the anchor—she'll die.

Rather than press my luck, I let the conversation die. Better to not push too hard. Especially in his condition. Plus, I'm not going anywhere.

# 44



JUGGLING A FULL cup of coffee in one hand and fishing the phone out of his pocket with the other, Henry closed the car door with his leg. He huffed at the text on the screen, set his coffee on the roof of the car, and slumped against the vehicle.

Eugene: *Have the girls arrived yet?*

"Seriously? Not even a good morning?" Staring up at the sky, Henry mumbled an expletive to himself.

Henry: *No, not yet. How are things going out there?*

Eugene: *They should arrive within the next couple of hours. Find out what Jean knows. I want everything, Henry.*

Henry: *And the child?*

Eugene: *She'll be delivered to a separate containment unit on the south-side of the complex. Anything on the Nocturnae blood?*

Henry: *Yes, the male Nocturnae told Jean the truth. When the deceased female Nocturnae blood and saliva are mixed and combined with a human patient's saliva and blood mixture, we get the results we've been striving for in*

*PHANG. Are you still coming back today?*

Eugene: *No, I won't be. I want you to send everything you've found pertaining to the PHANG Program to Langley.*

Henry: *You're going back to Langley?*

Eugene: *Yes, as much as I hate to, I must. This work is too important. Have you looked at the notes on the Book I gave you?*

Henry paused, realizing the word 'Codex' must be classified.

Henry: *It's on my agenda for this morning.*

Eugene: *Read quickly Henry. When the girls get there, Jean is your top priority.*

Henry: *And the child?*

Eugene: *Observation and non-invasive, non-stress inducing tests only. Just Stage 1. We'll begin Stage 2 when I return. I'll be back by Wednesday. I want the interview with Jean by then, and I want everything Henry. Everything.*

Henry: *I'll take care of it. See you in a few days.*

Henry stuffed the phone in his pocket and grabbed his coffee. Walking toward the facility, he whistled Elton John's *Cold Heart*.

The steel blue-gray door on the side of a seemingly abandoned building drew little attention from onlookers. Holding up his badge to the door frame beside the handle, he waited until the door popped open. A subtle alarm beeped and a ten second countdown appeared on a small 8-bit screen.

"Ah, shit! What was the damn PIN? Pin, what was the pin?"

– 9 – 8 – 7 –

"Earth? No, not enough letters."

– 6 – 5 –

"It definitely was a planet though."

– 4 –

"Saturn."

– 3 –

Henry typed 72-88-76 on the keypad and hit ENTER. The countdown stopped with one second remaining.

"Shit, that was close. Almost got locked out."

Without flipping on the lights, he walked to his desk. Setting the coffee on the far side of the desk, he took a seat and flopped his bag onto the desk. He turned on the fluorescent lamp at the head of the desk and peeled back the zipper on the bag. Without pause, he pulled out the leather book and the associated documents Dr. Shelley had given him to go through.

Bypassing the Codex, Henry opened the manila folder to a bright yellow page that read:

```
WARNING: The Artifact known as "The
Codex" is very dangerous and should be
handled with extreme care. Use with
latex gloves when handling to prevent
injury to the reader. In the event the
reader's blood touches any part of the
item, the individual is to immediately
call base emergency services and inform
them there's a CODE INDIGO at their
location.
```

Henry eyed the leather book. "Yeah, fuck that. Not touching you again." Pulling a t-shirt out of his backpack, he threw it over the book.

He peeled back the warning page to find two, hand-written

paragraphs at the top, followed closely by two columns—the page was autographed with "VI." The left column was written in pen in one handwriting, and the right column was in very faint pencil in a completely different handwriting.

The first paragraph of column one read:

```
    Our forefather said, "Stay in the light,
safety is in the light."
    He knew light protected us and darkness
was their ally, separating our worlds.
    He came every evening under the cover of
night and left before the morning sunrise.
```

Then he read the first paragraph of column two:

```
    Then God said, "Let there be light, and
there was light."
    God saw that the light was good. God then
separated the light from the darkness.
    God called the light "day," and the
darkness "night." Evening came, and morning
followed.
                              Genesis 1:3-5
```

Henry stopped reading and looked up at his faint reflection in the dark blank computer monitors. "Bullshit ... It can't be that simple or obvious ... can it?"

He laid the papers in his lap and pulled out his phone. He searched for *King James Bible, Genesis Chapter 1* and clicked on the first search result. "Well, all those years of Sunday School may have just paid off."

Henry pulled a small black notebook from the front pocket of his backpack and wrote:

```
Direct comparison of a handwritten document
of unknown origin by an unknown author to
The Creation Story of Christianity (KJE).
```

TWO HOURS AND thirty-eight minutes of reading, web searching, and note scribbling had passed when his cellphone rang twice "Henry Ingvar. The Company, Directorate 3."

"Mr. Ingvar, your package has arrived," a man said on the other end.

"I'll be right out."

Scooping up the documents, Henry packed them back into the folder, and slid them messily into his bag. Carefully cradling the Codex in his t-shirt, he placed it into his bag and slung the bag over one shoulder.

Henry approached the main entrance, but no one was there. Peering through the small window in the door, he clocked a long, thin shadow coming from the large hangar doors. "Hello?"

"Mornin' suga'! You Henry?" a female captain in ABUs asked, standing in front of a woman with her hands cuffed in front of her and a bag over her head.

Henry pushed through the crash bar and entered the hangar bay, peeking at the six armed men, two of whom held the prisoner. "Yes. Is that Jean?"

The captain glanced over her shoulder and down at her

clipboard. "Allicines, Jean M. PsyD. I'd say so."

"That bag over her head is pretty useless."

"Standard procedure," the captain said.

Appalled, Henry pressed. "She's blind."

"Standard procedure. Sign here." The captain handed Henry the clipboard.

"And the child?"

"Bravo team is handling the transfer. She was still sedated when we landed, but we'd rather not take any risks—"

"I understand." Henry backed away from the large doors. "We're taking her to Interrogation Room 1."

"How fitting," Jean muttered snidely from inside the bag.

One of the MP drove his elbow into her back and Jean let out a painful yelp.

"Careful!" Henry pointed at the man. "She may be a prisoner, but she's still Dr. Allicines. Have some fucking respect."

The MP stared at Henry and elbowed her again. "Move. Freak."

Henry lunged at the MP with a fist raised, but the captain stopped him. "Sorry, suga'. Can't have that." She tapped Jean's shoulder and said, "Keep it moving inmate."

"She deserves—"

"She don't deserve nut'in. She ain't human." The captain gently smacked Henry's shoulder. "Now, ya'h gonna show us where Interrogation Room 1 is? Suga'."

Henry badged them into the hangar; but two MP stayed behind. They wound through the corners of the warehouse within the hangar until they came to a door that read: INTERROGATION ROOM 1.

"We're here." Henry opened the slate gray windowless steel door to a ten-by-ten-foot room. "Give her to me," he said to the MP and turned into the room.

"Sorry sir," an MP said. "Gotta see the transfer all the way through. Dr. Shelley's orders."

The two MP escorted Jean to a chair and slammed her down, ripping the bag from her head.

Shaking her head with squinted eyes, she stopped with her head turned toward the MP on her left. "Can I pee first?" she begged, squeezing her knees together. "It was a *really* long flight."

"Dr. Shelley said *sit*. So, sit," the MP barked while forcing her deeper into the seat and ripping her sleeve with his metal watch band.

"Ow!" Jean gasped, holding her upper arm. A small drop of blood ran down her arm from the accidental cut.

"Lieutenant, that's enough!" Henry scolded and turned to the captain. "Seriously?! Captain—"

"We have orders suga'."

Henry rolled his eyes and looked at Jean's arm. He reached into the bag and pulled out his t-shirt, ripping a strip off. "Let me see your arm." He knelt down to wrap it. "I'm sorry, I only have this t-shirt."

Jean faked a smile. "Thank you, Henry."

"Uncuff her," Henry demanded. The captain gestured with her chin and one of the MP removed her restraints. "Thank you. You can go now."

The MP leave the room, but the captain looks back. "We'll be right outside."

"No, you can leave the building. I don't need you."

"Sorry suga', we have our orders." The captain closed the door behind her as she exited the room.

"Bitch," Henry snapped under his breath and took a seat across the table from Jean. "Nice try with the *can I pee first.*"

The corner of Jean's lip curled up as she turned her face toward the wall to her right. "I didn't think it would work, but I had to try."

Henry silently sat across from Jean for a minute and then asked, "How you doin'?"

"That's a pretty stupid question."

"Yeah, I know. I guess I just … I haven't seen you since the attack and…" Henry softly laid a hand on hers. "Are you okay? Where have you been? What happened out there?"

Jean pulled her hands away. "I'm sweaty from being bagged." Using her teeth, Jean tightened the shirt on her arm and closed her eyes with a heavy sigh. "Where have I been since when and what happened out where?"

"Harrisville. Wright-Patt. And everything in between," Henry said with excitement and concern in his voice. "They're saying you've aligned yourself with the … the …"

"The Nocturnae? The one I was interviewing?"

"I know that's not true."

"Oh," Jean says with an evil giggle, "but it is. And he has a name. Sorin."

"Why would you align yourself—"

"Why?" Jean raised her voice. "Because I know you were experimenting on your own fucking niece."

"I never—"

"BULLSHIT HENRY!" Jean slammed both hands onto the table. "Your brother didn't know. Victor never knew I was pregnant. But you, you knew—"

The door swung open and the three MP drew their guns and pointed them at Jean.

"STOP!" Henry shouted, jumping out of his chair with his arms outstretched. "We're fine. Guns down!"

The captain stared at Henry a moment, then slowly closed the door behind her.

Henry reclaimed his chair. "I didn't know—"

"Bullshit!"

"—at first," Henry said, with both hands raised. "I didn't know, at first."

"When did you find out?" Jean doesn't let him answer. "When she could crawl? Walk? When she said her first word?"

"She was five when I found out," Henry said slow and calm.

"You expect me to believe that for five fucking years you watched an infant grow into a toddler and had no goddamn idea she was your FUCKING NEICE!?" Tears welled in the corners of Jean's eyes, but she was too angry and refused to blink. "When I lost her, you sat at my bedside with GG after I tried to kill myself. Both fucking times Henry!" She held up two fingers. "Both times. Do you know how that feels? What kind of betrayal that is?"

Henry let his head fall and hang. "Forgive me."

"Forgive you?" Jean jumped from her seat and positioned herself an inch from him, impeded only by the table pressing against her hips. "Fuck off Henry! You could have told me years ago. She's your brother's child!" She spat at him.

Henry wiped his face. "You were never supposed to know."

"Thank God Victor isn't here," Jean said, shaking her head. "Because he'd fucking kill you."

"Well, he's dead. So, I don't need to worry." Henry took a deep breath, sat back in his chair, and placed both hands flat on the table. "Let's start again. Yes, you are under arrest and will be detained. But I assure you, I will treat you well. I am a friend after all."

"A friend," Jean scoffed. "Did you honestly think I'd never find out? No, of course you didn't. You and Eugene lied to my face for years. For my entire adult life. For her *entire* life. You. Eugene. The Company. You all expect me to still be on your side? Fuck you. Fuck you all. I'm not on your side."

"So, you're on *his* side?"

Jean smacked the table. "He hasn't lied to me!" She smacked it again. "Not even when I was drilling him for information to help destroy him and what remains of his race. He told the truth, every time. Even if he knew I wouldn't like it. He found my… He found Rahne. He protected us! FROM YOU!"

Henry slid his bag across the table and reached inside for a notepad and a pen. He wrote:

```
Dr. Jean Allicines has aligned herself with
the Nocturnae. It appears as though she
cannot call Rahne her daughter—she just
stopped herself from saying, "He found my
daughter," and instead said, "He found
Rahne."
```

"What does the Nocturnae know about the child and the Lygos?"

"His name is Sorin. And the *child* has a name, Rahne. He knows as much as I do."

"Which is … how much?" Henry twirled the pen between his fingers.

"NOTHING!" Jean gave a hard shrug. "This is all new to me. To Rahne. To him. To you. Dr. Shelley. The Company. Fuck Henry, use your damn brain. I thought you were smarter than this."

"Why do you think he helped you and Rahne, even after she killed his Maker?"

Jean froze, clearly taken off-guard. "She did what?"

Surprised, Henry spared no detail. "Just after taking her Lygos form, Rahne ripped Sorin's Maker in half and then consumed her."

Jean took a moment to fight back the tears. She wrung her hands, digging her fingernails into the skin. "She killed his Maker…"

"Yes."

"…right before his eyes…"

"Yes."

"…and he still protected her. He still protected us. And was so gentle with her. Like she was Cora. His *Mo Chroí*."

"Cora." Henry took a note. "Sorin's daughter."

Jean took a hard sniffle and wiped her nose. "You have my notes."

"And the video."

"Then you know everything."

"Yes."

"And that means, you saw her Lygos form." Jean smiled in wonder. "The power she has."

Henry put down his pen. "Very. Which makes her a threat, but unlike anything we've seen before."

Fear washed over Jean at the thought of what Henry was implying. "She's a scared little girl who doesn't understand what's happening to her."

"She's still a threat."

"Well, no shit," Jean said rudely. "The only person showing her kindness, or interest in helping her understand her gifts, is a seven-century-old Nocturnae."

"What does that say about you as a mother?" Henry asked in a cold voice.

Jean felt like he'd ripped her heart from her chest. "That's low. Even for you. Can you just go away for a bit? Please?"

Unable to look at her, Henry quickly got up from his chair. "Yeah." He tapped the door twice and the door immediately popped open. "I'll be back in ten."

The door closed softly behind him.

With a heavy sigh, Jean dropped her arms flat on the table and used them like a pillow with one arm out straight. The tip of her finger caught something soft near the edge of the table. She perked up as her hand found the mouth of Henry's bag.

She pulled the bag toward her and its contents partially spilled onto the table. Her hand brushed against loose pages fanning from a manila file folder.

Quickly, she ran her hands over each page reading the depressed letters. The Roman Numeral six—*VI*— appeared often and the word CODEX was repeated throughout.

"Victor Ingvar," Jean gasped as the geography of her face rearranged into a hesitant smile.

She stopped a moment after reading a line describing the exterior of the Codex. She read it three more times and returned to Henry's bag to explore further. Her hands found a book bound in leather. She removed it from the bag and pushed the handwritten notes aside.

Slowly, she ran her hands over the exterior of the book—memorizing its shape and every detail. Opening the book from the back cover she searched for depressions in the page, but there weren't any.

"Are you alive?" Jean asked, flipping the pages and thinking of Victor's scent. "Come on… Tell me something. Anything."

The wound on her arm, no more than a scratch, suddenly bled like a deep laceration. In seconds, her makeshift bandage was soaked and blood ran down her arm, seemingly with a mind of its own. Jean searched the page from top to bottom unaware her blood was pooling on the page. Just as her finger approached the pool, the blood morphed into a red braille cell.

A blue ring formed around her eyes. She read the small dots as they formed on the page, made from her own hardened blood.

```
Victor is alive.
```

Jean lifted her hand from the page in shock. Could it be true? Hovering just over the parchment, Jean ran her fingers over one another and then returned them to the page, eager to discover more.

```
Over the course of a year, The Faceless
```

King, ruler of the Nocturnae, visited all the human kingdoms. The King promised them food, shelter, and water in His Garden and, above all else … protection from the horrors of nature. Humanity was welcomed into His kingdom of night. And the evening and the morning were the first day.

The humans were shown an expanse, where the King separated the waters below His Garden into the waters to drink and the waters to bathe. And the evening and the morning were the second day.

Jean cocked her head to one side and thought, "The Creation Story?" Turning the page, she continued reading, unable to feel the blood flowing down her arm and into the book.

The people were brought bags of seeds and the King said, "Let the earth sprout vegetation, plants yielding seed and trees bearing food," and we learned how to farm. And the evening and the morning were the third day.

Humanity was shown the lights that would illuminate His kingdom at night, built for them to see. And the evening and the morning were the fourth day.

They were shown new and better ways to fish the King's waters and hunt His lands, bringing true His promise that humanity would be fed better than ever before. And the evening and the morning were the fifth day.

The King brought forth animals they'd never seen in the wild and showed humanity how to care for them—he called them Domesticated Animals. The King turned to the humans and said, "I have given you every plant-yielding seed to grow herbs for medicine. I have given you the fish in my seas, the birds in the air, and the animals in my forests to fill your bellies. Everything you need for life. I only ask two things of you. The first being, that you tend my Garden. The second, you allow my Nocturnae children to drink from you from this day forward."

The humans agreed, and it was so. And the evening and the morning were the sixth day.

After being shown such new things, on the seventh day they came to their King and asked Him, "What of this day?"

The King sat back in His throne and said, "On the seventh day we rest."

Jean lifted her hands from the page in frustration, cutting the flow of blood to the Codex to a mere trickle. "What happened to the humans?" Returning her fingers to the page, braille appeared beneath them as they glided over the pages.

For the first few generations everything occurred exactly as it was prescribed. Until the King's Maker, Lamia, was killed. Angry and betrayed, the King renounced His deal and enslaved humanity within His Garden.

Human females were forced to breed until childbirth killed them or they couldn't anymore. If a woman became barren, she was doomed to feed the King's Nocturnae children until she died. This left the children to raise each other, in the absence of their mothers, either dead, or in birthing houses.

Once a child was eight years old, they were assigned gender-specific roles.

Young girls became responsible for nursing the sick back to health, cooking for their fellow humans, and cleaning the households. Once of childbearing age, the girls were forced into the birthing houses, shackled, and forcibly taken. Condemned to the unending physical and psychological torture until they were impregnated.

"Jesus," Jean said, shaking her head. "This might be the worst stain in history."

Young boys were forced to work in the mines. Extracting minerals, elements, and gems from the earth to power Nocturnae technology and decorate their elaborate structures. Many boys died from the harsh conditions, cave-ins, and disease—they were the lucky ones.

Every evening, half the men were fed upon by a Nocturnae. Not enough to kill them, but enough to keep their masters satiated.

The following day, the other half of the men were fed upon. The Nocturnae found this method was most effective in keeping the men healthy enough to work.

Once a week, ten men were chosen at random to fight in hand-to-hand combat in The Pit as entertainment for the Nocturnae. All the men were savage brutes, lean and strong from the daily physical labor and the high protein diet—comprised of human flesh.

The Nocturnae wasted nothing of a human carcass. Skin was dried and used as parchment, hair was used as thread, and the fat was rendered and made into soap.

The only break the humans were afforded came every twenty-eight days, when the moon was full. Meals were supplied at normal times. No work was done. A day of rest.

Generation after generation, lives began and ended in these conditions; knowing nothing other than this life of trauma, pain, anguish, and horrors from the depths of one's worst nightmares.

After many years, a man informed the King some of His people were planning a coup. When the man's intelligence was confirmed, and the coup was thwarted, the King gave the man a gift.

For the next three years, the man was the King's eyes and ears on the streets, in the mines, and everywhere else the humans roamed. Having yet to be caught by His fellow man, the King gave him a gift unlike any other, a name, and allowed him to take a wife all of his own.

The Encomiâ family was born.

"Seems like there's never been a time we didn't turn on our own kind," Jean mused aloud and turned the page.

The Encomiâ family was blessed with twin girls, Adamari and Eveline. Nearing adulthood and fearing their daughters' horrific future that lie just over the horizon, the family escaped the Garden using the sewer system. Traveling at high noon and covered in mud and excrement, the Encomiâ family would be gone for hours before the Nocturnae knew.

Once outside the Garden, they ran. They ran until Adamari and Eveline's feet bled, and their parents had to carry them. Just before twilight, they found a cave and took shelter deep in the cave until morning.

Adamari awoke in the middle of the night and noticed a stitched toy, a stuffed animal shaped like a pig, near a large pool of shallow water in the middle of the cave. She woke Eveline and, for a moment, the sisters admired the paisley patterns with flecks of silver and sapphire blue; but quickly scrambled toward the strange object.

In their excitement, the girls woke their parents. But before they could stop the children, the stuffed animal was in their hands and the room was lit up in deep blues and purples, while a shroud of the blackest-black sealed off the entrance to the cave.

The parents ran to their children, using their bodies as shields from the mysterious lights. At the edge of the pool, a large aura formed in the water. The family looked on in fear, thinking the worst. Emanating from the aura, three distinct tones rang in their ears.

A dark cloudy figure appeared. Swimming from deep in the shallow pool, growing in size as it neared the surface. It wasn't long before only what can be presumed to have been the figure's head could be seen.

"What is it?" Adamari asked her mother.

Taking a half step closer, the mother inspected the figure further. "I don't know sweetheart."

Two purple eyes appeared from the black figure as it spoke. The figure backed away from the water's surface and appeared to bow with one hand outstretched to the surface.

"It's here to help us," Eveline said.

Her father gasped, "No Eveline, we don't—"

"You're here to help us, aren't you?"

Eveline continued, interrupting her father.

The black figure nodded.

"See, I told you. Magic aura, magic aura in the water," Eveline began.

"Won't you save us from the Nocturnae?" Adamari asked, finishing her sister's question.

Jean's fingers stopped moving across the page. "'Magic aura, magic aura in the water' … sounds an awful lot like: Mirror, mirror on the wall."

The figure's eyes widened sternly as it swayed under the water, "SPIL DER SA EHT ESOR. RIAH KCALB SA YNOBE. NIKS ETIHW SA WONS. LUFITUAEB ERA EEHT HTOB. NO EHCRANEM THGIN. TA DOOLB SNOOM KAEP. YTUAEB LLIW EMOCEB TSAEB. A TSEAB OT ELTTAB TSEAB. EMOC HTROF NEHW DEDEEN. ECIFIRCAS OT DLOHPU. LITNU ENILDOOLB SDNE."

Jean read each word carefully, committing it to memory to decipher later.

The room illuminated again with purples and blues, forcing the family to cover their eyes. When they opened them, the King and a handful of His Nocturnae generals were standing in the entrance to the cave. The family didn't resist, there was no point.

The generals took them into custody and

escorted them back to the Garden. They paid no attention to the stuffed animal on the cave's floor.

The following night, the two girls' parents were made an example of in the center of the Garden. The Nocturnae cheered and carried on and the humans watched in horror as their friends were brutally murdered before their eyes.

Not long after, the twenty-eighth day came, marking a new day of rest for the humans. The humans gathered outside; as had become customary to do for they worshiped the moon. After all, the moon saved them from their torturous existence, but this moon was special.

Rather than its normal off-white appearance in the sky, this moon was a deep red from the time it appeared in the sky, through apogee, to the birth of the new sun. A moon of this kind only appeared once every sixty-six years or so and was greeted with great festivities, food, and music. Over the centuries, the Nocturnae had come to realize they benefited greatly by grand-standing this day as a holiday of sorts for these lesser creatures; morale is important even when the workers are slaves.

The festival reached its peak as the moon reached its highest point in the sky. Just as the moon hit apogee, Adamari and Eveline Encomiâ let out high-pitched screams of pain and fell to the ground; clutching each other's hands.

The crowd fell silent as all eyes moved from the sky to the ground. Even the Nocturnae who were partaking in the festivities, in their own ways, took notice of the commotion from their balconies.

The screams coming from the two twelve-year-old girls were both bone-chilling and heartbreaking; resembling the screams of a human being skinned alive. The once white dresses were now stained with dirt and grass from their writhing on the ground. Some nearby women tried to comfort the girls, but the girls took no notice of them. Nor comfort.

Then all was silent.

Just as quickly as the pain came on and the screams started, it was gone. The girls laid spread-eagle next to each other exhausted and motionless. Blood stains appeared on their gowns as menstrual blood flowed from them for the first time. They were women now.

Loud cracks echoed from the girls, like that of an axe splitting a thick piece of wood. It was so obvious it could have been mistaken as cracks of thunder. The pelvises of both girls shot to the sky as all their weight was positioned to their feet and shoulder blades.

Short, precise screams, never heard

before by human or Nocturnae, splintered from their cores instilling fear into all man and beast. Their eyes were clamped shut, obviously in pain, when second loud cracks came from the girls. An unknown, invisible force was shattering every bone in these girls' bodies.

Confusion swept over all who were present. The Faceless King, however, had an uneasy feeling about the spectacle and ordered His generals to kill the girls. The Faceless King's fear of the unknown masked as mercy.

Two generals leaped from their balconies—one with his hair tied in a chonmage and the other wearing a helmet with the face of a jackal. They made their way through the crowd at a quick pace, forcing their human cattle out of the path.

The Nocturnae slowed to a stop over each girl. They each clutched a girl by their neck, raising them high. Looking back to the King for the command. He nodded His head.

As the Nocturnae tightened their grips around the girls' throats, their eyes opened, revealing four bright yellow glowing eyes staring back into the crimson eyes of their executioners. The Nocturnae raised their other hand to their child's neck, to assist the first. Their efforts to strangle the girls were futile.

Adamari and Eveline screamed harder and the more they screamed, the more it transformed into a terrifying roar. Their teeth began to fall from their mouths and the bones in their faces protruded and elongated. Fangs took the place of their tiny human teeth. The girls' hands and fingers that wrapped around the wrists of their Nocturnae captors enlarged, sprouting long dark brown hair; matching their heads. Fingernails thickened, growing to points, forming razor-like claws.

As their hands grew, so did the rest of their four-foot, slender bodies. Their shoulders broadened to three times that of a grown man's. Ears grew to a curved point, round like a bear's but also pointed like a fox. The new muscles attached to the elongated ears and they twitched independently of the other. Their noses and mouths merged forming the snout of a wolf. Mouths only opened enough to reveal the terrifying canines that were at least eight-inches in length.

It wasn't long before the girls were no longer dangling helplessly in the air under the grip of a Nocturnae. Standing on paws three times the size of a lion, they flexed their new bodies. The tides had finally turned. Adamari and Eveline towered over all.

> At nearly ten feet tall, the two wolf-
> like girls shook the fur across their body,
> spraying those nearby with blood and
> remnants of their human bodies that became
> intertwined with their fur. The girls
> gripped their former suppressors by their
> necks, held them high, and let out blood-
> curdling cries.

Jean rested her face in her hands and stared into the pages. "Garden … The Garden of Eden. *Adamari* and *Eveline* … Adam and Eve. So that would make the King … The Faceless King … *God?*"

At the sound of the door opening, Jean snapped the book shut.

Henry gasped as he watched the blood on the pages of the Codex disappear into the binding of the book. Once Jean removed her arm, the blood stopped flowing out of her wound like a quill running out of ink.

"Shit." Henry pulled himself from the doorway and looked at the captain. "Call Base Medical. Tell them we have a Code Indigo."

The captain turned her head and silently gave the orders to the MP. The MP distanced himself and radioed it in.

Henry rushed to Jean's side.

The captain stepped into the room. "What's going on?" she asked with concern in her eyes.

Henry pulled his bloodied shirt from Jean's arm. The cut sealed itself before his eyes. Picking up the Codex, he looked at the captain with eyes wide like he'd seen a ghost. "She's an anchor."

# 45



DR. SHELLEY RUBBED his aching eyes and took a swig of his cocktail of whiskey and coffee. Shaking his mouse, the JWICS—Joint Worldwide Intelligence Communications System—computer came to life, and he read the most recent email from Henry:

```
Classification Level:
Top Secret/Paranormal Intelligence/No Foreign


Eugene! Where are you? I need your help.
```

Dr. Shelley smiled. He knew Henry had written 'the fuck' in there, but deleted it before sending.

```
Jean has anchored herself to the Codex.
She's been moved to a secure location in
accordance with Code Indigo procedure.
She's  under  24/7  video  and  audio
```

observation, but shows no signs of the degradation described in the Codex files.

No physical degradation after five days of being anchored was an anomaly. Dr. Shelley considered if rapid degeneration of the anchor was limited to humans and Jean was less affected due to her Lygos gene.

Dr. Shelley logged these thoughts in a notebook and continued reading:

Rahne is adjusting nicely to her new cell with very little push back. I had her cell made up to look just like her old room at WPAFB. There have been no outbursts or transformation events, but she is exhibiting signs of enhanced auditory and olfactory senses. The next full moon isn't until February 19, so I won't have any new observations until then; *if* the legends and myths are all correct. I believe the Super Wolf Blood Moon was the catalyst required for her first transformation, but not subsequent ones. However, confirmation through observation is required.

Would you like me to begin the physical and psychological testing on the child now or wait for your return? When are you coming back?

-Henry

P.S. Has there been any luck with the new "cocktail" for the PHANG Program?

Dr. Shelley closed his email and shut down the computer. He slammed the rest of his drink with a painful groan. Using the back of the chair and the table as supports, he stood up and grabbed his coat.

"Doctor," a woman yelled from down the hall. "Dr. Shelley! Come quickly!"

Dr. Shelley dropped his coat and ran down the hall as best he could. "What is it, Kristi? Is Diya okay? Kristi!"—he doubled his speed—"Kristi!?" He rounded the corner into Major Diya Kshatriya's room and stopped dead in the doorway. "Major Kshatriya … you're …"

"Standing? Yeah!" Diya beamed, looking down at her feet.

Kristi handed Dr. Shelley the chart for Major Diya Kshatriya: PHANG PATIENT-XIV.

Dr. Shelley couldn't believe his eyes. Decades of research. Countless bottles of Jameson. And the lives of hundreds of animals and thirteen humans sacrificed for this moment. Overwhelmed with emotion, Dr. Shelley hugged the chart to his chest.

Kristi cleared her throat. "Doctor."

"Right." Dr. Shelley studied the chart with pride. "I did it. I've replicated the process."

"So, what's next doc?" Diya asked sliding off the patient table. She stretched her legs like a runner preparing for a race, euphoric to be standing for the first time since Afghanistan.

"Begin Phase I of testing," Dr. Shelley instructed Kristi. "But don't exceed fifty percent of the Major's recorded maximum capability."

Diya smirks. "I can do more than that, Doc."

"Okay. Sixty percent. But no higher. It's been years since she's used her legs, so one would assume they've atrophied." Dr. Shelley looked Diya over in a way a scientist would when trying to solve a problem. "And yet, a normal patient couldn't stand right now. But she is. I'd hate to push her spinal cord past sixty percent of its weight-bearing capacity and put her back in that chair."

Diya began doing jumping jacks. "I've been waiting years to do this again."

"And that's why we're going to proceed with caution, Major." Dr. Shelley grabbed Diya's hand and urged her to take it easy. "So, you can continue doing this for a very, very long time."

Tears welled in Diya's eyes as she wiggled her toes. "Okay Doc, we'll do things your way."

Dr. Shelley patted her hand. "Very good Major. Very good. Now I've got someone else to see before my flight."

After giving final instructions to Kristi, Dr. Shelley grabbed his coat and made his way to another wing of the building. He stopped in front of a rusted red door with a black plaque.

**PROGRAM**

Phylogenetic Human Alteration
with Nocturnae Genomics

**PATIENT**

Nulla

Dr. Shelley badged into the room with his CAC and six-digit pin. It was dark, illuminated only by a faint blue light coming from a large cryo-tube. "Hello, my loves," he whispered. "I've missed you both."

# 46



LET ME OUT!" I scream and slam my hand into the door. Upon touching the silver surface, my hand crumbles into what looks like a half-baked chocolate chip cookie. "Stupid."

I shouldn't waste my breath or my hands. There's no chance I'm getting out of here. This isn't at all like being in that cell with Jean. Jean was my way out. As long as I could keep her interested, keep her coming back, there was a way out. This is like being back in that fucking cabin on the Cliffs of Étretat.

Suddenly, I catch the scent of blood coming from the spicket on the wall above the steel trough. Control over my own body escapes me, as I dive into the trough of blood to my right like a dehydrated dog finding water. Gagging on the third gulp of the sour, almost rotten, pig's blood, I try to stop but can't—I'm famished. Looks like aerosolized silver increases metabolic rate too—how wonderful.

Vile humans couldn't keep the pig calm when they killed it, they had to scare it. They toyed with it so much that adrenaline and testosterone circulated through its body and tainted the meat. And the blood.

I dry-heave. Blood spills out of my mouth, and I stumble backwards into the center of my cell. I close my eyes and cover my mouth, hoping it'll help me keep the blood down. Oh Maker, don't puke. You don't want to have to drink that shit again.

The blood circulates through my body and my strength returns. I open my eyes again and watch the bones and muscles in my wrist, fingers, and hand reassemble one cell at a time.

This is going to take at least an hour to have full use of my hand.


I HATE THIS place. Unable to raise my heavy eyes from my stumped hand, I sit in the center of the floor and bow before my demons. Jean needs me. Rahne needs me. Just like Fenix, Gaius, and Claret needed me. Cora needed me. And I failed all of them just the same.

"AHHH!!!!!" a voice screams from the floor above me. The voice is hoarse like it hasn't been used in years. It's masculine, of that I'm sure. And it's filled with pain.

I know that scream. It comes from the gut-wrenching psychological pain of helplessness and worthlessness. A pain-filled scream I've let loose twice in my life, but both were internal screams. The first was when Cora died. The second was when they took Claret.

I sit on the edge of my shitty mattress waiting for the horrifying scream to come once again. I wait twenty minutes—the time it takes my pinky finger to fully heal—and this time the scream lasts twice as long.

It's been a very long time since a man's scream has made the hairs on my neck stand on end. The last time was in 1591 France, not long after I gained my freedom from the Étretat cabin. A man named Capitaine Gaucherou de Palioly used his *pear of anguish* on a wealthy couple as he and his accomplices robbed them. His victims' screams were horrifying, even for me.

"Phaeton. Why do you think he's screaming?" Silence. "C'mon, don't ignore me—"

"Watch your tone *neophyte!*" Phaeton scolds, his voice a whisper. "Probably because he's in pain. But it's an Ubiet, so why do you care? The lullaby of humans screaming should rock you to sleep as the sun rises."

Good point: Why do I care? "In all the months I've been down here—"

"Eighteen days," Phaeton says quickly.

It hasn't even been month? My mind starts to spin. Between the silver, being unconscious, and this so-called blood dispensed at irregular intervals, my internal clock is way off. "How do you know that?"

"It's … a gift."

"However long it's been, this is the first time I've heard any kind of a scream."

"I simply don't care if the cattle scream as they're being slaughtered. I don't care if this is his first scream or his thousandth. I don't care if the screams last through the day—although, I hope they do!"

Humans amount to nothing more than food to him—no surprise there—but getting such pleasure in their pain means they must have tortured him.

"The question is," Phaeton says in a slithering tone. "Why do you care so much about them?"

Unable to find the words, I come to the uneasy realization that I do care for Jean and Rahne. I turn the tables on him. "Why do *you* hate them so much?"

"Hate them?" Phaeton says, raising his voice with a hint of mockery. "I don't *hate* them, I need them. But I'm not foolish enough to believe Ubiets have an ounce of dignity or dare I say, humanity, in their blood. Afterall, haven't they harmed you in some way? Killed a comrade?"

Gaius. Fenix. Claret. All victims of human cruelty, but not all humans are cruel. "I've seen promise in some."

"Ah, so you *do* care for the Ubiet." Phaeton stretches out each word with malice.

"I never said that."

"Blasphemy! You are no Nocturnae—aligning yourself with an Ubiet! You ought to be left for the rising sun to incinerate." Phaeton spits with force. "Curse the ashes of your Maker."

"How dare you!? Who do you—" I stop myself at the sound of gearing turning behind a metal door across from mine.

"I had high hopes for you," Phaeton says softly.

A door latch squeaks up, freeing the door of the bolt, and the door whistles open as metal rubs on metal.

"But I see now," Phaeton continues, "that you are a traitor to your kind."

I scramble to my feet and run to my prison door. I press my face to the small gap in the window—ignoring the pain—and see a tall, dark-skinned man in a tattered robe standing in front of an open cell door.

"Not everything is as it seems." Phaeton flashes his crimson eyes at me.

I blink and he's gone.

# 47



HOW'S OUR GIRL doing?" Dr. Shelley entered the observation room with a cup of coffee in his hand.

"No change," Henry replied without taking his eyes off the computer monitor.

"Really?" Dr. Shelley joined Henry at the desk and scanned the screen. "Respiratory and heart rates: normal. Temperature: normal. Blood pressure: 140/90. Hm, that's a little high." Henry nodded as Dr. Shelley studied the screen. "Well, she looks fine—all things considered. What about her brain waves?"

Henry clicked the mouse, bringing up a new window. "Delta, alpha, and beta waves are all within normal ranges."

"And theta waves?" Dr. Shelley asked.

Henry advanced to the next dataset. "She slept last night for seven hours and twenty-eight minutes. Her theta waves appeared consistent with her past sleep cycles."

Needing a moment to think, Dr. Shelley pulled a misshapen

boutonniere from his pocket. "What do you make of this?" He handed it to Henry. "The strike team found it in the Nocturnae's pocket." Henry shrugged behind a blank look. "Add it to his file and make a note of it. It may come in handy." The slight distraction freed Dr. Shelley's mind to come up with an idea for Jean. "Have you put the Codex in the cell with her?"

Henry spun around in his chair and eyed Dr. Shelley. "Absolutely not. That's a classified artifact."

"So?"

"So … what if something happened?"

Dr. Shelley raised a finger. "What *if* something happened indeed?"

"No Professor, what if something happened to the book? The Company could cut our funding or cut our program entirely."

"A risk we've taken many times over the years my dear boy," Dr. Shelley said, barely hiding his smile. "Tonight, I want you to give her the Codex an hour before her normal bedtime along with something comforting. Maybe a cup of tea or a glass of wine. Whatever it is, it should relax her."

"Gose or another sour beer. I'll try and find the orange citrus one that's her favorite," Henry offered.

"Fine. I'd like you to pay particular attention to the gamma waves."

"Isn't that all just brain noise?"

"For a long time, yes, it was dismissed as background. Unimportant."

"Then what am I looking for?" Henry asked, looking up at Dr. Shelley.

"I'm working on a theory that gamma waves modulate perception and consciousness. A higher presence of gamma is indicative of an expanded consciousness."

Cocking his head to one side, Henry tried following Dr. Shelley's train of thought. "What would cause an expanded consciousness?"

"Based on the item's archives, I believe that with Jean anchored to the Codex, there's some kind of a reaction that occurs when she taps into its power."

"Granting her a kind of second sight."

"Precisely. Thus, expanding her conscious and unconscious minds to a higher level." The image of his old friend wrapped in a straitjacket sitting on the floor of a padded cell flashed in his mind. Or another world entirely.

"And therefore, increasing her gamma wave activity. Professor, that is brilliant!"

"It's a little early for applause. It's still merely a hypothesis at this point." Dr. Shelley patted Henry on the shoulder as he turned to leave. "Let's go see my daughter and the monster she's been keeping locked up inside of her." Dr. Shelley beckoned.

The two men made their way through the winding halls and stopped in front of a pair of rusted yellow double doors with black lettering that read:

**PROGRAM**

Jekyll & Hyde

**SECURITY LEVEL**

Omega

**PATIENT**
Delta Zero

Dr. Shelley glanced back at Henry. "A little on the nose, don't you think?"

"I don't like acronyms." Henry scanned his badge on the reader beside the door until the door beeped open. "The government uses them too much as it is and ends up with acronyms within acronyms."

They stepped into the room and set their eyes on Rahne's new containment cell—a transparent dome fifteen feet high.

Dr. Shelley looked back at Henry. "What happened to the cell? It was supposed to be a perfect replica of the old one."

"She broke it." Henry translated the look on Dr. Shelley's face. "Two days after I told you she was adjusting fine. She kept asking for Brenda and no one knew—"

"Her Dr. Barbie doll."

Henry nodded. "Yeah, but I didn't connect the dots until it was too late. She was fine. Normal. Just a little girl. No visual signs of mutation. But when she got upset, she literally smacked the face right off one of our technicians. Then she roared like the monster inside wanted to be freed from its tiny prison."

"And you chose a dome for the new design?" Dr. Shelley asked, cocking his head toward the cell.

"Not just any dome, it's a geodesic dome—a dome made of triangles. DARPAs latest and greatest design for deep-water living. I figure if it can withstand 140 cubic tons of pressure, it can withstand the child."

"Has she transformed at all since she's been here?"

"Not fully." Henry shook his head. "She didn't transform in Michigan either when captured."

"Full moon is tonight. The first one since her initial transformation."

Henry's eyes traced the wall behind Dr. Shelley, stopping on the young girl innocently playing in the center of her cell. "You think…"

"Yes, I think the moon plays a role, but I doubt it's *exactly* what the stories and legends claim. You're going to balance your time between Rahne, Jean, and the Codex. Understanding Jean and her ability to use the Codex is very important; but understanding Rahne and … the Lygos, is equally as important."

While it excited Henry to make breakthrough discoveries, he feared being eaten alive or sliced in half by giant Lygos claws. The technician Rahne attacked had died a horrifying, painful death.

Dr. Shelley slowly walked up to the plastic barrier separating him from Rahne and tapped on the hard, textured surface. Rahne turned her head slowly, revealing swollen red bags under her eyes and a red nose. A smile quickly appeared on her face as she scrambled to her feet.

"Daddy!" she shouted, slamming herself against the wall separating them.

"Hello sweetheart," Dr. Shelley placed his hand on the clear wall between them. "Are they treating you well?"

"Please, can we go outside?" She grew more and more upset with each word. "It's so beautiful out there. I don't like it in here or in my room."

"You don't like your room?" Dr. Shelley used his most soothing tone with her. "Henry spent a lot of time getting it just right for you."

"NO!" A roar gurgled up from the pits of her soul. "I want to have dinner with Mr. Sorin by the fire again and play hide-and-seek and stare up at the stars."

Dr. Shelley closed his eyes and let out a heavy sigh. "Mr. Sorin's not here, Rahne."

"But Ms. Jean is here! Can't I go see Ms. Jean? She wasn't as fun as Mr. Sorin—she didn't eat the deer with us—but she's really nice."

"How about you tell me everything you, Mr. Sorin, and Ms. Jean did while you were outside and then we can go see your friends? How does that sound?"

"NO!" Rahne snapped and stomped her foot. The lights flickered, the dome shook, and the concrete ground crunched beneath her tiny foot. "You lied to me daddy!"

"What do you think I lied about?" Dr. Shelley raised his chin.

"You said bad people would hurt me if I ever left."

"And they did…"

"No. You're the bad man, daddy. You do bad things. Your people hurt me. Mr. Sorin protected me."

Dr. Shelley slowly pulled his hand from the glass. Rahne watched her supportive and caring daddy's face morph into the stone-cold scientist, Dr. Eugene F. Shelley.

"Prepare her for Testing Phase II."

Henry blanched. "Is that wise with the full moon tonight? We don't know for any certainty that this facility will be able to contain her."

"Wait until tomorrow then. Run all tests to stimulate and trigger the transformation. I'll call the commander and tell him to put the base on FPCON DELTA until testing has been completed."

"DAAAAAADDDDDDDDDYYYYYY!" Rahne screamed, slamming her fists against the transparent wall over and over.

Her eyes flickered between a soft blue and a fiery yellow as the wall flexed under the powerful force of her tiny hands.

"I've never seen her eyes shift like that." Henry gulped. He didn't have a great feeling about setting Rahne off.

"Seems like many of the physical attributes of the Lygos are maintained in human form." Dr. Shelley adjusted the glasses on his nose. "Document everything up to the full moon. Use your best judgement on when to begin the second phase of testing."

"I'm a little jealous you got to see her in her Lygos mutation state."

"Breathtaking," Dr. Shelley said, curling one side of his face into a sinister smile.

JEAN PACED IN her room, recounting every moment with Victor from the night they met in that shitty bar to the day she got the call that he'd been killed. A sudden low rumble shook the ground under her feet, shaking her free of her memories with Victor.

"Rahne," she said softly, listening for a scream … a cry … anything that would convince her it was Rahne and not something heavy like construction equipment hitting the ground outside.

She didn't know what The Company was waiting for, or what they hoped to find. She wondered where they kept Sorin, and also why she cared so much. She couldn't stop thinking about the book and questioning if it was the Codex and why it contained braille.

The intercom in the room came on. "Jeanie, it's Eugene. How are you?"

Jean stopped two steps from the door and refused to answer.

A hatch flipped up from the bottom of door and a small cardboard box slid into the room.

"One step forward and two steps to your right is a small box. I'd like you to open it," Eugene said over the speaker.

Jean turned toward the box, but didn't move, as possibilities raced through her mind of what might be inside.

"Go on and open it."

She slowly walked to the door. But stopped again. "Give me today's date and time and I'll open it!"

"It's six fifty a.m. Pacific Standard Time on February nineteenth. Open the box."

Jean squatted down, over the box, lost in thought. It was almost the next full moon. She hoped Rahne was safe. When her fingertips grazed the item inside the package, she realized it was the book from before. The Codex?

"Remove the item from the box, Jeanie."

"Don't call me that," she mumbled under her breath and lifted the book.

Cradling the book in one hand, Jean explored its edges and binding before opening it to an unmarked page. Slowly she caressed the page with the tips of her fingers. No braille.

Dr. Shelley watched intensely, swirling the Watch with his thumb in his pocket. "What do you see?"

"See? I'm blind, you old loon. Did Sorin scare you stupid down in the catacombs or did experimenting on children finally get to you?"

Eugene ignored Jean's taunting. "The Codex has shared its secrets with you once before, Jeanie. We have the recordings."

"Good. Then you know what it said."

"The braille cells are too small for us to decipher—"

"Sub-pixel image registration."

"Don't be a smart-ass Jean, you know that wouldn't work with those shit cameras in interrogation."

"That may be true," Jean said, "but I stand by the fact that I don't know what you're talking about. This book"—she held the book high and shook it—"doesn't *speak* and has never spoken to me."

Jean had always been a fucking word-salad smart-ass, good at answering *exactly* the question and giving nothing more. It frustrated Dr. Shelley to no end. "You're not going to help me, are you?" Dr. Shelley asked.

Jean sat on the ground and crossed her legs. She placed the book on her lap, raised a closed fist in the air, and flipped him the bird.

Dr. Shelley stepped away from the microphone and took a seat in his worn tweed chair.

"She's obviously lying Professor," Henry said.

"I'm aware."

"Then what's the plan?"

"I'm thinking we make her uncomfortable. Have them drop the oxygen in the room to fifteen point four percent and the temperature to forty-two degrees Fahrenheit. I want to stress her system by simulating high altitude conditions."

Henry eyed Jean sitting on the floor of her cell in a short sleeve shirt, thin cotton pants, and flip flops. "She'll freeze."

"Do it my way. Find your own way. I don't care, but get it done. I have my own work to attend to. Project PHANG specifically." Dr. Shelley grabbed the handle and opened the door to leave. "You're on your own this time. I'm happy to provide input and my opinion when you ask, but I'm not going to do it for you."

Dr. Shelley left, closing the door behind him.

Henry looked from the exit door to the viewing window of Jean's cell and then over to the thermostat. After a moment, he walked to the thermostat and dropped the temperature. "You chose the Nocturnae and that abomination. I choose humanity and the survival of *my* species."

# 48



A DOOR SLAM echoes through my cell block, waking me. Footsteps come ever closer. They don't slow. They don't even change direction. Someone is here for me.

"Hello, Sorin," a guttural voice says from the other side of my door.

Phaeton. "How did you free yourself?" I ask, hurrying over to the door.

"Free myself?" Phaeton laughs. "I never had to free myself. I am here because I choose to be. There is much more at play here than you know. Much more."

"Why don't you let me out and explain it to me then?"

"In time. First, I need to know where your loyalties lie. Your concern for the Ubiet and the Lygos troubles me."

"Keep your friends close and your enemies closer." He probably won't buy that, but I have to try.

"You don't fool me."

"There's nothing to fool."

"Right you are, that's why you're in the box and I'm not." Phaeton clears his throat with a hideous cough. "Tell me about your Maker. You tell me what I want to know, and I *may* let you out of your cage. Or, you can refuse and I most certainly will *not* free you."

Asshole. Who is this guy? "Her name was Claret."

"Was … so, she has experienced the true death?"

"Yes, just before I was imprisoned here."

"How?"

I can't tell him about Rahne. "Silver bullet to the head."

"A lie. That's your only warning Sorin. Do it again and I walk away, never to return." The sound of Phaeton wringing his dry hands on the other side of the door sends a sudden chill down my back.

Shit! I don't have a choice. "A Lygos tore her in two and devoured her remains."

"Pity," Phaeton wheezes behind the door. "She was the last female Nocturnae. I know the kind of pain you're feeling, I once had it myself."

How would he know that? I didn't even know that. Did Gaius or Fenix know? Why didn't they tell me if they did? "Oh. I thought you didn't know my Maker."

"I never said that. I told you to tell me about her." Phaeton pauses a moment as if waiting for me to say something. "Do you know why her being the last is of such significance? Because without a female, the Nocturnae race will inevitably cease to exist. It's only a matter of time."

"There are no more females? How do you know?"

"Do you stand beside me and your Nocturnae brothers or the Ubiets?"

"You make it sound like there's a war—"

"THERE'S ALWAYS BEEN A WAR! They have committed genocide on our kind for millennia, driving us to the brink of extinction. And now, it is inevitable. The Ubiets must pay for their transgressions."

"As far as I can tell, there are two of us and about eight billion of them. Outnumbered is an understatement and with those odds, this shithole of a cell is looking more and more like the Taj Mahal. This is the stupidest thing I've ever heard." I shake my head, laughing to myself. "You can't fight a war without an army. No females, no army."

"A minor inconvenience disguised as a major one to the narrow-minded," Phaeton says, clicking his tongue in disappointment. "The Ubiets will pay and they will be reminded of their rightful place in the fields or on my plate like the cattle they are."

"That's never been."

"Ah, but it has. The arrogance of Ubiets is thinking nature bends to their will and not vice-versa. This world is tainted and wrong because we Nocturnae, the strong, have had to take refuge from the weak, the Ubiets. It won't be long until the Ubiets are the ones that need to seek refuge."

"I don't understand, Nocturnae have always been running. My entire existence I've been running."

"Except for the century-and-a-half you spent shackled to the floor of the cabin at the edge of the Étretat Cliffs. One of the Atrocities, the Pearl, kept you hidden."

How would he know that? "I've never been to Étretat. Are those the cliffs in Ireland?"

Phaeton coughs, hard, three times. "I said no lies and yet, you lie. So here you will stay to either slowly starve on the Ubiets' concoction of artificial pigs' blood or be forgotten about as their kind die as time moves on." His feet scrape across the floor as he pivots.

"It was a reflex," I say, "it's been so long since I've been around one of my own that I don't trust anyone." Not completely a lie.

"No one." Phaeton stops moving. He swallows as if he's tasted something rotten. "You trust no one, but the Ubiet."

"Trust is such a strong word."

Phaeton swirls around and slams his hand hard onto the door of my cell. "Stop! Enough games." I back away from the door and square my stance, preparing for a fight. "My child, you are being foolish. The Ubiets hate you for being what you are. Why *not* join me?"

Fuck it, he already knows. "Humans and Nocturnae don't have to be enemies. I'll never join you, never."

"That's too bad. Truly tragic, yes," Phaeton scoffs and softly knocks twice on the door with his knuckle. "You are an idealist Sorin. And I am a realist. There is a dark past between our kinds, from long before you were born, that has been forgotten by the Ubiets but haunts me still—the event that began the genocide against us." Quickly, Phaeton turns around and walks back to his cell. "We are the future Sorin, not them."

His cell door slams closed.

"Shit," I mutter. "Now what?"

# 49



PACING IN HER cell, Jean began to grow winded, like she was walking up the side of a mountain. With every breath, the air grew a little thinner and her heart beat a little harder. Tilting her head in the direction of the air vent, she listened for a faint whistle echoing through the ducts.

She assumed they performed their beloved tests. Perhaps this test attempted to determine if she would transform under harsh conditions. But if she limited her activity, she could make it harder for them. She sat on the edge of her mattress-less bed.

"Something wrong, Jean?" Henry asked over the intercom.

Knowing she couldn't let him know she was onto them, she denied everything with a simple, "Nope. Why?"

"Ugh, nothing." There was a brief pause on the intercom before Henry came back. "Never mind."

Using the Codex as a pillow, she laid back on bed with her hands behind her head and closed her eyes. The hard pallet beneath her dug into her back, but she faked a contented smile.

From the observation room, Henry watched as small clouds of warm air left Jean's nose and dissipated into the frigid room. He buried his face in his hands and he studied her from between his fingers. He had turned the temperature down to a chilly thirty-three degrees Fahrenheit and cut the oxygen level to that of Everest's Base Camp. The scrubs she wore were so thin they might as well have been made of tissue paper. He examined her body, surprised to find that her nipples hadn't hardened.

Meanwhile, Jean pondered the idea of Henry and Dr. Shelley trying to trigger some kind of mutation in her. If it were her doing the experiment, she'd thin the air and drop the temperature. But Jean didn't feel at all cold. She wondered if she could transform like Rahne. It would definitely make escaping easier. Her stomach gurgled with hunger. Perhaps they were attempting to starve her. Would that stress the body enough?

HENRY SOFTLY TAPPED on a silver-coated steel door. Dropping to one knee, he opened the small hatch at the bottom of the door and slid a tray into Jean's cell. Her breakfast was an eight-ounce bottle of water, a piece of warm toast, wilted spinach, and two hard-boiled eggs with dollops of Dijon mustard on them.

Jean rolled over on her bed and put the Codex on the desk. Swinging her legs over the edge of the bedframe, she let out a heavy sigh as she shook her head.

Peering in through the viewing window of the door, Henry asked, "Is everything okay?"

Jean lost her patience with Henry's constant badgering. "When

I get out of here, I'm going to find Victor … and when I do, prisoners gutting you with a toothbrush shiv is going to look like a good time compared to what Victor's going to do to you."

"He died years ago," Henry said and slammed his fist into the door. "He's dead. That, I'm sure of."

"Better hope so." Jean retrieved the tray and sat down with it on her lap. Carefully, she explored the tray's contents with the tips of her fingers. She flipped the tray off her lap and onto the floor. "You think recreating my typical breakfast is going to make up for anything? Come on Henry, I thought you were smarter than that."

"Jean," Henry said over the intercom. "You need to eat. If you don't, I am required to report you and have a medical team come in to sedate you and pump liquid food into your stomach through a feeding tube. I don't want to do that, but if you don't eat anything by the end of today, you'll have made the decision for me."

Jean leaned over her legs and patted the floor until she found the toast. She snatched the slice of bread and tore into it with her teeth, chewing aggressively. She swallowed and showed her empty mouth. "There! Now you don't have to call anyone. I ate something. Happy?"

"Yes. Thank you."

"Fuck off Henry."


JEAN YAWNED AND wiped the sleep from her eyes. When had she fallen asleep? And on the floor, no less? She figured they must have drugged her toast. But to what end? Apparently, starvation wasn't enough of a stressor to induce transformation, if she even had the ability.

Jean's stomach made a low glugging sound and it felt like it was turning over on itself. She grabbed her belly and winced. She'd need to eat to be strong when, or if, someone came to rescue her. Not that she had much hope of that. If Sorin or Rahne were coming, they'd be here by now. If she was going to escape, she'd have to do it on her own. If Victor really was alive like the Codex said, she was going to find him.

Her hands glided over the surface of the desk until they found the Codex. The book must answer questions that The Company wants answers to, and definitely should *not* have. They'd be unstoppable. Sir Francis Bacon said it best: Knowledge is power.

Sliding her left hand down the spine, she opened the book, but just as it opened, an extremely sharp pain shot through her body from the tip of her finger.

It hurt a ton, but she tried not to wince as she was likely being watched. She breathed out the pain and spread her fingers wide over the first blank page searching for the words, not knowing how the Codex worked nor that her blood was the ink it needed.

With her mind, she asked the book how she could help Victor, envisioning the shape of his face in her hands and remembering how his crooked smile felt under her lips.

Slowly, blood from the papercut on her finger moved onto the page as she searched for a Braille cell, like she'd found before. The blood slithered under the paper until it reached the top-left of the page where it stretched out and formed characters that read:

The Crown.

Jean shook her head, faking disappointment when her fingers reached the bottom of the page, and she began again.

She asked the book for the location of the Crown, hoping the book would understand the meaning behind her simple question.

Running her fingers over the words, she felt the cells change. It was a strange sensation almost like water bubbling up from under a blanket and suddenly hardening in place.

```
Here... Let the song guide you.
```

She reached the bottom of the page and faked disappointment once more. Shaking her head in false frustration, she slammed the book closed.

"What are you expecting this thing to do?" Jean yelled for effect. "It's just a stupid book of blank pages."

The intercom squealed as Henry pressed on the microphone. "The same thing that happened in the interrogation room."

"Nothing happened." Jean threw up her hands in mock frustration. The Codex toppled off her lap and landed hard on the floor next to her.

"Something happened the first time. I know it, and you know it. I'm not sure what it was, but it looked like you were reading Braille from its pages."

Picking up the book, she opened it wide so Henry could see the blank pages. "No Braille." Jean licked her fingers and flipped the pages wildly, and ran her hand over the page, once again, in search of characters. She performed the charade one more time and slammed the book closed. She dropped it on the floor. "There. You happy? Can I go now?"

"Don't be a smart-ass," Henry said in a muffled voice over the intercom.

"I just proved to you that you were wrong," Jean said and tapped the binding of the book with her toe. "Now let me go."

"You know I can't do that Jean," Henry said. Then he lied, "At least, not until you tell me everything the Codex told you."

Just then, the door opened, and Dr. Shelley joined Henry in the observation room. He updated his protégé on Diya's promising progress.

"That's wonderful things are going well on PHANG, but I haven't made any progress with Jean," Henry said, glancing at her through the window.

Dr. Shelley paused a moment, evaluating Jean through the glass. "Maybe you've been thinking about this all wrong. Look at the problem from another angle."

Henry crossed his arms and furrowed his brow as he reanalyzed the situation. "Growing up, my grandparents had Labradors. And, being in northern Ohio, we got our fair share of snow. The dogs loved it and could play in the snow all day, but when the summers got hot, the dogs never wanted to stay outside longer than they had to."

Dr. Shelley refused to take his eyes off Jean, but Henry could see the edge of his smile. "Go on."

"Cold won't work." Henry walked over to the wall with the thermostat. Putting his hand on the dial, he forced down what little moisture was in his mouth and turned the temperature up to eighty-seven degrees Fahrenheit. "It has to be uncomfortably hot."

"Good thinking," Dr. Shelley said with a crooked grin. He placed his hand on Henry's shoulder. "You did good. Now let's see what happens."

Before Henry had time to bask in Dr. Shelley's rare praise, one side of Dr. Shelley's face drooped like someone had cut the strings holding it in place. His smile melted, his cheeks wilted, and his brow sagged. "I dhon't fheel rhight…" Dr. Shelley said, wrapping his hands around Henry's arm for support.

Henry flipped the phone off the receiver and still gripping Dr. Shelley, awkwardly pressed the red EMERGENCY button. "Hold on Professor," Henry begged. "I've got you."

The phone rang once before being answered. "Edwards Air Force Base Emergency Services; How—"

"Dr. Eugene Shelley is having a stroke," Henry said in a panicked voice. "We're in the south side of Building A51 level B2."

"Sir, there's no building with that number on this base."

"Of course there is! I wouldn't be able to call you from an internal line if there wasn't, now would I? Trace the phone or something! Just get EMS here now!" Henry slammed the phone onto the table and began pleading, "Please don't die."

Dr. Shelley looked into Henry's eyes and pulled the Watch out of his pocket. "Hold onto this for me. Just in case. Keep it safe." Then he fell unconscious.

Panic enveloped Henry as he stared down at an unresponsive Dr. Shelley.

ROUGHLY 140 MILES east in the Sandbox, on Level Omega, Phaeton stood in the corner of his cell. His eyes were closed as he focused on the conversation between Henry and Dr. Shelley in Jean's observation room.

The Watch that Dr. Shelley carried with him everywhere was anchored to Phaeton and allowed him to use his Nocturnae gifts from great distances if in the hands of a human; but the Watch was also a kind of one-way receiver, a trait Phaeton came to find very useful over the centuries.

"Jean is smart," Phaeton observed aloud.

Suddenly, Phaeton gripped both sides of his head and keeled over. His mind twisted inward on itself as it ripped and tore in every direction. "Gah, nooooo! Not now!"

"Are you okay?" Sorin yelled from his cell, but Phaeton couldn't answer. "PHAETON!" Sorin beat on his prison door.

Phaeton thrashed around his cell. The pain was unlike anything he'd felt before.

Dr. Shelley felt compelled to touch the pocket Watch and, in that moment, a bright sapphire ring illuminated the edges of Phaeton's crimson eyes as he quickly entered the old man's mind. *"Give the boy the Watch. Tell him to keep it safe."*

The pain was too great for Phaeton to hold the connection any longer. All he could do was hope he'd done enough. Then as quickly as it manifested, the connection and the pain were gone. Slumping back into his bunk, exhausted, he closed his eyes and forced the remnants of pain to retreat.

"Phaeton, are you okay?" Sorin yelled again.

Phaeton faced his door and said, "No need to shout, just a bad dream. Nothing to be worried about."

The moment the pocket Watch hit Henry's hand, Phaeton knew

it. Being inside a young mind feels very different from an old one. He looked forward to using Henry as his puppet, as he had done with the old man.

Henry's mind resembled a massive gaming store. Organized by subject and time, row after row of comic books filled the floorspace of the room. On the walls hung pictures of people he'd met once or twice but didn't know their names, and places he'd visited just long enough to know he was there, and things he'd lost that were never found again.

While Phaeton thumbed the rows of comics, a light flickered in a stairwell in the far back of the game store. The basement, otherwise known as the deep, dark recesses of Henry's mind.

Perusing the store like he was a patron, Phaeton made his way to the back and down the stairs. The staircase was old, rickety, and covered in cobwebs and dirt.

Phaeton stepped onto the basement floor and sensed something different about this young man, something he hadn't expected.

UNAWARE OF DR. Shelley's condition on the other side of the one-way mirror, Jean laid on her bed with her hands on her chest. She dissected the Codex's meager eight words into three distinct pieces.

The first piece was *Crown*. The second piece, *here*, a single word she feared had to mean more than it seemed.

She flashed back to 2007 to the dive bar where she met Victor for the first time. She chuckled recalling that she had chipped black nail polish to match her Avril Lavigne crop-top. She had been deluded to think that was cool.

The distinct smell of stale beer and billiard chalk gave way to cedar and musk as she relived walking up to the bar—purposefully following this mystery man's scent. As she tried to figure out a way to talk to him, she tapped her thumbs to the rhythm of Something Corporate's *Konstantine*—the song that had been playing at that moment.

Yellow light flashed outside her cell. Level by level, the hallways filled with flashing yellow lights and all the doors silently unlocked. Two EMTs raced by her cell, followed by another two wheeling a gurney into the room adjacent to hers. But through it all, she stayed focused on her memory.

It was something about girls being old-fashioned that finally got Victor to talk to her.

*Let the song guide you.*

The phrase echoed in her mind like a song stuck on repeat. Her fingers played the repetitive right hand on the piano she imagined in front of her, and the hard bass of the left hand boomed in her ears. She could have sworn she was listening to the song on very low volume through a pair of headphones.

"Wait." She quickly sat up and swung her legs over the side of her bed. "Let the song guide you." She tilted her head until the song grew slightly louder—it was coming from her cell door. She wondered if the Codex meant *let the song guide you* literally. Like a beacon.

Slowly, she made her way across the cell until her hand hit the door handle. No way could this work. She was locked in.

Jean took a deep breath and pulled on the handle. To her amazement, the door opened. With a slight chuckle, she followed the song out of her cell and down the hallway. With each step the song grew louder and she grew evermore curious.

As if in a trance, Jean allowed her fingers to drag on the wall while she walked. She kept count of the number of steps she'd taken before the song pulled her down another hallway. She passed an archway with a thick yellow line painted on the floor, marking the border of the next section of the facility.

The music suddenly softened like someone turned down the volume. Jean took two steps back and searched the door for the knob. She opened the door and the music blasted like she'd just busted into a concert venue with a rock band in the middle of their set.

Although the music was loud, it didn't hurt her ears in the slightest, nor could she feel the bass in her chest like she'd been able to at any concert in the past. The music just hung there. With one hand searching the air in front of her, she took half steps into the room.

The room was shaped just like hers, but instead of a bed, desk, and toilet, a pillar stood four feet high in the center of the cell. Atop the pillar sat a vine elegantly braided to form a crown, but the long sharp barbs protruding from it in every direction shrouded its beauty in horror.

Jean took her last step before the Crown, thrusting her hand into its thorns.

Although she quickly recoiled her hand, it was too late. For the first time in more than 10,000 years someone had anchored themselves to more than one Atrocity. An inaudible *bell* rang throughout the multiverse.

A handsome man locked in a padded room smiled his crooked

smile. His eyes glowed purple, as he glanced at the small window of his cell where his invisible friend flashed sparks of purple.

Phaeton, sitting cross-legged on his prison floor, broke from his meditative state with a slow, deep breath. "Hmm, haven't felt that in centuries."

A grieving man with writer's block in Seaside, Florida noticed something different about his cat, Tweety, and suddenly had an idea for his next story.

The alarm was heard far and wide, by those with magical abilities. In this world and the next, and the worlds existing between worlds—where a man with a thin, skeletal face put on his hat of hats and walked deeper into the Void leaving his prison outside of space and time behind him.

Not everyone was sure what had happened or what it meant, but they all knew something was different. Something, had changed. And something was coming.

A hand gripped Jean by the arm. "JEAN!" Henry yelled, tightening his grip.

"Ow. Henry, you're hurting me."

Henry loosened his grip enough to return the color to her arm. "How'd you get out of your cell?"

"I don't know. I was in my cell and then in some hallways and then here. Something sharp like a knife—" She quickly stuffed her bloody finger in her mouth.

Henry looked past her at the Crown. "Are you bleeding?" he asked with great trepidation.

She shook her head without removing her finger.

"Jean, show me your finger," Henry demanded.

Reluctantly, Jean removed her finger from her mouth and showed it to Henry like a child does to a parent. But to Henry's surprise and Jean's dismay there was no blood, nor a wound of any kind.

She quickly wrapped her hands around his, appealing to his affection for her. "I'm so scared. What's going on?"

Henry carefully slung Jean's arm through his and patted her hand. "It's not your fault. Something happened that I must attend to, but first let's get you back to your cell."

Jean let him lead her back. She couldn't explain the relief or confidence she felt in the moment, but she knew, somehow, she just helped Victor escape whatever prison was holding him.

# 50



DR. SHELLEY'S EYES slowly fluttered open. Blanketed in confusion, they darted around the room pausing on the wires, tubes, and machines monitoring his body's every action. The technology helping to keep him alive. He tried to speak, but winced in pain.

"Shh," Henry said softly, wrapping his hand around Dr. Shelley's. "You're at Ronald Reagan UCLA Medical Center. You've had a tube down your throat for a while. They performed two embolectomies to remove the piece that traveled to your brain and the primary clot. They removed them, but during the second surgery you had an adverse reaction to one of the medications they pushed—sorry, I don't remember which one. They finished the surgery, but you've been out for five days."

Dr. Shelley looked at the ceiling and breathed deeply. He looked back at Henry and mouthed, "Two?"

"Two surgeries? Yeah. You probably don't remember me being here after the first one. You were still feeling the effects of the anesthesia and by the time the effects had worn off, you were already being wheeled into your calf surgery," Henry said, watching fear grow in Dr. Shelley's face. "But don't worry. They got the entire clot out of your leg, no problem. They recommended daily exercise and no more bacon or other high cholesterol foods."

Dr. Shelley smiled and mouthed, "Jeanie."

Henry's hand touched the Watch in his pocket and as if it had a mind of its own, a voice said, *"Don't tell him about the Crown. No reason to worry the old man."*

"Her room temp is up to ninety-six degrees now. She passed out four times yesterday and we had to pump her with fluids last night."

Dr. Shelley cocked his head to one side and glared.

"What? I didn't want her having heatstroke."

Dr. Shelley shook his head and mouthed, "Hallucinations."

"Did she have any hallucinations?"

Dr. Shelley aggressively nodded.

"It was all nonsense. There was Genesis chapter one, the Encomiâ family, a Faceless King, the Chaste Tree, Adamari, Eveline … and then some gibberish."

Dr. Shelley's eyes begged Henry for more.

"I'll try to remember. Spilder. Saeh. Tresor? It might have been 'tesor,' but I could be wrong. I'm telling you it was—"

Dr. Shelley gestured, repeatedly pointing at Henry's jacket.

Henry looked down toward where Dr. Shelley pointed. Of course. He wanted Henry's pen. Henry handed it over.

Using a napkin left on his nightstand, Dr. Shelley scribbled down the letters:

Dr. Shelley studied the letters and Henry studied Dr. Shelley. Suddenly, Dr. Shelley crossed out the first 'R' in TRESOR and wrote five words in a single column.

"Rose … The … As … Red … Lips …?" Henry asked. "I don't get it."

Dr. Shelley rewrote the five words; but this time, in the correct order.

"Lips … Red … As … The … Rose. Lips red as the rose. LIPS RED AS THE ROSE! … Wait, isn't that …?"

"Snow White," Dr. Shelley mouthed.

"What does Snow White have to do with—"

The old man shrugged and pointed to the drawer beside his bed. Henry opened the drawer and found a black leather-bound book.

"The Holy Bible: King James Version," Henry said and opened the book. "In the beginning God created heaven and earth. Professor, it's the creation story." His eyes glanced at the clock on the wall and closed the Bible. "I'm sorry Professor, it's almost midnight and I need to get back and check on the Patient before I grab some shuteye."

Dr. Shelley snatched the young man's hand before he could pull it from his bedside. Shaking his head he mouthed, "No," and gestured for him to sit. Using the same napkin, Dr. Shelley wrote *Adamari* and *Eveline*. Turning the napkin for Henry to read, he pointed to each name.

"I'm not following," Henry said, looking back and forth between the napkin and Dr. Shelley. "Yes, she said those names."

Frustrated, Dr. Shelley rolled his eyes and aggressively pointed with the pen at the bible on Henry's lap. Then pointed to the names on the napkin. As he underlined *Adam* in the first name and *Eve* in the second, Henry's eyes widened.

"Holy shit." Dr. Shelley quickly wrote *Encomiâ* under the two names and circled them. "Adamari Encomiâ and Eveline Encomiâ." Dr. Shelley nodded. "They were sisters." Henry's eyes darted over the room like he was mentally drawing on a whiteboard how the pieces fit together. "The Creation Story. It's not about man, it's about the Lygos."

The old man in the bed smiled and rested his head back on his pillow.

"Four of the five words are connected to the Lygos," Henry said, questioning the words Jean muttered as if they were a riddle. "How does a tree fit into this?" Henry pulled out his phone and searched the internet for *Chaste Tree*. "Huh, the flowers kind of look like lilacs."

Henry showed the screen to Dr. Shelley who agreed and mouthed the caption, "Vitex agnus castus."

Turning the phone back around, Henry's eyes raced over the screen as he thumbed through links. "Huh," Henry said, causing Dr. Shelley to sit up with curiosity. "I found an article from 1991 in *Pharmacy in History* that says, 'Pliny the Elder (A.D. 28-79) wrote that the Greeks called the Chaste Tree *lygos*, or *agnos*, because, quote: the Athenian women, preserving their chastity at the Thesmophoria, strew their beds with its leaves.' They're named after a flower? And who, or what, is a Faceless King?"

Dr. Shelley shrugged as he stared at the napkin, tapping it with the pen.

"What is it?" Henry asked, realizing something was bothering him. Leaning over to see the napkin, Henry noticed the cluster of dots under where the pen had repeatedly pressed. "Encomiâ? What about it?"

Beside the word, Dr. Shelley wrote *Allicines* and drew arrows connecting the two names.

"You think they're related?"

Shaking his head, Dr. Shelley wrote under *Allicines*:

ILLE CANIS

"That's Latin. *Canis* sounds like canine, but…?" In parenthesis, Dr. Shelley wrote the translation. "Man. Dog." Henry looked at Dr. Shelley in disbelief as the old man deciphered the anagram *Encomiâ* before his eyes.

"Câine Om," Dr. Shelley said in a straining voice. "Romanian for Dog Man." Wincing in pain, he coughed and cleared his throat.

"I told you not to talk," Henry reminded him, and noticed Dr. Shelley was drawing a line between the two translations with his finger. "Dog-man. Man-dog." Then it clicked. "Werewolf. Jesus Christ, it was right in front of us this whole time. Professor, you're a genius."

Dr. Shelley held his head in shame, shaking it softly and pointing to his chest.

"What do you mean, it wasn't you? You just solved the—" Dr. Shelley looked up at Henry with eyes he reserved for only one specific, difficult topic. "Oh … Victor figured it out."

Watching the pain and grief rise up in his young protégé over the loss of his older brother more than a decade ago, Dr. Shelley didn't even consider sharing his dark secret.

479

# 51



Jean … Jean…"—Henry tapped on the window of the prison door—"Jean, it's time to wake up."

With the back of her hand, Jean wiped her eyes. "What? Where am—"

"You're still in your cell. But I need to know about your Lygos heritage. At any point in your life, did you experience anything close to what Rahne did? Did your mother? Your father?"

She sat up. Burying her face in her hands, she rocked back and forth in frustration. "I already told you. I don't know anything about werewolves or Lygos. I never changed nor did my parents."

"I believe you."

"Then what's the issue?" Jean asked, getting up and walking to the door. "And when are you going to tell me how my door got unlocked?"

"I told you," Henry said with a heavy sigh. "There was a power surge and some of the systems went offline for a moment."

She didn't believe him, but continued asking the same question every day to see if he'd slip up and she could catch him in a lie. "If you believe that I don't know anything about the Lygos, then what's the issue? Let me go."

Henry chuckled and wiped the irritation his brow. "I cannot take the risk of you transforming into a Lygos—you birthed one, after all."

"Oh, come on Henry. That's bullshit and you know it," Jean said knowing her argument was weak, but she needed more information and over the years she found arguing with Henry was a good way to get information from him.

"Jean, stop. You know the protocols. The safeguards. The reasons why." Henry cleared his throat in an attempt to hide the pain of her conviction in his voice. "You are an existential threat to the human race and are no longer privy to the rules and laws governing the treatment of prisoners. You are no longer considered human."

"Let me guess… From the moment I was captured in Michigan, I was considered property of the United States."

"Correct."

Jean recalled when she'd used those same words on Sorin and suddenly the situation felt more morose than ironic. "And Rahne?"

"Rahne is resting comfortably in her new home."

"Thank you, Henry," Jean said, forcing a smile. Sauntering to the far corner of the room, she mumbled to herself. "A home every child dreams of: bars, guards, and twenty-four seven surveillance. What if … I never get out of here? Never have the courage or the opportunity to wrap her in my arms and tell her…"

"If you never get out, she'll hate you forever," Henry said quickly. "Therefore, you have to talk to me. Help me understand. And then, I'll get you out."

Jean stopped suddenly, just a few steps from the far corner of the room. "There's no way he heard that," Jean said in an even lower tone.

"Of course, I did." Henry had an arrogant chuckle in his voice. "This is a state-of-the-art containment cell." He rapped on the door with his knuckles. "There's nothing in there that you can say or do that we won't know about. But don't worry, we're keeping her safe."

"*Her* safe? You mean, to keep *you* safe and your potential *weapon* secured. Like you did with Claret and tried to do with Sorin."

"You've come to see through the veil quite well since the incident at Wright-Patt. Claret? Who is Claret?" Henry snapped his fingers. "Ah, the Maker. Subject 252-7-38. That's right. He carelessly broke in, in an attempt to rescue her as memory serves. Is that right?"

"You tell me," Jean said and took a seat on the floor in the far corner of the room, tucking her back tightly against the walls. "That was a state-of-the-art containment cell. There was nothing that went on in that room that you didn't know about."

"Mm...," Henry groaned in agreement.

"I've always seen through the veil, Henry," Jean snapped. "I've always known there was more going on than you or Dr. Shelley told me. 'We'd like to better understand them' is what you two told me when you asked me to join your team."

"And that's true, we do want to better understand them.".

Jean shook her head. "A lie hidden within the truth. We were government employees, working at Wright-Patt. It didn't take much to conclude you and Dr. Shelley were trying to weaponize them. Wright-Patt is home to Air Force Material Command who builds all the toys for our military."

"That all may be true, but it's different now."

"Why? Because I know the truth about Rahne?" Jean asked in a condescending tone. "Because I've got you second-guessing yourself on Victor's death? Or perhaps because I prefer the company of a Nocturnae over you?"

"Now that you're one of them." Henry glared through the small window with hate burning inside him. "Now that you're a Lygos. Another Subject under that subcategory of Homo profectus."

Smirking, Jean toyed with him. "You think I'm perfect?"

"I did once," Henry said sadly. "Now you're disgusting."

"That may be true in your eyes, but you were the one yearning for the girl you couldn't have. The girl that was in love with your brother."

"And where is he now? Huh? Where's Victor? Dead. He's dead, Jean. And has been for what ... almost eleven years? Eleven years Jean."

"He's still alive."

"They found his fucking body Jean. DNA and dental records confirmed it was him."

"A freak accident on the base?" Jean smacked the ground. "Come on! That's as bad as saying he died during a 'routine training exercise.'"

"And what was The Company supposed to tell the media, that

Victor's body was found drained of blood?"

"Is that what happened?" Jean asked, leaning forward.

"I don't know," Henry erupted and paused long enough for Jean to believe him. "I don't know, if a Nocturnae got him. But if it was a Nocturnae, it could've been your good buddy Sorin."

"He wouldn't do that."

"Oh, no? I think he would. A moody, *woe is me* Nocturnae with a grudge against humanity? Yeah, pretty sure he would have. Seems like he didn't have a *change of heart* until he met you. Why is that?"

Jean folded her hands on her lap. "I don't know," she lied. She began to see him change after she gave him the boutonniere. He probably would've drained Victor years ago, but she felt sure he wouldn't now.

"Look, this can go one of two ways. You can continue being a pain in the ass while not helping me, and I can continue rationing your food, drugging you, and making your living conditions inhumane. Or, you help me and things go back to normal."

"You'll let me out?"

"I never said that."

"But you'll drop the temperature?" Jean rung the corner of her sweat-soaked shirt out onto the floor.

"Absolutely. You know what, as a sign of good faith I'll do it right now." Henry nodded at the camera outside her cell.

Instantly, cool air blasted through the air vents. Jean couldn't help but shiver in the pleasure of it. How did humans ever survive without air conditioning?

Cradling his notebook in his arm, Henry pulled out a pen from his pocket. "Walk me through the events that took place that day.

Did you let the Nocturnae out of its cell?"

The foggy image of Sorin emerged in her mind like a piece of a nightmare she'd long forgotten. An uncomfortable chill fell over her. "No ... well, not of my own volition."

"So, you *were* compelled."

"Yes. Well, I believe so," Jean confessed, rubbing the goosebumps on her arms.

"What did it feel like?"

The feeling of utter terror shook Jean to the core. "What do you mean?"

"Was it like being drunk or drugged? Did you feel like the puppet to her puppet-master?"

"No, not at all." The dancing shadow with purple eyes in the world of darkness had seemed neutral. Not friendly exactly, but not malicious either. "It was nothing like that. It was peaceful," Jean said. "Like that first sip of a good chilled Riesling on a hot July day."

"And the Lygos? How did she get out of her cell and escape the facility at Wright-Patt unscathed?"

"It all happened so fast. My MP lie dead all around me when Sorin—"

"The Nocturnae?"

Henry was pissing her off. He knew Sorin's name, and yet steadfastly refused to say it. "Yes, *Sorin*. When *Sorin* exited the cell and made his way to your lab. I alerted security immediately. MP were running down the halls in seconds. One of them told me to stay put, so I took cover in the cell."

Henry rolled his wrist and looked up from the page. "And then what happened?"

"A roar echoed through the halls. The whole building started to shake followed by crashing and banging. I could hear something huge making its way toward the cell, so I pinned myself against the wall. All went silent, until a giant fur-covered hand exploded through the wall and wrapped itself around my waist. I screamed as long and as hard as I could, but it didn't help. Then it became very, very cold."

"You were outside, with the creature?"

"Rahne. And, yes, we were outside, and she … cradled me."

"But didn't harm you?" Henry asked, scribbling on his notepad.

"No, never. It was like she was trying to protect me."

Henry raised his eyebrow at that notion, as if these abominations had empathy. "And the Nocturnae? When did he show up?"

"It's kinda hard to keep track of time when you've just been pulled through a top-secret government building by a giant humanoid wolf."

Ignoring her sassy comment, Henry continued his line of questioning. "The Nocturnae, what did he say to you on your journey to northern Michigan? Did you walk together? You got there awfully fast."

"No, Sorin carried me," Jean said quickly like it was no big deal. A feeling of calm spread over her recalling how cozy she'd been cradled in his arms. And how gentle he'd been with her.

Henry assumed the Nocturnae carried her as a means to an end rather than being nice, but he had to clarify. "The Nocturnae carried you? Of his own accord?"

"Yes. I didn't ask him for help, if that's what you're insinuating."

"Huh," Henry grunted and took the note. "Was there anything

about the Lygos? Did he know anything?"

Curious as to why Henry didn't already know all of this, since everything was in her notes, Jean quickly deduced her notes were somehow damaged or destroyed when Rahne tore through the cell.

Jean paused, weighing how much to say. "No, but he seemed to be studying her. Like he didn't know Lygos existed until that day. It wasn't like he was measuring her up but more … was intrigued by her?" A soft smile spread across her face at the thought of how sweet he was with her. How patient he was. How *human* he was.

Henry scribbled an underwhelmed note and looked up from his pad. "How is it that sunlight doesn't affect him?"

"It never came up." Jean shrugged. "I was a little preoccupied coping with the fact my … that Rahne was alive, well, and only one hundred yards from me for years after you psychopaths ripped her from my womb and told me she died."

Henry ignored her provocation. "It never came up during the interrogation?"

"No," she lied, still betting on her theory that some, if not all, the data was damaged or destroyed. "I don't think that *ability* is something he wanted The Company to know until after he took advantage of it."

"Let's talk about your daughter, Rahne." Henry stuffed the pen into his pocket and placed both hands behind his back, holding the pad. "For all those years you two played together, you never knew she was your daughter? Never the slightest wondering, inkling, or hint of *mother's instinct*?"

"No."

Henry tilted his head slightly, not believing her. "Are you sure?"

His patronizing tone made her want to punch him in the face. She couldn't believe she used to think he was nice. "Henry, stick to molecular biology and genetics. Leave the psychoanalysis to me. You're terrible at it."

Henry scowled. "I think that'll do for now." He closed the small window in her door and left. Five steps down the hall, Henry reached into his pocket and a question formed in his mind. He turned. "When you were brought in from Michigan, you were wearing a necklace. A necklace that you didn't have on that day at Wright-Patt. Where'd you get it?"

She felt the soft spot at the top of her chest, but the necklace wasn't there. "It was my mother's. I found it at the cabin, and I put it on to feel close to her."

"Then you should have it." Henry opened the small hatch at the bottom of the door and carefully set the necklace inside. "I put it just inside your cell door, on the floor."

Bewildered by Henry's kindness, she lifted herself on unsteady legs. Waiting for the other shoe to drop, she walked across the room, but the shoe never dropped. She picked up the necklace. "Thank you. You don't know how much this means to me."

"It should be with you. I know how much you miss them." Although Henry viewed her differently now, he couldn't help but empathize with her when it came to the loss of a parent. After all, he was only six when his mother committed suicide and he cherished every trinket of hers.

Jean chuckled. "Yeah. Right."

"I plan on seeing Rahne today. Is there anything you'd like me to tell her?"

Her absentee-mom guilt weighed on her. Sure, it wasn't exactly her fault that she hadn't been in Rahne's life, and couldn't be there now. But it hurt all the same. "Just tell her I'm sorry."

Henry said nothing. He closed the access door to her cell and his footsteps receded followed by a steel door slamming shut.

"I'm sorry," Jean called out into the universe, hoping Rahne could somehow feel her. The pendant danced on the necklace woven between her fingers like a marionette. "I'm so sorry…"

AFTER PASSING FOUR armed guards, Henry swiped his access card and entered Rahne's classified room. The extremities of the room were black as night, a stark contrast to her brightly lit transparent cell in the center.

"Hello Rahne."

Turning away from her television, she pushed the hair out of her face. "Henry!" She still acted excited to see him, despite everything. A pity Jean wasn't more like her daughter.

Henry smiled. "What are you watching today?"

"Blue Planet." Rahne turned back to the television.

"Ah, another David Attenborough documentary."

"I like his voice. It sounds funny," Rahne giggled.

"I like his voice too." Henry stepped up to the red line draw on the ground that read: DO NOT CROSS. "What's this one about?"

"The ocean." Rahne whirled around with her arms stretched wide. "It covers a lot of our planet. And there are whales and dolphins and daddy horses that have babies!"

Looking past her, Henry watched an octopus squeeze into a soup can on the screen. "Wow! That's really cool."

"Yeah. I'm going to see it someday. Have you seen it?"

"I have. It's very beautiful."—Henry pushed his glasses higher on his nose—"Rahne, why the sudden interest in nature?"

Rahne shrugged. "I like it."

"Because of your trip to Michigan?" Henry pulled a small notebook and pen from his pocket.

"Mmhmm." Closing her eyes, Rahne tried to relive the experience. "I like the sounds, the smells, and the feeling."

Henry looked up from his notebook intrigued by her word choice. "The feeling? What do you mean?"

"The wind on my face. Snow and dirt between my toes." She looked down at her wiggling bare toes. "Heat from a fire. When can I go outside again?"

"Soon," Henry lied. "Rahne, do you feel different?"

"Different?" Puzzled, she tipped her head to one side.

"Do you feel stronger or smarter since that day you woke up in the field?"

"When Mr. Sorin showed me outside?" Her eyes lit up with excitement.

"Yes." Henry wrote in his notebook: *Subject has an affinity to the Nocturnae.*

Rahne looked at the door Henry had entered. "Sometimes I can hear things people really far away are whispering or smell things that I couldn't smell before."

"What do you mean?"

Rahne pointed at the floor in front of Henry. "Your left shoe smells minty." She returned her attention to the television.

Henry lifted his foot, but saw nothing. Jamming the notebook under his arm, he took off his shoe for a closer look and there, wedged in a deep crevasse of his loafer was small speck of gum.

"That's quite a gift, Rahne," Henry said. "What kinds of things can you hear now that you couldn't before?"

"I don't know. It only happens sometimes."

Henry made a note and rested the end of the pen on his chin. "But you can always *smell* things you couldn't before?"

"Mmhmm."

"When can you hear things then?"

"When I'm not thinking about anything."

"So, when you're in a meditative state," Henry mumbled, writing frantically. "This is great. When else?"

Rahne tapped her lips with her finger. "When I'm thinking about someone, I can sometimes hear them?"

"What do you mean?"

"A little bit before you walked in, I was thinking about Ms. Jean, and I heard her talking about a necklace that was her mother's. And then a little later she kept saying she was sorry. What was she sorry about?"

Henry lost grip on his pen and it fell to the floor with a dull ping. He scooped down to pick it up. "I don't know. How did you …? There's no … Wow," he said, having a pretty good idea of what Jean was apologizing for.

"Next time you come visit, could you bring me some crayons and paper?" Rahne asked sweetly. "I miss the drawings I had in my old room."

Henry smiled away his fear of the little girl and said, "Sure thing. Twenty minutes, and I'm turning out the lights."

"Except for the night light!"

He checked to make sure her unicorn nightlight in the outlet nearest to her cell was on. "Except for the night light. Goodnight."

Henry turned and headed for the exit.

"Night Henry," she said, climbing into bed; her eyes still glued to the television. "Night Fred."

The heavy door slammed shut behind Henry and he scribbled a small note in the margin of his notebook and folded it over his pen.

```
Subject 072-4-63 has regressed since the
transformation event at WPAFB and has
started talking to her imaginary friend
once again.
```

# 52



IN THE CENTER of his padded cell, on Level Xi of the Sandbox, a man sat with his legs crossed, meditating calmly. Motionless and out of breath from his recent Houdini escape act, he stared into the dark corner of the room with his discarded straitjacket on the floor just out of sight. The cell was twelve by fifteen feet and almost devoid of any light.

"Why now?" he asked the dark corner.

In the man's mind, a faint, airy voice spoke. "EULB NOOM FO NIAHMAS."

"The second full moon in a calendar month and this one, happens to land on Halloween—a once in a lifetime event." The man paused a moment to think and looked to the dark corner. "But it's May 2019. Blue Moon of Samhain isn't until October 2020. And that's seventeen months from now."

"EHT TEKNIRT LLIW DEEN EMIT WOLLOF TI DNIF REH."

The man searched the darkness. "Okay. Which cell is it in?"

"NEVES EERHT XIS ENIN ROUF ROUF ROUF NEVES."

"That's not the one—"

"ON EHT WOKITHIW SI A TSAEB FO STI NWO."

"Okay good. That thing creeps me out." Turning his head, he looked at the handleless door—the cell's only exit—nested flush to the wall, wondering how he could get out. "Gonna need a little help, Fred."

A streak of purple flashed over the small window of the door. The latch softly clicked as the bolt came free from its strike plate, allowing the door to float open.

Unfolding his unsteady legs, the man slowly brought himself to his knees and shimmied his shackled hands over his head. "It's going to be a little difficult with these—"

The restraints snapped open and fell from his hands.

"Thank you," the man said, ringing his wrists.

Calmly, he made his way to the door with the long plexiglass window down one side and gently pulled open the handle enough to look down the hallway to his right. All clear, as far as he could tell.

Opening the door further, he peered around the doorframe and down the hallway to his left. The guard who normally sat by the door was gone, but a red light on the security camera above signaled it was on.

Slowly pulling his head back into the room, he whispered, "I can't get past that camera without triggering the motion alarm."

The camera lenses, windows, and other reflective surfaces in the hallway flashed purple and everything went black. Three seconds later, the hallway lit up red as the emergency power kicked on, but the camera light stayed off.

"Show off," he said to no one, with a chuckle.

"LLEWRIATS."

Quietly, the man made his way to the end of the hall, not bothering to close his cell door behind him.  As he checked down the next hallway, he smiled—the coast was clear. With his eyes closed, the man checked the door to the stairwell. It was unlocked.

"This is going to be easier than I thought," he said to himself and snuck into the stairwell, closing the door softly behind him.

The purple eyes followed the man by darting from the window in a door to the lens of a security camera like they were windows of a house, and it was the ghost that haunted the home.

A faint cloud of dust floated up from the ground behind him as he walked through the long, large red lit passage of the lowest level of the prison—Omega Level. He stopped when he came to an enormous pair of steel doors with yellow letters spray painted in the center.

**WARNING**
Enter at your own risk.
Prisoners of this ward are considered
Omega Level threats to the human race.
Prisoners span the Darwinian, Arcane, and
Celestial Divisions of The Company.
In the event a convict becomes free of
its restraints or cell...
...may God help us all.

"Politicians and government personnel do everything they have to, to keep *their* hands clean. Fucking dirty lying pricks." Turning his head slightly to look over his shoulder down the dark, empty hall. "Don't you think?"

The darkness staired back, silently.

Focusing on the door, he squinted at the lettering and muttered to himself, "At least they wrote it large enough for those of us to read who are *too dangerous* to have our glasses."

"Now what? Base lockdown procedures lock doors and exits, and I would bet they have extra security measures for this area." The man shrugged. "At least, that's what I would do."

He scanned the hall for a pool of water, a window, a mirror, anything that was even relatively reflective, but couldn't find one. He wondered if the lack of reflective surfaces was meant as a deterrent or if it was simply luck for the military assholes.

The man continued scanning his surroundings frantically, looking for anything to spark an idea. Finally, he spotted a discarded pen lying flush against the crease of the wall.

"Fuck it, I don't have another option." He hurriedly grabbed the pen and clicked the ballpoint end open. This was going to hurt.

Closing his eyes, he stabbed the pen into the center of his left forearm, dragging it three inches up his arm. He gritted his teeth in an attempt to mute his groans of pain. Then, he lowered his hand so the blood could run into his cupped hand. Dropping to the floor, he flattened his hand to the ground, until a decent-sized pool of blood formed. Once enough had spilled out, the man flexed his hand, folding his bleeding arm in on itself to stop the bleeding. Eyes fixed on the pool, he stood, taking one step back and waited.

"Come on," he pleaded. Slowly a purple hue formed in the center of the pool. "There you are."

Keeping his eyes on the purple ones centered in the pool of blood, he pointed at the doors behind him. The locks shook the ground and air hissed past them as they opened. Their hinges groaned until the doors suddenly stopped, creating an opening between them *just* large enough for the man to squeeze between.

"EVOM YLKCIUQ SEREHT EROM NAHT MIH OT RAEF NI EREH."

At the sound of rusted hinges, Sorin sat up in his cell. "Phaeton, did you hear that?"

The Nocturnae moved to the edge of their cells, positioning themselves as close to the door as they could without touching silver.

"Hello? Who's there?" Sorin called out from his silver cage.

"Speak less neophyte." Phaeton shook his head. "You may not wish to know."

The free man walked along the edge of the prison, pausing in front of each door muttering to himself. "Seven three six. Seven three six. Seven three six. Seven three six."

Sorin wondered what the man was looking for, how he'd gotten down here, and if he might be able to break him out.

Nearly outside Sorin's door the man stopped, "73…7-274-46. Nope, not this one. Close though."

"Help me," a sweet, gentle, almost angelic voice cried.

Concerned, the man stepped toward the door and placed one hand upon it. "Hello?"

"EVAEL TI TI SEOD TON NRECNOC UOY."

Compassion overtaking him, the man ignored Fred's warning. "Are you okay, miss?"

Confused, Sorin listened again; harder, this time. For breathing. A heartbeat. Anything. But he couldn't detect anything coming from that particular cell. Who could the man be talking to?

"You can hear me?" she asked the man. "No one has been able to hear me for a very long time."

"Of course I can," the man said, though his voice cracked with uncertainty. The military had called him crazy for so long that sometimes he doubted his own senses. "What's your name?"

Sorin heard nothing, but the man answered. "Nice to meet you, Sera. I'm Victor."

Sorin's mind raced. What kind of being might be so quiet not even a Nocturnae with heightened senses could detect it? And what was so special about the man outside that he could?

"Let me out. Please," Sera said with a quivering voice.

Victor leaned into the door, his hand reaching for the lever on the door that could free her. He couldn't help but feel bad for the girl, and he wanted to do what she asked. He knew all too well what being caged in felt like.

Stampeding boots echoed from the stairs above.

"ON EMIT."

Victor dropped his head. "I'm sorry. There's no time." Regretfully, he let go and moved onto the next door. "I'll come back for you."

"EVOM TI."

He jogged past many doors.

"EREH."

Stopping at the opposite side of the room, the man read the door:

**736-94-447**

```
WARNING: Charming and exquisitely horrid
Subject contained. True physical form is
     unknown. Do not speak to Subject.
  Exchanging words with the Subject may
  lead to hallucinations, early onset of
   terminal diseases, and/or infertility.
    If subject has escaped, call 727-0239.
```

"Are you sure you want to open this door?" Victor asked the empty room. "Whatever's behind it sounds … well, exquisitely horrid."

A purple aura enveloped the edges of the door's viewing window, followed by a sudden purple flash around the door seal. The latch unlocked and the door drifted open.

"Well then … I guess we're doing this." Victor took a deep breath and prayed, "Please Lord, don't let me die." Gripping the door, he slowly pulled it open. "Hello?"

"UOY TNOW EID I TNOW WOLLA TI."

Victor feared the worst as he stepped into the dark abyss of the cell. A single light appeared in the center of the room revealing a metal pedestal.

Resting unrestrained atop it was an old, ratty, hand-knit animal. Its eyes were made of black buttons and its mouth and nose of black string. Its body was the color of red wine with blue and yellow paisley curls.

He stopped. "Seriously? We did all of that for a damn stuffed doll. What is this thing, a pig? A hippo?"

The parade of footsteps grew louder.

"YLKCIUQ WON."

"Right."

Grabbing the doll from its podium, Victor turned for the hallway.

"Now what?"

"TIAW."

"For what? If I stay here, I'm going to die and you don't get your…"—looking at the doll under his arm uncertainly—"…this."

Two men in full tactical gear came into view near the rear entrance. One dropped to his knee and without warning fired upon the man.

"Fuck! Shit!" Victor covered his face and ducked back into the cell for safety. "ARE YOU HAPPY!?" he screamed at nothing.

Gun shots rang out as more soldiers arrived. Bullets ricocheted off the walls near the door and Victor dove into the corner, folding himself tightly around the stuffed animal.

"Hold your fire!" a soldier called out after nearly a full minute of shooting.

A feeling of encouragement swept over Victor, as though he *had* to look out of the cell at something; but he knew it was Fred. Peering out of his cell, he could clearly see the main door was severely damaged by the gun fire. A stray bullet had gone through the security system and the door stood ajar.

"Well, I'll be damned," Victor said. Suddenly, a rancid odor like that of a thousand corpses filled the air nearly causing him to vomit.

He scurried back to his corner.

"EHT WOKITHIW."

Victor cupped his ears and clutched his eyes shut as hard as he could, muttering, "The tricks of the Wihtikow. None of it's real. Not the smell or the visions. Just stay calm. None of it's real."

"UOY REBMEMER."

"Of course, I remember." Victor opened one eye to peer into the darkness.

The men outside begin coughing and gagging on the smell quickly filling the giant room. One by one, the men fell victim to their own greatest fears.

A daughter who died at the age of five to leukemia cried out to her father from the hospital bed. A best friend, a marine, exploded before the soldier's eyes. A woman screamed and clawed at her body as ants appeared all over her skin.

The aroma shifted about the room and focused itself on the soldiers. Pushing them deeper and deeper into chaos. Throwing them into their own circles of Hell.

"WON."

Without hesitation, Victor tucked the doll under his arm, leapt to his feet, and sprinted toward the door. He pulled it closed behind him.

"Thanks Fred."

He was free at last.

# 53



LORD GOD HELP me," a soldier cries out as his feet dangle freely over the ground.

Phaeton pulls the man's face to within an inch of his own and snarls, "I *am* God. How dare you ask for my help, Ubiet."

The unmistakable sound of a hand pulling wet and sloppy intestines from a person plagues my ears as the soldier wiggles and screams. "Phaeton stop this," I shout from the depths of my cell. It's one thing to kill a man and feed on them, is another thing entirely to play with one's food until it dies simply because you can.

Discarding the corpse like it was nothing more than a piece of trash, Phaeton moves to my cell door in an instant. "How *dare* you tell me to do such a thing? Have you already forgotten what it's like to be hunted? Or how the humans killed Fenix while he was protecting you? Or how Gaius sacrificed himself to save you?"

"How do you know that?"

"How about your Maker? Have you forgotten about her and

what torturous horrors she suffered for six centuries while you were lying on your back in a cabin at the edge of the woods overlooking the ocean? …Have you?!"

Silently, I stand on the other side of the door with a heavy head. Speechless. He is right.

"You disgust me, Sorin. A traitorous Nocturnae such as yourself has no place in the Kingdom of The Faceless King! And I had such high hopes for you." He slams his fist into my door, denting it.

My eyes shoot back to the door. "Phaeton, you can't leave me here! Please."

But his footsteps quickly move away from the door. He has left me to fend for myself.

I put my back as close to the back wall as I can without touching it and propel myself at the door. In one singular, fluid motion I link the kinetic energy coursing through me into my fist. My skin melts instantly on the silver surface. But I wasn't punching the door. I was punching through it.

Gritting my teeth, I scream through the pain. The bones in my hand, wrist, and forearm collapse in on one another. Tiny bone shards splinter through my skin and my ulna pops through the back of my arm. Fuuuuuuuuuuck that hurt.

My flaccid arm dangles uselessly at my side. Stumbling back to the center of my cell, I kick something hard on the floor—the olecranon from my boneless arm. In my desperation, I've been stupid. It'll be hours before more blood is dispensed in my feeding trough.

My blood covers the floor, but I sit on it anyway. I inspect the door for damage, but it stood unblemished other than the dent

Phaeton put in it. How was Phaeton able to impact it, when I can't?

THE THROBBING IN my head could be confused with the bagpipes of Scotland. My memories of Germans from University on holiday in 1992 would say, it's like the worst hangover after the best party on the shittiest day with your favorite mates.

I must have bled out enough to pass out. Slowly, I peel myself from the floor and wipe the sleep and dried blood from my eyes, freeing them to flutter in the darkness. My body's too busy trying to heal to flip through the wavelengths. I lift my arm from the shoulder, but it dangles lifelessly against me. This isn't ideal.

There's a rapping on my door. "Mr. Harker!" a man says from the other side.

Where the hell did he come from? Is this a dream?

"Mr. Harker." The man knocks again. "Answer me."

"What?" My voice is far more hesitant than usual.

"I'm surprised to find you still here." His fingernail traces the center of the door. "Impressive dent. The other Nocturnae try and bust you out?"

"I don't know what you're talking about," I lie.

He scratches the silver. "Remarkable what materials scientists can come up with these days. This much damage to the door, and it's still barely compromised."

With a groan, I bring myself to my feet. "Yeah, these things are 'built Ford tough.'"

"Hope you didn't try to punch your way out after you saw the door was dented," the man says with a chuckle. "Takes quite a creature with unmeasurable strength to do this."

"Oh, but I did." My wet noodle of an arm flaps against my hips.

"Prison's done you good, Mr. Harker." The faint sound of metal rubbing on metal whistles through my cell. "You're more talkative, more compliant than you were back at Wright-Patt." The man clicks his tongue like he's sucking food from his teeth. "But, then again, Jean has that effect on people."

"Who are you?" You're not that monster Dr. Shelley. The voice is too young. You're not his associate, Henry, either. Nor Victor, the man who talks to empty cells. No, I don't know this voice. You're someone new.

"Me?" the man asks in a darker tone. "Oh, that's not how this works."

I reach for the viewing window in the door with my good hand.

"I wouldn't do that," the man snaps. "You'll only sear more flesh from your body, and I'm willing to bet you don't need anything else taxing your regenerative gifts." The man slides the window shutter closed, locking it.

There must be cameras in my cell. I can't believe I haven't found them yet, but there's no other way of him knowing that I was reaching for the window. He knows Nocturnae too, at least to some degree.

"I wouldn't breathe too deeply either," the man adds, as I hear him put something back in his pocket. "Cayenne pepper. Takes scent dogs out for a week. So, I'm betting it'll *really* fuck your kind up—heightened senses and all. Don't worry, we'll clean it up when we're all finished."

"What do you want?" Seems like he knows Nocturnae quite well. I'm going to have to be careful with this human.

"I'm here to make sure everything gets cleaned up and put back in place," the man says, clapping his hands together. "There are some pretty nasty things locked away in here. Two of them got out. You wouldn't happen to know anything about that would you?"

Haughty? Really? He's not the least bit scared of being this close to a creature as dangerous as me. No, he's borderline conceited. "Ah, see that's not how this works," I say with a smirk. "I don't just *give* out information. There's a cost."

The man lets out a single, hard laugh. "You're quite the character, but I don't negotiate with your kind. If you change your mind, just holler," the man says and the soles of his shoes scrape across the ground like he's pivoting on his heels.

"How would I do that?" I ask.

"Just say you're ready to talk, and I'll get the message." Three steps from the door, the man stops. "Funny isn't it."

"What?"

"How everything changes when the human doesn't care what the Nocturnae has to offer in a game of quid pro quo…" I open my mouth, but no words came out. "We'll talk soon, Sorin. I'll put in for some extra blood for you. Real human blood this time. Not that pig shit. Think of it as a gesture of good faith."

Not such a bad guy after all. Ironically.

# 54



Yellow warning lights suddenly filled the rooms and hallways of The Company's Arcane division building as a pre-recorded voice came over the intercom system. "Intruder alert. Intruder alert. Intruder in Sector C, Cell Block Omega."

Henry looked up from his desk with a sense of dread. "Fuck!" He pointed to the guards near the lab's north exit. "You two, get to the child. NOW! Protect her at all costs."

The guards hurried through the door.

Turning on his heels, Henry made a break for Jean as quickly as he could. "That fucking Nocturnae," he thought to himself. "He's escaped before. If he did it again, he'd come for her."

"Intruder alert. Intruder alert. This is not a drill. Begin lockdown procedures. All civilian personnel are to seek cover in the appropriate predetermined locations. All military personnel are to follow lockdown procedures."

Henry pushed past the panicked crowd of military and civilian personnel, making his way through the main hallway difficult. The access hallway, however, remained empty. His shoes clicked as he stepped down metal stairs and onto the grating. He tripped over his feet as he approached a rusted door guarded by two MP. Flashing his badge, he barked, "Open it up." Once inside, Henry called out for Jean. "Are you still here?"

"Well, that's a stupid fucking question. Where else would I be?" Jean grumbled.

Henry stood in front of her cell door huffing from the exertion of the past few minutes. "I see the freezing water we pumped in for you hasn't improved your mood."

Jean pulled a foot out of the water and kicked it dry. She'd been confined to her bed for days to avoid it, which made her even more stir-crazy. But she wouldn't give Henry the satisfaction of knowing it bothered her. "What are you talking about? I love the stuff."

"If you cooperate and tell me what I want to know, I can remedy that minor inconvenience."

An alarm sounded.

"There's an intruder in Sector-C, cell block Omega." Jean cups an ear toward the intercom overhead as it repeats the alert. "When we captured Sorin we classified him at Apex Level, so it's worse than that. A stronger Nocturnae? Something else?" When Henry made no reply, she asked, "…it's something else, isn't it?"

"Do you know anything about it? This…?" Henry asked, pointing at the flashing lights. "Who broke in? What they're looking for?"

"How would I? I've been in here this whole time. And I need a damn shower. A nice hot one." Through the window, Henry watched, patiently waiting for a twitch or a shift in her bodyweight to tell him she was lying. Suddenly, Jean's eyes opened and fixed on Henry like she could see him. "It's Victor," she said.

A chill ran down Henry's spine. "My brother is dead. Besides, if it were Victor, which it can't be, wouldn't he come for you?"

"Who says he's not?" Jean asked. Her voice rang out higher than usual, with a sing-song quality to it that spooked Henry even more. Why on earth did he ever agree to work in paranormal intelligence? It would be the death of him for sure.

Henry decided to humor her. "Okay, he is coming for you. In that case, why would he choose to come through the most heavily defended section of the facility?"

Jean barely restrained herself from smiling. "He's probably after Rahne. Unless you have someone else here considered *Omega Level?*"

The flashing warning lights went out and the intercom dinged three times, followed by a voice over the loud speaker. "Threat has been neutralized. Repeat. Threat has been neutralized. All medical staff to Sector-C, Cell Block Omega."

"Well, whoever was out and about failed at getting in." Henry laughed, mostly in pure relief, and walked away from Jean's cell.

THE WALK WAS long. Full of twists and turns. Badge scans and PINs. Security checkpoints. Security Forces everywhere. Medical staff lined one side of the halls with equipment and beds for the injured, and dead or dying.

"What happened here?" Henry asked a nurse.

Suturing a minor head wound, the nurse glanced back. "Umm, I don't know. You'll have to ask the gentleman from the Celestial Directorate. He's in a red suit."

Henry searched the hall and doorways, and finally stopped when the man in the red suit stepped in front of him, seemingly from nowhere.

"Henry?"

"Gabriel?" Henry gave his colleague a once over. "You're the man in the red suit?"

"I am a man," Gabriel said with his arms spread like wings as he eyed himself. "And I am wearing a red suit, yes. Why?"

"I just didn't expect to find anyone from the Celestial Directorate here. This is an Arcane site."

"You're here, aren't you? And you're Darwinian Directorate. I'm here because a cloaked figure broke into this wing."

"What? Who?" Henry went through his mental paranormal database trying to remember if any of the contained creatures were known to wear a cloak. Or could it be someone from the outside?

Gabriel snapped his fingers. "That's the million-dollar question. Whoever it was, they weren't afraid of being seen or of killing anyone in their path. Satellite imagery shows the assailant punched their way in."

Henry's eyes widened. "Punched?"

"Mmhmm," Gabriel said with a nod. "I should clarify, a singular punch."

Shocked, Henry said, "So it wasn't Rahne?"

"The kid?" Gabriel waved him off. "No, she's fine. Last time I saw her she was enjoying macaroni 'n cheese with little hot dog pieces."

Henry placed his hand flat on the exterior wall. "Aren't these three feet thick with a three-inch steel core?"

"Five-inch core," Gabriel said. "We upgraded this hallway eight years ago when we transferred the Crown from Golgotha."

Fearing the worst, Henry asked, "What's Golgotha?"

"Another supermax prison like the Sandbox, but where the Sandbox resides in the middle of the Mojave Desert, more than 200 miles away from a dense population, Golgotha is located outside of Jerusalem. It being in Israel makes it a little more difficult to keep it away from civilization, but we did our best."

Shocked, Henry fell silent. "And they took it? The Crown? It's gone? Who took it?"

"A Nocturnae," Gabriel said, not giving the full story. "Looks like it's the only thing he came for. He was in and out before the satellite imagery data could be sent down, processed, and viewed. That's how fast everything happened. Luckily, we had a little notice after recent break-ins at the other Omega Level prisons."

"There are more prisons than Golgotha and the Sandbox?" Henry asked.

"Three others: The Colosseum in Rome, Shinto in Japan, and the Nile in Egypt. Each break-in was separated by about eighteen hours and was quickly followed by the genocide of a nearby village or town."

"Another Nocturnae." Henry fumbled his hands through his hair. "How old was it? As old as Subject 252-7-38? Or Subject 076-7-46?"

"Older."

"Best we could tell Subject 252-7-38 was born—as a human—

between 110 A.D. and 125 A.D.," Henry said excitedly. "Even older than that?"

"Oh, not much then," Gabriel said. "This one was born—also as human—between fifty B.C. and thirty B.C." Gabriel stuffed his hand into his inner jacket pocket and revealed a small silver coin-like charm. "When we found him in a sarcophagus-like coffin, this was tied around his neck with a leather string."

Taking the charm, Henry studied the object. "Why would a Nocturnae be wearing silver?"

"We were stumped on that one too. Best guess, it was used to subdue him and trap him in his coffin."

"Too small to subdue a Nocturnae," Henry said, flipping the charm in his hands. "It would just piss them off, and they'd just pull the thing from their body. Jerusalem you say?" His eyes widened with amazement.

"Yeah," Gabriel said. "This guy was alive when Jesus Christ was born."

Henry squinted and rubbed the charm. "There's a word on here. Hebrew maybe?"

"You're close," Gabriel said, impressed. "Aramaic."

Bringing the charm into better light, Henry asked, "What does it say?"

"In Aramaic: *Muth*. In Hebrew: *Mot*."

Henry shivered. "*Mot,* as in the personification of—"

"Death."

# 55



FIVE WEEKS LATER, the halls of The Pentagon were strangely empty, an anomaly, for in the U.S. Department of Defense, terror never sleeps.

"Where are we going?" Dr. Shelley tightened his grip on his walker. "I hate this stupid contraption. It makes me look like an old man."

Henry scoffed internally. Dr. Shelley *was* an old man, and it had only been a little over three months since his surgeries. "You're in luck. Looks like we're here."

Gabriel came out of his satellite office to greet them. "Henry. Dr. Shelley. Sorry for all the cloak and dagger. We didn't put the actual location in case the paper was intercepted. Let's walk."

Their pace was slow so that Dr. Shelley could keep up. After a short walk, they reached their destination.

The door unlocked and Gabriel pulled the door ajar. "Just because we're in The Pentagon doesn't mean someone couldn't be a whistleblower. And telling the world vampires are *real* would instantly make them a household name like Daniel Ellsberg, Mark Felt, or Edward Snowden. Every tour of The Pentagon would go something like, 'On your left, you'll see The Hall of Heroes. And down here on your right, is where the government discusses the movements of the things that go *bump-in-the-night* that your parents said were make believe.' But we don't have to worry about that." Gabriel gestured into the room. "After you."

A second hidden entrance flew open. One after the other, three service members in dress garb entered the room, followed by a gentleman in a blue suit and light brown shoes with a matching belt.

"Ardie," Dr. Shelley said with a smile. "Oops, I guess it's Director Ziegler here." He gave a wink to his life-long friend and lost the smile.

Standing behind the head seat of the table, Director Ziegler placed his hands on the back of the chair and eyed each person in turn. "Thank you, all of you for joining us on such short notice. Especially you, Dr. Shelley. I'm glad you're recovering quickly."

"Director, would you mind if we did an around-the-room first? Henry hasn't met the leadership here," Gabriel said.

Director Ziegler gave a nod. "General Grissom, Secretary of Paranormal Intelligence for the United States of America, and the two Deputy Directors: you already know Gabriel Glass, Head of Celestial Division, focusing on higher-dimensional beings, and Colonel Letitia Wyatt, Head of Arcane Division, focusing on the Artifacts." He put his hands on his hips. "It's rare to have all three of you Deputy Directors together in one room, so thank you for coming." He took his seat at the head of the table.

"Take it away, Professor," Gabriel said.

"Right," Dr. Shelley said, sitting up in his chair. "I'll keep this short and sweet. After the Nocturnae infiltrated the Wright-Patt facility and was captured, we learned the missing piece to the PHANG Program."

General Grissom leaned over the table with intrigue. "And what might that be?" His eyes locked on Dr. Shelley.

"To put it quite simply, only female Nocturnae can create new Nocturnae from human hosts—for lack of a better term. They do this by mixing their blood and saliva in a ceremonial kind of … kiss of death, if you will," Dr. Shelley said, interlocking his fingers on the table.

"Is this a theory, or do you have tangible evidence?" Gabriel asked.

"I had a feeling that question might come up, so I flew Patient-XIV in from Langley AFB where I've been testing PHANG." Dr. Shelley slowly stretched his arm out toward the front entrance with an arrogant grin. "Let me introduce to you, Major Diya Kshatriya. With the undisclosed meeting location, I had her follow us with her recently improved senses."

The lock on the door suddenly disengaged. Major Kshatriya stepped into the room in her ABUs and took her place behind Dr. Shelley.

Dr. Shelley continued, "Diya endured extensive physical and psychological trauma after an IED explosion paralyzed her from the waist down during a routine perimeter sweep in Afghanistan. Her body was covered in scars from the fire and shrapnel that accompanied the explosion."

"After being medically discharged, I heard rumors of a secret program that could help people like me," Diya said. "So, I started making noise."

"Quite a bit of noise," Dr. Shelley chuckled. "But she got my attention, and after a considerable amount of prescreening, she was entered into the PHANG Program."

"And her ability to stand and walk are proof the … *transformation* was a success?" General Grissom asked.

Diya refused to look at the General and shifted her weight between legs.

"She can stand—run—jump—her scars are gone. But, I had a feeling demonstrating I'd given her back her human abilities wouldn't be enough," Dr. Shelley said, removing his glasses. "Go ahead, Diya. Show—"

To Diya, time slowed to a trickle as she tapped into her new Nocturnae gift of speed. Gabriel's eyes remained closed in mid-blink. The glasses in Dr. Shelley's hand appeared to be frozen in time. Calmly, she walked across the room and sat on the table in front of the General.

"—him."

General Grissom gasped and threw himself back from the table. Toppling over in his chair, he tripped over his own feet and fell to the floor as he quickly tried to distance himself from Diya. "How did she? Where? What just happened?" he stammered, pointing.

Colonel Wyatt, Gabriel, and Henry were all out of the chairs looking at the trembling General on the floor; but Director Ziegler and Dr. Shelley remained seated, merely exchanging a short, subtle glance.

"That General, is proof that the PHANG Program is successful." Dr. Shelley returned his glasses to his nose. "I don't think further proof is necessary at this time. Do you?"

General Grissom, regained his composure as Henry helped him to his feet. "No, I think that will suffice for now."

Diya hopped off the table and stood behind Dr. Shelley. To the untrained eye it might have looked like she was his bodyguard or his attack dog—and they'd be right.

Since Dr. Shelley restored her ability to walk, Diya had become extremely protective of him. In fact, during one of her physical tests, a staff member got mouthy with Dr. Shelley and stuck his finger on the doctor's chest; but before Dr. Shelley could respond, Diya ripped the man's finger clean off. Needless to say, that ended her testing for the day.

Once everyone was back in their seats, Gabriel said, "Where do you plan on taking PHANG from here, Professor?"

"My plan is to move onto the next phase of my work." Dr. Shelley's eyes moved from Gabriel to Director Ziegler. "As was agreed upon Christmas of '87."

Director Ziegler held up his hand with a heavy heart. "I remember the agreement. You are cleared to begin the administration of the PHANG serum to Patient Nulla once Major Kshatriya's training and field tests have been completed."

Dr. Shelley gave a short smile and turned back to Gabriel. "What are you really asking, Gabriel?"

"Do you plan to have her"—Gabriel pointed at Diya—"Hunt down the remaining Nocturnae and kill them?"

Sporting an evil grin, Dr. Shelley gave a quick tap of his knuckle on the table. "Precisely." He relaxed in his chair. "After all, you don't bring a knife to a gun fight."

Diya was dismissed from the meeting.

Colonel Wyatt cleared her throat. "Our bigger problem is the Xi Level inmate who escaped his cell and stole an Artifact before disappearing into the dessert."

Director Ziegler held up a finger. "Let me handle this part." He turned to Henry. "Henry, your brother Victor didn't die in an accident back in 2008. His whereabouts were kept secret from you, and Gabriel, for security reasons."

Henry fell silent as his eyes welled up. He couldn't believe it. All this time. More than ten years. Victor was alive. He wondered how he was going to tell his friends and family. His father. *Their* father.

Dr. Shelley laid a hand on Henry's back. "I'm sorry. I wanted to tell you for years."

"You knew?" Henry asked, rolling Dr. Shelley's hand off him. "You knew and you never told me?" One by one, Henry looked at each person in the room. "My brother, is alive?" Henry ran his hands through his hair, recalling how adamant Jean was that Victor was alive. "Jesus Christ, he's alive. Victor, is alive."

"What was so important for you to keep this from us," Gabriel said, barely containing his anger. All that time spent comforting Jean, and Victor had been alive this whole time.

"You're not read in," Director Ziegler said, quickly. "And you're still not."

Gabriel decided to play the game. "Of course."

"Unfortunately, it only gets worse," Colonel Wyatt said, shaking her head, "during Victor's escape, one of the Omega Level prison cells was compromised and its contents also escaped."

Dr. Shelley gasped and sat forward in his chair. "Do you know which cell?"

"We do my friend," Director Ziegler said, dropping his head. "And you're well-acquainted with him already."

"No ... not ... Subject 053-8-79."

Henry's eyes widened and he leaned over the table, glancing between the Director and Dr. Shelley. "Phaeton? Isn't he the cause of—"

"Yes," Director Ziegler said folding his hands on the table.

"And the Artifact?" Dr. Shelley asked softly.

"Victor took the Trinket," Colonel Wyatt said.

Confused, Henry glanced around at the sober faces, almost afraid to ask, "I'm sorry, The Trinket?"

Colonel Wyatt and Dr. Shelley locked eyes. She gave him a nod. He swiveled his chair to face Henry. "Colonel Wyatt and her team are leading the way on understanding these items. Throughout history, humanity has been periodically in contact with them— usually, in the hands of the voodoo shamans or priestesses."

"We've concluded there are six Artifacts, although we've only ever been in possession of three," Colonel Wyatt said.

"The Trinket is one, the Crown, and I'm assuming the Codex is the another," Henry said, counting on his fingers. "That's three."

"Correct," Gabriel said.

Henry looked past the silent Director and the General, and into the eyes of those in charge of each Directorate. "What are the other three?"

"The Pearl," said Colonel Wyatt. "But the last known record of its location was the day we gained control of the Codex—November 28th, 1414 at the Étretat Cliffs of France."

"A pocket watch," said Gabriel. "An Artifact that was in our possession back in 1986."

Henry stuffed a hand into his pocket as a terrible awareness washed over him. This watch was *the Watch*.

"It disappeared." Director Ziegler stood, his eyes winced shut in pain, and he grabbed his lower back as he stood. "One day it was there and the next … *poof!* It was gone." Keeping his back to the table, he walked to the far side of the room and grabbed a bottle of water.

Sweat dripped from Henry's forehead as panic began to settle in. He couldn't touch the Watch ever again, but even as he thought this, the tip of his finger brushed the Watch in his pocket.

*"If you flinch, I'll pull your spleen out through your nose,"* the voice warned in Henry's mind. *"What's the sixth Artifact?"*

Removing his Watch-touching hand from his pocket, Henry dried his clammy hands on his pantlegs. "What's the sixth Artifact?"

Everyone else in the room exchanged looks. One by one, they turned to Henry's mentor.

"Henry," Dr. Shelley said with a heavy sigh. "You are intimately aware of the sixth Artifact."

Confused, Henry shook his head. "…intimately aware of—What are you talking about?"

"When you were a young boy, did anyone in your house do or say anything that was a little odd or out of the ordinary?" Dr. Shelley asked.

"I mean, what kid doesn't say there's a monster under his or her bed? Or that their imaginary friend is playing with them? Or sits in front of…" Henry asks rhetorically.

"The Mirror," Dr. Shelley said, finishing the young man's thought.

"No. That mirror had been in my mother's family for generations. Someone in the family would have figured it out at some point in their lives."

"Non-corporeal beings communicate though the Mirror. You can't touch them or hold them. They're not like us," Colonel Wyatt said. "We believe they're creatures with a collective consciousness that exist outside of our plane, experiencing the past, the present, and the future all at the same time."

"Fourth dimensional beings?" Henry asked, his mind reeling over the things his mother and brother claimed to see.

"From what we can find, they are known by the name Penyihir," Colonel Wyatt said. "It means 'witch' in Indonesian."

Henry suddenly felt the weight of it all and held up his hands. "Wait. Wait. Wait. Stop. Hold on. You're telling me, my brother is not only alive, but also escaped from a super-secret prison and stole *The Conjuring's* Anabelle doll…?"

Gabriel cleared his throat. "It's more of a pig—"

"It's really more of a dog," Colonel Wyatt said.

Dr. Shelley interrupted. "I think it's a hippo."

"Whatever!" Henry waved his hands, cutting them off. "Victor stole a doll. And on his way out, he 'accidentally' freed a powerful Nocturnae—who I've heard terrifying stories of over the years. Two prisoners from the same supermax prison escaped and took an Artifact. Therefore, could be in cahoots." Henry gasped for air. "Then, another powerful Nocturnae breaks out of a different super-secret prison on the other side of the world and breaks into Edwards AFB to steal the Crown." Henry looked around the room. "Is that right?!"

"Yes," said Dr. Shelley.

"Oh, and how could I forget," Henry said, throwing up his arms. "There are six magical items that we call *Artifacts* and we only have one! The Codex. Do they all fit together in a magical glove and allow one of these Thanos-like Nocturnae to snap their fingers and wipe out half the planet?"

The men at the table chuckled.

"Well, they're not Infinity Stones, Henry," said Gabriel.

General Grissom leaned over the table. "But they could destroy the world as we know it."

"I'm still not convinced there are only six," said Dr. Shelley. "I still think there may be seven Artifacts. And before you all jump down my throat, I realize there's no evidence."

"Seven?" General Grissom asked, intrigued. "Why do you think there are seven?"

Keeping his mouth shut, Dr. Shelley looked at the Director and his equals knowing full-well the subject was a minefield and could cost him dearly.

Director Ziegler broke the long silence at the table. "Go ahead Eugene, tell the general."

"Numerically, there's no significance to six. But seven … There are the seven wonders of the world. Seven continents. Seven oceans. Seven days in a week. The seven chakras in Hinduism. The seven days resulting in the creation of the world, in Genesis chapter one."

"The seven deadly sins," Henry said.

"Yes." Dr. Shelley sighed heavily. "And the seven sacraments. But I think the most convincing and supportive reason there are seven Artifacts can be found in the understanding of the numbers three and four."

Colonel Wyatt threw up her arms. "Here we go again."

Dr. Shelley held up three fingers on one hand. "The number three is a symbol of equilibrium. It's exemplified by the trinity." He held up four fingers on his other hand. "The number four represents the material and terrestrial world; X, Y, Z, and time. The sum of these two numbers is seven; existing in a place between the two worlds, the world of life and the world of death."

"Great theory, but like you said there's been no evidence to support it," Colonel Wyatt said. "Now, can we get back to what these series of incidents means for the nation. And how in the hell we're going to regain control of the situation."

Director Ziegler smiled. "That's what we're here to discuss."

DR. SHELLEY AND Henry left through the door which they came.

"What's wrong, Henry?" Dr. Shelley asked as he held the exit door open. "You're pretty silent."

"Other than the obvious?" Henry stood there, chewing on his lip—a nervous trait he'd picked up from his grandfather as a kid. "That you lied to me all these years about Victor?"

Dr. Shelley put his hands up. "You know how classified information works, Henry. I couldn't jeopardize my work. Not even for a friend."

They walked halfway down the hall in silence. Henry knew Dr. Shelley's excuse was reasonable, but it stung nevertheless. Childhood memories came flooding back. "I didn't know…"

"What didn't you know?" Dr. Shelley asked.

"That they were telling the truth. All those years. So many arguments. Screaming matches in the dining room, living room, and the kitchen. Once, dad scooped me up from the *Teenage Mutant Ninja Turtles* puzzle I was doing on the floor only to rush me to the car and buckle me in."

"I'm not following."

"I don't remember if we ever pulled out of the driveway. We must not have, but—"

Dr. Shelley softly gripped Henry by the shoulders. "What are you talking about?"

"My mom," Henry's eyes quickly welled up with tears as guilt overtook him. "She was telling the truth. For all of those years. We didn't believe her. I didn't. Dad didn't. But—"

Then Dr. Shelley realized, "But Victor did."

Wiping his eyes, Henry nodded silently. "He said he could see them too. But I didn't believe him. I didn't believe either of them. Ever. How could I believe them? I called them crazy. Nutcases. Hell, I screamed in my brother's face that I was happy mom finally killed herself. All the while, he was telling me that a monster killed her."

"You were a child."

Henry turned away from Dr. Shelley, mad with grief and disappointment in himself. "A child? A child?! Professor, my brother was already working with you. He had already met Jean when I said all of that. I wasn't a child. I was a grown man."

Dr. Shelley looked at his feet. "I guess I too have a confession. I agreed to work for The Company in hopes of saving my wife and child."

Confused, Henry said, "But your wife's dead."

"In all known scientific standards, yes; but she's not technically." Dr. Shelley waited for Henry to put the pieces together.

"Your wife and unborn child, they are what started all of your research. That's the agreement you made with Director Ziegler Christmas of 1987..." Henry's eyes darted back and forth as he connected the dots. "Isn't it?"

"They are Patient Nulla."

"But you said—"

Dr. Shelley pointed to the bench pushed up against the wall. "How about we sit? And I'll tell you the whole story. The real story."

# 56



ON A BEAUTIFULLY clear, early fall afternoon at one o'clock on the twenty-sixth day of the tenth month in 1985, Dr. Shelley had the honor and privilege to marry his best friend and true love, Michelle A. Grime.

He awoke in a state of panic. It was his wedding day. An outsider would have never known he'd been calm and collected with a clear mind through their entire engagement by his state that morning.

His best man, David Brodie, picked him up for breakfast at seven o'clock that morning, as previously arranged, and it was exactly what Dr. Shelley needed. David had been wed to Michelle's close friend Kat just five months prior, and she was already pregnant.

Needless to say, David had words of wisdom despite being so new to married life. Dr. Shelley and David laughed a lot, reliving stories from college before they entered medical school and the military.

They finished breakfast around nine with plenty of time to get ready for the big day. Dr. Shelley's and Michelle's parents sent out more than 550 invitations, and they all came back 'yes.' Every single person invited was coming to the wedding. Michelle was the fourth of her parents' five children to be married, but Dr. Shelley was the first of his generation on both his parents' sides. It was a big deal for an Irish-Catholic family.

Dr. Shelley had asked Michelle to marry him the previous December. He figured he needed to do something with the wedding ring he'd purchased the previous summer.

One August afternoon he found himself in a shopping center. He strolled into a jewelry store—he couldn't recall which one if you paid him—for a unique pair of earrings for Michelle's birthday in the coming months. As he perused the showcase, a young salesman asked if he could help, or if Dr. Shelley had any questions. The salesman must have misinterpreted Dr. Shelley's look of confusion and panic because he asked Dr. Shelley if he wanted to look at their wedding bands.

Dr. Shelley had never seriously thought about it, but after a brief pause, he said, "Sure."

After looking at a few uninspired sets, Dr. Shelley saw one he actually liked. He asked the salesman for a closer look, and the price—which quickly ended the conversation. Dr. Shelley asked the salesman if he could hold them for a few days. The clever salesman apologized. Regrettably, he could not hold *this* set as it was the only one they had, and it was against the store's policy to hold merchandise without a deposit. Dr. Shelley was feeling boxed-in so he thanked the salesman and made his exit. The air suddenly seemed thin on oxygen.

Dr. Shelley was surprised to find that he couldn't get marriage out of his mind. He truly loved Michelle, but could he live with her, forever? Could she put up with him, forever? Could he put up with her? He liked the way he felt whenever he thought of marriage with Michelle.

The thought always brought a smile to his face. That was the deciding factor. Dr. Shelley went back to the jewelry store—he could have sworn the salesman smirked when he walked into the showroom—and bought Michelle's engagement ring and wedding band. He felt really good about it, but now what?

The engagement ring and wedding band purchase was his secret for a few weeks. Dr. Shelley was still getting used to all of this. Whenever he and Michelle went out, he couldn't help weighing her current behavior against their future together. She passed his scrutiny with flying colors. Unknowingly, she eliminated all of his doubts.

Being a traditionalist, Dr. Shelley wanted to ask Michelle's father for permission and his blessing. Eventually, Dr. Shelley grew a pair of balls large enough to ask her father, Jim, if they could speak privately.

Jim replied, "Sure. When?"

The asshole.

Dr. Shelley told Jim that now would be fine. Jim said he wanted to show Dr. Shelley something from one of his collections—he had so many—and he motioned for the nervous Dr. Shelley to follow him into his bedroom; Jim didn't sleep in the same room as his wife.

After listening to Jim expound upon his good fortune on acquiring his latest treasure for what seemed like hours, Dr. Shelley finally told him that he wanted to ask him something. Dr. Shelley told Jim he loved Michelle and wanted his permission to ask her to marry him. He told Jim he'd always take care of her. Dr. Shelley reached into his pocket and pulled out the set of rings to show Jim.

Jim looked at them for a few moments, looked up at Dr. Shelley, and said, "Well, good! That's great! I would love to have you in the family." A large smile spread wide on Jim's face.

Dr. Shelley thought his knees would give out from under him. Jim could be a rather stern, serious man. And he was big. To say that Dr. Shelley was nervous doesn't begin to describe his anxiety. He had no idea how Jim would take this. Dr. Shelley asked him if he would keep this secret—Dr. Shelley intended to ask Michelle in December. Jim agreed to keep the news between the two of them, and he did.

The day came to ask Michelle to be his bride. Dr. Shelley had it all worked out. He'd call her after work and invite her out for a romantic evening of wining, dining, and dancing. The evening would be capped off with his asking her to marry him as they left the dance floor. This would be, by any standard, an extraordinary evening. Dr. Shelley couldn't wait.

When Dr. Shelley called Michelle that Friday evening and told her he had made dinner reservations for two and wanted to make an evening out of it, she said, "Oh, not tonight. I've had a rotten day. All I want to do is get into my sweats and lounge around. Why don't you come over and we'll watch a movie or something?"

Dr. Shelley was speechless and so irritated that he almost hung up on her.

Michelle couldn't figure out why he was so angry. Dr. Shelley didn't know how to explain his frustration without blowing the whole surprise. After some increasingly heated exchanges, Dr. Shelley conceded to come over to her parents' house to watch a movie or something.

The night turned out okay, but it certainly wasn't the night Dr. Shelley had planned. Toward the end of the evening, he told Michelle he had something for her. He gave her the wrapped ring box and when she opened it, he asked her if she would marry him.

Michelle was beautiful in her sweats and stockings with her hair tied back in a bandana. She sobbed and choked out a *yes*, made some strange noises, and ran upstairs to tell her parents. Dr. Shelley was left sitting alone in the basement family room.

She came back down with both her parents. Michelle was crying. Red, Dr. Shelley's soon to be mother-in-law, was crying. Even Jim got a little emotional with a stiff upper lip and a slight quiver on the bottom; he'd never admit it though.

Dr. Shelley had truly surprised Michelle.

He had a lot of fun telling them of his original plans for the evening. Both Red and Michelle were surprised Jim had known for so long and hadn't said anything. Receiving a subtle nod of appreciation from his soon to be father-in-law confirmed for Dr. Shelley he'd done right by asking for Jim's blessing and keeping with formal traditions—no one would have had it any other way.

Michelle wore the engagement ring to Dr. Shelley's parents' house the next day. They decided on a subtler approach to announcing their engagement to his parents. They sat at the dining room table with Mr. and Mrs. Shelley, talking and laughing.

Mrs. Shelley hadn't noticed the ring until Michelle made some elaborate gesture with the fingers of her left hand extended. Then she saw it, hugged them both, and began crying—of course. Mothers are strange that way.

The following ten months were a blur, and their wedding day came upon them before they knew it. The wedding party was a mix of friends and family. The wedding was beautiful. Michelle was beautiful. She walked down the aisle like she owned it, never taking her eyes off of mine.

Poor Jim, hands shaking as he walked, filled with emotion. His eyes were wet and red when he gave Dr. Shelley her hand, but she didn't seem to notice. It was her wedding day, and Michelle was having the time of her life.

When they exchanged rings, they kissed and Michelle leaned forward as she whispered, "Gotcha!" in Dr. Shelley's ear. It took everything he had not to laugh, which he hid behind a smile and another kiss. Even for an Irish-Catholic wedding it went long, ninety minutes, from having more than 500 people receive communion.

The reception was the biggest party they ever threw and had to be held in a gymnasium to account for all that attended. Everyone was there. Michelle and Dr. Shelley wanted everyone to dance, so they started the reception off with a bang.

The band introduced them as they entered the hall, and they went straight to the dance floor, slow dancing for about a minute when—right on cue—the band broke out in a rousing rendition of *Wipe Out*. The bride and groom cut some impressive rug and set the mood for the rest of the night. The party had begun.

Although their reception was large, it wasn't fancy. They had a buffet of cold-cuts, cheeses, hot and cold vegetables, baked beans, and potato salad. Their priorities were the music, a large hall for guests, a suitable dance floor, and a full bar—of course. Jim and his firefighter buddies took care of the bar.

They didn't want a grand march, but at the dollar dance they offered all participants a shot of Jameson's Irish whiskey and a Backwoods cigar—Dr. Shelley's cigar of choice. David and Dr. Shelley's sister collected the money and doled out the vices.

The happy couple couldn't believe the pile of cash they were given. It paid for the majority of their honeymoon. The newlyweds left the reception around eleven thirty that evening to consummate their marriage. The party lasted well beyond that.

A little more than thirteen months later, they were pregnant. They were ecstatic. They read every pregnancy, newborn, and parent book they could get their hands on. By the tenth week they'd settled on Katie, if it was a girl, and Michael, if it was a boy.

In all honesty, they didn't care about the gender. They just wanted a happy, healthy mommy and baby at the end of the pregnancy.

During the twelfth week they met with their Gynecologist and everything checked out. Michelle was healthy and so was the baby. There didn't appear to be any complications and they were doing everything right.

That evening, after dinner, Michelle and Dr. Shelley took their evening walk through the neighborhood and the park near their house. There was a little walkway hidden next to an old white Cape

Cod house they liked to walk down. The owner of the house had hundreds, maybe even thousands, of beautiful, sweet morning glories intertwined along the fence. They stopped to smell and admire them.

Michelle's grip on her husband's hand quickly changed as she fell to the ground, convulsing and foaming at the mouth. Dr. Shelley's heart sank. Dropping to his knees, he turned her on her side and began talking to her, praying she could hear his voice.

Dr. Shelley screamed, "HELP! SOMEBODY HELP ME! CALL AN AMBULANCE!"

A middle-aged woman ran out of the house, with a throw pillow and a towel in hand, to help them. "My husband has the medics on the phone. Help is on the way."

She propped Michelle's head on the pillow, so the concrete didn't continue scraping her head. The woman placed her hand on the small of Dr. Shelley's back. He was sure she said something, but Michelle was the only thing he could see, hear, or think about.

Three minutes passed and so did the seizure. Dr. Shelley didn't think he breathed once through the whole episode. The woman and Dr. Shelley slowly coaxed Michelle to an upright and seated position. The woman called for her husband to bring water.

Dr. Shelley rubbed Michelle's back and held her hand. "You're going to be okay, my love." He kissed her worry-filled forehead. "The ambulance is on the way."

With that, the ambulance came into view. Dr. Shelley knelt there next to his wife, holding her hand while the medics went down their checklist. Heart rate. Pupil response. What is your name? What is today's date? Do you know where you are? Who is the current president of the United States of America?

The world moving around Dr. Shelley had gone silent. A million potential diagnoses screamed through his mind. None of which were good. She was scared. He was terrified.

Preparing Michelle for transportation to Toledo Hospital, one of the medics turned to Dr. Shelley. "Would you like to ride along, sir?"

Dr. Shelley thought it was the dumbest question he'd ever heard. He said nothing, just nodded his head. Sitting inside, he held Michelle's hand, stroking the hairs off her brow. He didn't want to be separated from her for even a second.

Whispering the empty promise that everything would be alright, the medic began filling out her chart. Michelle and Dr. Shelley answered questions on medical history, the pregnancy, and the events leading up to the seizure until they reached the hospital. They didn't have to wait in the lobby, having come via medical transport. A small perk for the almost eight-hundred-dollar *cab ride*.

An hour passed waiting for the doctor to come to their room. By this point, Dr. Shelley had called their family members to tell them what had happened.

The doctor entered with a smile. "I hear you gave your husband a bit of a fright this evening Mrs. Shelley." He winked at her to try and calm her nerves. It didn't work.

Michelle went over the evening and her husband went over her chart with the doctor, confirming all the facts were correct. Dr. Shelley knew it was necessary, but he just wanted answers. The doctor ordered a CT scan with contrast, an MRI, an ultrasound to confirm a viable pregnancy, and a slew of blood tests.

The entire testing process took a painful five hours and twenty-two minutes.

When they got back to the room, a nurse informed them the doctor wanted to keep Michelle overnight for observation. This was both a relief and another thing for Dr. Shelley to be concerned about. If the doctor wanted to keep her overnight, then he was worried, to some level, that she may have another episode.

Michelle and Dr. Shelley sat together awkwardly that evening, flipping through the channels, unable to focus on anything for long. Their conversations were just as strange and fake as they were short. Limited to only a few words or a sentence and on subjects neither of them gave a shit about. Clearly, they both were obsessing over the same thing.

Dr. Shelley didn't sleep at all that night. If he did, he didn't realize it and it didn't last for long. He laid in a pseudo-recliner counting the holes in the drop ceiling of the hospital room. The bustling sounds of the hospital didn't stop the entire night. Codes being called over an intercom system and nurses and doctors stampeding down the halls in response.

He studied his wife as she laid there dreaming happily—he hoped—and was thankful for her reprieve, even if brief. When he wasn't counting the craters on the ceiling, Dr. Shelley was memorizing every curve and blemish of Michelle's face.

Dr. Shelley awoke the next morning to a nurse on the opposing side of Michelle's bed. He was surprised he ended up getting some sleep after all.

The morning shift change had occurred and the oncoming nurse whispered an introduction, trying not to wake her patient. She checked Michelle's vitals and wrote them next to her name on a whiteboard hanging on the wall.

"The doctor will be in shortly," she said to Dr. Shelley, looking at Michelle only to confirm she wasn't disturbed. "Is there anything I can get for you at the moment? Coffee?"

Dr. Shelley declined. The nurse left with a smile, closing a curtain behind her to obstruct the view of passersby into their room. The door to the room, however, was left open.

Michelle's lashes began to flutter, and she awoke from a restful night's sleep. Dr. Shelley raised himself slightly from the chair to kiss her forehead, combing her hair back with his palm. He didn't know why he was doing this. He'd never done it in the past, but for some reason it just felt right.

They faked a smile for each other, trying to remain positive and hide their fears. Dr. Shelley told her he loved her; concern poorly hidden in his words. Michelle said nothing. She just blinked slowly and looked to where the door would have been, had the curtain not obstructed her view. The doctor entered with a simple good morning that was oddly quick.

"Good morning doctor," Dr. Shelley said, standing. "Have you gotten the test results yet?" He was eager to hear nothing was wrong and they could return to their carefree life, and prepare for their baby.

"Yes, I do. Please," the doctor said, gesturing for Dr. Shelley to retake his seat. "The results from your blood work look great. White blood cell count is where it should be, and your cholesterol is better than the average woman your age. Your CT results looked suspicious." He paused a little too long at this point and Dr. Shelley knew something was wrong. "Your MRI results revealed a mass growing on your frontal lobe. This is the region of the brain that controls your speech and memory. I have consulted with our neurologist and our oncologist who have diagnosed the mass as a glioblastoma."

Dr. Shelley's heart sank. He almost threw up. Of all the possible diagnoses it could have been, this was by far the worst. It was pretty much a death sentence. Historically, it's killed ninety-nine percent of all diagnosed patients within five years.

"Due to how aggressive this cancer is, we recommend beginning treatment immediately."

The doctor went onto explain that if they chose not to treat the cancer, the baby would not make it thirty weeks before the cancer took Michelle's life. If they chose to treat the cancer, the baby would be lost due to the chemotherapy and radiation, but Michelle would be lucky to live another ten months due to the tumor's location.

Over the next four months or so, they saw twenty-eight different doctors, all leaders in their field. The majority of the doctors were neurologists and oncologists, but they also met with dentists, occupational therapists, psychologists, and cardiologists to help treat the side effects of her limited treatments and the disease itself.

Michelle's first clinical trial treatment took place at the Cleveland Clinic in Cleveland, Ohio. This trial used a matrix of electro-magnets spread evenly across the cranium, emitting low-frequency pulses at timed intervals in hopes of breaking up the cancer cells. This treatment yielded inconclusive results as the tumor neither grew, nor shrank.

Her second clinical trial, also at the Cleveland Clinic, involved opening the skull and administering the chemotherapy directly into the tumor. The doctor's thought process was that the chemo was having trouble traversing the cerebrospinal fluid when administered intravenously. The results were more promising as there was a clear retardation in tumor growth over the following months.

The third and final clinical trial took place at MD Anderson in Houston, Texas. Here the doctor wanted to infect Michelle with the polio virus, which, in theory, would attach itself to the tumor. Once the doctor was convinced the virus had progressed far enough, the vaccine would be administered, curing her of polio and—hopefully—cancer.

The trial was unsuccessful. Upon receiving the bad news, Dr. Shelley's beautiful wife looked at him. She said nothing. She didn't have to. He knew what was next. She was done trying to beat the disease. She wanted to spend what little time she had left at home.

She made it to a little over a year, 370 days. After which, Dr. Shelley quickly fell into bottle after bottle of Jameson and remained there for two years. Eventually, Michelle's parents intervened and convinced him to see a psychologist who convinced him yoga would be good to reset the mind.

THAT WAS THE official story. All of that, was bullshit. Except for the first clinical trial. And the drinking. He was definitely drinking and most assuredly had a problem.

But Michelle never died.

The day everything changed was a few weeks after the results of her clinical trial came back. Dr. Shelley was taking a walk through the park, tipping a bagged bottle of cheap Canadian Whiskey.

He stumbled and the bottle flew from his hand, smashing on a rock as he caught himself on the cold, snowy ground.

"You okay mister?" a man asked.

Dr. Shelley didn't even look at him. "I'm fine."

The man reached out to try and help him to his feet.

"I don't need your help," he snapped.

"Never said you did. Just look like a man down on his luck, with a lot on his mind," the man said, patting Dr. Shelley on the back. Adjusting the fedora on his head, he smiled and stuffed his hands into his long, black cashmere coat pockets. "You try and have a good day mister."

Dr. Shelley said nothing audible—he mumbled something heinous to himself as he brushed the dirt and snow from his hands and knees, but he couldn't tell you what. The man gave a subtle nod, dropped his head and carried on with his stroll through the park.

Dr. Shelley watched as the man walked away from him. The thought of his wife telling him to apologize for his rudeness took over him, and he hung his head, ashamed. "Wait."

The man looked back. "Yes?"

"Eugene. My name is Eugene," he said, holding out his hand.

"I'm Ardie. You look like you've got a lot on your mind. Can I buy you a cup of coffee?"

The men walked back to the entrance of the park and across the street to a little coffee house that hasn't been there since the early '90s.

Sitting across from each other at a two-top, Ardie cradled the paper cup between his hands and stared into the steam that rose from Eugene. It was awkward the first minute or two. But he never pushed or prodded.

It made it easy for Eugene to tell him everything. How Michelle and he met, their life plans, his occupation, time in the military, and so on.

Ardie never said a word, but he'd nod from behind his cup every once and a while. He could have said anything. Literally, anything in the world and it wouldn't have mattered or helped or made Eugene feel better. Except he said the one thing that could. "Maybe I can help." From within his long coat, Ardie pulled out a file folder stamped:

TOP SECRET/PARANORMAL INTELLIGENCE

Coming from the military Eugene knew classification levels and the proper procedures of handing such information. "What is that?

"Dr. Eugene F. Shelley, you've been cleared. And everyone in this coffee shop works for me."

"Cleared? What? I never told you I was a doctor. How do you know my middle initial? Who are you? What the hell's going on?" Eugene scrambled out of his chair.

The barista behind the counter revealed a pistol from under the register.

"Stop! Everyone stop! Lower your weapons. I'm not in danger," Ardie said, holding up his hands. He leaned over the table and lowered his voice. "This might be a good time to admit you're not going to harm me."

Eugene looked at Ardie like he was crazy. "Hurt you? No, why would I—"

"See…," Ardie said, looking around the room. "Everything is fine. Stand down."

The undercover agents put their weapons away and returned to acting like normal citizens.

"I can help you. More importantly, I can help your wife. And child." Ardie gestured for Eugene to retake his seat. "Please, sit. Let me explain. If you don't like what I have to say, you're free to go; no strings attached. But once you walk out that door, the deal is off the table, and you'll never hear from or see us again."

Finally, a glimmer of hope. It was like someone lit a candle in the pitch-black house of horror Eugene had been living in since Michelle was first diagnosed. He wasn't even the slightest bit skeptical. He just wanted to save his wife and child. After all, it was just a conversation. Ardie said no strings and Eugene could leave whenever he wanted.

Eugene took his seat, nodded and listened intently with folded hands.

"I work for The Company, a secret organization operating within every government across the world. The public has come to call us a 'shadow government' or more recently, a 'cryptocracy.' In short, we operate outside the rules of the real world as we fight for humanity's survival." Ardie said all this nonsense with a straight face.

Eugene couldn't help but laugh—it was ridiculous. A government that's not a government operating across the world protecting its citizens from invisible, make-believe threats.

"I had the same reaction." Ardie sat back in his chair. "But I promise you, I'm telling the truth."

"Okay, assuming that's hypothetically possible, what do you want from me?"

"There's a species called the Nocturnae that is far superior to humans. I'd like to reverse engineer them." Ardie slid the folder across the table.

Eugene opened the folder and skimmed the first classified page: Increased strength and speed; Rapid regeneration capabilities; Immortality. He grew up reading comic books and it was all right there. "You want me to weaponize them?"

"No, I want you to cure your wife." Ardie slid his coffee cup to the edge of the table. "Anything beyond that is not your concern."

A woman came around and filled his cup, never taking the pistol hidden in her apron off Eugene.

Thumbing through the pages, Eugene felt overwhelmed with excitement, curiosity, and above all else, real hope. "There are decades of research here that would need to be completed, she won't make it another six months."

"Not to worry." Ardie placed a pen on the table. "As soon as you sign the last page in the folder, a team will be sent to retrieve your wife and move her to a classified facility at Langley Air Force Base."

"Virginia? But, how will I ever see her?"

"You're welcome to visit as often as you'd like, as long as it doesn't interfere with your work." Ardie held up a finger. "Now, there is a catch."

Eugene tried not to roll his eyes; but in that moment, they had a mind of their own. "Of course, there is."

"It's nothing bad my friend," Ardie said with a chuckle. "All that I ask is you don't tell anyone outside of myself and those working in her facility about her."

"You want me to lie?"

Ardie's head swayed back and forth like he was listening to a compelling tune. "I would label it more as an omission, but call it what you will."

"What would you have me tell them, that she's dead?"

Ardie nodded behind a long shrug. "Wraps up all the loose ends quite nicely, doesn't it? You get to save your wife, and we gain a better understanding of the Nocturnae." He downed the rest of his coffee and held out his hand. "What do you say? Do we have a deal?"

It was in that moment that Eugene knew Ardie owned him. "Yes."

# 57



HURTING AN ANIMAL, human, or creature was the one thing Henry hated about his job. It wasn't so much empathy as it was he simply didn't enjoy the cries of pain the Subject or Patient would let loose. He kept telling himself today was no different, but it was. He liked Rahne and had wonderful memories playing with her and coloring pictures and watching cartoons. Nevertheless, he had a job to do.

Henry entered the well-lit, white-walled room with his hands in his jeans and a blank look on his face, rocking a Metallica t-shirt covered by a white lab coat. "How are we looking?"

"She's all hooked up," the nurse said. She'd seen a lot of things on the job, and she'd never say it, but this was barbaric.

Henry flipped the cover sheet and medical history and stopped on the page labeled: COERCIVE PERSUASION.

Stuffing the chart under his arm, Henry made a pass around the Subject strapped to a chair like she was a wild animal. Blood and drool spilled from a mouth that housed a silver ball gag and tears streamed from eyes that remained locked on him.

"Good morning, Rahne," Henry said, checking the silver restraints at her bare wrists and ankles. "I'm going to show you a series of images and Ms. Carrie,"—gesturing to the nurse—"is going to watch your vitals. If you react incorrectly, I'm going to take one of these and drive it into your body." Henry reached into the pocket of his lab coat and pulled out a solid silver spike the size of a pencil and waved it in the air. "Nod if you understand."

Rahne screamed from behind the metallic sphere in her mouth and her eyes flickered yellow. Questions raced in her mind as she panicked. What was he doing? He was her friend. What happened? Why is he doing this?

"Ah, ah, ah," Henry said swishing his finger back-and-forth and glanced at nurse Carrie. "I wouldn't do that."

From the top drawer of a nearby crash cart, Carrie pulled a syringe filled with a thin fluid. It shimmered under the bright lights as she removed the cap housing the large needle.

"If you even begin to show the slightest sign of transforming into that hulking thing, we're going to sedate you with a new cocktail I like to call: *Full Stop*. After your Nocturnae friend broke into the facility, we began working on this little beauty. It won't kill their kind, but they wouldn't like life for quite a while. I have no idea how it'll affect you. So, don't make me find out."

Henry set down her chart and picked up a small remote. "Now, let's begin."

He pressed a button and an image of Sponge-Bob Square Pants showed up on the wall in front of her.

"Next," Carrie said.

Henry clicked the button. Dr. Barbie showed up on the wall.

"Next."

A unicorn.

"We have a baseline. You can proceed," Carrie said from behind the monitors.

"Okay Rahne, we're going to begin. Remember, if you react incorrectly there are going to be consequences."

Henry reached into the bottom drawer of the crash cart and pulled out a hammer.

"Here we go…"

He clicked the button and an image of Jean from two years ago appeared on the wall.

"No change," Carrie said.

He clicked the button again, changing the image of Jean to a more recent one.

"No change," Carrie said.

An image of Jean curled up in the corner of her cell with bags under her eyes and sunken cheeks. Rahne's eyes widened, and she lunged forward in her seat.

"Mild change, but still within acceptable bounds," Carrie said. "Go onto the next image. You're okay."

A grainy image of the Nocturnae Subject in the halls of The Company's Darwinian division facility at Wright-Patterson Air Force Base filled the wall.

"Significant change."

With a single strike, Henry drove the spike through the top of Rahne's hand, splintering the wooden arm rest underneath. Rahne groaned as bubbles of blood and puss erupted around the silver spike like hydrogen peroxide on a fresh wound.

Setting down the hammer on the crash cart, Henry looked at Carrie and gestured to the door.

"Don't go anywhere," Henry said to Rahne, patting her bloodied hand.

He followed Carrie into the hallway and closed the door behind them.

"Is everything alright?" she asked.

"Yes, everything is fine, but we can't continue. Protocol says we have to wait two hours before continuing. I should say, starting over. Otherwise, we risk triggering a catastrophic response."

"Okay … and then what?" Carrie asked and gulped down a haunting presence resembling heartburn.

"We do it again," Henry said, hatred growing in his voice. "And again. And again. Until she responds to the photos like we want."

"And we want her—"

"We want her to respond *aggressively* to the sight of Sorin or any Nocturnae. Then, we move onto the next phase."

Carrie recalled her training manual which outlines the horrific tests and inhumane sequences for psychological conditioning and reprogramming. "The trigger phase."

Henry gave Carrie a quick glance. "Exactly. I prefer to call it the *Trigger Scent* since it's a specific scent placed on the target which sends the Subject—Rahne in this instance—into a mindless berserker rage."

"Sounds dangerous."

He took one of his latex gloves off. "Well, we're building a weapon, not an entertainer for children's birthday parties." He pulled out the sapphire-blue Watch from his pocket and checked the time. "I'll be back in two hours. Page me if anything changes." He made for the exit.

"Henry…?"

"Yeah?" Henry responded with one hand on the door.

"What about the spike?"

"Protocol says leave it in," Henry said with a smile. He pivoted on his heel and pulled open the door. "She needs to learn."

THE STEEL DOOR crashed closed behind Henry as he exited the room housing Rahne's prison and he sprinted for Jean's cell. A few minutes later and two hallways to go, he heard faint screaming and quickened his pace.

"What the fuck did you do to me Henry?" Jean screamed from her cell. Her screams echoing down the halls. "HENRY!"

Henry broke into a sprint. When the guards were in sight, he gestured for them to open her cell door.

One of the guards held out his hands, signaling for Henry to stop. "But sir, that's breaking—"

"I don't fucking care. Open the goddamn door!"

The door swung open and Henry stopped abruptly at the sight of Jean in the far corner. He searched the room for the Codex and found it sitting on the edge of her bed.

Jean looked up from the blank pages of the book with trails of blood running down her face. "Henry … What's happening to me?"

Henry stepped forward with a confused look on his face. "Is that blood?"

"Yes, Henry. What the fuck is going on with me? What did you do?"

"I ... I don't know ..." he stammered.

Jean's eyes flashed yellow as she let out a terrifying and sudden, guttural growl. "HELP ME!"

Henry gasped, and the MP standing guard pulled him out of the room, slamming the door. "Are you okay, sir?"

"I'm fine," Henry said, picking himself up off the floor. "Thank you. Thank you both. Really."

One of the guards pointed at the cell, but refused to look through the small window in the door. "What's going on here, doc?"

"Guys, I've told you, I'm not a doctor," Henry said, stepping up to Jean's prison door. "And to be quite honest..." Henry studied Jean through the window as she rocked herself fearfully in the corner, clutching the Codex like it was the means to her salvation. "...I have no idea."

In that second, Henry caught a glimpse of small bloodstain on the sleeve of her shirt.

"Unless..."—he looked at his own hand, eyeing the spot where he'd stabbed Rahne—"...they're connected somehow."

"HENRY," Jean screamed from the confines of her cell. "HELP ME!"

Henry rushed to the window and watched as her blood flowed into the Codex. Text rippled over the pages in more languages than he could identify, and then suddenly, red light filled the hallway.

"SECURITY ALERT. SECURITY ALERT. CONTAINMENT BREACH IMMINENT IN SECTOR C, CELL BLOCK OMEGA."

"Shit," Henry said, flinging himself away from the door. As he ran down the hall he turned back and pointed. "Don't let her out of your sight. I want to know everything that happens in that room. Call security and IT, make sure they're recording everything. Take notes if you have to. I don't care. Just get me that data!"

"WARNING. SECURITY ALERT. SECURITY ALERT. OMEGA LEVEL THREAT IMMINENT IN SECTOR C, CELL BLOCK OMEGA."

Huffing air like an Olympic sprinter, Henry bolted down the hallways hurdling trash cans and rounding corners with grace. He scanned his badge and punched in his PIN. Ripping open the door to the room with Rahne's prison, he slowed his pace and buried his emotions.

"Henry, I don't know what happened," Carrie shouted at first sight of him. "It was like a demon was coming through her."

"What do you mean a demon?" Henry asked.

Slowly, Carrie's quivering hands came to her face and fluttered. "Her voice grew hoarse, into a low, deep animal-like growl. Foam spewed from her mouth. She threw her head back and her neck was bulging like something was tunneling up from deep within her. Then, her eyes flickered a yellow hue, and she jerked hard on the restraints."

"And that's when you hit the alarm?"

Her head nodded in a quick and shallow manner.

Henry opened the door to the outside hallway and pushed her through. "Get a coffee from the break room. I'll come join you in a few minutes."

Rahne's heavy breathing greeted Henry when he entered her prison, her body pulling hard on her restraints. A low growl gurgled from her throat and her beading yellow eyes locked on Henry, refusing to blink.

Half-squatting on his rear leg, Henry surrendered his open hands out in front of him. "Rahne. I just came from Jean's room."

Rahne's ears perked up and the growling stopped.

He looked at Rahne's injured hand. "Rahne, honey, I think you're hurting her somehow. You need to calm down."

Rahne's body relaxed in her seat, and the smoke and smell of burning flesh wafting from the silver binding her wrists and ankles ceased.

"Good. Now, let's slow your breathing. Ready? Breathe in, two, three. Hold, two, three. Breathe out, two, three," he chanted.

The yellow glow of her eyes faded into a thin yellow ring around the edge of her irises before disappearing completely.

"I didn't mean to hurt her," Rahne said.

She hated Henry for what he was doing and would never forgive him; but somehow, she was hurting Ms. Jean and *that* needed to stop. Even if it meant burying her dark feelings about Henry.

"I know you didn't, sweetheart," Henry said and swiveled the chair over beside her. Taking a seat, he pointed to the silver spike in her hand. "How about we get this thing out of your hand and get you back to your room?"

Rahne nodded and watched Henry grip the silver spike. He paused, fearing it was the only thing keeping her from fully transforming and tearing him and the facility to pieces; but he knew greatness comes with risks. In one quick, smooth motion, he removed the spike.

She winced at the pain, but refused to look away. Her clenched fist slowly relaxed as the hole closed before their eyes. "Can I have ice cream?"

Dropping the spike into a large metal bowl, Henry chuckled. "Of course." One by one, he removed her restraints, hiding his fear. "Let me get these off of you and then I'll go get you some ice cream. Rocky Road?"

She rolled her wrists and flexed her feet. "Vanilla and chocolate."

"Vanilla *and* chocolate? Like a swirl?"

"No, a scoop of each." She stood up from the chair of pain with a big smile and a fully healed hand.

"You got a deal."

# 58



GABRIEL GLASS SAT alone at his desk, head buried in one hand as thoughts, memories, and theories haunted his plagued mind. Startled by the sound of a new email on his classified computer, he opened the message.

```
Classification Level:
Top Secret/Paranormal Intelligence/No
Foreign
To: Eugene Shelley, Ph.D., Colonel
Letitia Wyatt, and Gabriel Glass
From: Henry Ingvar
Subject: Jekyll & Hyde


All,

    Since our meeting at the Pentagon in
August, I've been working through the
reprogramming process of Rahne, Subject
Delta Zero, former prime Subject of Project
```

Innocence. During the Coercive Persuasion session, the Subject exhibited a kind of parent-child symbiotic link with Dr. Allicines.

At first, I thought the link was one-sided, emanating from Delta Zero. But in my analysis of the video, I've concluded the link works both ways and Dr. Allicines may have initiated the chain reaction unknowingly.

The Codex was in the hands of Dr. Allicines during the event, but it's still unclear if the Artifact played any part in creating this link. However, for a fraction of a second, Jean's eyes flashed yellow during the link—I saw it with my own eyes.

My working theory is that the two Subjects have some kind of a latent psychic connection that was triggered at the moment of Delta Zero's initial transformation at Wright-Patterson Air Force Base on January 20, 2019. This would explain why she instinctively rescued and protected Dr. Allicines from the facility before removing her from the area without causing her harm.

The question is: Did Delta Zero's initial transformation trigger something dormant within Dr. Allicines?

Moving forward, I recommend proceeding as if Dr. Allicines has the same abilities as Delta Zero until proven otherwise. I will initiate testing and analysis to assess.

--Henry Ingvar

Gabriel sat back in his chair. He still couldn't believe Jean was Rahne's mother or how he didn't see that. The Company had kept him just as much in the dark about that as it had Jean. Maybe this link Henry proposed added to why Jean attempted suicide after believing she lost her child.

He couldn't help but mentally flip the bird to his old college days. When he and Jean were kids, ignorant to the horrors of the world.

Swiveling around in his chair, Gabriel faced the corkboard on his wall. The HVAC kicked on, rustling a board of pages, his case board, covered by articles and bits of colored string. It was all connected somehow. But to what end?

There was a soft knock on his door.

"Yes?"

"Sorry, sir," a Major in ABUs said as the door swung open. "You're needed in the War Room immediately."

Surprised, Gabriel immediately nodded and buttoned his purple sport coat.

"You taking point on this Neil?" Gabriel asked the man while keeping an eye on the other servicemen.

"Yessir. Ready when you are," Neil said.

Gabriel stepped behind Neil, but kept two paces between them. "Let's go gentlemen."

"Mogul is on the move," Neil said into the microphone on his wrist. "I repeat, Mogul is on the move."

The servicemen escorted Gabriel through the building, keeping in constant communication with the service members ahead of them. In only a few minutes, they made it from one end of the building to the other—nearly three quarters of a mile.

Rounding the last corner, Neil pulled his wrist to his mouth once more. "Mogul has arrived. Open the Labyrinth."

The doors to the War Room opened only wide enough for Gabriel to walk inside, and they quickly closed as security measures re-engaged.

The room was small, only large enough for six people to comfortably sit at a table. Gabriel pulled out the seat at the head of the table, alone. At the other end of the table was a monitor with The Company's logo spinning in the center: *A caelesti et innaturali defende*. Defend from the heavenly and the unnatural.

Gabriel clicked a remote on the table. "I'm here."

A small device, the size of a pill, popped out of the top of the monitor and scanned the entire room with a red light. The scanner descended back into the monitor and a face appeared on the screen. The face was blurred for security purposes.

"Gabriel Glass. Director of the Celestial Division," the censored face said in the altered voice generated by a vocoder. "We have new intelligence suggesting you have an Insider Threat in your division. For the past three months, multiple Human Intelligence reports were submitted from agents across the intelligence community with startling information. These reports identified a high-ranking member of The Company as an insider threat at the National Level. It may even reach to a Global Level, if accusations are correct."

"Have these accusations been confirmed?" Gabriel asked, shocked by the allegations.

"Yes," the electronic voice said quickly. "Our Signals Intelligence satellites, outfitted with sensors capable of picking up virtually any signal floating in the air, confirmed chatter on multiple channels and have collected images of a mysterious man who was seen entering a classified building on foreign soil. Historical analysis identifies the same man entering the institute a half-dozen times in the last eighteen months."

Gabriel anxiously rubbed his chin, grumbling, "Not often enough for our analysts to catch. Why was he there?"

"Reports outline him handing a small vial of an unknown substance to an employee, Zheng Shi. The Company raised the threat level when the vial was identified as containing something labeled: SARSC0V179. We believe it's a strain of SARS virus being researched for gain-of-function."

Gabriel reeled. It always amazed him how scientists never seemed to think, or care, about the impacts of their research. To him, scientists only ever seemed to care about advancing science, being published, and finding the next 'cool' thing—no matter the repercussions. "A biological weapon?"

"We have to assume that's the case. No further details are available on the virus, but our analysts estimate a test is imminent. We don't know what kind of test."

Growing frustrated, Gabriel took a breath to regain control of his emotions. "Have we identified the mysterious man?"

"Yes sir. That's why we came to you and only you."

"It's a Celestial being?" Gabriel asked, crossing his arms.

"No, sir." There was a short pause. "You were identified as the least compromised senior director with the longest good standing in The Company. We did extensive background checks, but, in short, we know you're trustworthy. Keep in mind, we have multiple sources identifying this man at numerous points in the last eighteen months at the building; but intelligence isn't perfect and there's still a chance we're wrong. It goes without saying, you are not to act any differently when around this individual."

Gabriel nodded. "Understood. Who is it?"

When they told him, Gabriel nearly convulsed from the shock of it. Director Ziegler? It didn't seem possible. Gabriel took a deep breath and studied the ceiling for a long time as the face on the screen watched him. He lowered his eyes to the monitor and sighed. "Where do we go from here?"

"We will continue observing and if he returns to an Institute of Virology, we will intercept and bring him into custody. You will do nothing new. Go about your day as normal. Act no differently toward anyone. Give no indication of the insider threat."

Rolling his eyes, Gabriel glared into the screen. "That's all? Really?"

"Almost, because you will protect this nation and The Company at all costs from all enemies foreign, domestic, paranormal, or otherwise, we need you waiting in the wings to take over as Director of The Company when Director Ziegler is taken into custody."

"I'll be ready," Gabriel said.

When the communication ended, Gabriel sat silently at the six-top table, staring into the blacked-out monitor. Removing his oversized lenses, he rubbed his eyes and buried his forehead in the palm of his hand. "Fuck."

Suddenly there was a knock at the door, but before Gabriel could say anything, a man entered the room. "Excuse me sir. This just came for you." Setting a manila envelope on the table, the man backed out of the room, securing the door behind him.

It was evident the contents were gravely important since a man just broke three security protocols to leave it in front of him. With a heavy sigh, Gabriel opened the envelope and found a large photo with a second, smaller photo paperclipped to it.

"God help us," he gasped.

# 59



IT WAS A routine day at the Bio-Weapons lab, until it wasn't.

Mr. Xiao glanced behind him just as his mop handle pulled a test tube rack off the workbench. He watched in horrifying slow motion as the test tubes flew out of the rack and tumbled toward the floor.

Dr. Shi quickly backed out of the room, smashing the red EMERGENCY LOCKDOWN button to her left. She crossed her arms as the air vents and doors slammed shut, trapping Mr. Xiao inside. Scared out of his mind, Mr. Xiao stood still with his eyes locked on Dr. Shi, silently screaming for help.

A loud alarm erupted and flashing red lights swirled throughout the complex.

"EMERGENCY ALERT: BIO-SAFETY BREACH, LEVEL-4 IN JIANGSHI SECTOR. EMERGENCY LOCKDOWN PROCEDURES INITIATED," a prerecorded, electronic voice said over the loudspeaker in Chinese. "REMAIN CALM AND FOLLOW POSTED BSL-4 EMERGENCY PROCEDURES."

Mr. Xiao panicked and flailed about the room wildly. In his flurry, more glass cylinders bounced chaotically onto the floor only to shatter into thousands of pieces, spilling their contents everywhere. Mr. Xiao ran to the door, begging for Dr. Shi to let him out.

Dr. Shi watched with cold eyes as he banged on the glass frantically. Pulling a phone from her pocket, she typed:

```
Mr. Primis- there's been an incident at the
lab. Multiple vials have been compromised.
Vials in refrigeration remain intact. One
infected Subject. Virus and the Subject are
contained.      Beginning      human      trial
protocols.
```

She selected the voice recorder on her phone and spoke loudly. "On November 3rd, 2019 at 8:27 p.m., while mopping, janitor Li Xiao accidently knocked over the vials of SARSC0V179 which Mr. Primis brought on his last visit. I, Dr. Zheng Shi, will observe the Subject and the effects until further instructed."

The phone vibrated in her hand. She read the text message.

```
I'll be there as soon as I can. Keep this
information    quiet    and    the    Subject
contained. No records except your personal
notes. -Natu S. Primis
```

She restarted the recording and peered through the tempered glass.

A MAN IN a tailored suit silently entered the room. He was a tall, slender man with swarthy skin and he stood with such confidence, it screamed royalty. He interlocked his hands behind his back and observed.

Watching the monitors, Dr. Shi clocked the janitor's oxygen level. "His respiratory system is in critical condition," she said into her recording device from behind tempered glass. "At this rate, he won't make it to Monday. But there's something else, something strange in his blood. It's almost like—"

The suited man in the room cleared his throat.

Dr. Shi jumped up from her chair with a gasp, "Ah!" Realizing who he was, she quickly bowed. "Mr. Natu S. Primis. I am sorry, I didn't hear you come in."

"Good morning doctor," Natu said with a bow, releasing her. "It's quite alright. You were deep in thought, and I didn't want to interrupt anything." Slowly, he walked toward her. "Forgive my tardiness. Things have been rather difficult on the home front."

"The incident was twelve days ago, I was beginning to think you weren't coming," Dr. Shi said, her eyes still studying the janitor.

"Don't insult me doctor," Natu sneered. "If I say I'm going to do something, I always come through."

With her phone still recording, Dr. Shi turned toward Natu and caught his eye. "Forgive me," she said, apologetically. "I meant no disrespect." She gave a shallow bow.

"I know my dear, we never *mean* to do anything that could jeopardize our race." Natu slipped a metal chopstick out of his jacket sleeve and slid it into the doctor's eye socket, lobotomizing her. "And mine has lived in the shadows for too long."

Natu caught her limp body in his arms as his eyes flashed crimson.

"Thank you for everything, doctor. You've been an essential component in the rebirth of my race." Natu cleaned the small amount of blood that pooled in the corner of her one eye and slowly licked it from his finger. "Mm, delicious."

He dropped her body and peeled the phone from her warm, dead hand. Realizing the device had recorded their conversation, he crumpled the phone into a tiny wad of metal and plastic like it was a sheet of paper.

Sitting down, he eyed a control panel with thirteen buttons. Six read OPEN, six read CLOSE, and one in red with the words: EMERGENCY EVACUATION.

Natu pushed the lonesome button and a series of loud *thunks*, *clicks*, and *squeals* erupted outside the room. He brought himself to his feet, smashed the computer, and pulled the fire alarm as he walked out of the room.

Water spickets, lights, and sirens went off in unison, soaking Natu.

"Help! Somebody- please help me," the janitor screamed from the laboratory which had become his prison cell.

Natu smiled and jogged down the hall. "I'm coming. Where are you?"

"I'm here. Here. Help!"

Natu forced open the door to the lab and found the old janitor lying on a table with a mask hanging off of his face and an oxygen tank beside him.

"Oh, thank you sir. Thank you," the janitor wheezed.

Natu rushed to his side. "You'll be just fine, mister…?"

"Li Xiao."

Natu knelt beside the man and placed the oxygen mask back over his nose and mouth. "Okay Li, I'm going to get you out of here, but you have to keep this on you so you can breathe. Okay?"

Li nodded.

"Okay, good."

Natu scooped the man into his arms, grabbed the oxygen tank, and rushed into the hallway. He followed the EXIT signs until he found a herd of workers traveling down the hallway to the building exit.

"Help! Someone please help," he cried, stumbling and faking exhaustion.

Six people turned around and ran back to help him; five tended to Li and one helped Natu stumble through the building's exit.

Just outside, a medic ran up. "Are you okay?"

"I'm fine," Natu said. "I found him abandoned in the medical wing. Please, help him."

"We'll take it from here guys," the medic said. "You guys probably saved his life."

Natu disappeared into the crowd of chaos with an evil grin.

# 60



A MAN CLEARS his throat on the other side of my door.

"If I didn't know any better, I'd think you were cat-calling me." Sitting on the floor, I pull my knees to my chest. "Mister Nameless Man."

"You're not my type." I can't tell, but I'd be willing to bet he smiled or maybe even blushed. "I think we got off on the wrong foot last time. I'm Gabriel Glass. As for the cat-calling, I apologize. I didn't want to be rude if you were sleeping."

"Rude." I smile. "How thoughtful of you. I don't sleep much to begin with but down here with the monsters, I sleep even less."

"Afraid of the dark are you, Mr. Harker?" Gabriel mocks.

Taunting a Nocturnae. He's either very stupid or exceptionally brave. "Is there something you need? Dinner is about to be served and I only ordered enough for one. Sorry."

"A few months ago, there was another inmate here," Gabriel says, from the other side of my prison door. Little bits of dirt and grit grind against the hard floor as he turns on his heels, as if he's turning to look at Phaeton's empty cell. "Did you ever happen to speak with him?"

Is he talking about the prick that left me here or the kind-hearted mystery man with the imaginary friends? Intrigued by where this conversation might go, I bring myself to my feet. "I've spoken to at least two of your inmates. Which one do you mean?"

"Two?" Gabriel asks as his heart rate spikes. "I was speaking of a Nocturnae who goes by the name Natu, but if you spoke to two—"

"Is there a purpose for you flying to this pit in the middle of butt-fucking nowhere of these Useless States of America?"

"I need your help," Gabriel says, without hesitation.

Well now, the prison with no exit suddenly has an exit. What did that gospel-guy say...? 'Ask, and the Maker will give you,' or something like that. "A human asking a Nocturnae for help..." I smile, tonguing a fang, "...that must feel weird."

"That's enough Mr. Harker," Gabriel says with a twinge of angst in his tone. "Are you going to help me or not?"

I turn away from the door and pace within my cell, tapping my cheek. "I don't know. What's in it for me?"

"Playing games again, I see," Gabriel says, irritated.

"Just being fair."

"How do you figure?"

I count the events on my fingers. "You tracked me and two others to a cabin in the woods. Entered the house with silver aerosol knock-out gas. Locked me in a cage with only coagulated blood to feed on and nothing but the memories of my victims to keep me company. And you took a mother and her child and did

Maker knows what with them, leaving me here to rot."

"Everything was done to keep humanity safe."

"If you prick us, do we not bleed?"—*like Claret did when you experimented on her*—"If you tickle us, do we not laugh? If you poison us, do we not die? And if you wrong us, shall we not revenge?" Revenge never tastes sweeter than when paired with blood and fear.

"Shakespeare's *Merchant of Venice*, how fitting. But it doesn't change the fact that you're still… a monster designed to be the perfect killer in every way. You are stronger. Faster. Smarter. And damn-near immortal. As frail human beings, we took the measures deemed necessary to ensure the safety of everyone involved." Catching himself getting spun up, Gabriel paused. "What's it going to take for you to help me?"

Oh, he is desperate. "Why ask the *monster* for his help?"

Gabriel sighed. "Because, now, there's a bigger threat than you, Mr. Harker. *Much* bigger."

An enemy of my enemy is my friend scenario? "Out of curiosity, what gave you the idea I'd help you and your kind?"

"Because for as much as it pains you to admit it, you care about Jean. And I think you'd do anything to protect Rahne. Because she reminds you of…" Gabriel drifted off like he was debating saying his next words. "…your daughter Cora who died during the Black Plague in Northern Ireland—"

"Enough!"

"—back in the fourteenth century, but you lived and became … this." By his tone, I have to assume he gestured to the door like I was standing before him.

"I said that's enough," I say solemnly. "I don't work with humans."

"You cooperated with Dr. Allicines. Why not me?" Gabriel pleads.

"Technically," I say, raising a finger, "she's a dormant Lygos."

"But you didn't know that when you confided in her at Wright-Patt."

"I needed something."

"Natu's going to kill Jean and Rahne," he blurts out.

I stop. "How do you know that?"

"Intelligence sources all point to Natu being active for years, but greatly increasing his presence around the world shortly after Rahne's initial transformation and your escape from the base."

"What do the girls have to do with any of this?" I ask, not hiding my concern.

"Big picture: I don't know. All I know is everything points to them being Lygos."

"And," I ask, "if I agree to help you, what's in it for me?"

"You're freed from this cell and pardoned by the President of the United States of America."

"I'm not human." I never thought Jean's speech she gave me when *The Fellowship of the Ring* was trying to take me into custody would come in handy. "Therefore, and according to Dr. Allicines, your laws don't apply to me. Try again."

Without pause, Gabriel tries again. "You will be scrubbed from The Company's archives and databases. Any digital or physical evidence pointing to your existence will be destroyed."

"Better." I nod and resume pacing within my cell. "And the girls?"

"They will be released into your custody with the understanding that you're to protect them from Natu, The Company, and any other adversary that wishes, or would wish, to do them harm."

Well, someone came prepared; but it's still not good enough. "Their existence needs to be scrubbed as well."

"Okay. Do we have a deal?"

A human came to me, a monster, a creature they've hunted for nearly 700 years, for help. Then, gives me everything I ask for without reservation. This is too good to be true. "No, no deal."

"What's the problem?" Gabriel huffs.

"I don't trust you."

"Fair enough," Mr. Glass says and fumbles with his badges.

A loud *beep* fills the room and the locks on my cell door release.

I stop and slowly look over my shoulder. "Well, I'll be," I mumble, walking over to the door. Using just the tip of my finger, I push open the door. "You're either very brave or very, very stupid, Mr. Glass. Opening the door to a thirsty monster with no one to save you."

Gabriel cast his hand about in search of the words. "This won't work if there's no trust. Think of this as the first step toward building that trust."

"And the second?" I step to the edge of my cell.

His heart is racing, but he's not trembling. "Drink," Gabriel says, rolling up his sleeve. "You'll see I only want what's best for Jean. And Rahne."

He's willingly offering himself to me? What's the catch?

Slowly, I step out of my cell and into the open air of the cellblock. I look down at his wrist, salivating at the liquid pulsating just beneath his skin. "A human has never willingly offered themself to me."

"Is that a problem?" Gabriel asks, looking at his wrist with a confused look on his face.

"A problem? No," I say, smitten with the thick vein running down his arm. "I'm just contemplating what the probability is that you have silver flowing through your veins and what might happen to me if I ingest blood tainted in that way."

"What?" Gabriel asks, genuinely taken back. "I'm trying to establish trust between us. Trust that I'm one of the good guys and only want what's best for Jean and Rahne. Trust that you won't drink me dry or drink your fill and snap my neck anyway."

"Oh, I wouldn't simply *snap your neck*, I'm much more creative than that." Our eyes lock and the fear within him is simply intoxicating. "But, that's not the point. The point is, humans are deviously creative. You could have some kind of Nocturnae-poison booby trap infused in your blood. All The Company would need to do is disguise it as a vitamin, an enzyme, or a vaccine."

"There's nothing wrong with my blood. It's not tainted or booby trapped," Gabriel insists.

Another push. But is there another option? Freedom for me and the girls at the cost of being an indentured servant once again. Is it worth it?

I press my finger firmly into Gabriel's sternum. "If you're lying, I'm going to rip your arm from your shoulder before I'm crippled by your poison. You understand that right?"

"I understand."

Holding his forearm in one hand and his palm in the other, I sink my teeth into his ulnar artery. The fresh human blood is euphoric like biting into an apple for the first time. His blood is thinner than I expect—baby aspirin—and mildly acidic on the front end, with a hint of citrus on the back.

The dark prison fades away, and I enter Gabriel Glass's mind. It's been so long since I've fed on a human, I'd almost forgotten what it was like—euphoric.

Slowly, a dark room comes into focus and I find myself standing in a bedroom littered with tissues, pizza boxes, and take away containers. I choke on dense fog of rotting food and body odor.

A beam of light illuminates the room for a second as a car passes by and I catch sight of an overturned Lexapro bottle next to a fifth of vodka. Alcohol and anti-depressants, looks like a party.

A shadowy figure moves from under the blankets to the attached bathroom like the scene is being fast-forwarded. Following the shadow in the bathroom I see a sickly-looking postpartum brunette sitting on the toilet drinking her vodka as the breast pump sucks and slurps the tainted milk from her.

Who are you? Is this Jean?

"Bye honey. I love you," Gabriel says from the doorway.

Closing the door behind him, the memory suddenly goes black and the smell evaporates. He wasn't here so he doesn't know what happened. A door slams in the distant darkness and footsteps stomping up a set of stairs. Must be a time jump.

"Jean, I'm home," Gabriel says. "I picked up some chicken and veg from the store on my way home because I'm starving and haven't eaten since lunch. There's plenty if you're hungry."

You were her roommate? Gabriel Glass. GG. You're the GG Jean had mentioned during our patient-psychologist sessions.

I don't know how much time passes, but Gabriel calls out again. This time, with concern in his voice.

"Are you still up?" he asks, rapping on her door. His heart is racing. "I'm making chicken and veggies but I'm not super hungry. Why don't you come join me?"

The hairs on his back and arms stand on end. Gabriel knocks, hard, three times.

"Jean!" When she doesn't answer, he slowly opens the door. "Jean. I'm worried. I'm coming in."

His face quickly morphs into one of disgust as the stench punches both of us in the face like an iron fist. Turning, Gabriel notices a light coming from under the bathroom door, but there's a shadow, like something's slightly obstructing it.

Oh no.

"JEAN!" In two steps he's at the door, beating on it. "Jean!" The door flexes under his thumping fists. "JEAN! Are you in there?" He twists the doorknob. Locked.

His eyes drift to the frame above the door where the edge of a key is barely visible. He grabs it and unlocks the door. He rushes to her body on the floor.

Gabriel cups his face in shock. "Oh, Jean. What have you done?"

Blood. Lots of it.

Pooling between her knees, blood flows from between her legs. Gabriel's eyes travel from Jean to the bloody knife in her hand.

"No Jean. No, no, no, nonononono. Come on baby girl, don't do this to me," Gabriel begs.

He pulls a phone from his pocket and blindly dials 9 – 1 – 1. He licks his index finger on the other hand and places it under her nose, testing to feel for her breath.

Good thinking, human.

"9 – 1 – 1, what's your emergency?" a woman asks on the other end of the line.

Gabriel puts the phone on speaker and sets it on the floor. "I just found my roommate in her bathroom, bleeding on the floor."

"Is she conscious?"

"No, but she's breathing," Gabriel says, panic in his voice.

"That's good," the woman says, calmly. "What is your name and address?"

"Gabriel Glass. 4505 Corkhill Drive. 45424."

"Okay, Gabriel, a team has been dispatched to your location."

"Please stay with your roommate. Have you been able to locate the source of the bleeding?"

"It's coming from between her legs," Gabriel says, shakily.

"Is she pregnant?"

"No, she lost her baby a couple weeks ago." Gabriel eyes the knife. "I found a knife next to her."

"Sir, you need to find the source of the bleeding and apply pressure until paramedics arrive."

"Is she going to be okay?"

"Sir, you need to stay calm and maintain pressure on the wound. Have you found the source of the bleeding?"

Gabriel kneels between Jean's legs, spreading them just enough to see she's cut her inner thighs. Taking a deep breath, he places his hands firmly on the wounds and watches as the edges of his palms become stained with blood.

"Yes."

"Good. Keep pressure on the wound. Paramedics are 8 minutes out. An officer in the area should be there momentarily. The officer will identify themselves as they enter the home. Do not be alarmed. Simply call back and verbally direct them to your location."

"Why is an officer coming?" Gabriel asks, looking at the phone.

"Officers have medical training and with the location of the wound I want to get you help as quickly as possible."

Dispatch is concerned she may have cut her femoral artery—the main blood vessel supplying blood to your lower body.

Time speeds up again.

The officer pokes his head into the bathroom from around the door. "Gabriel?" The officer steps into the bathroom and places his hands on top of Gabriel's. "You can let off the pressure. I've got it from here."

Gabriel nods and gets out of the way of the officer, taking a seat on the toilet and stares overwhelmingly at his bloody hands.

Time speeds up again and three EMTs come into the bedroom, dropping their equipment near the bathroom door and glove up. The blonde woman squeezes behind the officer and takes over. The silver-haired man sits just inside the bedroom, receiving the report from the officer and taking down his assessment on Jean's wounds.

The blonde woman looks at Gabriel. "What's her name?"

"Um, Jean. Her name is Jean," Gabriel says, looking at the officer and other EMTs.

"Jean, can you hear me?" the blonde woman shouts as the black man shines a light into Jean's eyes.

"Pupils are sluggish, Paige," the black man says, putting the light back in his pocket.

"Bleeding has slowed," Paige says, taking pressure off one of the wounds. "Dee, she barely missed her artery. We need to get her to the Valley, now. Call them and tell them we're coming."

"Okay, let's prep her for transport gentleman," Dee orders, sticking his head out of bathroom. The officer and the silver-haired man nod, and quickly wrap up.

Paige looks at Gabriel. "You're coming too."

"Oh, I don't...," Gabriel stammers.

"That wasn't a question," Paige says, gently. "She's going to need you when she wakes up. You were the first one on the scene and will be able to give the doctors and nursing staff the best depiction of what happened here. You're coming."

"Okay. Let me put some pants on and grab my coat." Gabriel slips past Jean and the EMTs.

Time zips forward and we're all in the back of the ambulance.

This is cozy. Glad I'm not claustrophobic.

The night air is cold and still. The neighborhood lights up in red and white and is completely empty except for a black suburban parked halfway down the block.

I lean over Jean and shift my eyes through the wavelengths until the license plate is perfectly clear:

U.S. Government

**C067269**

For Official Use Only

Mother. Fucker. A Company car.

The ambulance doors slam shut on my face and time speeds up again.

Jean is rushed to the ER. Gabriel and I follow closely behind. The EMTs relay her status and current vitals to the nursing staff. Gabriel is guided to the waiting room while a team of nurses triage her and switch her over to their monitors.

I'm staying focused on you, Jean. What did Gabriel see and hear that his human mind couldn't process on his way to the waiting room?

The nurses start spouting off measurements while the trauma doctors are barking orders. "Call the blood bank and get some emergency release blood. Let's get some trauma labs and an ABG."

A nurse shouts, "BP is eighty-five over fifty-five and dropping."

The medical team blurs into a single, cohesive smear of dark blue scrubs.

Here we go again. Time jump.

"Mr. Glass?" a nurse calls into the waiting room. "Is there a Mr. Gabriel Glass out here?"

WAKE UP!

"What?" He looks around the room like a kid that fell asleep in class. "Yes, I'm here." He scrambles to his feet and rushes to the nurse. "Is she okay?"

"Yes, Mr. Glass. Your roommate is recovering as we speak, but we'll need to keep her here for a seventy-two-hour observation hold in the Psychiatric Unit. You will be able to see her, but only during visiting hours. Before I take you to her, I need to go through some paperwork with you. These questions are for our records and police records to ensure we have a clear and concise understanding of what happened. Do you feel comfortable answering a few questions?"

His mouth hangs open.

HEL-LOOO. Answer the woman.

He nods, his mouth still hanging open.

"Thank you," the nurse says looking at her clipboard. "This shouldn't take long. The EMTs said you found her in her bathroom, bleeding on the floor with a knife nearby. Is this correct?"

"Yes."

The nurse checks a box. "Do you know if she's been depressed?"

"Yes. She had a stillbirth a week or two ago while at work. She hasn't told me a lot about it, but she's been cooped up in her room ever since. I've made her meals. I've been there for her and everything. I didn't know it was this bad. I thought she was getting better."

You didn't know? She lost her child!

"It's okay, Mr. Glass. Try not to blame yourself. You didn't know." The nurse checks her clipboard again. "Has she ever done something like this before?"

"No," Gabriel says, shaking his head. "Never." He looks at his feet like shame was setting in. "At least, not that I'm aware of."

You really didn't know? I don't believe this. Humans are so oblivious.

"Is she on any drugs or medications? Is she allergic to anything?"

"She's taking something for the depression, but I can't remember the name of it. And a fair amount of vodka to take the edge off."

The nurse checks two boxes. "Last question. Has her family been notified, or do you have their contact information?"

Gabriel suddenly becomes surprised by the question, almost offended. "I'm her family."

You care about her. She's not *just* a roommate or a friend, you're her *best* friend.

"I understand you're a close friend of hers, but I'm referring to her blood relatives, parents, siblings, anyone we can call," the nurse clarifies, pulling the clipboard into her chest.

"She doesn't have anyone. I'm all she's got."

You really do care about her. You love her like a sibling. But did you know about The Company? What they did with Rahne? That they were parked right out front?

The dimly lit prison we're standing in becomes ever more real and slowly shifts back into focus as the ten-year-old memory fades away like a mirage.

Releasing my bite from his arm, I wipe my lips with my thumb. "You were her friend. Are her friend. Her"—I suck his blood from my thumb—"*best friend.*"

Lowering his eyes, he nods. "Yes, we've been friends a very long time."

"You looked out for her."

"As friends do."

"You were concerned for her safety and well-being," I quickly say like we're playing a game of speed chess, but with words.

"I still am."

Gotcha.

"If that were true, then why was there a black SUV parked outside your house with a government license plate that, in T9 predictive text, spells: COMPANY."

"What?" Gabriel's head shoots up and his wide eyes lock onto mine. "But … how did you … that's not the memory—"

"You don't get to choose what I see when I drink. That's not how it works" I close the little distance between us. Gabriel stutter-steps backwards trying to keep some distance, but I continue advancing. "If you lived it—saw it—heard it—smelled it—tasted it, it's fair game."

Gabriel stared back at me with a confused look on his face. "Oh, no…" he says with wide eyes.

Were you trying to show me a memory about someone else entirely? It's not important, the memory I saw tells me everything I need to know.

"I didn't know The Company was there. I didn't know Jean was different. I didn't know they took Rahne," Gabriel rattles off quickly with his hands raised near his face.

Oh, no? Then why did your heartbeat just change?

I step on the tip of Gabriel's shoe, sending him tumbling over his own feet and falling onto the floor. "Lying wasn't smart, GG."

"I didn't know!" Gabriel says, raising his voice. "When Jean tried to kill herself, I had no idea. I didn't even know Nocturnae were real." I take my foot of his shoe, freeing him to take a few steps back. "By the time I knew, Rahne was already grown, and I was too deep in The Company to do anything—"

Too deep? Couldn't do anything? Pathetic.

"—that wouldn't get me killed. Or worse."

Okay … that's a motivator.

"Explain," I say.

"How I didn't know?" Gabriel clarifies, shocked I'd ask such a question. "Jesus Christ, it's not like I started with The Company in this position. I advanced and was read into more programs and was provided higher and higher clearance levels. I was a lot like Alice, tumbling further and further down the rabbit hole."

"Do better," I say and flash a fang, "or the first thing I'm taking from you is your tongue, so you can't poison this world with your words anymore."

I wonder what it tastes like, his tongue.

"When I was read into the program—"

"What program? What's the name?" I ask, quickly.

"Project Innocence."

Taking the innocence of a child and having the arrogance to call it Project Innocence is evil in its truest form.

"When you were read into the Project Innocence program…?" I question, mockingly. "What do you mean by that?"

"I was introduced to the child, Rahne, and back-briefed on experiments performed, medical history, the known evolution of the Lygos … everything about her from her favorite color to the date and time she took her first steps—"

They know everything about her because they watched every second of her life like she was the star of The Truman Show.

"—but I wasn't told anything about her biological parents or how she'd come into the care of The Company or when she was born—"

The 'care' of The Company. How perverse.

"—The Company left everything out of her files that could lead back to Jean or the baby's father."

"Who's that?" I ask.

"That's the memory I intended to show you." Gabriel took a deep breath. "Jean, Rahne's father, and I were friends in college. We knew he had an internship at Wright-Patt, but it was normal for engineers to get internships over there—it was only a few miles from campus. If that."

"But you didn't know he worked for The Company?" I cross my arms.

"No, and that's the thing about The Company … you don't know you're working for them when you start. You just think you've got this great, high-paying job right out of college." Gabriel takes a few breaths. "It's only when you no longer can tell the difference between the darkness and the light, that they reveal themselves."

Where'd he come up with that? A welcome pamphlet?

I yawn and remind him that I'll eat him, by tonguing my fang, if he doesn't convince me he's not going to double-cross me or the girls.

"They loved each other," Gabriel says, desperately. *I guess he got the message.* "They still love each other. A love unlike any I've ever seen."

"How so?"

Gabriel held out his fists and opened one. He looked at it, saying, "She was the smart, independent blind girl who didn't need a man." He opened his other hand and looked at it. "He was the bad boy with a heart of gold who had every girl eating out of the palm of his hand. He was the epitome of handsome and therein lies the problem, no one could see past his pretty face. No one actually *knew* him." Gabriel closes his hands and looks at me. "No one wanted to approach her, but everyone knew her. Everyone approached him, but no one knew him. It was a fairytale love."

Barf. "Okay, say I believe you that you want what's best for Jean and Rahne. And say I trust you'll hold up your end of the deal when I'm done helping you," I say, counting on my thumb and forefinger. "Why do you think it's Natu and why do you fear him so much?"

Gabriel reaches into his back pocket. "Take a look at this."

He hands me a large, folded photograph with a smaller photo paperclipped to it. "What am I looking at here?"

"This is the Wuhan Institute of Virology in Wuhan, China," Gabriel says, pointing with his pinky. "The woman here is Dr. Zheng Shi."

"And the man she's with?"

"Ardisson Ziegler." Gabriel runs his hand through his hair. "We intercepted a message sent to Dr. Shi's phone, signed by a Natu S. Primis—"

"*Natus Primis,* in Latin means *born first.*" Firstborn. "Who is Ardisson Ziegler?"

"He's the Director of The Company. We doubled our surveillance at the Wuhan Institute," Gabriel continues, "and for eleven days we saw nothing. But on the twelfth day, we snapped this photograph."

Gabriel taps the small photo tucked between my fingers.

I look at the photo. The man in the photo was weathered and olive-toned.

"And this is your Director Ziegler?" I confirm. "And it wasn't doctored or edited in any way?"

"Mmhmm, that's the director. And no, this is the raw image."

Studying the photo with my Nocturnae eyes, I project the two-dimensional image into a three-dimensional plane in my mind. Then I see it. "Well, that's interesting." I follow the light source, and confirm where shadows should and shouldn't be in the photo. "Do you see the light? Here," I say, pointing with my fingernail, "on his face. This section here, behind his ear, is a shadow, but the ear itself is not and should be the same color as the rest of his face. Instead, it's black."

"Holy shit," Gabriel gasps. "How'd my guys miss that? How'd I miss it?"

"It's something that could easily be overlooked. It means your Director Ziegler can change the pigment of his skin."

"Have you ever seen that or heard of someone doing that? Because I haven't. This is a long shot, but what if Director Ziegler and Natu are the same person?"

I start pacing to help me think. "That's a scary thought. That would mean a Nocturnae has a camouflage-like ability."

Gabriel's eyes widen as he realizes the story we're concocting. "Can you do that? Can Nocturnae—"

"I can't, and I've never known of any who could." But that doesn't mean it couldn't be their unique gift.

Something in the depths of my Nocturnae mind kept running possible scenarios as we spoke, trying to find the ties between The Company, their Director, a Nocturnae, Jean, Rahne, and a virology lab. When suddenly Rahne in Lygos form tearing Claret in half comes to mind, and the dots connect.

"Jean and Rahne. Where *are* they?"

"In our classified facility at Edwards. Why?"

"We need to leave. He made a virus that can kill a Lygos." I step toward the door. "Now!"

Gabriel slams his hand into my chest. "Woah. Woah. Woah. Slow down. That's not the deal. There's—"

Wrapping the lapels of his sport coat in my grip, I lift him from the ground and raise my upper lip, revealing my fangs. "Natu, your Director Ziegler, is headed that way right now. If you want my help and want to keep Jean and Rahne safe, we need to leave right now."

Gabriel winces, afraid for his life.

"Nod if you think we should leave."

Gabriel nods and I drop him.

"Glad we agree."

He keels over, coughing to catch his breath.

"But first, I'm going to need a shower, a new suit, and fresh human blood," I say, closing my eyes imagining blood's succulent beauty.

"Seriously?"

"You wear the same suit and eat fake food for months, and then tell me how you feel. But … if you insist." With a hand on his skull and the other on his shoulder, I expose his neck. "Okay, I'll take it from you and skip the shower."

"Okay! Okay! Okay! Shower. Suit. Blood. Got it."

Hovering my lips just above his neck, I whisper, "What kind of blood?" I pinch his skin between my teeth.

"Human! Human blood! Definitely human blood! As much as you want!

"Perfect." I let go of him and walk to the door.

Fear is such a good motivator. It's good to be back.

# 61



THE SIKORSKY HH-60 Pave Hawk, escorted by two F-22 Raptors and four F-15 Eagles, touches down outside The Company's Hangar at Edwards AFB.

The wind rips past me as I open the helicopter's door and find Gabriel inside taking his headphones off. "It's about time you showed up."

Gabriel steps out of the helicopter. "Not all of us can free-jump out of a perfectly good helicopter, fall half a click, and live to talk about it," he shouts over the whipping of the rotor blades. "Are you sure he's coming here?"

I don't answer because he's already here.

Gabriel throws up his arms. "Who knew. Nocturnae are moody."

We walk from the helicopter to the entrance. Gabriel scans his badge and punches in the code, but the door doesn't unlock. "That's weird."

"Is there a problem?" I ask, looking over my shoulder.

Sweat drips down his neck. "No, no problem. Just hit a wrong button."

I don't think he did. I slam my hand into the door, sending it hurling down the hallway. "Unlocked."

"You know that door costs as much as my truck, right?" Gabriel points at the misshapen door at the end of the hallway.

"Seems like you need a better truck."

We weave in and out of hallways, staircases, and hidden rooms until we come to the entrance of a sub-building. It lies ripped open and balled up like it was just a piece of paper.

"Jesus," Gabriel says.

Not Jesus. Nocturnae. "Stay here," I say without looking at Gabriel.

His hand slams into my chest. "That's not how this works."

My patience is wearing thin, but I'll stretch it for Jean. I look at his hand and back at him. Slowly he removes his soft, tiny human paw from my chest. "Most Nocturnae are much, much meaner than I am. Especially the one that's in there. So, unless you want to know what it feels like to be fed your own intestines, you should stay here."

"Yeah, I think I'll just stay here," he gulps.

"Good idea."

The room I enter is dark except for a flickering light in the center that makes it hard for my eyes to focus. Concentrating, I filter the annoying blinking light and a destroyed room comes into a shadowy focus. This was no accident.

"Hello," a voice says from the darkness.

"Natu?" I call into the darkness. "What are you doing here?"

Scanning the room from one end to the other, I cycle through wavelengths. A perfectly put together child's room, contained within a dome-like cage comes into focus. In the center, playing with her dolls, sits Rahne. I can't help but smile at the sight of her. A wave of relief washes over me that she's okay.

"See for yourself," Natu says in a way that I cannot tell where his voice is coming from. "The child of prophecy. Amazing isn't it."

"What?"

"All of this…" Natu gives an evil laugh. "…over a child."

She's not just a child.

"Leave her alone." I step up to the prison, trying to position myself between Rahne and Natu.

"You abandoned your kin. Sulked for centuries. While drowning your guilt in blood like an Ubiet in their booze. All that time with them and yet," Natu says and pauses, "you hardly know a thing about your own kind."

That word: Ubiet. I only know one other person who's used that word. "She's just a child!"

"Silence! You know nothing, neophyte. Deserter. Traitor to his kind."

Shocked by Natu's words, I say, "Deserter? Traitor? I've never…"

Natu's thin figure appears in the shadows, just beyond the lights reach. "Tell me Sorin, did you forget the sacrifices made by your brothers, Fenix and Gaius? Was Claret really the only one you cared for? Searched for? Wanted revenge for?"

I wonder how he knows so much. "I could never forget—"

"But you didn't search," Natu says, emphasizing his disappointment with his hands. "Not for any of them. You condemned them to their fate in search of your Maker."

A stiffness suddenly encapsulates my head, preventing me from looking away from the figure.

This is strange. What is doing this to me?

"I didn't condemn anyone," I say, while second-guessing my actions.

"Oh, but you did," Natu says, elongating each word. "Your eyes never laid upon their bodies. Your feet never walked through their ash in the sun-soaked snow. And when you did return to each site of their deaths," Natu disappears and reappears with his lips only an inch from my ear, "did you ever ask yourself, *why?*"

I can feel his unwavering crimson eyes on me. "I—"

Natu grips my head with both hands. "You, what?" His dry, sharp fingers dig into my skull. "Never thought of it? Assumed they were dead?" He forces me to lock eyes with him. "Took her word on it? Or … was it even a thought at all?" Natu shakes his head. "I don't think it was. At least, I don't think that's *quite* true; but you're certainly thinking of it now." Natu slowly turns his head toward the door I entered. "Maybe we should ask your new friend, the Ubiet, what happened to Fenix and Gaius."

The grip on my head is loosened enough for me to catch a glimpse of Gabriel peeking around the door frame. "Gabriel, RUN!"

Gabriel turns to run, but something stops him before he can start.

"He's not going anywhere. My associate will keep him company." Natu's crimson eyes look down the hallway. "Thank you, Amen."

Amen? What's an *Amen*? "Leave Gabriel out of this," I groan.

Natu releases me and disappears back into the shadows.

"My child you're being foolish," Natu says, his voice echoing throughout the chamber again. "Ubiets hate you. They fear you for what you are. And will use you to their advantage until they no longer have a use for you. Then, they will turn on you and put you back in the prison they freed you from." An open ebony hand, reaches into the flickering light. "Why not join me?"

"No! Humans and Nocturnae don't have to be enemies. Jean showed me that."

"Ah, yes," Natu says with a gargling voice. "The mother of that dog."

"I'll never join you."

"That's too bad," he says with an airy voice and removes his hand from the light. "Truly. Tragic. Yes. After all this time. All my effort. Everything I've sacrificed."

"What are you talking about?"

"Many years ago, when your Maker was still a neophyte, my sister, Amicia, was killed by Gilead."

My Maker, help me, this … this is The Faceless King. Natu is The Faceless King. "I've heard this story," I snap.

"I doubt you've heard the *whole* story," he says as crimson eyes lock onto mine.

My cheeks twinge in irritation as the invisible grip tightens on my neck.

"Claret was not aware of *why* my sister was killed," Natu says. "She had no reason to know."

No reason to know … I seriously doubt that. "Get to the point," I squeak through his grip.

"The Company learned how we—for lack of a better term—*procreate* and, under the command of the Gilead family, sought out to kill every female Nocturnae across the world." Natu goes silent a moment and I cannot help but wonder if he's purposefully leaving something else out. "Will the Ubiets kill us all? I don't know, but with the death of Claret, the Nocturnae race is inevitably doomed for extinction. And makes you the last Nocturnae ever to be created."

"But when I was at The Company's facility in Ohio, they didn't know anything about how to turn humans, or even that the females were the key," I call him on his lies and deception. "How is that possible? They didn't just *forget*."

"That's exactly what they did," Natu says, pride in his voice. "They forgot in 273 AD. When I burned the Library of Alexandria, the archives of The Company, and all of its contents. Their knowledge of Nocturnae, the Lygos, the Atrocities, and everything else that haunts them still—gone."

"But destroying their knowledge, didn't solve the bigger problem that Nocturnae would die off, in time," I say, seeing the bigger picture.

"No, it didn't," Natu says as his voice changes like a young boy going through puberty. "So, I took matters into my own hands…"

Stepping out of the darkness, the mysterious figure's bones began to break, rearranging themselves in a peculiar manner. His dark skin lightened, and black hair grew from his bald head and body. The once tall, slender man was now short, rugged, and weathered under the light.

Recognizing his face, I gasp. "It can't be…" He looks at me, solemn. "…you were Sir Gilead that day in Étretat."

Natu smiles a devilish grin. "I took over The Company and with it, the search for a way to save our kind. But that would take time. Lots of time. For the Ubiets to evolve and their technology along with it. And to do that, civilizations would have to rise and fall, and wars, countless wars, would be fought to push scientific discovery. All to ensure that *MY* race didn't die and leave these filthy Ubiets to inherit the Earth."

"You imprisoned Claret." The disgust and humiliation of his betrayal grows within me. "You had her experimented on. How could you?" I consider attacking, but I restrain myself.

"The death of a few is necessary in survival of the many," Natu says in a tyrannical tone of proclamation. "No more hiding. No more suffering." He curled his hand into a fist. "Our kind has lived in the shadows of shame and fear for long enough. Imprisoned and hunted while Ubiets thrived. I ensured our survival with the development of a mutagen. A virus that will allow males of our race to procreate like our sisters once did."

The comforting thought of my kind surviving is like a cup of warm blood, but the thought of the consequences hits me like a fist.

"You manipulated humans into making a weapon that will, inevitably, be their own demise." I spit on the floor. "Good thing Amicia can't see you now. She'd be ashamed."

Natu closes the gap between us, tearing through my chest like it was a Kleenex. With my spine tightly wrapped in his grip he slams me into the floor. "I tried it her way! Lived among them in peace. Think of the person you've loved most in your life. Your Maker. Your brother. Daughter—"

Mo Chroí.

"—the Ubiets, they took everything away from me." Natu snarls. "My Maker. My sister. My kingdom. And in that moment, I swore I would take everything from them."

His Maker? There's something older than a Firstborn?

Blood erupts from my mouth, and I cough from the pain. "Killing the humans and killing me won't bring back what you've lost. It will not bring you peace." Who am I? Maybe there's some truth to what he's saying. Maybe Jean and Rahne have had an effect on me.

He lifts me by my spine and we hurl across the room and hit the wall hard. His crimson eyes glare at me and his hand is still wrapped around my insides.

"Peace was never an option," Natu says in an eerily calm fashion.

Past the tyrannical expression on his face, I glimpse over at Rahne. She's in the middle of a cell, playing with her toys, completely unaware of the chaos around her. *Strange.* And it clicks.

I look back at him with rage growing in my crimson eyes. "What have you done to her?"

"The child? She's fine, lost in the Void until I release her. I needed a moment alone with you, Sorin. It's been such a long time since our talks in opposing cells nestled deep within the Sandbox."

"Yes, Phaeton LéTry. I already figured that out."

The bones in his face break and shift, but he doesn't grimace or recoil from the pain. His skin quickly darkens and the hair on his Sir Gilead body retreats until it's completely gone.

Standing a good two feet taller than he was a moment ago, Phaeton smiles. "You can call me, The Faceless King." With his free hand, he takes three quick punches at my face, caving in my eye sockets. "The Nocturnae rebirth has already begun."

The Faceless King's hand snaps to his side with three of my thoracic vertebras tightly in his grip. "Make sure you're on the right side, neophyte."

My paralyzed body falls to the floor.

Slowly, he lowers himself to my level peering into my eyes. "I could kill you, but you are still Nocturnae. So, I'll give you a chance to redeem yourself." He lifts my head up by the chin so he can see my face. "On the first day of the second month, bring the child and the Codex to the place of your new birth."

"And if I don't," I gargle through blood and spit, holding myself up with my hands.

"My horsemen will find you and kill you." The Faceless King stands and in a blink he's at Rahne's cell. "Bring the girl." He speeds to the exit. "And bring the Atrocity."

The Faceless King's gone before I can respond.

Rahne shakes her head and at the sight of me, calls out, "Mr. Sorin!"

I cough up blood, but will it back down my throat. "Hi little one," I say, begging my body to heal quicker and keep her from seeing me this way.

"Why are you on the floor?" Rahne asks, concerned.

Footsteps quickly approach from the hall. Gabriel.

Looking up at her with a forced smile, I lie, "I tripped. I'll be alright." I turn away as blood erupts from my mouth.

Rahne's eyes narrow when Gabriel entered the room. "Who are you?" she asks with a curled nose.

"I—" Gabriel sees me on the floor. "Jesus, Sorin what happened to you?" He rushes to my side.

"Like I told Rahne, I tripped," I say and gave Gabriel a painful wink.

Unsure of what to do or how to help, Gabriel says, "You just walked in here and the next thing I knew, I heard Rahne call your name."

"Damn it, you were compelled," I say, groaning.

"I was what?"

Rahne watches from her cell, unapologetically eavesdropping.

I let out a sigh of annoyance. "A Nocturnae told you to forget everything that happened."

"I had my mind wiped?"

"Mmhmm," I say, nodding. "Ugh, and I need to heal."

Gabriel takes a seat next to my beaten body. "Then we have more than enough time for you to fill me in." He raises a finger and shakes it at me. "And don't skimp on the details, even for her sake," he says, thumbing at Rahne.

# 62



GABRIEL CROSSES HIS arms. "Well shit. A shapeshifting Nocturnae. That's pretty fucking terrifying."

"Language," I say, pointing with my chin at Rahne.

Gabriel nods, guiltily. "Phaeton, Natu, and Director Ziegler were all the same person. The Faceless King."

Healed enough to stand, I stretch my stiff, regenerated body. I can't feel the floor beneath my feet. Imagine the worse sciatic pain fathomable and that's the tip of the iceberg of what it's like to stand without three vertebrae.

"The better question is," I say, looking at Gabriel and popping my neck. "Who *else* has he been pretending to be?"

"The first day of the second month? That's strangely specific," he says, deflecting his own unease.

Not really. "It's the day of Imbolc." I say, tilting one ear into the air.

Footsteps. Faint ones. Barefoot. Now what… Who else is here?

"Imbolc?" Gabriel asks.

"A cross-quarter day following midwinter that,"—I sniff the air—*Human* "marks the beginning of spring." The human stops, just outside the door. "It's a Celtic pagan holiday dedicated to the goddess Brigid, the exalted one, with shallow roots in witchcraft," a soft, masculine voice says from the doorway The Faceless King had exited.

Can't fight. Not now. My spine isn't anywhere near healed enough. Broken bones and torn muscle are easy to mend, but growing entirely new ones takes time. Time that I don't have right now.

I turn my head toward the man. "Heart beats like a human. Blood swims through his veins like one." I sniff the air again. "Can't tell if he's AB+ or AB-, but I'm getting a waft of cranberries and rosemary with earthy overtones." Smells like something else too.

Pulling a revolver from his ankle, Gabriel jumps to his feet. "Hands up! And walk into the light. Nice, and slow."

Don't know what it is, it's unlike anything I've ever smelled before; but it reminds me of death. I gulp down the saliva pouring into my mouth. The fight with The Faceless King has left me ravenous.

Rahne shrieks in fear and hides under her bed.

"Everything's fine little one. We won't let anything happen to you." I tongue my fangs. I could use the blood right now.

A man wearing a flannel shirt over a hooded sweatshirt with a *Hocking Technical College* ball cap slowly enters the room with his hands held high. He stops just outside the light, but that can't keep me from getting a look.

He's a handsome man with the cleanest shaven face I've seen in all my years—not a nick to be found. He's taller than me and his skin looks softer and newer than a two-day-old baby.

"Hold it right there," Gabriel orders. "Who are you?"

Slowly, the man interlocks his fingers on top his head and pulls back the hood protruding from under his shirt. "Hi, Gabriel."

I know that voice. The mysterious man who talks to invisible people.

"Victor?" Gabriel squinted to get a better look. "Is it really you? Where have you been all of this time?"

Jean's love. I see why she'd like him.

Victor shifts his gaze to me. "Tell him." He winks.

I think back on all the strange things that happened while I was incarcerated by The Company in that pit of hell. The screaming at night. The gentle voice that spoke to the empty cell next to me like there was someone in it. Sera.

I lock eyes with Gabriel and gesture to Victor with my head. "He was another inmate at the Sandbox."

"You've been in the Sandbox this whole time?" Gabriel's mouth gaping.

Victor's head tilts slightly, noticing Rahne as she peeks her head out from under her bed. "Yes, to protect Jean."

I wonder if he knows Rahne is his daughter.

Gabriel holsters his gun. "To protect her from what V?" he asks with concern in his voice.

It didn't take any of my Nocturnae gifts to see Gabriel was more than surprised. A situation comparable only to getting the chance to hug a loved one years after they'd passed—an impossible wish come true.

"From me," Victor says, "and everything I know."

Rahne scurries out from under her bed and presses her forehead against the glass. "Who are you?"

Reluctantly, Victor looks up but refuses to make eye contact with her.

"Wait, I know you!" Rahne's face lit up. "You're Tweety's dad!"

Tweety? The bird? The Looney Tune character?

Gabriel and my eyes dart from Rahne to Victor and back again, repeatedly, anxiously waiting for one of them to elaborate.

Victor pauses a moment like he's not completely sure how to answer the question. "Yes, I am. I—"

This is taking too long. We need answers, now. Real ones.

His eyes carelessly lock with mine, midsentence.

He's mine!

The room's flashing lights slow and fade into darkness as I enter Victor's mind.

The beckoning blacks of the Void swirl with unforgiving blues and clouds of ominous grays cascading into a collage of purple hues—a state I've never seen in the Void. As the mental projection of my psychic self stands in the middle of the Void's unusual landscape, I concentrate on the words Claret spoke to me all those years ago: *Envision a small room in your mind.*

Just outside my reach, my wooden box with a heart in the center appears. I beg time to slow as the purple flowers bloom on the hinges and a twisted wooden spoon grows from where the knob would be.

Cora.

A spark ignites in the center of the box. First, moving outward. Then moving together again. Constantly burning and darkening the memory of Mo Chroí. The fire continues to burn and grows until it overtakes my coffin, erupting in purple flames. The flowers curl inward quickly charring to ash and the spoon blackens into two purple eyes.

I try to cut the tie between Victor and me, but something has hold of me. Something I can't see. Something I can't smell. Something I can't sense. Who or what is it?

Slowly, a shadow grows from within the flame and squelches the purple fire in its cloak. The shadow takes the form of a dark cloud and curiously shifts into a hooded figure. From deep within the hood, a pair of purple eyes come into view and it pushes a single word into my mind: OUT!

Darkness, swirls of blue, ominous grays, and purple hues repeal into the lights flashing around the static darkness illuminating Rahne's cell.

Instinct consumes me—that apex predator shit the humans accused me of—and I quickly close the gap between me and Victor. I grab him by the shoulders and smash my nose into his, growling. "WHAT ARE YOU?"

"Jesus. Shit," Gabriel shutters and grabs his arm.

Must have grazed Gabriel on my way. He'll be fine.

A cocky smile spreads across Victor's face and he winks. "I'm a little *more* than human." My eyes flash crimson. "Not gonna buy me a drink first?" Victor chuckles and kisses my nose. "You already tried entering my mind." My crimson eyes darken and I tighten my grip. "Try compelling me again, but it won't do you any good. You can't compel me. Hell, most of your Nocturnae gifts won't work on me. Suppose that's why The Company liked me so much. I could work with the Nocturnae and never become compromised."

"Explain," I snap.

"A long time ago, I worked for The Company as a—"

"I don't want your resume. Why can't I compel you?" It's not silver. I'd smell it.

"Magic," Victor says, fluttering his hands about whimsically.

Are you fucking kidding me? Magic? This is the real world, not Dungeons and Dragons.

Gabriel takes two steps forward and puts an arm out in warning. "Don't fuck with this guy V. He's got a bit of a temper."

Good boy. You'll get a biscuit later.

"What? I answered the question." Victor shrugs.

My fingernails pierce his skin as I tighten my grip. "You expect me to believe you can shoot fireballs from your hands, make force fields around buildings, and shoot laser beams out of your ass?" I can smell his blood.

"So narrow-minded. Shoot fireballs out of my hands," Victor says, laughing as he speaks. "Force fields. What do you think this is, *Castlevania? The Witcher?* Laser beams out of my ass? Really? That sounds painful!"

My hands rotate on his shoulders. "How does it work?"

"Let go of me and I'll tell you. No tricks." Victor holds up open hands. "Honest."

His shoulders pop a little when I pull my nails from his skin. Blood pools at the surface of the puncture wounds, but hangs there. Taunting me. Begging me to bite.

"Talk," I say, licking the blood from the tips of my fingers.

The strange scent definitely isn't silver. It tastes awful. I gag on the small bit of Victor's blood I put in my mouth, reminding myself not to spit it out.

Victor shrugs. "It's not like a fucking owl swooped in with an acceptance letter to a school for magic on my eleventh birthday."—*this makes no sense*—"I never said it made sense." Victor looks at me. "If it did, there'd be a handbook or something, but there's not. Trust me, I looked."

Did he just?

*"Read your mind?"* a voice calls in my mind. *"No, not exactly."*

"Did you just?" I ask, pointing at Victor.

"Yes." Victor teetertotters his head like he's debating with himself. "And no, I don't have time to explain it. We'd be here for three days. And no, you may absolutely *not* drink from me to download my memories." He pats my arm. "Besides, I'm not even sure they'd allow you to get any further than you just did."

"Who are *they?*" I ask.

Walking to the dome in the center of the room, Victor looks over his shoulder and says, "The Penyihir, but I don't have time to go into that either."

He kneels in front of Rahne's prison, put his hand on the glass, and smiles. Rahne, clutching a hideous stuffed animal, mirrors Victor's hand with her own.

Gabriel pushes past me, pointing at the doll in Rahne's arms. "Where did you get that?"

Rahne recoils her hand from the glass.

I've seen this thing before. The night of November 25, 1414 in

Bruges, Belgium when I met the young girl, Genevieve, who had a nightmare and I had no choice but to feed on her.

Victor didn't flinch. "She got it from me … sorta."

"I figured you stole it when you'd escaped, but how'd *she* get it?" Gabriel asks.

"I just told you."

Oh, for fuck's sake, you're so annoying. "Do better," I bark.

"The stuffed animal," Victor says, "is known as the Trinket and it's tied to her, in a way. A very ancient way."

"What do you mean?" Gabriel and I ask in tandem.

Victor shifts impatiently. "Lygos were born from this Atrocity. I don't know how or when exactly, but there was a deal made, and I don't think the first Lygos knew anything about it. Think of the Atrocities as the most direct way for the Penyihir to interact with our world; but for anyone here to make the connection, there's a cost."

"Their life," Gabriel says, snapping his finger. "That's why people died when using the Codex."

Victor nods. "Exactly, but for people like him"—he points to me—"or her"—he points to Rahne—"it won't kill them, they'll just need to feed more; but, and this is the important part, their gifts are amplified."

"How'd the damn pig get in her cell then?" I ask.

Victor chuckles into his hand. "It's a hippo and to be honest, I can't explain how *that* Trinket does the things that it does; but this isn't the first time it's appeared out of thin air, and I expect it'll disappear into thin air as strangely as it came into her cell."

My eyes lock on the black cloth, button-eyed stuffy tucked tightly between Rahne's arms.

"If you think you're going to watch it evaporate, you're sadly mistaken. It'll go when no one is looking. In the brief fraction of a second when no one is thinking about it."

How does he know this?

"This is what you were studying all those years ago when you were working on base … wasn't it?" Gabriel asks.

"Unfortunately for me, yes. Fortunately for you guys, someone knows what's going on in the worlds beyond this world." Standing, Victor brushes his hands on his pant legs and turns for the door. "I'll see you all in thirty-seven days."

"Where are you going?" Gabriel asks.

"I have some things I need to take care of," Victor says and looks back at Rahne. "Besides, it's better I'm not here for the time being. My presence could complicate things. Best not to mention to anyone that I was here."

Stuffing his hand into his pockets, Victor walks to the doorway.

"Are you coming back?" I ask.

Victor turns his head slightly like someone, or something, is whispering in his ear. Then he smiles. "I'll see you in Dundalk, Ireland."

As he spoke, a purple glint flashed in the corner of his eye. The flash was too quick for a human to see, but for me, it was clear as night.

Something, indeed.

Halfway through the door, Victor points southeast. "Jeanie's that way. Better get her out of her prison after you free the little one. She's going to need a shower, clean clothes, and a good vegetarian meal; but she'll be fine."

With one hand on the wall of her prison, Rahne waves. "Bye Mister Victor—"

Ha! Mister Victor.

"—bye Fred!"

Fred? Who the fuck is Fred? As strangely as he appeared, he was gone. No sound. No scent. Nothing.

He was just gone. And so was the Trinket.

# 63



STEAM FLOODED FROM the bathroom door like horses stampeding down a mountain as Jean stepped out from the military shower. Her hand fumbled for a towel until she found one. She dried and bound herself with it, securing one of the corners between her breasts. She grabbed a second towel and wrapped her hair in it like a ceremonial headdress.

"Gabriel, can you please come in here and pass me my clothes?"

Gabriel entered the bathroom, happy to help. Grabbing her pile of clothes, he walked them over to her and set them on the bench just inside the door. "They are right here." He tapped the wooden bench with his knuckle. "And in the order I know you like them."

His shoes squeaked on the floor as he turned to leave.

"You don't have to go," Jean said, taking a half-step toward him.

"Sweetie, we're besties and everything, but watching you get dressed doesn't really do it for me."

Jean smiled. "I've missed you."

"I've missed you too." Gabriel sat on the bench beside her clothes with his back to her. "Okay, I'll stay, but I'm looking the other way."

Pressing the towel into her chest, Jean chuckled. "Well, it's not like you haven't seen all of *this* before." She gestured to herself from head-to-toe.

"True, but I don't need to see it again," Gabriel said, averting his eyes even more.

Jean swung an open palm at Gabriel, hitting him in the shoulder. "No wonder you're still single. You *are* still single, right?"

"Yes, baby girl," Gabriel said behind a heavy sigh. "I'm still single. Not sure why *that's* what you want to talk about when we have everything else that—"

"Because I want a distraction. I *need* a distraction," Jean said, sliding her socks on. "I don't want to talk about Sorin."

"He is dreamy though," Gabriel said behind a hard blink. "Do you think he'd ever play for my team?"

"No." Jean slipped her leg into the pair of jeans. "He doesn't fuck his food." Startled, Gabriel's eyes widened. "And might I just say, fuck Henry. He's become a hateful, terrible person. You wouldn't believe everything he did to me while I was a prisoner."

"That bad, huh?"

"And before you say anything about it," Jean said and raised a silencing hand, "I don't want to talk about Rahne either."

The dreadful stories the Codex shared with her at the smallest questioning thought and everything about Rahne's life since birth was too heartbreaking to think about anymore. She'd been obsessing over it all for months while in her prison and just wanted a break from it all.

"Have you talked to her about your relationship to her?" Gabriel asked, ignoring her request.

Jean answered without looking up. "She already knows."

"I understand that, but have *you* told her?"

There was a long pause, as Jean completed dressing. "No."

Gabriel stood and grabbed Jean's hand. "Maybe you should when she and Sorin get back."

"Where'd they go?" Jean asked.

"To get food," Gabriel said, like it wasn't a big deal.

A sudden and short burst came from Jean. She covered her mouth, but couldn't hide her smile. "Sorry, hope I didn't spit on you. You know 'getting food' means wild game and not cheeseburgers, right?"

With apprehension in his voice, Gabriel inquired, "What?"

"Don't get me started," Jean said, throwing up a hand. "On our way to Michigan it was either eat the meat or don't eat at all. So, prepare yourself. I guarantee, we're going old school for dinner 'round the campfire tonight."


GABRIEL ESCORTED JEAN down the halls back to the room with Rahne's cell.

He patted and rubbed her hand as they walked and only took his eyes off her to stay on the path. He'd missed their inside jokes, her witty comebacks, and how her nose wrinkled when she laughed. He'd missed his friend. Talking like no time had passed since they'd seen each other, Gabriel realized the agony he felt the last year coming home to a house without her.

"Jean," Gabriel said, dropping her arm from the nook of his elbow. They stopped in the middle of the hallway and he held both her hands in his. "I cannot keep aligning myself with The Company. Not after what they did to you and to Rahne."

"I'm sure you did everything you could in your position to help us." She tried to shift her weight and continue walking down the hall, but Gabriel stopped her.

"I've been trying to figure out how to bring it up, but—"

"Just say it."

"The Director is a Nocturnae and he wants Rahne and the Codex. We're supposed to meet him in Ireland on the day of some pagan holiday. Imbolc, I think."

Jean ripped her hands from his. "Ardisson Ziegler is a Nocturnae?"

"Sorin says he has the ability to shapeshift."

"Shapeshift as in, changing your form at will?"

"We have a photo of Director Ziegler mid-transformation," Gabriel said. "He's been going by other names as well: Natu S. Primis, Phaeton LéTry, and The Faceless King."

Maintaining her composure, Jean recalled the story of the Codex and the horrors of The Faceless King. "What does Director Ziegler want with Rahne?"

"Not a clue. All I know is that it can't be good, and we need to be ready," Gabriel said with a shaky voice.

"There's more, isn't there?" Jean pressed with worry in her voice.

Gabriel scoured his brain for *something* to tell her that wasn't '*Victor is alive, and he told me not to tell you.*' His palms sweated. "Yeah, there's something else. Remember how during your interrogation with Sorin you learned the missing piece to the PHANG Program?"

"Claret mixed her blood and saliva with Sorin's."

"What I didn't know—and maybe you did—was that the females are the only ones who can make more Nocturnae."

"I did know that. What's that got to do with it?"

"Everything," Gabriel said, elongating the word. "Rahne killed Claret, the last female, but Director Ziegler was already fabricating a virus in China that would alter human RNA allowing male Nocturnae—"

"To make new Nocturnae. Shit…," Jean said, covering her mouth with both hands. "I know what he's planning."

"And that is…?"

"He's going to make an army of Nocturnae and enslave the human race. If male Nocturnae can make new Nocturnae like their females could, their race is no longer on the verge of extinction. And humans are, once again, nothing more than livestock for them," Jean said.

Gabriel did not like the sound of that. "Jesus Christ. And Rahne and the Codex? What does he want with them?"

"Well, Rahne is a Lygos," Jean said. "And Dr. Shelley has been trying to convince leadership within The Company for years of his hypothesis that the Lygos gene is shared within a bloodline—"

"He believes Lygos evolved to hunt and kill Nocturnae."

Jean remembered hearing how Rahne killed Sorin's Maker right before his eyes. "Oh shit, that would make sense."

"And if Lygos hunt and kill Nocturnae," Gabriel said slowly, connecting the dots. "And Rahne, and you, are Lygos. Then I think Director Ziegler's plan—"

"To kill off the thing that hunts his kind," Jean interrupts with wide, fearful eyes. "Exactly like we, humans, did with wolves and bears for the last three hundred years. If we don't have any predators, we're the top of the food chain. It's not too far-fetched to believe Nocturnae think the same way."

"And the Codex?" Gabriel asked.

Shaking her head, Jean said, "I don't know. But whatever it is, it can't be good."

"We need to tell Sorin," Gabriel said and grabbed Jean's hand.

# 64

THE LOOK ON Jean's face when Rahne and I walk into the destroyed facility is like the one parents give their child who waltzes back into the house after sneaking out. "Welcome back," she says.

"Nice to see you too, my dear," I say with a big smile. "Now, if you don't mind, I'm going to get cooking so Rahne here can eat some *real* food." I drop my voice and mutter, "Almost a year living on noodles and cheese in a cup and peanut butter and jelly sandwiches. No wonder your kind is so unhealthy."

Rahne sets down the deer and smiles up at me.

"Now what?" I ask, testing her memory.

"We need something to burn." Rahne points at to an overturned wooden chair.

"That'll do just fine."

With his eyes locked on the dead deer, Gabriel saunters over to Jean and whispers, "Holy shit, you weren't kidding about…" He gulps. "Wild game."

"I told you," Jean whispers back.

"It's deer when it's alive," Gabriel says, covering his mouth with his hand, "so is it only called venison when it's dead?"

Jean shrugs. "I don't know."

Using a large piece of glass, Rahne skins and quarters the animal like she'd been doing it for years. The deer cooks up nicely, but it takes most of the wood furniture in the room. Rahne eats quickly and in silence.

I offer some to Jean and Gabriel. Gabriel looks at Jean, and by his face, appears to be hoping she'll turn it away so he can follow suit.

Jean shrugs. "Fuck it," she says softly and holds out her hand. "Sure. Been eating the shit since May."

"What?" Gabriel says with genuine surprise. "You have?"

I put a piece of meat on a mostly clean piece of paper and hand it to her. Then, I hand Gabriel some meat in the same fashion.

"It was either eat meat or starve." She gulps down the first bite after only three chews and takes another bite. "I tried the whole protesting food thing early on. It sucked."

Amazing what true hunger and real fear can do to a person. Maybe imprisonment did her some good.

Disgusted, Gabriel pushed the food around on his makeshift plate.

"It's not going to get up and walk away," I say, popping a burnt end into my mouth like it was popcorn. "Just eat the damn thing."

Pinching the very edges of the smallest piece of meat in front of him, Gabriel brings it to his mouth with his fingers sprawled like his nails were just painted. He stops and looks at me behind his suddenly pale face. "I don't think I can eat this."

"If you don't eat it," I say with a stone-cold face, "I'm going to stuff it down your throat."

Gabriel's eyes widen with fear. "Oh, shit." He looks at Jean for support.

"He'll do it," she says, downing the last of her food.

He quickly tears into his meal. "Holy shit, this is really good!" Gabriel confesses causing Jean and I to bust out laughing. "What?"

"I wouldn't have forced it on you had you not wanted it," I say, calming my laughter.

Gabriel turns to Jean. "But you said…"

"I know what I said," Jean says, still laughing. "And I wish I could have seen your face after I said it."

Reaching for another piece, Rahne catches the empty plate in front of me out of the corner of her eye. "Mr. Sorin, aren't you going to eat?"

I need Human blood, not this trash.

"No little one, I'm not hungry," I lie. "You go on ahead. Eat as much as you want."

Gabriel coughs, choking on his food with wide eyes like he remembered something but couldn't say it out loud. He glances at me and then to Jean, and back again.

I pretend not to know what he's getting at and give him the *'what?'* look.

He flamingoes his neck with a slight tilt of the head and glares into my eyes.

Don't tempt me with a good time.

My eyes flash red and I enter his mind. *"We're not telling her about*

*Victor. He said he'd be there."*

I exit his mind and see Rahne staring at me, a wad of food hanging halfway out of her mouth. She doesn't seem fazed by my crimson eyes.

Gabriel taps the side of his head and locks eyes with me again, mouthing: You?

The corner of my mouth curls and I see Rahne pat her stomach.

Rahne's fed. Good. Time for us to get going.

I stand. "Let's go, little one," I say with a smile, holding out an open hand to Rahne.

"Where are you going?" Jean jumps to her feet.

"I'm going to be frank," I say, helping Rahne up. "That Nocturnae, your Director,"—*Phaeton*—"could have killed me. He had every chance to kill Rahne, but he didn't. Why?"

Jean and Gabriel take a minute to think of an answer, but remain quiet.

"Yeah," I say, concerned. "I couldn't think of one either."

"So, you're going to take her and leave us here?" Gabriel asks, fearing his own words. "You're going to leave the defenseless humans alone?"

Jean crosses her arms. "No, he expects all of us to do our part. To fight a Nocturnae." Her tone is sarcastic, but begging for the answer to be no. "It took a dozen or so men to take *you* down when you broke into Wright-Patt and they were trained MP! Now you want us, a psychologist and a suit to help take down a Nocturnae who's stronger, older, and wiser than you. Are you out of your mind?"

"Help from the two of you in fighting your Director or The

Faceless King or whatever name we're calling him?" I ask rhetorically while pointing at Jean and Gabriel. "No." I turn my gaze to Rahne. "Her? Yes."

"No. No. Absolutely not!" Jean says, waving the idea off.

"I can't be the only one in the fight. As much as you humans might think it, I'm *not* immortal. I've spent my entire life running from and fighting *humans*. Not Nocturnae with gifts like mine. It's going to take more than little-old-me to bring down The Faceless King."

Phaeton threw me around like a softball and ripped out my spine with ease, for Maker's sake. Claret nearly killed me all those years ago, but she held back. Phaeton, The Faceless King, won't be so kind. He'll actually kill me.

"Rahne has gifts," Jean says, "but she's still just a little girl!"

"She's not *just* a little girl. She has a monster coursing through her veins, lying dormant right beneath her skin that, at any moment could tear through her flesh like a hot knife through butter." I press my nose against Jean's to make sure she hears me and lower my voice. "She ripped my Maker in half, right before my eyes. Then proceeded to eat her. So yeah, she's going to help. While you pathetic blood sacks sit on the sidelines."

Gabriel chuckles and says, "Did you forget we have weapons that took your arrogant ass down?"

"My arrogant ass recklessly went into that facility half-cocked," I say without raising my voice, but speaking sternly enough that Gabriel knows I'm serious. "If I'd been prepared, it would have been a different story."

"You both have a point." Jean sighs. She knows she can't fight me, so it's best to cooperate. "Where are you going to take Rahne?"

"Alaska," I say. "It's remote and we should be able to stay under the radar."

Gabriel nods. "I can keep The Company's satellites from surveying that area while you're up there. But what will you be doing? Like, do I need to keep local law enforcement away too?"

"Yes," Jean says, before I can answer. "He's going to be training her. At least, he's going to try and train her to control her Lygos transformation and have some level of consciousness while in that state. Isn't that right?"

"Mmhmm," I say. "If she can at least aim the creature, that's good enough."

Jean turns to Gabriel. "So yes, you'll need to keep the area clear of satellites and law enforcement, but also hikers and hunters. The last thing we need is collateral damage or seeing a photo of Lygos Rahne on the evening News with the headline: Abominable snowman or Werewolf sighting in Alaska."

"No, I suppose you're right," Gabriel says, scratching the back of his head.

"What are you going to do if she kills you when she goes all *Wolf-woman* on you?" Jean asks.

"That's a risk I'm going to have to take," I say, even though I have a feeling she won't. She didn't last time. "But Rahne and I need to go."

"I'll secure us some transportation to get us to Ireland too," Gabriel says, snapping his fingers and forming them into a finger-gun. "And some extra firepower."

Grabbing Rahne under the arms, I set her on my hip. "Tell Ms.

Jean everything will be okay."

"Bye Ms. Jean." She waves with a smile. "Mr. Sorin's going to take me on another adventure like the one we went on to get to Michigan."

Jean chuckles and droplets form in the creases of her face. "Yeah. Yeah, he is. You'll have lots of fun, but take it easy on him."

"We'll see you in a month," I say.

Gabriel joins Jean, putting his arm around her shoulder. "We'll be ready with the transports."

# 65



SILENCE. PERFECTLY CLEAR, unremitting silence. Humans don't realize just how rare this commodity is, in today's world of Uber, iPhones, and Spotify. But I remember this sound.

I long for it.

"Are you cold?" I ask.

The arctic wind whips past us, and Rahne's hair tussles about her face.

Peeling the hair from her face, she says, "Kinda."

"Focus on trying to change," I say, encouraging her to try the impossible—control something that doesn't want to be, or can't be, controlled. "You'll be plenty warm in Lygos form."

You may also tear me in two and throw the lower half of my body a half-mile up a mountain.

"I don't want to," she pouts.

Squatting to look her in the eye, I pull her jacket around her. "Are you sure you want to do this? Try to control it, I mean."

She nods. "Yes, I want to help so we'll all be okay and no one has to be locked inside." Sticking out her tongue, she catches a snowflake. "It's too pretty outside to be inside."

I cannot help but smile. "Isn't that the truth." I hold out my hand. "Come."

We walk out of the clearing and into the densest part of the forest where the wind is almost nonexistent, and the air is warmer. Rahne curls up in the thick roots of an old Sitka spruce and eyes an animal perched high above. "What is that?"

"That's a bald eagle. A beautiful animal and apex predator of the skies," I say, smiling at the irony. "And a lot like you."

Her head turns. "Like me how?"

I sit beside her. "They're gorgeous creatures and from far away they seem harmless, but then, when they're up close, you see their talons. With their top speed of almost one hundred miles per hour, there isn't much that can evade them once they've set their sights on them. But for a long time, they were on the verge of extinction. Kind of like you."

She doesn't respond. She lays back against the tree with her eyes aimed high. The eagle spreads its magnificent wings and takes to the sky.

"Rahne," I ask. "What is it about the…"—*Shit. What's the right word? Transformation? Lygos form?*—"…the other side of you, that you don't like?"

Her innocent baby-blues peer up at me like a puppy pleading for forgiveness. "It hurts."

"What hurts?" I ask, intrigued by the depth of her confession. "Does it physically hurt to transform?" She nods. "Is it painful to remember everything that's happened while you're in that form?" She nods. "Is it the rage, or anger, that comes with the power?" She nods. "Oh, I'm so sorry Rahne."

I reach over and pull her into my arms. She buries her face between my neck and shoulder and squeezes me tightly—a little too tight.

"It's okay Mr. Sorin, it doesn't happen often," she says, curling herself into me.

She's quite something. With everything she's been through, she still has a heart of gold. She really is so much like my Cora.

"How many times has it happened since I last saw you?" I ask.

She holds up two fingers. "But not completely."

Only two. Legends of the full moon are bullshit then. That's good to know. "Do you remember what set it off each time?"

She nuzzles herself closer, but remains silent.

"Were you excited?" She shakes her head. "Scared?" She nods and buries her face in my chest.

Fear is a trigger. That makes sense … she was terrified in the catacombs when I opened the door to her cell and a feral Claret pounced on her. So, the catalyst is a real fear. A mortal fear.

I caress her head. "What caused you to be scared? Did they hurt you?"

She nods again, sniffling and taking short shallow breaths like she's trying not to cry.

Pain. Of course, pain is a trigger. So, it's fear and pain, together, that starts the process. Humans. Monsters, purposefully harming a child. Cowards. All of them.

"I promise, no one will ever hurt you again," I say, drying her cheek.

She dries her eyes. "How do you know that?"

"Because I will be there," I say and we share a smile. "And I'm going to help you control the monster inside of you, for when I'm not there."

"How?"

First, I'm going to go back on my word. "Well, I'm going to put you in situations to trigger the transformation."

My Maker, please forgive me of my trespasses against her and guide her to forgive me. Please guide me away from my Nocturnae temptations, and to deliver us both from the evil whose eyes are set upon us.

I grip Rahne from the nape of her neck and hurl her into the trunk of the tree. Her arm dangles useless from her side and the broken collar bone piercing through her skin glistens red in the cold air.

Forgive me little one.

"Your enemies will show you no kindness, so neither will I." My eyes go crimson with the scent of blood.

This is going to hurt me more than it's going to hurt her.

Holding her arm she looks at me with eyes of betrayal. "W-W-Why?"

"Because I need to know you'll be safe when I'm gone." My fist hurls through the dry air with a shockwave forming in its wake. Three inches from her face, she stops me. Glaring through me, the blueness of her eyes ignites yellow.

Here we go.

Her hand clamps down on my fist and wrenches it back, breaking the small bones in my wrist. Her hand grows around mine.

Fur pops through the skin as it's stretched tightly over the creature tearing through. Large claw-like talons pierce her fingertips, splintering the tiny bones in my hand.

I grit my teeth. "Rahne! Stay in control!" The bone protruding from beneath her neck slides across her body like a knife for the creature to cut its way out. "RAHNE!"

Snaps, crackles, and pops erupt from every inch of her body, but she doesn't scream. A guttural growl groans through the ripping of flesh as the hulking, humanoid wolf-creature takes shape and Rahne is pushed out.

From my mangled wrist, the creature lifts me in the air until we're face-to-face.

"I don't suppose we can talk about this," I gulp.

Her small, sweet child face is gone and has been replaced with a head bigger than a bear's with big yellow eyes set far behind its wolf-like snout. The tips of teeth peak out from its saliva-soaked jowls, drenching the black-furred leg below. Snowflakes collect on the black hair covering its body giving it the most haunting of looks.

She licks her chops. The monster's mouth opens wide. She's going to bite my fucking head off. I shove my free hand into her mouth, grab her tongue, and pull with all my might. "RAHNE! STOP THIS!"

The tongue makes a loud *Pop!* as it snaps free.

Dropping me, Rahne turns away, covering her face with both hands. Snarls, groans, and howls radiate from the monster, sending shivers down my spine and echoing through the white taiga.

I flick my broken wrist a couple times in hopes of speeding up the healing process and look at it. The bones snap back into place and range of motion quickly returns. I flex my hands, fingers, and wrist.

I look up. The monster looks back at me, eyes filled with rage.

"Rahne, don't!"

The hairs on her back stand up. I need to run. I kick off with my front foot and take off. I don't care what direction. The monster gallops behind me, snapping tree limbs and shattering trunks as she closes the distance. She's gaining on me.

I drive my heel into the earth and turn with my fist blindly aimed at the creature behind me. My fangs slide over my lip, and I prepare for impact, but I hit only air. I tuck and roll, coming to a stop on one knee.

"That's a neat trick," I say, looking around for the creature. "One minute you were there, the next minute you're gone without a sound, but where'd you go?"

I scan the terrain, flipping between wavelengths. Nothing. I sniff the air but can't smell anything, and tilt my ears to either side, but there's only silence.

When you've lived—if you can call it that—nearly 700 years, and spent 150 of them stationary, in the same position on a dirty cabin floor, you gain a special kind of patience. One that humans will never understand.

I wait, motionless, and repeatedly cycle through my senses in search of the creature. The shadows lengthen at the edge of the frozen tundra as the sun grows ever closer to the horizon.

THE WAXING CRESCENT moon lights the open tundra in the cloudless night.

Suddenly, fifty meters into the woodline, a bird flies off.

You can change your scent. You can move like a shadow. But you cannot keep nature from doing what it does best, sounding the alarm to a predator.

Fixing my eyes on the area the bird flew from, I slowly stand. With my hands by my sides, I stare into the darkness. A shadowy figure creeps out from behind a weathered oak tree bringing into the moonlight the outline of a large, furry creature standing on all fours.

The hairs on my neck stand on end at the sight of yellow eyes set deep behind a long snout. My heart begins to race and my breathing grows shallow and rapid. Don't panic.

A corner of her lip curls up to show her glistening pearl white fangs under the moon's glow and I can't help but think she's smiling at me. I keep my eyes fixed on the creature's and widen my stance, preparing for her to strike.

Rahne's eyes slowly raise and float up the trunk of the tree as she unleashes a roar like I'd only heard in a memory not my own. Snow falls from the trees as they quiver under the weight of her cry, and the thin layer of ice on the forest floor crunches as animals scatter in every direction.

A hand three times the size of my own slides around the trunk of the tree as the beast hurls herself toward me, diving forward into a run on all fours, leaving the tree to fall alone.

This is it. I close my eyes.

The creature crashes through the trees and onto the tundra plain.

This is my true death. I bow my head. "I'm so sorry I made you do this, little one."

The thundering gallop suddenly stops. Hot breath pounds on my face and the hairs on my head tickle my ear.

Fearing the worst, I peek out of one eye at the monster standing before me. Both yellow eyes are fixed on the ground in front of me. I open my eyes fully and feel my chest to check for injuries.

What are you looking at? I follow her gaze to the tundra floor.

Well, I'll be damned. In front of me was the most hideous and horrifying of things that could be considered a stuffed animal.

The Trinket.

Keeping my eyes on the beast, I pick up the Trinket. The creature's gaze rises with the stuffy, but her body remains motionless.

Examining the doll, I say, "So, this thing is a relative to the Pearl. The Atrocity that confined me to that cabin floor for 150 years. And blood is your energy source…" I bite a chunk out of my hand and sigh. "Fuck it. Here we go again." I close my eyes and slam my bloody palm onto the Atrocity.

# 66



DARKNESS IS SOMETHING I've come to know quite well.

This darkness can only be one place, the Void. It's made of the kind of darkness that plays tricks on you, usually children. It seeps into your room late at night and makes you think your toys are turning their heads to watch you.

Ghost. Apparition. Presence. Whatever the term you choose, it always appears from the same place. A shiny, reflective place like a window or a mirror or sometimes a steam-filled room. A place where light bends and breaks the open veil between worlds.

"Penyihir, I'm here," I say with outstretched arms.

Far in the distance, a shadow dances in the sea of darkness and stops as if it just discovered me. A legless body floating within what looks to be a hooded cloak keeps its uniquely purple-colored eyes on mine and sways ever closer.

"Darkness is not your ally," I taunt. "I didn't walk in the light until I'd overcome an Atrocity, and by then I was alone in the world."

The Penyihir's head tilts left and right, studying me. "The one who walks in the light. The Dhampir."

Daywalker. Balkan folklore.

I raise my finger. "Not a Daywalker. Not a dhampir. Not half-human. Try again."

"Tangi flagitium," the Penyihir says.

Latin. Touched by an Atrocity. "Oh, that's a hideous term, but whatever. Why am I here?"

"Prophecy."

"What prophecy?"

"Verboten progeny. Rise of the King. Resurrection of the Progenitor."

I throw my head back and sigh. "I don't have time for riddles."

The eerie purple eyes vanish and columns of images whiz past me, but the air remains still.

No wind, no air. No air means a dream? No, not a dream. An astral projection? Has the Atrocity, this one at least, allowed me to step into the world of the Penyihir and interact with these non-corporeal beings?

Looking around, the Void takes the shape of an art museum. Some images are framed in metals, others in wood, and a few are encased in plastic, but the pillars of pictures stretch as far as my Nocturnae eyes can see in every direction.

"What is this?" I ask, studying the images.

One, a large balding man finishing a pirouette in a ballet class. Another of a crying woman wearing only a towel with mascara stains on it. A third is of the shoes of a child in a yellow raincoat that fill the frame and hide his tiny, red head.

"You're watching them. All of them. Every reflective surface, every subtle change in how light works allows you a window into our world.”

The figure nods once.

Creepy and perverse, but aren't we all?

“And the Atrocity? This Atrocity, the Trinket is a more direct way of communicating, isn't it? Are they all this way?”

“In a way.”

Ugh, more fucking riddles.

I stop in front of an object unlike the others. The frame looked like flowing blood and the image was of a little yellow house on a neighborhood street, with a birch tree out front and flower beds dusted in snow.

“Why is this one different?” I ask, pointing. “There's no reflection here. My first thought was it may be a mirror or something nailed to a tree, but then I noticed it's moving. The movements are subtle, but they're there.”

The Penyihir floats behind the image and back around to face me. “Different for Vatic.”

“Vatic? What do you mean?”

“Born from Penyihir.”

More cryptic nonsense.

“Why did Rahne stop when she saw the Atrocity, the Trinket?”

“Born Lygos. Born Vatic.”

Jean is part of the Lygos bloodline, and so Victor is the Vatic? The moving image must be what Victor is seeing right now.

“Can a Nocturnae compel a Vatic?”

“No.”

“Because the Penyihir protect the Vatic?” I ask.

"In a way."

The framed images disapparate in a black cloud and the floating figure dances away, hissing, "Prophecy."

# 67



HALFWAY DOWN THE street, right in front of a break in the boulevard, sat an old yellow house on a small plot. The front porch could hardly fit two small chairs and still have room to open the door, but the blooming flower beds made you want to sit out there.

At least that's how Victor remembered it. That house. His childhood home.

From across the street, Victor stared at the house, now rundown, with snow-dusted flower beds and plants growing from its rain gutters. Memories of playing catch, learning to ride his bike, and watching fireworks from the yard cycled through his mind.

"EMOH."

Victor didn't answer his invisible friend. It wasn't exactly, but it was something *like* home.

In the center of the bay window stood a thin, old man wiping his face with a misshapen hand. The deformed hand was frozen, atrophied from a lack of nerve stimulation due to Lou Gehrig's disease.

The old man's face lit up when a dark blue sedan rounded the corner of the street. His face pressed firmly against the glass, and he waved through the window.

"RAC."

Victor pulled his hood over his head, stuffed his hands in the pocket of the Carhartt jacket, and stepped behind a large tree. "Thanks."

The car rolled into the narrow driveway, and it hadn't even stopped before the crippled old man awkwardly, but excitedly, came out the front door. The engine stopped and a tall, lanky man with a tidy beard stepped out and hugged him. "Hi dad."

Sorrow swept over Victor at the sight of his aged brother, Henry, and how time, and likely his disturbing work experiences, had battered him.

"Can I help you grab anything?" the father asked in a painfully throaty voice.

Henry reached into the car and stretched his long body across the center console, retrieving his bag. "Nope, I got it. Thanks though."

Victor observed the gentle way his brother handled their father and found it difficult to reconcile this sweet behavior with the horrors Henry perpetrated for The Company.

"WON TAHW?"

"Now we wait." Victor sighed and walked down the street, stopping only once to look back at the house.

THE SUN HAD set by the time Henry left with their father.

Victor approached a side door through the long shadows of a

detached garage. Lucky for him, the garage light didn't work and neither did the motion detector for the spotlight in the backyard.

The screen door squeaked loudly as Victor peeled it open. He checked the knob, but it was locked.

"Little help," Victor whispered, eyeing the security system controls on the wall.

A purple light flashed across the pane of glass within the large wooden door and the alarm system lights flashed. The doorknob and the deadbolt simultaneously unlocked, and the system deactivated.

"Good work," Victor whispered. He turned the knob and entered the home, closing the door behind him.

After wiping his feet on a tattered gray rug at the top of the basement stairs, Victor stepped into the galley kitchen. Yellow rock-like laminate flooring matched the pale-yellow counters and the home's exterior vinyl siding.

Just a few short steps and he reached the dining room with its large bay window. Victor stopped just inside the room and looked back into the kitchen. Visions of himself playing the drums on pots and pans on the kitchen floor while his mother cooked played out before him.

He moved into the next room. He passed the piano he'd learned to play on and the woodburning fireplace his father lit every day in the winter, and new furniture he'd never seen before. He headed up the narrow stairs. Puffs of dust clouds wafted from green carpeting as he walked up the stairs to his childhood room. The place needed some serious vacuuming.

"EREHT."

Victor stopped at the top of the stairs and looked to his left. The space between his index finger and thumb arched with purple bolt. After stepping onto the landing, he turned the corner and stood behind the banister. His breath caught in his throat as he viewed the Mirror of his childhood nightmares.

The Mirror was framed in a thick, dark wood. Its beautiful, intricate carvings featured faint flecks of silver and sapphire shown through the deepest crevasses and craters of the etchings.

Victor stared at himself in the Mirror. He'd aged decades since the last time he saw his face within the enchanted frame and his once smooth skin had sagged and grown sallow. "Magic Mirror on the wall—"

A blue aura surrounded his eyes, and his reflection slowly became clouded by a dense fog on the other side of the glass until he could no longer see himself in the Mirror. From the shadows, a cloaked figure with purple eyes reached out its dark hand.

The Penyihir stared back at Victor as it wrote on the fogged glass:

I AM THE FAIREST ONE OF ALL

Victor cracked a polite smile that another human would find condescending, but the Penyihir didn't understand its nuance. "Funny, but let's be serious."

The darkness cloaking the inside of the Mirror disappeared, and Victor saw himself again. "Take me to Clolachatro," he said.

Raising his hand, Victor rolled his fingers until a purple aura appeared around his hand and blue sparks crawled down his body from his eyes to the tips of his fingers.

"ERA UOY ERUS UOY TNAW OT RETNE NIAGA?"

The surface of the Mirror ebbed like water until dark purple ripples from the abyss took its place.

"We don't have a choice." Bolts of bright blue and purple lighting arched from Victor's hands to the Mirror.

The Penyihir floated toward the surface. From under its cloak, a skinless hand reached out for Victor. "TEL EM EB RUOY EDIUG."

Using the banister as a support, Victor stepped in and vanished.

# 68



VICTOR HAD NEVER gotten used to the type of darkness that permeated the Void. Even during his childhood when he'd spend hours playing with his only true friend, Fred, the darkness kept his senses on high alert, never allowing him to truly relax.

"Hello, Fred." Victor planted both his feet, trying to keep in control. The Penyihir's ghostly shade-like form solidified into its humanoid shape right before Victor's eyes. "It's been a long time since we've been this close."

Victor preferred Fred's ghost form over this skinless monstrosity that stood nearly ten feet tall and had a mouth two sizes too big for its noseless face. The last time Victor had seen Fred this way was the day his mother died, when he had been a young boy of eight. Why was Fred appearing like this now? It unsettled Victor, but he followed Fred deeper into the Void anyway.

"Not much has changed," Fred said. "Even your body hasn't changed in this place. You're still a young boy, no more than eight."

Victor eyed his small hands and forced a smile of acknowledgement.

They passed a three-legged stool centered on a brick wall with chains running from it and broken near the stool. Dread washed over Victor. "Wait. Stop. Isn't this where Matt Rhead was chained up?"

"Yes," Fred said, looking down at Victor with its dazzling eyes.

The dozens of hat racks that surrounded the prison stood bare like winter trees. "And his hats?"

"He took them, of course." Fred sighed. "When Jean became anchored to the Codex and the Crown, she broke the spell that bound him."

"Where did he go?" Victor had a few ideas of Matt's possible locations and none of them were good.

Preying on the innocence of Victor's childhood, Matt tried manipulation and coercion for years to secure his freedom from the shackles that bound him to the Void. Had it not been for Fred, Victor would already be dead—or worse, a prisoner in the Void.

Fred shook his head. "His hats make it nearly impossible for us to find him."

"Shouldn't we do something?" The limp chains that once bound Matt troubled Victor greatly.

"He is a concern, but not *the* concern." Fred held out a hand. "Come, we still have far to go until we reach Clolachatro."

Together they walked in silence for what seemed like a lifetime until they reached the sands of Clolachatro. Rolling hills of sand as far as the eye could see with two large piles of broken glass resting at the top of the tallest mound.

Fred transformed back into its shade-like appearance. "What do you want to see?" Fred asked, floating beside Victor.

Victor answered without hesitation. "The day my mother died."

"The past." Fred raised its left hand and a purple flame erupted around it. The shards of glass on its left floated into the air and formed a broken window. "And what point in the future?"

"Tomorrow. The man that was with Gabriel and the young girl at Edwards AFB."

Reluctantly, Fred raised its right hand and a flame ignited, matching the one on its left. The heap of glass on its right levitated and reconstructed itself.

Victor crossed his arms and forced himself to gaze upon the first window, into the past.

The still image of a small bathroom came into the focus. Centered in the room between the tub and the vanity was a cloaked figure clutching a brunette woman. Just outside, in the hallway at the bottom of the staircase, was eight-year-old Victor scared stiff with one hand clutching the railing.

"Show me my perspective," Victor ordered, his eyes fixed on the scene.

Rotating its wrist, Fred changed viewing angle of the image to child Victor, standing in the hallway, which revealed that the first perspective came from the wall mirror above the vanity.

"I need to see his face. Play the scene."

Fred curled its hand into a fist to play the scene and it started with a high-pitched scream ringing out from Victor's young self. The scream startled the cloaked figured who looked back at the boy and froze. The creature's blood-soaked face and crimson eyes had long been etched in Victor's memory, but this time, Victor wasn't looking at his eyes.

"Pause here." Victor walked up to the image. "Can you brighten the face?"

"I will try," Fred said and pitched its hand.

The shadows retreated enough for Victor to see a scar running across the creature's face.

"Perfect. Can you hold this image and bring up the one of tomorrow?"

Fred nodded with a hum and did as Victor asked.

"I just need to see the man's face."

The day cycled past the window like it was on fast-forward as Fred rotated its hand at the wrist. It stopped with Sorin's face centered in the frame.

Victor stepped back far enough to see both the past and the future at the same time. "They're the same." His eyes darted between the images. "The scar on his face. The eyes. They're…" His voice quivered and grew raspy. "…they're the same." Victor wanted to teleport himself to wherever the crimson-eyed man with the scar currently mucked about and strangle the life out of him, like he had done to his mother.

Fred watched unaffected by Victor's pain.

"Did you know Sorin killed my mother?"

"Yes."

Victor's heart burned with the betrayal of it all. How could Fred expect him to work with his mother's killer? He turned and walked back the way they came. "I'm leaving."

Fred rotated the world so Victor was walking toward him. "You can't go. There is much you do not know."

"I don't care," Victor yelled, pointing at the portrait of the crimson-eyed man with a scarred face and his dead mother. "Nothing will change the way I feel. I hate him!"

Fred dropped its hands and the images of the past and future fell back into the sand in billions of tiny pieces. It snapped its boney, fleshless fingers and trillions of indiscernible objects passed by them. When the objects came to a quick and sudden stop, four windows floated behind Fred. "I have much to show you. Observe."

The first window illuminated with Jean standing in front of a mirror.

"What are you showing me?" Victor asked.

"What you missed," Fred said and played the scene. "And why the crimson-eyed man with the scar may not be as bad as you believe."

Jean turned sideways in the mirror and Victor gaped at her swollen belly. "Jean was pregnant."

Fred nodded and the first image faded as the second image brightened on Jean alone in her bathroom with a razorblade in her hand and blood dripping from her wrists.

"Jeanie, no," Victor cried, cupping his face in his hands. He couldn't bear to watch the woman he loved hurt herself like this. And she carried his child … "The baby. What happened to the baby?"

"The baby is gone."

"She lost it?" Victor took a step forward like he was going to attack Fred, but Fred raised its hands in surrender.

"Not exactly. The doctors told Jean the baby was stillborn and for ten years, she believed that lie."

"What happened to my kid?" Victor growled behind clenched teeth.

"The Company took her."

"No." Victor dropped to his knees in anguish. The Company had already taken so much from him, and now his daughter too? Did their evil know no bounds?

"The Darwinian Division imprisoned her. Watched her. Studied her—"

With his eyes glowing purple, Victor balled his hand into a fist and snarled, "You're going to pay for this Eugene, my *old friend*."

"—until one day, the crimson-eyed man with the scar set her free. In the process, he willingly gave up everything he'd been searching for the past 600 years."

The second image faded out and Victor watched the third image come into focus. A hulking humanoid-wolf creature devoured two halves of a woman as the crimson-eyed man with the scar that haunted Victor's dreams looked on in terror.

"I don't understand," Victor said. "Is that a werewolf?"

"The Lygos, or werewolf as you put it, is your daughter." Fred imparted this startling revelation in a bored monotone, like it wasn't the most extraordinary thing Victor had ever heard. "The woman being devoured is the Maker of the crimson-eyed man with the scar, whom he'd feared had died in 1414."

"Is a Maker what it sounds like?"

"Think of a Maker as the mother of a Nocturnae," Fred said, bringing its hands together in a praying fashion. "Call it irony or call it fate, he killed your mother and in turn your daughter killed his."

Victor's rage flared up. He could never forgive his mother's murderer. Never. "An eye for an eye isn't good enough to redeem him for what he did."

The fourth image flew in front of the other three windows and grew to be twice their size. In it, Sorin ran with Jean and Rahne tucked under his arms, but the image quickly became distorted when a foot impacted the frame.

"A puddle? You're showing me this from the worst viewing angle possible?"

"Watch."

Victor looked back at the window just as the rippling water flattened and a helicopter flew through the frame.

"Roll back. Stop with the chopper centered on the frame," Victor ordered.

As Fred did, C067269—The Company's covert identification number—came into focus written on the side of the helicopter. Although surprised, Victor said nothing.

"He's been protecting them from The Company," Fred said and waved its hand. The windows and their frames disintegrated into grains of sand, rejoining the desert.

Victor took a deep breath. "Why is he protecting them?"

"You'll have to ask him. But I can tell you that Jean showed the crimson-eyed man with the scar empathy and compassion by bringing him a gift that symbolized a certain bond they share."

"And what bond might that be," Victor scoffed.

Shifting back into his humanoid form, Fred knelt before Victor to better look him in the eye. "The loss of a child. His daughter died of the Bubonic plague at age ten."

It was a bond Victor now knew he also shared with the crimson-eyed man with the scar. Ten years of his daughter's life stolen from him, but at least he still had the chance to save his own daughter, and hopefully have a relationship with her. "That's terrible. I have to help him, don't I?"

"Mmhmm," Fred said, standing. The two of them began their long journey back.

"I'm still going to kill him," Victor said after a few moments of silent brooding.

"I know." Fred put a skinless, slender arm around Victor. "Where to now?"

Victor's eyes glowed purple. "Dundalk, Ireland."

# 69



I sit on the side of a hill overlooking the vast greenery of rolling hills and grazing sheep. It feels both like home and like a recurring dream. These hills are where I ran reckless as a child. Where I fell in love with Cora's mother. Where I buried Cora's mother when she died in childbirth. So many memories of my brief human life, both joyful and sad. I wish I could have shared them all with my daughter.

"Hi, Mo Chroí. I'm sorry I haven't been here in a long time. I've been…"—I chuckle through the corner of my mouth—"I don't have an excuse. I'm sorry."

"Mr. Sorin," a whisper comes from a mile away. "Who are you talking to? I don't hear anyone else's heartbeat."

She is incredible, my little one.

"Cora, meet Rahne. She reminds me of you, in a lot of ways. Her innocence, how utterly mesmerized she is with the world, and her unbelievable strength."

"Thank you, Mr. Sorin."

"I tried, Sweetheart." I look up at the cloudless sky. "I really tried. Every year since 1350, I stood and watched the sun rise. Begged the sun not to burn the flesh from my body. Defied my Maker and kin and instead tried to keep my humanity. I pleaded with the gods to let me peer through the veil of death. All for a chance to see my little girl's face again. Your face."

"You had a daughter," Rahne gasps. "And she died."

Plucking a flower from the patch of lavender beside me, I study it. "You know what they call these, Mo Chroí? Well, the flowers that look just like these? It's an interesting story actually. Between twenty-three and seventy-nine A.D., Pliny the Elder wrote that the Athenian women would line their beds with the leaves of the Chaste Tree to preserve their chastity."

"What are you talking about?" Rahne whispered.

"The people we worked for, the MacTíre family, would place them in their beds every so often. Turns out, they only did it when they had ill thoughts. The Greeks called it by another name though. They called it Lygos. Speaking of Lygos, I met someone when I was captured by some very bad people. Her name is Dr. Jean Allicines, and she's a wonderful woman. I think you would like her."

The wind picks up and ruffles my hair that's grown longer and scruffier than it was the last time I sat on these hills. The gust kicks up loose lavender pedals and leaves that flip and twist and, for a second, form a figure. It's small, but familiar.

Tears of blood run down my cheeks. "Cora?"

Purple sparks bolt from every leaf and petal in the outline of my Mo Chroí and a voice enters my mind. *"Rin."*

"RIIIN!" Rahne screams in a high-pitched shriek.

The outline of Cora dissipates and my heart screams as if I've lost her all over again.

"Sorin, where the *fuck* are you?!" Jean yells over Rahne's ear-piercing wails.

I dry my face without letting go of the flower and I rush back to the car. Gabriel and Jean stand side by side, but Rahne is nowhere to be seen.

"Where is she?" I ask, looking around in panic. And then I see her. An olive-toned woman has Rahne in a headlock halfway up the castle's hillside.

"Give me the Codex," she says to us, "and we'll be on our way."

Gabriel abandons Jean and steps toward the woman with his arms stretched wide and shaking his head. "Major Kshatriya? Diya. What are you doing?"

"Aligning myself with the winning side," Diya says, tightening her grip around on Rahne's neck.

Rahne kicks and screams, struggling to keep her windpipe from being cut off.

Not yet Rahne. Not yet. We haven't seen Phaeton.

A tall man, wrapped in a cream toga, with long dark hair and a beard to match appears atop the castle's curtain wall. His eyes flash crimson, revealing streams of blood running down his face and a crown of thorns woven with silver and tipped with sapphires, resting atop his head. A Nocturnae and another Atrocity—the Crown.

"And you are?" I step in front of Jean. "Because you're not Phaeton, The Faceless King." He knows we're coming; he has no reason to hide his face. His pride wouldn't allow it.

The crowned man says nothing and folds his arms. There's an old saying: Don't bring a knife to a gun fight. Well, our dumbasses brought a super-soaker to a nuclear war. I scoop Jean up in my arms and rush her to the car where I set her down. "Stay here. Do you still have the Codex?"

Jean climbs into the backseat of the car. "Yeah." She hugs her purse to her chest.

"Good. I'll keep them away from you." I shut the door a little too hard and accidently crack the window.

I hurry to Gabriel's side. "How do you know Diya?" His heartbeat changed for a second. Surprise. No, panic. But he doesn't want to tell me, so I force him to look at me. "The Company made its own Nocturnae using the intel they gathered during Jean's interrogation of me, didn't they?" Gabriel gives a heavy sigh and nods. "Fucking humans and their arrogance. Did you know?" Gabriel averts his gaze and that's all the answer I need to know he's been keeping vital information from us. I roll my hand into a fist, but restrain myself. "We're going to have a serious talk later."

A Nocturnae made by man. She's going to be just as destructive and clumsy as I was as a neophyte. Hopefully, she doesn't know how to use all of her gifts.

Struggling to free herself from the headlock Diya has her in, Rahne and I lock eyes. I push a thought into her mind. *"Duck."*

I close the distance between us and throw a punch where Rahne's head was a fraction of a second ago. Diya's eyes bulge and spittle flies from her mouth. Her grip on Rahne loosens.

Rahne slips out of Diya's grip.

"Run Rahne. RUN!" I yell and throw another jab and a cross to Diya's face. Hook to the body. Cross, jab, jab back up top. Finish with an upper cut.

Gabriel drops to a knee and waves Rahne over. Rahne runs into his arms and he scoops her up. "I've got you." Holding Rahne tightly against his chest, he sprints to the car.

Good. She's safe. For now. But the crowned man, why isn't he helping Diya? Is he watching her? Is he testing her somehow?

Diya stumbles back, wipes the blood pouring from her face with her sleeve, and smiles. "My turn." She comes at me throwing punches wildly. Sloppy.

Dodging the chaotic strikes, I throw punches of my own. Kidney, solar plexus, liver, spleen. Blood pours out of her like iced tea from a pitcher.

The crowned man appears behind her, his face clenched in frustration. "Pathetic." Wrapping his arms around Diya's head, he snaps it from her neck and carelessly discards it over his shoulder.

Didn't see that coming.

Gabriel raises the cuff of his shirt to his lips and says, "Alpha team, move in." A number of soldiers appear out of nowhere, all in tactical gear and reeking of silver. "Fire at will. Take 'em down."

Throwing his arm around Rahne, Gabriel covers her as he drops to a knee.

"Jean! Duck!" I scream and throw myself on the ground as silver bullets zip through the air, whizzing past my ear. One nearly clips my shoulder.

Jean's muffled screams from the car tell me she's tucked tightly somewhere in the vehicle.

The crowned man smiles with a huff of amusement and takes off in the direction of the largest pod of soldiers. Seven soldiers fall and he reappears at the base of the castle. Not a scratch on him.

He's so fast, I can hardly track his movements.

"Got any other ideas?" I urgently ask, glaring at Gabriel.

"Where are my 50-cals?" he screams into his cufflink.

Three Humvees barrel over the surrounding hills and unleash a barrage of ear-pounding gunfire from the mounted guns.

"MOVE YOUR ASSES!" Gabriel yells, waving them on, proudly.

The crowned man grabs the two soldiers nearest him and makes for the Humvees. He hurls one soldier like a javelin, piercing a windshield, and uses the other as a shield. Bits and pieces of his human shield—a hand, then a leg—are blasted off by the remaining Humvee's roof-mounted .50 caliber gun.

Throwing the remains of the mutilated soldier-shield at the vehicle's windshield, he drops to his knees and drives his shoulder under its front end, toppling it end-over-end. Soldiers spill out and one after another, he kicks them into oblivion like they're nothing more than wasps leaving their nest.

He tears into the belly of the vehicle and pulls out the engine. With one hand, he hurls the engine at the final Humvee like a softball. It rips through the center of the Humvee and leaves a smear of metal, blood, and body parts in the grass.

His head snaps in my direction and suddenly a sandaled heel strikes my sternum with a loud *crunch* and sends me back three steps.

"That all you got?" the crowned man taunts.

He breaks for Rahne, still wrapped in Gabriel's arms.

I can't let him get to her.  I move to counter with a punch, but he grabs my wrist and twists midair, slamming me into the ground. With a foot in the square of my back, he wrenches hard on my arm, pulling at the tendons and ligaments in my shoulder.

"AHHHHHHHHHH!" I cry. He's going to rip my arm off.

"Samael! That's enough," a familiar voice calls from the highest point of the castle. "Let him go. There's no reason for us to act like animals." Phaeton.

Samael grunts, throws my arm to the ground, and calmly steps away from me.

"I see the child, now where's the Codex?" Phaeton jumps down from the pillar.

I grunt as I stand. My shoulder pops back into its socket and the connective tissue stitches back together. "You're not getting either of them."

Samael appears behind Phaeton.

Phaeton laughs. "You can either give them to me willingly, and we'll be on our way. Or, we can drink the Ubiets dry and leave you torn limb from limb. You'd be a torso with a head—helpless and afraid—unable to do a thing. Just like when Claret and Gaius were taken from you."

I look back at Rahne. "I'm pretty sure two against two is a fair fight."

Rahne nods. After Alaska, she's ready for this.

"You? And the pup?" He laughs. "Don't insult me."

Three more men appear from the shadows and join Samael at Phaeton's side. The first one is a short Japanese man in a Gi with his hair in a chonmage and a katana fastened to his hip. A samurai.

Beside him stands a tall, built man in a loin cloth with a mohawked helm covering his face, and a dory spear in one hand, shield in the other. A Spartan warrior. The third and final man is a shirtless dark-skinned man with a full-length skirt flapping in the wind and a golden jackal headdress encompassing his entire head and neck and a golden scythe strapped to his back. Anubis?

Suddenly, Samael takes his place at Phaeton's left and cocks his head to one side as if cracking his neck. Phaeton reaches out his hands beseechingly. "Give me the girl and the Codex."

"No."

Phaeton shrugs and pulls his hood over his head. "I guess we'll do this the hard way, then. You are brave neophyte. Arrogant, ignorant, and stupid—but brave."

"What's that have to do with any—"

"STELIOS!" Phaeton yells, looking at the Spartan warrior.

The Spartan lunges, soaring through the air with his shield covering himself from thigh to neck. He pulls back his spear, ready to strike, and his eyes go crimson.

"Come on!" I throw a punch as soon as he comes near.

Stelios swats away my attack with his shield. I catch my footing and look back in time to watch a man in flannel tackle him. Victor. Their bodies summersault over the grassy knoll. Stelios drives his shield into the earth, stopping himself, and Victor pops off the ground like an expert martial artist. Where'd he come from?

A voice, unlike any I've ever heard, enters my mind. *'EW THGUORB MIH."*

Panicked, I look around but cannot find the source. "Oh, I don't like this. Invisible entities speaking to me. I don't like this at all."

Victor throws three quick punches and dodges the tip of Stelios's spear from piercing his face.

"No way!" I gasp, mesmerized by Victor's movements. "He's so fast!"

The two square off and Stelios snarls. "A Vatic. It's been some time since I saw one of your kind."

The Company didn't make this one? I look back at Phaeton and the three other Nocturnae beside him. These aren't neophytes. These are old, possibly ancient Nocturnae.

"Oh yeah?" Victor acknowledges with a smile and bounces on the balls of his feet like a boxer. "I promise you, I'm not like the rest."

Stelios grunts. "That's what they all say." He cracks his neck.

He lunges and his spear narrowly misses Victor's face. Victor twists down the spear's shaft, purple sparks climbing up his body from the earth, and he lands a backhand hard against Stelios's helmet, severely denting it. What is that? Is that magic?

Stelios peels the helmet from his head and his jaw snaps back into place. Discarding the helmet-shaped scrap of metal, he throws a punch with his shield.

Victor folds back, and the shield narrowly misses him as he loses his footing. "Shit."

Taking two steps, Stelios jumps high into the air and brings down his spear on Victor, but Victor raises his forearm like he holds a shield of his own. As the spear tip descends, a purple ring appears in front of Victor's arm, blocking it. Yes, definitely magic.

Victor rolls back onto his feet, checks Stelios's kick, and purple sparks appear again. Stelios thrusts the spear repeatedly, but Victor dodges the attacks with ease almost like he knows where the attack is coming from before it happens.

I look to Phaeton, but neither he nor any of his generals seem worried. They look like they're enjoying this. Almost like this is a tournament.

Stelios hurls his shield at Victor like a frisbee. Folding backwards Victor dodges the shield, but the tip of the spear is right near his face as he comes back up, and he loses balance and falls to the ground. The hurling spear zips past Victor and finds a different target. It pierces soft tissue, tearing flesh and breaking bones as it slows. A loud gasp escapes from a man behind me and a little girl's screaming sends chills down my spine. Rahne!

I look back to see blood covering one side of Rahne's face. I follow her eyes to Gabriel who is clutching the shaft of the spear sticking out of his chest.

Victor looks over his shoulder. "GG!"

He clambers to his feet, but Stelios drives his knee into his back. A solid purple shield goes up around his body just in the nick of time. He falls flat on the ground, and Stelios delivers blow after blow with relentless ferocity.

I step to come to Victor's aid, but as I do, Samael appears in front of me. "Don't you dare, neophyte."

Purple bursts shine from Victor's back. He can't take much more of this.

Rahne, trying to keep Gabriel from sliding down the spear, screams for help. Her face and arms are covered in his blood. Panic floods Gabriel's eyes as his breath becomes shallower with every wheeze. The spear punctured his lung.

I look back at Samael. "Try and stop me." I push past him.

"With pleasure." Before I know it, I'm tied up in a choke hold with my arms pinned in his grip.

Rahne's crying eyes jump from Gabriel to Jean in search for help. Jean, covering her ears in the front seat of the car, has no idea what just happened to her friend. Rahne's eyes jump to Victor as he falls unconscious, then she looks to me, in a headlock under Samael's arm.

Her eyes flash yellow and connect with mine. My eyes flash crimson, and I push a thought into her mind. *"It's okay little one. Let it out."*

*"Gabriel, he loved us,"* her mind pushes back. *"He gave everything to save me. To save us. I let him die. I can't do that. I feel it slipping. I won't watch this anymore!"* She screams a high-pitched cry of anguish and sorrow.

*"That's it, let it all go."*

"Stop it! That's enough!" Her scream shifts up two octaves, growing in intensity. The ground splits beneath her. Tears stream down her face and her wails continue.

Samael lets me free and Stelios stops his attack on Victor.

"This is it," Phaeton mutters to himself with pleasure.

Rahne's screams deepen and she pounds her fists into the ground, narrowly missing Gabriel.

I rush to Gabriel, snap the ends off the spear, and carry him to the car. Ripping the door from its hinges, I yell, "Jean, it's me. Sorin." I prop Gabriel up against the side of the car as Jean uncovers her ears. I grab Jean by the hand. "Gabriel's hurt badly."

She climbs out of the car and investigates Gabriel with her

hands. She stops on the handle of the spear and her hands quiver. "Oh, Gabriel. No…"

The two generals keep their eyes locked on Rahne as her bones break and the flesh peels away from her body revealing long, black hair.

"Incredible," Phaeton says.

Rahne's screams deepen and the innocence fades from her eyes leaving them furious and yellow.

Jean looks to me. "She's changing,"—her eyes flash yellow—"isn't she?"

"Yeah, she is."

The beast's hulking body towers over Samael and Stelios.

"It sounds terrifying," Jean says.

Rahne's fur shimmers under the waxing crescent moon as she rears her massive head back and lets out a long howl. "Oowwoooo!" She lowers her gaze to Stelios and the diamond-shaped snowy patch of fur at the nape of her neck glistens.

# 70



THE HULKING WOLF pumps her arms at the ground and stomps toward the pair of ancient Nocturnae, Samael and Stelios. Exposing her bone-crushing teeth and fangs designed to not let go, I swore I saw her smile.

Get 'em Rahne.

Leaping forward, she runs on all fours at Stelios. Her claws tear at the ground, pulling up chunks of earth with every booming impact they make. Clouds of steam vent from her nose and saliva pours from her jowls as she grows nearer to her prey.

Her onyx claws swing at Stelios, but hit only air as he ducks and drives the full force of his shoulder into her chest. Their bodies shoot toward the sky and quickly tumble to the ground.

Samael takes a step forward and Stelios snaps, "Don't you *dare* intervene!" He throws three hard jabs to the beast's ribs, fracturing them. "It's been so long since I've had this much fun and been able to—" Rahne slashes at his face, pulling out an eye and tearing off half his nose. Raising his mutilated handsomeness to Samael, a smile of pure joy spreads wide on his face. "It's been so long since I could really let loose."

Fun? Getting your face ripped off is fun? Who are these guys?

Samael takes two steps back with a nod. "Of course, my friend." He folds his hands behind his back.

Cartilage, muscle, and tissue stitch a fresh nose back on Samael's face, and he sets his new eye on Rahne. "Bring it on, little girl!"

She snarls, chomping at the air and swings.

He counters with a hard upper cut to her jaw, dislocating it. He takes her under the arm, pinning it against his shoulder, and grabs her wrist with his free hand. Stepping between her large muscular legs, he flips the beast over his shoulder and slams her into the ground.

"Hey," Jean says. "Can you still fight?"

I scoff. "What kind of question is that?"

Stelios has Rahne's arm pinned to her side.

"What are you doing?" Jean asks, annoyed. "You can see. You can fight. Get out there!"

Prison gave her some stones. Amazing how living life on the other side will change your perspective.

A loud snap of Rahne's humerus echoes across the Irish land and she howls in pain. Her scapula is one good twist away from snapping, too.

"I can't," I say, taking a step back.

Snap. There goes her scapula. Rahne throws a mean blow on Stelios's hip, causing his whole leg to wiggle loosely like a fish out of water. Arrogance leaves his face and Rahne slams him to the ground, taking top control.

She rolls the arm of her injured shoulder. Aligning the back of her arm with her rear deltoid and latissimus dorsi, the injuries heal before my eyes. She's recovered. Good.

"What do you mean you can't?!" Jean's voice sounds shrill. "Get out there and help her!"

Lowering myself, I grab Jean by the shoulders. "I'm Nocturnae, remember. Lygos were born—" My eyes drift over to the unconscious Victor.

A purple hue appears behind him, and a voice enters my mind. *"EDAM."*

"—no, made. Lygos were made to hunt and kill Nocturnae. They're faster than us. Stronger than us. And have control over their pheromones. She could kill me without realizing it now that she's in this hulking werewolf form. I can't do that to her."

"Bullshit!" Jean wiggles free. "If that were true then she would have killed you in Alaska."

She almost did. "Jean, you wouldn't believe me if I told you." I stand and lean against the car. "If shit goes south, I'll jump in. But it doesn't look like that's going to happen from where I'm standing."

"What do you see?"

"Rahne's got Stelios—the Spartan—pinned to the ground under her massive knee and is pummeling his face into bloody cottage cheese faster than he can heal. The ground under his head cracks and a small bowl in the earth appears where his head continually bounces after Rahne's strikes."

Stelios's heart rate slows. Rahne strikes him three more times.

His breath becomes shallow. Two more strikes. He exhales, but doesn't inhale. She did it.

"Never submit! Never withdraw! Fight until true death!" Phaeton yells from the castle. "Show her what it means to be—"

Stelios deflects Rahne's next punch sending it hurling into the earth beside his mangled body. He pulls her close and wraps his legs around her torso, tucking his arms under hers as the bones in his face reconfigure.

Phaeton steps forward, but his confidence in his soldiers keeps him quiet.

Stelios' drops his head under Rahne's armpit and he spiders over her body. With his feet driving into her inner thighs, he wraps an arm around her neck and grips his own bicep with that hand, placing the other on the back of Rahne's head.

Stelios grunts, tightening his hold on her neck.

Rahne reaches for him, but her massive body works against her. Clawing at his grip, blood spills from his forearms, and her neck and chest. She drops to her knees, her eyes rolling back. Her heartbeat slows. Her breaths are shallow and short. Her muscles relax.

Is this the end? It can't be. She's just a little girl. She's too young to die. Like my Cora was too young.

Suddenly, her skin excretes an odorless, oily substance. She falls forward, catching herself at the last second with her forearms. The oil runs down every hair on her body, and just as she's about to pass out, Stelios lets go.

Rahne gasps for air, clutching her throat.

Stelios stumbles over to Samael like a drunken baby walking and vomits. "Help," he gasps, wiping the chunks from his face.

Samael catches him, saying, "I have you, brother. You forgot about the Lygos pheromones, didn't you?"

Pheromone secretion as an automated defense mechanism causing the attacker to become disoriented and extremely sick. I hadn't observed that before, but I like it. It could turn the tide. I become more hopeful by the second.

Rahne charges them and kicks Stelios in the back. His back breaks and his ribs burst through his chest.

"Yes," Stelios gasps on his knees, blood running from his mouth. "Let's kill her now." Pushing his ribs back into his chest, the wounds quickly close. He stands and squares off against Rahne.

Samael widens his stance on the other side of her.

Rahne looks left—Stelios—and right—Samael. She lets out a war cry and barrels at Stelios.

Sliding his head to the right, Stelios slips the first swing. And the second. And the third. Rahne roars in frustration and swings her claws wildly, disemboweling him in her fury.

Samael tackles Rahne. They slide across the ground, bouncing over the hills like a stone skipping across water, exchanging blows along the way. He kicks off of Rahne's head and lands gracefully on his feet. Her head comedically sticks in the dirt, folding her body over onto the ground. Muscles tear. Bones shatter. Tendons snap.

"Not as tough as I remember." Samael blitzes Rahne, kicking her in ribs. Blood bursts out of her mouth, staining the snowy ground. He kicks her again. "Not." Kick. "So." Kick. "Tough." Kick. "Now." Kick. "Are you?" Kick. "Little Lygos."

He's gonna kill her if I don't so something. But what? Light glints in the corner of my eye. The spear. "Forgive me," I say, grabbing the spear.

"What?" Jean winces in pain, cutting her hand on a jagged piece of metal hanging off the car.

I don't answer and rip the spear from Gabriel's lifeless body. It burns my skin. My Maker. It's made of fucking silver? I hurl the spear at Samael and run after it. He'll dodge the spear at the last second and that's when I'll lay him out.

Out of nowhere, Stelios appears. He rips the spear out of the air, twirls it around his body, and—

"Shit." I cough. My mouth fills with blood and my hands move to my belly. The tips of my fingers burn as the spear's shaft melts my insides.

Stelios rotates the spear. "Still susceptible to silver, neophyte? Pity, you'll never learn the ancient secrets." Lifting me in the air, he slams the blunt end of the spear into the ground and steps back from my dangling body with a chuckle. "I've always liked how an impaled body looks on the moon lit horizon just after midnight."

Vlad Tepes. I try to speak, but only gurgles of blood escape my lips.

"What's that?" Stelios gets his ear as close to me as he can.

I try to speak, but fail again.

"Ooh, why am I doing this to my own kind?" Stelios laughs. "That's quite simple really. You see, when you aligned yourself with *that*"—he points at Rahne being slammed into the ground left and right like a rag doll by Samael—"and that"—he points at Jean holding Gabriel's corpse—"and that"—he points at an unconscious Victor—"you forfeited your right to be called Nocturnae."

I wheeze and gasp for air. One lung has collapsed, and the other is quickly on its way. If I don't get off this spear soon, I'm done for.

My arm falls limp as the spear tears further into my shoulder, back, and stomach. "Damn … it …" I gasp.

A giant ball of black fur whistles past me and lands twenty feet from Jean. The broken and bleeding Rahne skips to a stop. This is it. Samael and Stelios laugh and begin their slow walk to finish the job, enjoying every second of Rahne's suffering. The end.

Jean releases Gabriel. Slowly, she crawls toward Rahne.

"Rah—ne" I cough. "Get—up"

The purple aura around Victor is gone. Is he dead? I can't hear his heart, but I can't hear Jean's either, and she's alive. Fucking silver.

Rahne's hulking hand reaches for Jean. Catching the necklace with her claw. The jewelry falls from Jean's neck, between Rahne's massive hands, and into the dirt.

Jean stops next to Rahne and kneels back on her ankles. Grabbing the massive hand with her own, she holds it close to her chest. "I've got you."

Rahne coughs, throwing Jean off balance. She slams her bloodied hand onto the ground catching herself—right onto the necklace.

A faint purple cloud appears behind the pendant wrapped in Jean's hand. The Pearl.

Jean's eyes flash blue, and she disappears for a fraction of a microsecond, then reappears. What just… How? Did Samael and Stelios see that? My Maker I hope not!

The mysterious voice returns to my mind. *"EMOCREVO*

*TSETAERG REAF."*

Jean buries her face in her hands. I don't understand and I don't care, if this means what I think it does.

Steam vents from Rahne's Lygos body as her dark-haired coat stains the snow red around Jean.

With a trembling hand, Jean clutches the blood-soaked fur and a yellow fire ignites behind her eyes. "What did you do?" Jean asks with tears streaming down her face. "What did you do to her?"

The bones in Jean's legs, arms, and back snap and elongate. It can't be! Her chest shoots toward the sky, and she screams a scream I've heard only once before. The maternal scream.

"That's my DAUGHTER!"

Jean's eyes shift into a solid yellow, and she kicks off the ground. Before her other foot even hits the ground, the flesh of her human form is gone revealing a perfect Lygos body, with snow white fur.

Stelios and Samael are caught off guard by her speed. Jean tears through them, severing Stelios's arm at the bicep and peeling the flesh from Samael's face.

"There are two?" Stelios asks rhetorically, holding his dangling arm in place so it can heal quicker. He looks back at Phaeton, and then at Samael. "But only a Vatic can ignite a dormant Lygos. And he's still down."

"Then it was an Atrocity," Samael says.

Jean swings wildly at Stelios and Samael, and, narrowly misses them.

They split up. Samael centers himself with Jean while Stelios circles around to her back. Stelios lifts his fist from his side, but before he can even consider his next movement, he's on the ground and Jean is tearing into him. Samael charges at Jean.

Without looking, Jean reaches out and grabs Samael's leg. She whips Samael at the car which sends it flying and subsequently dislodges the spear from the ground. I don't think she did that on purpose, but I'll take the help.

The car spins like a top and flips backwards. Jean's purse flies out of the car and plops on the ground on its side with the Codex partially exposed.

Pointing at Jean's purse, Phaeton looks at his jackal-headed general. "Amen, get what we came for." Eyeing his samurai, Phaeton points at Jean. "Oda, end this."

Amen and Oda disappear.

Suddenly, Jean roars loudly in pain. Amen plucks his blood-soaked scythe from her back, revealing a gaping wound from shoulder to hip, crossing her back.

Amen disappears and reappears next to the Codex. He grabs it. "Fool," he says and pulls Samael from the car. Slinging him over his shoulder, they disappear.

Jean cries out again. Circling her in sporadic, calculated movements was Oda slicing her with invisible blow after invisible blow. Lingchi—death by a thousand cuts.

Leaning back so the blunt end of the spear is as high off the ground as I can get it, I take a deep breath, and rip it from my chest in one clean movement. I cough uncontrollably, but I force myself to push on. Raising myself to one knee, I hurl the spear at the samurai, my hand burning.

*Please don't hit Jean.*

Narrowly missing Jean's face, the spear stops the samurai in his wake. He wipes his blade on his sleeve and sheathes the katana. With praying hands, he bows to me and disappears with the unconscious Stelios. Phaeton and his generals are gone.

And so is the Codex.

# 71



I TAKE A moment to heal.

Victor lies unconscious. Rahne and Jean, also unconscious, are still in Lygos form. Best not to startle the beasts and become their breakfast.

The first rays of light hit my face. Maker, it's morning already?

I push myself off the ground with a heavy groan. "Victor it is."

I creep over to Victor, fearing that if I run or move just a little too fast, I'll wake a Lygos. Halfway over to him, something shimmering on the ground catches my eye. I reach down and pluck the object from between the blades of grass. "The Pearl. Once again, we meet. I better hold onto you." I stuff the Atrocity into my pocket and continue my slow, cautious walk to Victor. I tentatively slide my foot under Victor's ribs. "You still alive?"

"You tell me." He moans and rolls over. "You're the one who can hear heartbeats."

Touché.

"Yeah, but this way makes me seem less…" I roll my hand in search of the right words.

"Of a blood-thirsty monster who has the same level of self-control around humans as an alcoholic does in a liquor store," Victor says like he's been rehearsing it in his head for some time.

"I'll let that slide this one time because you showed up and helped, but just this once. Take a tone with me like that again and—"

"And what?" Victor stands, dusting himself off. "You'll drink me dry? Sounds like my overly simplified stereotype was on the nose. Plus, I didn't *help*, I fucking kicked ass."

Who bit his neck and let him live?

"Actually, you got your ass handed to you and wound-up face down in the dirt."

Victor steps into my face while purple flashes flicker behind his eyes.

I return the taunt with fangs and crimson eyes. "Anytime, pretty boy."

Something else is going on with him. He's arrogant and an asshole sure, but that was hatred in his eyes.

A blood-curdling scream erupts from behind me. It's Rahne. Her scream has a faint howl in its echo and is quickly followed by another scream, just as horrifying. It's Jean. I've heard that cry before.

Victor and I watch in horror from only a couple dozen yards away as the two Lygos beat the ground beneath them.

He whispers, "What's going on?"

"Watch." I nod in the direction of Jean and point at Rahne.

First one beast, then the other, roll onto all fours and dig their claws into the earth, grunting heavily. Extending their backs to the heavens, their howls change to agony as chunks of fur and flesh fall from their once monstrous bodies. Their bones pop and shrink. The terrifying roars of unbearable pain turns into horrified screams as the monsters return to their human selves—naked and bloody.

Victor's heart skips a few beats at the sight of Jean.

"You ok?" I ask.

He doesn't answer at first with his mouth slightly open. "Jeanie?"

On her hands and knees, Jean clutches her naked chest. Blood, fur, and fluids coat her body. She alternates between gasping for air and coughing up chunks of flesh, white fur, and red fluid. Gross.

Slowly, Victor walks over to Jean.

I look over at Rahne, lying on her side in the fetal position blanketed in the biogenic ooze of horror that was her Lygos monster. Walking toward Rahne, I look over my shoulder and see Victor crouching next to Jean.

"Jeanie?" he whispers, placing a hand on her back.

Jean's nose twitches like she's got a scent. She shoots up onto her feet, aggressively rolling Victor's hand off her. "Rahne. Where's Rahne? RAHNE!" she pushes past Victor, sending him flying through the air.

Oh, my Maker, I'm glad I saw that! Serves that prick right.

She sprints to Rahne's side without a single misstep. Exhaustion, confusion, guilt, and even blindness don't stop her—a sign of a *true* mother.

Repeatedly, she mutters the same words into Rahne's ear, "I'm sorry," pulling her closer and tighter each time.

With heavy eyes, Rahne flops her head into the nook of Jean's shoulder. "Ms. Jean?"

Immediately, Jean laugh-cries. "Yeah. Yeah, it's me Sweetheart." She strokes the back of Rahne's head without pulling back from her. "But you can call me … mom."

A groan from behind me catches my attention, it's Victor.

The wind blows from Victor's direction, and Jean catches the scent. She pulls herself away from Rahne and sniffs again. She stands. Sniffs. Her head snaps to Victor.

"Jean DON'T!" I yell.

Even in her human form, she moves faster than a normal human and pins Victor to the ground. Studying him through blind eyes, she sniffs his neck.

With one hand on my chest and the other outstretched, I approach her with caution. "Jean, he's with me. Don't hurt him."— *Why am I looking out for a human? Wait, Vatic?* —I wave her off. "Scratch that, you can hurt him." I walk over to Rahne. "Hell, you can eat him if you want. I know I could use a snack."

Jean sniffs his neck like a rescue dog locked on a scent.

"A snack?" Victor yells behind a laugh. "Not funny, man. Not funny at—"

She didn't…

I look back, hoping to find Jean gnawing at his ribs, but instead, I find them in a deep, passionate kiss. Gross.

I take my jacket off and wrap it around Rahne. "How are you doing, little one?"

"Hungry." She says while peeking around me. "What are they doing?"

Victor's body presses firmly into Jean beneath him, and their lips fuse together.

"Uh…" I look back at the two love birds as Jean's hand travels south. "Hey you two! There's a kid over here."

"I never thought I'd hold you again." Jean whispers to him.

Victor smiles. "I didn't either."

"Where have you been all these years?" She lays her forehead on his.

"Somewhere I wouldn't wish on my worst enemies." Victor looks at me out of the corner of his eye and winks. "Or my newest friends."

Maker, kill me now.

"We can do this later," I say. "Two grown men with a couple naked females, one being a little girl, and a dead body is *not* a good look at all. We need to go."

Jean sits up, moving Victor off her. "Oh my god. Gabriel. How could I forget about GG?"

I can answer that. Victor's engorged member pressing firmly into your thigh…

She runs to Gabriel's body, but I stop her just before she gets there—barely. "Jean, you can't."

"Sorin, move," Jean says and tries to push past me and she nearly does.

"No. We need to leave."

"Move!" She pushes me back.

There's a little more Lygos still in there than I would have guessed.

"Jean, he's dead," I say with both hands out in front of me.

"Long dead. We can't do anything for him."

Tears run down her face. "But I have to—"

"You can't do anything," I say as she falls into my arms overtaken by grief. "He's dead. We're not moving him because the car is trashed and carrying a dead body on your shoulder as you walk into town is a great way to draw attention to yourself. We're not burying him because we don't have time, and we're not sticking around here any longer than we have to."

Thankfully, Victor pulls Jean from me before she starts to cry. Rubbing her back, he looks at me. "So, then what's the plan on getting out of here, all-great-knowing-one?"

"Why can't you just carry all of us?" Jean asks, drying her eyes.

I shake my head. "No. I'm too weak from the fighting. Not to mention there are three of you and that's a little awkward."

"And I'm not being carried," Victor says and points at me. "Especially not by him."

I look at Victor. "Glad we agree. Didn't you teleport here or something? Can't we just do that?"

Amazed, Jean looks at Victor. "You can do that?"

"Me, no," Victor says. "I used one of the Atrocities, the Mirror, and it's a one-way trip." Of course, it is.

I sigh. "Our best bet is for you and I to leave the girls here—"

"What?" Victor and Jean say in unison.

"Let me finish." I hold up a hand to shush them. "We leave the girls here to flag down a passerby and have them call the cops. Their story will be simple and believable: They got into a car accident and their friend"—I point at Gabriel—"was killed."

"One problem," Victor says with a finger up. "They're naked!"

"The people who found them acted like they could help, but instead attacked the women after the crash, attempting to have their way with them."

"Where are we going to be?"

"We are going to wait here until everyone else is gone. The girls, the cops, the civilians. Gone. Then…" I eye him from head to toe. "Then we're getting you—and me—some new clothes. And flannel shirts and hoodies aren't on the list."

"You sure 'bout that?" Victor asks, dusting the dirt from his sleeve. "Seems like I'd fit in quite well around here … cottages … sheep with painted butts … and flannels."

"Jokes? Really?" Jean spins in front of Victor and stares blindly into his eyes. "How can you be okay with this?"

"Because it keeps everyone safe and is our best option," Victor says, shooting me a subtle thumbs-up.

Jean looks back. "But Gabriel—"

"Gabriel's dead, Jeanie!" Victor grabs Jean's hand. "He's dead."

"Car." I clear my throat and point to the road. "If we're going to do this, we need to do it now."

Jean, although clearly not happy with the plan, agrees.

"When they ask, tell them to take you to Ballymascanlon House. It's a hotel. There will be a room under your name and clothes waiting for you in the room." I put my hand on Rahne's head, and we smile at one another. "Money will be under the pillow closest to the door in the master suite. A car will be waiting for the two of you out front at eight p.m. to bring you to us."

Before Jean or Victor or Rahne can say anything, I put Victor on my shoulder and disappear at hyper speed. In the next moment, we are already a mile away, blending in with the trunk of a tree.

Victor kicks himself away from me. "What the fuck man? I don't get to say goodbye?"

"Shut up," I snap, slumping against the tree. "And keep it in your pants."

I look down over the hills and grassy plains at the car coming to a stop in front of Jean and Rahne.

"Hey … it's working," Victor says, surprised.

"I told you it would."

# 72



AS WE WALK alongside the old brick buildings on the corner of Vincent Avenue and Dublin Street, the town silently tells stories of the last century. Thin lines of moss grow between the large concrete slabs making up the narrow walking path along the one-way road. Small cast iron potters are tucked tightly to the base of the second-story windows.

"What's good here?" Victor asks.

"When I was here in the fifteenth century, the mutton was quite good, but I'm sure the menu's changed since then."

His head snaps to me. "Jesus Christ you're old! If you haven't been here since then, how'd you know it was still here?"

"I had a European couple for dinner a decade or so back. They told me about it."

"So, you drank them." Victor rolls his eyes. "Great."

"Humans are cattle to me. My food." I stop beside the light pole and look up at the entrance. "We're here."

As we enter through the narrow doorway, a woman carrying a tray smiles at us in welcome. "Evening gents. Take a seat wherever you'd like. Someone'll be right whit'cha."

"Is there a fireplace somewhere?" I ask.

She nods and points down the length of the building. "Follow this all de way down and it'll dump you right into de library. Tink, dere's only one ot'er person back dere."

"Thank you," I say with a smile and hold up two fingers. "We're expecting two more. A woman and her daughter. Will you—"

"Course love," the woman says. "I'll tell 'em where to find ya."

We enter the library through double doors and find the fireplace roaring on the far side of the room. The fireplace is framed in a hand-carved bookshelf spanning wall to wall. Above the fireplace sits a recessed mirror and a stained-glass window depicting two glasses filled with red wine—*or blood.*

"Now this is what I'm talking about," Victor says, taking a seat at the table directly in front of the fireplace.

"You're not going to let the girls sit with their backs to the fireplace?"

A bald-headed black woman sitting in the corner knitting laughs at my question. "Chivalry is dead."

How right she is. She looks to be maybe a decade older than Victor.

"What can I get you two?" a young man asks from behind me.

A pint of O-negative and your liver served with fava beans because you smell like nectarines and pineapple.

I take my seat. "Purple Guinness."

"A *what*-Guinness?" Victor asks, leaning over the table on his elbows.

"A pint of Guinness with a splash of blackcurrant juice. It's really quite lovely."

Victor turns up his nose. "Gross."

The server looks at Victor. "And you, sir?"

"Guinness." Victor stares at me. "A regular one." He quickly scans the tap list. "And a Carlsberg. That's a pilsner, right?"

The server confirms and leaves.

"Two beers…?"

Victor shakes his head. "Only one is for me."

"That's very sweet of you."

Victor chuckles and slings his arm over the back of the chair beside him. "It's not for Jean either. She's a sour ale kinda girl anyway. Or gin."

"I'm not—"

"Before the girls get here," Victor says, cutting me off, "we need to talk."

This should be good. "About what?" I fold my hands on the table in anticipation.

Victor leans back in his chair and closes his eyes. "It's been almost twenty-eight years since you killed that woman in her bathroom only to realize, too late, her eight-year-old son was standing there the whole time. And before the boy could scream, you were gone."

I am speechless.

Victor's eyes flash purple. "I will never speak of this again. And Jean is never to know. But when we're done—when the girls are safe—when the bad guys are all dead—I'm going to kill you."

I wish you luck. I've tried. "I welcome the day I can see my Cora again," I say with a heavy sigh.

"They're here." Victor stands.

I follow his lead and turn. "Good evening, ladies."

Jean and Rahne enter the room hand in hand, smiling. Jean is wearing distressed denim and an oversized cardigan with knee-high boots, while Rahne is sporting jeans, tennis shoes, and a large hoodie.

Victor pulls out the chair he was sitting in and gestures for Jean to sit. "Wow. You look amazing."

"Thank you." Her cheeks flush and she tucks a loose clump of hair behind her ear.

A new server approaches our table.

"Alright, I've got a purple Guinness for the overdressed lad. And a regular Guinness *and* a Carlsberg for the chap from the farm." The waitress sets the three pints on the table. "What c'n I get you two ladies?"

She smells of vodka, cigarettes, and bad decisions. Oof, the memories I'd imprint off her would haunt me for a lifetime.

"Do you have any sours?" Jean asks. The waitress shakes her head. "Gin it is. Hendrix if you have it. On the rocks and with a lime. And a water."

The waitress nods while chomping on her gum like a cow eating grass. Livestock.

"And for you little miss?" she asks, looking at Rahne.

Rahne looks at each one of us with a panicked look on her face.

I place my hand on Rahne's and smile. "She'll have a water and a Coke. We'll also have a roast rack of lamb, Peking duck breast, roast rabbit, your Windsor chicken, bangers and mash, and"—I point at Jean—"a vegetable stir-fry for the vegetarian."

The server's eyes widen as she writes down the smorgasbord of an order before reading it back to me. I smile and thank her.

Rahne places her hands on top of one another on the table and rests her chin on them, staring deeply into the pint of pilsner sitting between her and Victor. It could have been my imagination, but I swore I could see a tiny purple cloud float behind the pilsner.

Silence hovers over the table for an awkwardly long time.

"So … how'd you two meet?" Victor asks, pointing at Jean and me.

I chuckle behind my pint. "We met in a dank, dark room with me a little tied up and a whole lot bloody."

The server silently drops off the rest of our drinks and heads back into the main dining area.

"I'm sorry, you were what?" Victor asks.

Jean wraps Victor's hand in her own. "He's messing with you."—*no I'm not*—"He broke into the facility at Wright-Patt and was captured. I was tasked with interrogating him."

Victor gives a half smile. "Not very good at breaking and entering, huh?" He gives me a wink.

Caught by eight-year-old him. Caught by The Company. Clever. "I guess not," I say, shallowly.

Jean looks at me. "Who were those guys?"

"I met the leader at the Sandbox. His name is Phaeton, The Faceless King."

"And the other four?" Victor asks.

Jean shrugs and I shake my head as Rahne chugs her Coke.

"I can answer that," the bald woman says from the corner of the room.

I sniff the air to be certain. Human. "Who are you?"

"A friend," she says with hands raised. "I mean you no harm."

Her comment earlier was funny. I'll bite. "I don't have many friends, so I'm going to need more than that or you're going to be my lunch."

The bald woman gets up from her table and takes a seat at ours. "Asha." She doesn't flinch at my comment. "My name is Asha."

"Asha, my name's Jean," she says, gesturing to herself. "This is Victor. The little one laying by the fire is Rahne. And you've already met Sorin."

Rahne points at the pilsner pint. "And this is Fred."

It *is* a Penyihir.

Unsure how the woman would have the slightest idea what we're referring to, I call her bluff. "Who were the men with Phaeton?"

"They are the Horsemen of LéTry," Asha says

As she says this, I suddenly recall the castle and the hillside with four horses: one pale, one white, one black, and one red.

"The Horsemen of the Apocalypse," Victor says, behind a gulp of beer. "Pestilence. War. Famine. Death."

"Correct," Asha says. "Pestilence, the white horse, is Oda Kamakura, the first Samurai. War, the red horse, is Stelios Iraklidis, the Herculean. Famine, the black horse, is Amen Ka, the great unifier of Egypt, founder of its first dynasty, and right hand of the Faceless King. Death, the pale horse, is Samael Zornitsa and the left hand of the Faceless King."

She knows a lot for a human.

I put a hand on Rahne's back and ask, "Why did they want her?"

"To bring back His Maker." Asha looks at each of us. "Phaeton has been searching for a way to bring back His Maker for thousands of years, but he needed two things. Neither of which are easy to find."

"The Codex." Jean nods. Her blind eyes dart back and forth. "The Codex answers any question you ask it with complete unbiased honesty. He doesn't know where His Maker is so he's going to use it to find her."

"And the blood of a Lygos." I recall the fight. "But not just any Lygos, the oldest living Lygos. They were targeting Rahne from the beginning, but when Jean transformed, she became the new target." I tap Jean. "Amen took your blood with his scythe and Oda took it when he delivered 1,000 cuts with his katana."

"Very observant, Sorin." Asha smiles. "I see what she saw in you."

"She who?" Rahne asks, innocently.

"Clar—"

Grabbing Asha by the throat, I snarl, "Don't you dare say my Maker's name. Now, who are you?"

"Easy Sorin," Asha says, placing a hand softly on my hand around her neck.

I sniff the air. The scent of a human slowly dissipates from her, revealing a uniquely familiar aroma. I release my grip on her and get up from the table. "You're Nocturnae."

"That's right," Asha says with a mysterious smile. "And I am your Maker's Maker. And I've been keeping my eye on you."

Kneeling before her, I bow my head. "Amicia," I say, overwhelmed with a mixture of emotions. "Forgive me. I didn't realize."

Amicia places a finger under my chin and forces me to look at her. "You were not supposed to. There will be time for me to answer all of your questions later, but right now we have much work to do."

# 73



DR. SHELLEY STARED into the fogged glass of a cryogenic tube, twirling a vial of Nocturnae blood and saliva between his fingers. Over and over, he relived his stroke and the hospital and the damn walker in his mind and could only come to one conclusion.

"After all of these years." He ran his hand over the silver plaque centered on the tube labeled, NULLA. "I've finally done it."

Reaching into his pocket, he pulled out a razorblade.

"But, there's only enough for one of us." The blade slid effortlessly across his old, cracked lip—the cut was painless. "And there is much work still left to be done."

He thumbed the cork out of the vial. "Forgive me, my love." The tip of the vial rested softly against his lower lip. Metallic aromas wafted into his nose. He was ready to be powerful, instead of a wreck of an old man. He was ready to fight for his country, instead of merely being a player behind the scenes. He was ready for the next stage of his… evolution.

He needed more time to save her and be with her.

To Be Continued…

# ACKNOWLEDGEMENTS

I may have authored this book, but I couldn't have done it without the love, support, and guidance of so many people. Thank you:

To my wife, Jenna. You are goodness, to the core. I couldn't have chosen a better person to be the mother of my children, walk through Hell and back with, and I have the privilege of spending the rest of my life with you. Damn, I'm lucky.

To my daughters, Amelia and Grace. You are both absolute perfection and I cannot wait for you to meet Sorin, Jean, and the rest of my characters; but I cannot tell you this story until you're older. Much older.

To my dogs, Neila and Hadley. Whether you were curled up to my left on the floor or at my feet as I sat at my desk; or next to me on the big green chair in the living room; or nudging my elbow when I had writer's block; you were there through it all. All of the writing, researching, reading, thinking, and frustration. You, my fur babies, played a pivotal role in not only helping me write the story; but never would I have guessed you'd both play such a huge role in shaping the Lygos appearance. From the white diamond at the nape of Hadley's neck to the jet-black hair covering Neila.

To my mother. Although you weren't around to see the completion of the story or, really, more than the first four chapters, I couldn't have done it without you. Your bravery through everything in your last year gave me the strength to keep writing even when I thought I was done. Thank you for encouraging me to start writing at such a young age. I never would have developed into the writer I am today without your guidance. I love you and miss you.

To my father. All of this… The story. The world. The characters. All of it, started because of one conversation in your living room in February 2012 when I was complaining about sparkly vampires falling in love with teenage girls. From your chair, you looked up from the Tom Clancy novel on your lap and said, "Why don't you write your own story? You're a good writer…" Thank you for your mind, your love of thrillers, and stories about monsters, but most of all for helping me name the vampires in this book, Nocturnae. It pained me to watch as ALS slowly took your mind and body while my story became clearer and more complicated. It's hard to not be able to share this with you in person, but I know you'd be proud.

To my brother for encouraging me to continue writing in the hardest of times by simply saying, "I can't wait to read it." It's been a lot of fun listening to you try and figure out where the story is going.

To my mother-in-law. You took my family under your wing from the very beginning and then went the extra mile when my parents, prematurely, fell ill. Thank you for your support, care, and guidance through it all.

To my father-in-law. Although you don't give yourself the credit, you're one of the most intelligent and inspiring men I've ever met. The amount of respect I have for you and the weight your words carry are immeasurable. Your support and encouragement in everything I do means the world to me. I couldn't have asked for a better father-in-law. Fucker.

To Bethany Lauren James, my developmental editor and teacher. Thank you for supporting this book, and my vision and dream. Thank you for the countless hours, late nights, early mornings (sorry), and many, many unnecessary words deleted.

To Emily Young and Lenore Appelhans, and everyone at Angelella Editorial. Thank you for your perspectives and recommendations.

To Alyssa Matesic for helping me craft a compelling query and synopsis.

To Kerry Ellis for capturing the essence of this story and creating a beautiful cover.

To Chelsea Bobulski for providing guidance, wisdom, and compassion to this, dare I say, mentee. I hope everyone enjoys your stories as much as I do.

To Laurie Hartford, my high school British Literature teacher. Thank you for supporting and encouraging a young mind, constantly reminding me that anything is possible if you believe. I still have the glass shamrock you gave me all those years ago. May you rest in peace.

To the Special Security Office of Headquarters Air Force Global

Strike Command—specifically, Sue Trevino and Kimberly Porras—for taking the time to read and review this story to ensure security had no objections to its publication.

My beta-readers and early supporters: Michelle Bostater, Amanda Cogan, Natalie Tyrey, Sydney Ledesma, Arthur "David" B. James, Lenore Marks, Jennifer Mitchell, Hunter Russo, Susan Weaver, and Andrew Welter. Thank you for taking the time out of your lives to read this story in various stages of its life—I know the early versions were [really] rough. Your feedback was extremely helpful in molding this piece of literature.

Finally, I raise a glass of whiskey and rye—or AB-positive if that's what you're into—to you, the reader. Thank you for taking a chance on this first-time author. I hope you enjoyed the story and are looking forward to what's yet to come.

# ABOUT THE AUTHOR

MICHAEL TERRANCE IS a native Ohioan and author of the urban-dark fantasy novel *The Last Nocturnae,* his debut novel and the first book in the series, *Atrocities of Blood & Moon.* Michael holds a Master of Science in Engineering and has worked in the Defense Industry since 2008. His experience in various R&D and leadership roles spanning numerous programs, allows him to craft realistic environments in classified rooms, motivations, and military oversight for his scenes.

At a young age, Michael wrote poetry and lyrics as a form of emotional therapy after his mother—a hobby poet and journalist herself—made the recommendation. Having grown up playing *Magic: The Gathering* with a father who loved comic books, science fiction, and fantasy, it's no wonder his debut novel is in this genre.

Michael has been happily married since 2014 to a woman just as ambitious and together they have two brilliant and beautiful daughters. They look forward to the success of his debut novel, *The Last Nocturnae,* and witnessing the *Atrocities of Blood & Moon* series come to life.

Follow him on social media:

    Instagram: @michaelterranceauthor

    Facebook: @michaelterranceauthor

    Twitter: @MTerranceAuthor


Visit his website:

    www.michaelterranceauthor.com


Get in contact with him:

    michaelterranceauthor@gmail.com

# GLOSSARY

| | |
|---|---|
| ABU | Airman Battle Uniform |
| CAC | Common Access Card |
| DARPA | Defense Advanced Research Projects Agency |
| FPCON | Force Protection Condition |
| GEO | Geosynchronous Earth Orbit |
| IED | Improvised Explosive Device |
| JWICS | Joint Worldwide Intelligence Communications System |
| MP | Military Police |
| NASIC | National Air and Space Intelligence Center |
| NIPRNET | Non-classified Internet Protocol Router Network |
| NOFORN | No Foreign |
| NTTR | Nevada Test and Training Range |
| OPIR | Overhead Persistent Infrared |
| PHANG | Phylogenic Human Alteration with Nocturnae Genomics |

| PI | Paranormal Intelligence |
| PII | Personally Identifiable Information |
| PMEL | Precision Measurement Equipment Laboratory |
| SCIF | Secret Compartmentalized Information Facility |
| SSgt. | Staff Sergeant |
| TS | Top Secret |
| WMD | Weapon of Mass Destruction |
| WPAFB | Wright-Patterson Air Force Base |